Riddle Me Home

B.D. Bucher

Copyright © 2018 B.D. Bucher

ISBN: 9781983356513

This book is dedicated to my family. Brad, you are my rock! I am so blessed to be married to my best friend. You have been supportive and patient with my 4:00 a.m. quiet departures from bed to get up and write.

Drewby, you have stood by my side through all of my educational and life endeavors. I often think about the times we sat and did homework together. When I first told you I was writing this novel, you said, "Of course you are writing a novel."

Morgan and Luke, thank you for encouraging me along the way. Remember, this novel started with a family vacation to Florida.

Acknowledgments

I would like to thank the following individuals who provided expert information for this novel. Former FBI Agent, Tom Gibbons, thank you for your law enforcement expertise and suggestions. Thank you to my husband, Brad Bucher, for your legal expertise and amazing editing skills.

I would also like to thank my editor and friend, Deborah Huffman, for reading several drafts and providing excellent advice and suggestions before reading the final draft. You encouraged me to keep pushing on when I was exhausted.

I offer a special thanks to my first readers, Peggy Pohlman and Marci Irvine.

Thanks to everyone who bought an early copy and provided feedback. Ken Mitchell, your notes were amazing. I have learned so much about the self-publishing process, even after I released the first copy of Riddle Me Home.

Thanks to Peyton for being a wonderful model for the cover photo. I feel blessed to be your family photographer.

Finally, I would be remiss if I didn't acknowledge my MANY students who have cheered me along on this journey over the past five years. To you I say, "BELIEVE YOU CAN DO IT, AND YOU CAN!"

1

The Masters family packed their flip-flops, hopped on a plane, and kicked off summer vacation with a trip to Orlando, Florida. Ella and the kids were much more enthusiastic than Davis, but at least he agreed to join them this year.

Ella, William, and Willow ended the month of May and welcomed June with two jam-packed days at Disney World, where Willow posed for pictures with all of her favorite princesses and William rode every roller coaster. Davis Masters stayed back at the condo, insisting he had too much work to do. Ella knew amusement parks weren't her husband's thing, so she didn't press the issue. The truth was that she knew they would have a more relaxed time without him.

Exhausted from their fun-park adventures, they decided to spend Monday resting at the condo, with plans to drive to the beach on Tuesday. Ella watched the kids swim in the morning, made them an early lunch, and got them settled into their afternoon reading and rest time. Davis was holed up in their bedroom working, so he didn't hear her say she was heading out to run some errands.

William said, "Don't worry, Mom, I will take care of Willow, and I will let Dad know where you went if he ever comes out of the bedroom."

Ella winked at her son and said, "When did you grow up on me? You were a toothless little boy just yesterday!"

William Gates Masters was a little old man at twelve years old. Ella's Momma said her only grandson was an old soul from the time he was born. He was tall and lean, with fair skin, thick, sandy brown hair, thoughtful blue eyes, and a face full of freckles, which popped out in the summertime like stars on a clear night. He was only four years old when his sister, Willow, showed up, after what seemed like years of being in his mommy's growing tummy, and found a spot in their family portraits. He took it upon himself to ensure his little sister's safety from the time she was born. He told his parents, his dog, Beau, Nana and Papa, Aunt Emilie, and even perfect strangers, exactly how to take care of his Willow.

Willow Rose Masters was everyone's little angel. She was born with a thick head of black ringlets, which turned into light brown tufts as she got older and her hair grew longer. Ella kept her little girl's gentle locks cut just below her shoulders to avoid a tangled mess. Willow's skin had an olive tone, and only a few freckles dotted her face. The pudgy little girl with chubby cheeks had thinned down over the last year and turned into a miniature version of her mother. She had a slight, but muscular figure that had been developed by dance lessons, yoga with her mom, and all of their outdoor hiking adventures. Her big blue eyes, outlined with long, dark lashes, stole the show of her sweet face.

Ella tapped Willow's nose with her pointer finger. "And you, little lady, better not follow in his footsteps! You better stop growing up right this minute, do you understand?"

The three giggled. As Ella closed the door, she said, "I might just bring you a surprise home if you are good and don't bother your father while he is working."

"I've got this, Mom!" William insisted. "Now get out of here so I can boss Willow around!" He mussed his sister's curly locks, covering her eyes with her hair. The three laughed again, and Ella shut the condo door behind her.

Shortly after she pulled out of the parking lot, Ella's cell phone buzzed in the console. She looked at the number and inhaled deeply. She knew it would not be a pleasant phone call, and she didn't want it to ruin her day, but she reluctantly answered anyway.

"Hello," she said, with a mix of irritation and caution.

She was correct; the one-sided conversation was not pleasant, and she ended it as quickly as she could. Her cheeks reddened, and her ears burned.

She pulled up to the Redbox movie rental kiosk at the 7-Eleven in the E-Class Mercedes Benz that her husband, Davis, insisted on renting for their week-long Florida vacation. The rusty, tan Honda Civic pulled in behind her and parked under a trio of palm trees in the corner of the lot. Ella's mind was still reeling from the call, and she was oblivious to her surroundings.

Donny, however, was NOT oblivious to her. He lost himself in thoughts of what he wanted to do to her, as he watched her Mercedes for the several minutes it took her to emerge from the vehicle. He closed his eyes and began his fantasy. He fantasized seeing high-heeled sandals stepping out of the car, followed by long, lean, suntanned legs. He imagined her in a skimpy, blue-jean miniskirt that, when she leaned over to pick up her movies out of the passenger seat, revealed white thong underwear surrounded by an evenly suntanned ass. He completed the picture in his mind by imagining a tight white tank top with beautiful breasts oozing out the top.

Donny was especially short-fused today. The June Florida heat was baking him in the sweltering rat-trap of a car he had been driving around for four days. The windows were rolled down because the air conditioner had kowtowed to the scorching heat three days earlier. The fan was on, but it felt like dragon breath as it did little more than move the stale summer air. The longer he sat behind the newspaper he was pretending to read, the more irritable he became.

Donny brought himself out of his fantasy, wiped the sweat off his upper lip and spoke aloud, "I know exactly what I am going to do to you." Gyrating his pelvis, he said, "And I will enjoy every minute of it!"

Sexual thoughts surged through his head as the slender woman stepped out of her car. She wore cut-off blue jean shorts, a baggy, black tank top, flip-flops, and a beige ball cap.

Short brown curls peeked out the bottom of the cap. She was unremarkable, and Donny was disappointed.

"Damn!" he muttered. "Not what I expected-- not at all what I expected!" The woman who emerged from the car did not match his fantasies. She had a small, narrow, yet muscular, frame; her chest was clearly that of an athlete, not a model. He watched her leg muscles tighten as she stretched across the driver's seat to gather items out of the passenger seat. He resignedly said, "I can still think of plenty of things to do to you, bitch."

Impervious to the fact that she was being watched, Ella hustled to the Redbox to return the videos her children had rented the previous day. She scanned the list for their most recent requests, pressed the corresponding buttons, inserted her credit card, and completed the transaction. Thrilled that the kids' selections were available, Ella momentarily lost herself in thoughts of them. She imagined Willow giving her big brother, William, a high-five when she walked in with their favorite movies. She loved how close the two were; they rarely had disagreements, mostly because William gave into Willow's every whim.

The clearing of a deep voice a bit too close to her ear interrupted her thoughts. She turned and was face to face with a handsome Italian man, dressed in perfectly-ironed khaki shorts, a navy polo, and Navy Sperry topsider shoes. The smell of cologne wafted toward Ella as he kindly asked if she was finished with her selection. She couldn't discern if he were making eye contact behind his Oakley sunglasses, but he was standing closer than comfortable to her. His smile, however, was oddly disarming. The air between them was palpable, and the already-hot temperature turned her body temperature up a few degrees.

"Oh, yes, sorry, I was thinking about how happy my kids are going to be that both of their movies are here." An immediate rush of embarrassment crossed her face as she smiled nervously and apologized for babbling. She quickly turned to walk away, but the man's arm brushed her back, sending a chill down her arms that caused the DVDs to tumble out of her hands.

The heat rose in her cheeks as she once again apologized, without making eye contact this time. Before she could gather her composure and reach down to pick up the DVD's, the man scooped them up and handed them back to her. He assured her, "It is absolutely not your fault. I was obviously standing a bit too close."

Ella took the DVDs and hustled back to her car, without looking back. The interaction left her off-kilter, something that didn't usually happen to her. She wanted to get a closer look at the guy, but she had already acted like a bumbling fool and didn't want to add insult to injury. She could feel the penetrating looks of the stranger burn through her skin as the distance between her and her Mercedes Benz narrowed. She wasn't sure if she felt flattered or frightened.

Mr. Honda Civic sat behind his newspaper watching the show, and it pissed him off. "Pretty people and their fake fucking interactions make me sick," he muttered. He knew that if he were in line behind her, she wouldn't give him the time of day. "Well, little bitch, you will give me the time of day soon enough." As he grinned, he caught his cigarette-stained, snaggle-toothed smile in the mirror. He swirled his tongue around his cracked, rough lips and flicked it in and out in a sexual gesture toward Ella, as she cluelessly walked to her car.

Still jolted by her interaction with the stranger, Ella hastily got back into her car and placed the DVDs onto the passenger seat. A yellow sticky note peeked its way out between the two movies. "I WANT TO HELP YOU!" was written in blue ink pen. A strange panic washed over her, and she looked around nervously. "What the heck? Where did the note come from?" She knew the only explanation was the Italian man, but who was he and why had he given her that note? Had he been following her? Her mind raced as she scanned the parking lot for the stranger who was now nowhere to be found. The only car in the lot was a tan Honda Civic with a scraggly looking guy sitting in the driver's seat reading a newspaper. Conflicted between concern over the words that stared her in the face and feeling the need to get back to the kids, Ella tucked the slip of paper into her wallet, surveyed her surroundings one final time, and pulled out of the 7-Eleven parking lot.

She felt discombobulated. She was unsettled from the phone call that still gnawed at her, and now, this strange exchange left her head spinning. She was completely unaware that the Honda Civic had pulled out right behind her and was following her. Ella pulled back into the condo parking lot. Donny parked along the street very near her car. A row of palm trees lined the street and provided a cover for him. He smiled when he saw there were no other people in the lot. He waited for the woman to gather her belongings. As she emerged from the car, he placed his hand on his door handle. Just as he was about to open the door, he caught a glimpse of the video camera aimed directly at her car.

"Fuck!" he muttered. He looked around to see several other cameras placed carefully to capture all areas of the parking lot. Sweat dripped down the side of his face as he searched for cameras that might capture an image of his car on the street. He was glad he had kept his hat on, but he had stolen the set of plates earlier in the day. He instinctively pulled his hat down to cover more of his face.

"I'll be back, my pretty," he cackled. He slowly backed up, pulled away, and drove off.

Ella walked into the condo to see both children reading. She had left them with strict instructions to stay inside to take a break from the pounding Florida sun. They were ecstatic when their mom tossed each of them the DVD cases and exclaimed, "Score!" She popped some popcorn and made a cheese and fruit tray. She knew Davis was working back in their bedroom, so she snuggled on the couch with the kids as the three of them watched part of Willow's movie.

Davis sat at the large desk in the bedroom of the rented condo staring at the yellow legal pad, cell phone, and several pieces of paper splayed out in front of him. He ignored the fact that he was supposed to be on vacation, and he disre-garded his children in the next room. His business world was about to crumble, and he was becoming more financially desperate as each hour passed. He had taken significant risks to obtain the necessary funds for the upcoming deal, but as he stared at the numbers in front of him, he was woefully short. He read over the notes he had doodled as he made one rejecting phone call after another.

Davis chastised himself, "If tomorrow's deal falls through, I will be out of business for good, and seriously bad guys will come knocking on my door with real-life threats." He was sickened at the thought of having to come clean with Ella and grovel at her feet to ask her daddy to help them out until they could recover from his financial mistakes, and he knew it would likely bring up evidence that he had already pilfered money from his father-in-law's bank accounts. Davis felt the walls of his extravagant secret life closing in on him. If only he could think of some diversion to hold off the deal at least one more week, he might have a chance. The air conditioner in the room was pumping cold air, but Davis was sweating.

The upcoming meeting between Gianni Russo, the bigwig Chicago businessman, and the developers with whom he had been involved for the past two years, was now less than twenty-four hours away. Mr. Russo had grown impatient that Davis wasn't producing his part of the final funds to make the restaurant development along the Chicago River come to fruition. Davis knew his window of opportunity was slipping through his fingers, and the added stress left him with a less-than-agreeable attitude most of the time. This was his make-or-break week. The developers had given him and Gianni a Friday deadline, and he knew if he didn't have proof of his additional funds, Davis would lose every dime he already had wrapped up in the deal. Gianni would move on to another investor, leaving Davis a washed-up, has-been in the investment world.

He stared at the paper that already had four of six phone numbers crossed off. He had put the last two numbers off as long as he could, one of which was his final desperate call to obtain the necessary funds. If this phone call did not go well, he would be forced to make the inevitable call to Gianni, the last number on the list.

Davis poured himself a glass of liquid courage-- Scotch on the rocks. The liquid slid over his tongue and down his throat, and the cool burn was soothing. His fingers traced the 3-1-2 area code on his legal pad, his heart quickened, and sweat dripped down his temples. He would rather be getting another vasectomy than make this phone call. He took a deep breath as he punched the number into his phone. After only two rings, the female voice answered, "I know exactly what you are up to, and you better be ready to do more listening than talking." Davis attempted to get a word in edgewise but was cut off each time he tried to speak. As he endured the conversation, he was oblivious to the fact that his wife had returned from her errands.

Willow's heavy eyelids finally gave way to sleep, and William repositioned his sister's head on the decorative pillow. Ella peeled herself away from the kids and went to check in with Davis. She slipped quietly into the room and carefully closed the door behind her so as not to interrupt her husband's telephone call. He appeared to be finagling another business transaction. He hadn't heard her enter. He spoke in a hushed tone as he quietly argued with the person on the other end of the telephone. "I don't think you understand; the timeliness of this transaction is of utmost importance. If this thing doesn't happen by tomorrow morning, I am fucked!"

Davis sat fidgeting as he listened to the response. He replied, "I have exhausted all other possibilities! Trust me, this is the LAST phone call I wanted to make." After listening for a few seconds, he hissed in an exasperated voice. "I know. I know." He began to say something else but abruptly stopped his words, as the person on the other end had hung up on him.

"Fuck!" he muttered, as he smacked the flip phone shut and shoved it in his pocket.

A visibly startled look fell over his face as he turned around to see his wife standing behind him. "Fuck... when the fuck did you walk in? You just scared the shit out of me!" His words came fast as he over-explained, "One of my big deals in Chicago is about to fall through because I have incompetent morons working on the project. I'm in Florida when I should be in Chicago closing the deal." His mind frantically scrambled to try to figure out what he had said in the last several minutes and how long his wife had been in the room. Sweating profusely, he rattled on about the phone call, which was out of character for Davis.

When Ella stared at her husband without a verbal response, he finally stopped rambling. This was followed by an awkward momentary silence between the two. He waited for his wife to question the flip phone, but she didn't. *She must not have seen it,* he thought, with a sigh of relief.

Ella was still keyed up from her experience at the Redbox, and Davis' erratic behavior was now causing her to question the allegations spewed at her over the phone earlier in the day. Right now, she didn't want to overthink anything, so she told Davis she was going to take advantage of the kids being entertained by taking a lavender bath. Her husband's demeanor quickly changed. He raised his eyebrows, walked over and locked the bedroom door, and said with a cunning smile, "How about you change that bath to a shower?"

Ella was frazzled and in no mood for what her husband had in mind, and her reaction made it very clear. She despised the way he could turn his emotions on and off like the flip of a switch. "Davis, I have been running errands all afternoon, and I am exhausted. The kids are right outside our room, and they will probably want more snacks. Can I have just thirty minutes to myself to wind down?"

Davis turned on her. "That's the problem with this fucking marriage! Every fucking thing revolves around THOSE fucking kids. It is never about me or about us. I am just about fed up with this shit."

His words stung, and Ella couldn't restrain herself. "THOSE kids, Davis? THOSE kids are your children!" she retorted. "I'm oh so very sorry if they get in the way of you enjoying your life."

It was uncharacteristic for Ella to come at her husband like this because he was a loose cannon. All she wanted was a vacation where she was allowed to relax without having to walk on eggshells around him. She knew the kids' presence in the next room insured Davis would not hit her. This gave Ella a false sense of security that allowed her to say things she would never have said if the kids were not there.

She continued in a hushed yell, "The ONLY time you pay any attention to me is when you want sex! Other than that, I don't exist, and I can't remember the last time you spent quality time with our children! It is like you regret ever having them."

Ella's words fell hard on Davis, and it was his turn to play the blame game. "You are not going to put this one on me! You and I don't have a relationship when the kids are around," he snapped back. "The only time I feel like you give me the time of day is when they are gone, and even then, I can tell you are thinking about them. Let's face it, Ella, you love those kids more than anything, and I am just somewhere in the backseat, waiting for a little affection from you. His voice rose to a yell. I am fucking sick of this life, and I am sick of you! If only..." He stopped his words before he said something that might come back to bite him!

The children cringed as they heard their father's words on the other side of the bedroom door. William wanted to throw open the door and tell his father to leave his mom alone, but both children sat frozen on the couch, as they heard their mom's response in her own raised voice.

"Davis, how can you be in the back seat when most of the time you aren't even in the car. You are hardly ever home, and when you are, you are on the phone making the next big business deal…or whatever you are doing on the phone." Ella surprised herself by the caustic tone of her words and the fact that she was standing up to her husband.

Davis knew the accusatory gist of her final remark. He opened his mouth to respond, but before he could verbalize his comeback, Ella marched into the bathroom and slammed the door so hard that the pictures on the wall shook. She quickly locked the door.

As she lay restlessly soaking in the tub, Ella played back the scenario at the Redbox. She closed her eyes and saw the small yellow piece of paper and the man behind it, "I WANT TO HELP YOU." She didn't get it. *What does it mean? Why do I need help? Maybe the man mistook me for someone else.* She was out of sorts, and she knew this is why she came at her husband harder than she typically would have.

She played back her fight with Davis and the words that could never be taken back. She pictured her husband's shocked face as he turned to see her in the room. She heard the snap of the closing cell phone. It dawned on her, *Wait, an iPhone doesn't click closed!* She hadn't noticed it in the heat of the moment, but now that she replayed the event in her head she could clearly see the small flip phone in his hand. Her mind spun out of control, rushing back and forth from the accusations of the phone call to Davis' secretive behavior.

In an instant, her anger turned to worry. She flinched as she heard the wiggling of the locked doorknob. She knew her words had not fallen on deaf ears and that she would eventually pay for the way she had spoken to her husband. Davis did not forgive or forget, and he always had the upper hand. She thought of the consequences she had endured in the past when she stood up to her husband. Ella instinctively rubbed at her upper arms. She knew she would be wearing long sleeves over this fight and blaming it on eczema.

The knock on the bedroom door, followed by her husband's harsh voice, both scared and relieved her. "Your mom is in the bathtub!" he scoffed. "Aren't you two old enough to fend for yourselves for thirty minutes without needing your mommy?" The scolding words made Ella cringe. She quickly dried herself and threw on her robe to intervene between Davis and the children to save them from the wrath she knew her husband would take out on them. She made a mental note to investigate the phone issue later.

Ella emerged from the bathroom, grabbed her pile of clothes and hustled past Davis. He narrowed his gaze at her and gave her a sharp look that told her their fight wasn't over; the threatening glare made Ella glad the kids were there. Both children looked at their mom with pained expressions, but she smiled a gentle smile as if nothing had happened and said, "I think it is pool time." The trio changed into their swimsuits, gathered their pool toys, and exited the condo. Ella's stomach ached as she hustled William and Willow down to the pool.

Davis seethed as he heard the condo door close. He took the Samsung flip phone back out of his pocket and stared at it, knowing he had to make the dreaded phone call to Gianni Russo. He was relieved when he heard Russo's familiar voicemail; this meant he could postpone the inevitable news until their previously arranged 9:30 phone conference.

Davis mixed another Scotch on the rocks and swished the liquid around in his mouth in a feeble attempt at easing the pain of what he knew he had to do. He had burned too many bridges, which left him boxed in a financial corner. He opened the Samsung back up and dialed Natalia's number. He knew he had a good hour to escape his miserable reality, and he knew Natalia had plenty of ways to take his mind off his troubles; the woman did not disappoint. Forty minutes later, Davis felt a little less edgy, and he promised to call her back later in the evening.

Ella sat on the edge of the pool and dangled her legs in the cool water while she slathered sunscreen on the kids. Eight-year-old Willow wiggled impatiently as her mom rubbed suntan lotion on her smooth sun-kissed skin.

Willow wrinkled her nose under her mommy's relentless, suntan-covered fingertips. "Mommy, that's enough, that's enough! By the time you get done slathering me up, it is going to be time to get out."

Ella topped the chore off with a kiss on the tip of Willow's nose and a tousling of her beautiful curly locks, and teased, "Go play, now will ya'. We don't have all day!"

Willow giggled, "Mommy, you were the one taking so long," on her way to jumping into the pool.

William waited patiently for his mom to finish with his sister. He insisted on putting on his own sunscreen since he was now twelve, but he reluctantly agreed to still allow his mom to finish the job on his back, face, and ears. Unlike the very few freckles on his sister's face, William's freckles had popped up like dandelions in the Florida sun, despite the plethora of suntan lotion his mom used each time he walked out the door. She loved counting his freckles and telling him the special characteristics that each spot represented. "These three," she would say, "represent how kind you are to your little sister because they come together like a heart. And this one shows what a bright future you have because it sticks out from the rest." Although William acted annoyed as she tapped at each of the freckles, he secretly liked having this special bond with his mom. When he had asked, on more than one occasion, where he got his freckles, when neither she nor his father had them, she replied, "God puts freckle-dust on his hands and gently blows it in the wind. It finds the most joyful little boys and sticks to them. The more joy the boy has, the more the freckle-dust spreads across his face."

Ella put the finishing touches on her son, and he cannonballed into the pool, splashing his mom before she had a chance to find refuge behind her towel. He popped up out of the water and said, "What number was that?"

Wiping the water from her face, Ella teasingly scolded, "That was a ten. You just drenched me! For that, you get NO dinner." Willow laughed her hearty laugh as she told her brother she would be eating all of the pizza by herself. William splashed at his sister, and the water fight was on.

Ella snapped pictures and videos of her children splashing in the pool, and she temporarily pushed the details of the past few hours to the back of her mind. Her kids loved the pool, and she adored watching them pop in and out of the water like fish.

She was about to capture a video of William coming out of the water with Willow on his shoulders as they readied themselves for a game of chicken with their new friends when her sister's number once again appeared on the rattling screen. Ella didn't have the emotional energy to deal with any of this right now. She had not bounced back from their earlier conversation or from her recent fight with Davis. "I JUST want to enjoy some time with my kids. Is this really too much to ask?" she mumbled under her breath.

She reluctantly answered the phone and listened to her sister's angry words on the other end of the line, smiling the whole time, so she didn't draw attention from the parents on the other side of the pool, who sat in lounge chairs sipping wine and holding hands while their children frolicked in the pool. The kids occasionally looked over to see their mom smiling and nodding as she talked on the phone. She didn't want them to have any knowledge of the harsh words that were filling her ears. She did her best to protect them from the domino effects of their father's actions, which was once again the topic of this current berating. She finally ended the one-sided conversation by saying, "I promise I will get to the bottom of this when we get home from Florida. I have got to get the kids out of the pool before Davis comes looking for us." She disconnected the call and nervously looked at her watch; it was 5:30. "Damn!" she said under her breath. The time had completely gotten away from her, and now she would have to put off the kids' baths until after dinner. Davis had made it clear that he needed to be back at the condo by 9:00 for his 9:30 business call, and Ella knew she already had hell to pay for her earlier words. She didn't want to incite any more anger in her husband. She had endured all the verbal abuse she could handle for one day. "So much for a relaxing day," she thought.

She hustled the kids out of the pool and asked them to please hurry in getting themselves ready for dinner. She said, "Daddy is a bit cranky today, so let's do our best, best, best to make him happy, happy, happy." Neither of the children had forgotten the words their parents had flung at each other a short time earlier, so they did as she requested and got ready for dinner in record time.

2

The drive to the Gastone's Pizzeria was filled with apprehensive silence, and the wait for a table, once they arrived, took longer than expected. Ella could feel Davis' anger radiating through his fake smile. Finally seated an hour later, Ella sat with William and Willow scrunched tightly on either side of her in the booth opposite of her husband. She wondered how she could have ever fallen in love with this handsome stranger across the table.

Davis Masters turned heads when he walked into a room. As he sat under the glow of the hanging light, he looked more like a model in a GQ magazine than a husband and father of two. His full head of brown hair had just enough peppering of gray to add to his sophisticated look. His brown eyes, chiseled jawline, and toothy white grin were highlighted by his summer tan. Tight pectoral muscles bulged out of his white linen shirt, and equally-impressive leg muscles were accentuated by his Ralph Lauren khaki shorts. Ella got why both women and men stared at her husband. Davis was tall, dark, and handsome, and he spent an excessive amount of time at the gym to keep himself looking that way. Sadly, Ella wished he would spend half as much time on her and their children.

Her husband was more distant than usual tonight, and it kept Ella on edge. She knew he was still seething over their fight, and she could feel the non-verbal fight that continued as they sat in the crowded booth; her husband's aloof behavior only added to her anxiety headache.

Ella had hidden the note in a secret compartment in her wallet, but the words, "I WANT TO HELP YOU!" were etched

in her mind. She once again tried to make sense of the note--
and the strange man behind the dark sunglasses who must have
slipped it between her movies as he picked them up off the
ground. It had been a surreal experience, and it was absolutely
the only explanation for the note. *Why would a stranger approach me
while I'm on vacation and give me a note like that*, she anxiously
wondered. *It just doesn't make sense.*

Willow's fingers tugging on her mommy's shirt brought
Ella out of her fog. "Let's play riddles," Willow's sweet voice
begged.

Ella moved the curls out of her daughter's eyes and said,
"You go first." Willow giggled her first riddle out, "What has to
be broken before you can use it?" Ella paused a moment for
effect and then said, "I have NO clue!"

Willow yelled, "An egg, silly."

William was next. "How do you double your money?"
For a brief moment, Davis' ears tuned in to the conversation,
but when William excitedly answered his own riddle, "Put it in
front of the mirror," Davis gave a disgusted exhale. The rude
interruption to their fun game sent a momentary awkward
silence across the table.

Ella watched her son crumble under his father's
judgmental sigh, and she quickly picked up the emotional pieces
by taking her turn in the riddle game. "What has a face and two
hands but no arms or legs?" In unison, the kids said, "A clock!"

Willow excitedly said, "My turn, my turn! What did the
chewing gum say to the shoe?" She laughed a hearty laugh that
rolled from the depths of her belly up to her precious face
before she even got the answer out; this caused a chain reaction
of giggling with Ella and William. "I'm stuck on you! Get it,
Mommy?" She could not stop giggling, and her infectious laugh
spread to her brother and mommy. Ella and the children
continued their riddle games as they patiently waited for their
deep-dish pizza.

Davis was absorbed in his own thoughts, as he blankly stared at his beautiful wife and the two children he had never wanted, wondering how long he would remain stuck in his miserable life. He requested they go to a seafood restaurant since they were in Florida, but the kids insisted on pizza, and, so, pizza, it was. He had learned years ago it was always one against three when it came to going out to dinner. His agitation and annoyance rose as the minutes slowly ticked by. He had the worry of the upcoming phone conversation running through his head, and he was wasting time waiting for a freaking pizza! His head was spinning from the sing-song riddles that were playing like a broken record and from the dull roar of voices as families throughout the restaurant competed for speaking time at each of their tables. Impatient, Davis rose and headed outside for a cigarette. He had been smoking for the past ten years, excusing the nasty habit by saying it was the only way he could relax. Smoking disgusted Ella; the stench of nicotine on her husband's clothes was such a turn-off. She didn't understand how a man who spent so many hours at the gym could harm his body by smoking.

As Davis walked toward the front door, his iPhone vibrated on the table, and a mailbox image appeared on his phone. "Great," Ella thought, "Now he will be responding to emails throughout the rest of our dinner." She realized it didn't matter, however, because whether he was on his phone or not, he was still only a body at the table. The recollection of the flip phone in his hand earlier in the day left her nauseous, and she tried to brush away the questions it stirred inside her. Sadness for her children and for herself made her heart hurt as much as her stomach, as she watched him walk out the front door.

Davis slipped around the corner of the restaurant away from the front door and large picture windows. He took a Pall Mall out of its pack, lit it, took a deep drag, and removed the flip phone from his pocket. The text read, "When do I get to see you again?"

"Soon" Davis quickly replied, as he took another deep drag off his cigarette.

Immediately, his phone lit up in his hands, and the text reply read, "Not soon enough! I still can feel what you did to me the last time!" Davis felt the heat rise through his body as he thought of her and the details of their last encounter out on the rented boat.

"I can still feel what you did to me over the phone today!" he responded. "Wait until you feel what I am going to do to you the next time I see you," he typed away.

Her response came quickly, "You have NO idea how I am going to rock your world and turn it upside down!!??!!"

He wrote, "REALLY!!?? We will just have to see about that!" He tossed his cigarette and added, "I need to get back into the restaurant now. I'm stuck in a fucking pizza joint!"

A mix of jealousy and bitterness flowed through Natalia's fingers as she quickly typed, "Well, if you would follow through with all of your promises of getting out of your miserable marriage, maybe you wouldn't be where you are now, buried in misery and regret-- but instead…"

As he read her last text, he took out another cigarette, lit it, cockily put it to his lips, and inhaled deeply. He fired back a text that simply read, "I bought you a SPARKLY gift to help you while you wait for me! It's your favorite color… DIAMOND!"

He smiled to himself as he thought about the control he had perfected throughout the years over the women in his life. He found their weaknesses and exploited them to first get what he wanted and second to get rid of them when he was finished using them. He had always been able to keep the women in his life far enough at bay to keep him out of major trouble, but this latest hottie, Natalia, had been a bit more of a firecracker than the others. She was by far the most creative one, Davis thought, but she pushed the envelope a bit regarding Davis taking risky chances to be with her, and she always pushed Davis to leave his family so that they could have more fun together. Whenever

Natalia started down the road of asking Davis when they were going to be able to be together, he bought her a present, filled her ears with lies, and told her to be patient because it would all be worth it. He sensed Natalia was growing impatient; more of their conversations were about how much longer she had to wait for him and less about the sexy things she was going to do to him.

Maybe, Davis thought, *it's time to dump her.*

Davis did want out of his marriage, but not without the financial stability the marriage provided, and definitely not to turn around and put his money into a gold digger who couldn't contribute enough financially for his liking. After all, that was what attracted him to Ella; she had enough of her own money that she didn't have to rely on him for financial security. He was aware, in fact, that she, or rather her daddy, carried their family financially. Ella, on the other hand, was not exactly privy to that information.

Davis knew a woman like Natalia would never be permanent in his life. He certainly wasn't going to risk the wrong timing of getting out of his marriage for a woman like her. She was great in bed, though, so he was going to ride the affair as long as he could keep her in check.

He fired one last text back-- a lie. "Ella just sent William out to look for me. The pizza finally arrived. I can't wait to run my fingers through your luscious long blonde hair, and......" He knew that would give her enough food for thought to keep her content for a while. He had to compose himself before he could go back inside, but his mind was running wild with ideas of what he would do to Natalia when they hooked back up.

Davis returned just before the little brunette bombshell of a waitress brought the piping hot pizza. Her skin-tight uniform left little to a man's imagination. Nanette, he noticed, was her name. "Nanette-- what a name!" he thought to himself. He imagined her using a broken mirror to put on cheap drugstore makeup while sitting on a dirty mattress on the floor of a room she shared with multiple siblings in a filthy mobile home in a run-down trailer park. Her parents would most likely be throwing back cold Pabst Blue Ribbon beers and smoking cigarettes with the neighbors, as they chatted through stained or missing teeth about how difficult it would be to stretch their money to the next welfare check. He was able to envision the scenario because it had been the script of his impoverished childhood. But he had escaped that life...at least until tonight.

He wondered if Nanette was a student, or, if like his own mother, she had failed at all other endeavors, thus forcing her to wait tables for the rest of her life. He felt no sympathy or empathy for the girl; he merely acknowledged that she was a hot girl with cheap make-up and jewelry, waiting tables at a pizza place. He also knew that he could have her in the back seat of his car within minutes if he wanted. She was just like most of the waitresses he encountered, no matter if it was a pizza joint or one of the country clubs to which he belonged. She was the kind of girl who desperately looked for a man to take her away from her miserable life. She was merely one more girl who wanted something for nothing from men. He guessed her age to be about twenty-six; not necessarily too young for him. As he eyed her tight little body up and down, he thought she probably could offer a little something in return.

Nanette caught his glances. She made sure his wife wasn't looking before winking at the man and seductively biting her ruby red lips as she turned and walked away from his table. *He was hot*, she thought, *for an old dude.*

The dinner conversation consisted of Ella and the children chattering and laughing back and forth, making summer plans. Davis impatiently picked at his pizza and checked his watch. This was not his idea of a nice dinner, and the longer he sat there, the more stuck he felt-- in this restaurant and in his marriage. He was much better suited to a filet mignon or a porterhouse steak with an exceptional Cabernet Sauvignon to complement the meal. In addition to the slop these restaurants called food, the ambiance was not conducive to his general demeanor. Listening to boisterous families with even more obnoxious children was not his idea of a relaxing evening, and his agitation grew the longer he sat in the uncomfortable booth.

The kids tried to bring their father into the conversation by asking him riddles, but he was in his own world that didn't involve pizza places…or kids for that matter. His mind was on other matters…business matters. Ella made a mental note that her husband was much further removed from the rest of the family tonight. He was always removed, but tonight was different…unnerving. This was supposed to be a vacation, but this didn't feel like a vacation; it felt like work. Davis had a nervous tick about him that revealed itself through his shaking knee under the table.

Ella felt Davis' dissatisfaction, and as always, she found herself trying to balance her energy between William and Willow and her disgruntled husband. She made a futile attempt at a conversation about his current business ventures.

He cut her off, "Well, I'm sure not making any money wasting my time here," in a sharper tone and louder voice than even he expected. Ella felt her cheeks burn with embarrassment over her husband's harsh tone and words. She recoiled into her booth and tried to hide her humiliation, but her spirit was broken. She didn't care about herself, but this was not the life she wanted for her children. An awkward stillness fell over the table for the next several minutes, as Ella and the children quietly ate their pizza.

The careful, watching eyes from outside the restaurant made note that Davis sat all alone on one side of the booth while Ella and the children crowded into the opposite. *What a perfect little family*, the woman thought, as she browsed the menu posted on the front window, *except, Daddy doesn't really look like he belongs*. The stranger found satisfaction in seeing the displeasure the man was experiencing with the supposed family bonding time. She relished the miserable look on his face. *Daddy has no idea that soon and very soon, he will wish this night could be a do-over*, she thought to herself. As she walked into the restaurant, she couldn't resist walking right by Davis' table for a close-up of the perfect family. Davis had his nose in his emails, and Ella was still shaken by her husband's stinging words. She knew she was so well-disguised that Davis wouldn't recognize her. She settled into a booth across the room, but within eyeshot of the Masters' table.

Ella told her children she had a tummy ache, and she excused herself to go to the restroom; she needed a moment to gather her emotional wits, and the pizza she had barely touched was sitting hard in her stomach. She patted and kissed Willow's head as her daughter wriggled out of the booth to let her mom out. Willow snuggled back in next to William, and they continued playing their guessing games. Ella snaked through the restaurant past the other families happily celebrating the onset of summer with loved ones. She couldn't help but notice the contrast of the other fathers engaged in their family conversations; envy stabbed at her heart.

She stepped through the door that read, "Pull, pull, pull" and headed down the long hallway past the kitchen. Despite the cool breeze from the rattling air conditioning unit that was overworked due to the heat generated from the ovens, there was a waft of heat in the hallway. As she approached the last of several doors on the right, Ella looked at the open door leading to the alley. The sign posted on the door to the alley read, "This Door Must Stay Closed At All Times!" The door, however, was wide open. *Odd*, Ella thought. *Should it be open? Should I close it?* She thought about the door for a fleeting moment and then opened the door to the women's restroom.

Ella saw a pair of clunky black tennis shoes on the floor of the first stall. She unconsciously made her way to the handicapped stall. Inside, she carefully placed toilet paper on the toilet seat, a ritual she followed religiously when using public restrooms. She laughed to herself as she neatly made her nest, realizing she had no hesitation whipping down her pants and squatting to pee in the woods. *There is just something disgusting about putting my butt where other butts had been*, she thought.

With her shorts just past her knees, she heard a male voice quietly sing, "Olly Olly oxen free, you are going to leave with me." Before she could process what was happening, she was blinded by a red laser that was mounted atop a pistol. "Slowly finish taking your piss, pull up your shorts and open the door," the creepily calm voice stated.

She quickly pulled up her shorts midstream, and with trembling fingers, reluctantly opened the stall door. Before she had time to think, the man had Ella's face smashed into the metal frame of the door.

"I said, Olly Olly oxen free, you are going to leave with me!" he hissed through clenched teeth. His fingers gripped her hair tightly; she thought the stranger would rip it from her head.

Ella tasted blood and felt herself screaming, but no sound escaped her mouth. Her children's innocent faces were all that flashed through her mind. She begged the man to let her go, offering him any amount of money in exchange for a safe return to her family. She pleaded, "Please don't hurt me. We are here on vacation, and my husband and children are out in a booth waiting for me to return."

"Fuck your husband!" The male voice hissed, "Ella, IF you ever see your children again, it won't be for a very long time."

When Ella heard her name come out of the man's mouth, fear turned her legs to rubber, and he had to grab her around the waist to keep her from crumbling to the ground. She knew this wasn't a random act of violence and that she was in trouble! Tears stung her cheeks as she quietly begged the man to let her go.

He whispered, "We have some games in store for you. Now take off all of your clothes."

Sickness choked Ella. Her body shook uncontrollably as she fumbled to remove her clothes. The black tennis shoes remained perfectly still just on the other side of the dividing wall. *This woman would be able to tell her husband what had happened*, she thought. But the man HAD to know there was another person in the bathroom, and he wouldn't risk this behavior if... At that moment, Ella's fear became palpable. *Was this part of the setup?*

The man dropped something from a Ziploc bag into the toilet and then stuffed her clothes in. He shoved the empty plastic bag into his pocket and handed her a set of clothes. "You have one minute to put these on, or you will never see your children again!"

She quickly followed his orders as she fumbled to put on the outfit that was provided to her. She looked down to see her favorite gray "I hike" t-shirt and black yoga pants-- clothes she had not brought on vacation. Confused unreason closed off her vocal cords and left her speechless.

She knew she should scream, kick-- anything but walk out the door with the stranger, but the 9mm pistol shoved into her side persuaded her to do so anyway. The man quietly ordered Ella to giggle as he put his arm around her shoulders, kissed her on her neck, and hustled her out of the restroom, out the back door and into the backseat of a beat-up car. If anyone did happen to see the duo, they would assume it was just a couple having a summertime quickie in the bathroom.

Moments later, a second man hopped into the driver's seat, started the car, and took off down the alley. *Was this the owner of the clunky black tennis shoes?* Ella feared. If so, there was nobody around to witness her abduction. She knew she was in trouble, but she didn't know how to make the nightmare stop.

As the car made its way down the alley, the driver was agitated and uneasy. The Chicago Cubs baseball cap was pulled halfway over his eyes, and the collar of his camouflage jacket was popped up to further disguise his appearance. The man who had stuffed Ella into the back seat continued to jab the gun into her ribs. "Don't make a move or a sound, or I will empty this gun in you."

The car slowly turned from the alley onto the road in front of Gastone's Pizzeria. Ella looked through the front window of the restaurant and saw the angelic faces of her children lighted up by their iPad screens as they giggled at each other. It was at this moment that sheer fear overtook Ella and she began to sob.

"Shut the bitch up, or I swear I will blow her fucking head off right now!" screamed the driver. The sudden roar jolted Ella back to her senses; she quickly gathered her wits and gained control over her tears. She began praying under her breath for God to watch over and care for her babies.

The man next to her heard her prayers. He increased the pressure of the gun into Ella's ribcage and whispered into Ella's ear, "Olly Olly oxen free, your God is not as strong as me." Terror, as she had never experienced it, wrapped her entire body. A wicked laugh slowly rose from the man's mouth, and the driver soon joined in.

The sound of the men's cackling chatter and the vile smell of her abductor's breath made Ella's stomach roll. Before she could stop herself, projectile vomit sent her pizza all over her lap. Her captor's laughs quickly turned to anger.

"What the fuck? Dammit, Jax, the bitch just threw up all over. I'm going to fucking throw up if we don't get this stench out of here. Open the fucking windows!"

The louder he yelled, the more violently her stomach retched. Tears and snot ran down her face as she uncontrollably heaved up her entire dinner. The smell of her own vomit induced dry heaves when she had nothing left in her tiny belly.

The two men continued to shout obscenities at her and at each other. Jax hurled a stack of Arby's napkins into the back seat and said, "Make her clean herself up and throw that shit out the window. I'm about to start throwing my own guts up!"

Ella wiped her face the best she could, gathered the barely-digested chunks of pizza with the napkins, and threw them out the window as the car drove further away from the restaurant. Her back-seat neighbor handed her a bottle of water. She put water on the last two napkins and attempted to wipe the remnants of her vomit from her yoga pants and t-shirt. Frightened and humiliated, she slowly sipped from the water bottle in an attempt to get the vile taste out of her mouth. Her world became cloudy, and within minutes, she could not keep her spinning head upright; her chin fell to her chest.

The stranger next to her took the bottle of water out of her hands just as it was about to fall from her fingertips. He dropped another pill into the remaining half bottle of water and screwed the lid back on.

Looking through the rearview mirror to the back seat, Jax said, "Dude, we aren't tryin' to kill the bitch; we are just tryin' to keep her quiet on the long ride home. Go easy with those pills, Donny; she isn't very big. Maybe you better add some more water to that bottle."

Donny followed Jax's instructions and filled the remaining half of the bottle back up. As he listened to her deep breathing, he quietly chuckled to himself about how weak and vulnerable she looked when she wasn't so high and mighty flirting with a good-looking stranger or driving her fancy Mercedes Benz. His thoughts took him back to earlier in the day when he sat unsuspectingly watching her make her Redbox selections. He smiled a wicked smile through jagged teeth, knowing the games were about to begin. He scooched in closer to Ella, closed his eyes and continued his fantasies, as Jax parked the car on the side of the twenty-four-hour laundromat and waited for June.

3

Ten minutes after his wife's departure from the table, Davis looked at his watch and impatiently cursed to no one in particular. "Damn it! How long does it take a woman to take a piss? I told her I needed to be back at the condo by 9:00 to prepare for my 9:30 conference, and it is now 8:40!"

When he noticed that she had taken her purse, he muttered, "She better as hell not be back there primping!" This comment made no sense to the kids because their mom never primped. Sensing his agitation, both children offered to go look for her.

Willow said, "I will go since I'm on the outside and I can go all the way into the bathroom."

William rebutted in a teasing manner, "I am eleven; therefore, I am more mature, so I should go."

Davis did not join the competition to go looking for his wife. After listening to the two banter back and forth, Davis barked at Willow to go tell her mother that time was money and that he didn't have all evening to wait for her! He sipped the final drops of his less-than-acceptable red wine as he waited for Ella and Willow to return. His agitation became evident to the patrons around him as the minutes ticked by.

The Gothic-looking girl across the room found great satisfaction at the man's apparent annoyance. She sipped her coke as she eagerly awaited the rest of the show.

When Willow returned, her ashen skin and horror-filled eyes made her look as if she had seen a ghost. She attempted to open her mouth to speak, but no words escaped her lips. She was mute, which only further aggravated her father's less-than-patient attitude. "Well, what did she say, and where the hell is she?" By this time, other patrons were attempting to look inconspicuous as they watched the painful interaction between father and daughter.

Willow Rose knew that if her father saw tears, he would chastise her for acting like a baby, but for the life of her she couldn't make her mouth turn on and her eyes turn off. She stood in front of him with tears streaming down her cheeks and an empty glaze over her face. William knew this situation was getting worse by the minute, so he took matters into his own hands. He attempted to calmly wind through the tables full of families, but once through the door to the hallway, he bolted down the short hall and rushed into the women's restroom. He returned to his father with the same startled look on his face and an inability to speak.

Growing increasingly impatient and agitated, Davis quietly waived Nanette over and explained through a fake smile and a hushed voice, "There seems to be a bit of a problem, Nanette. My wife went to the bathroom fifteen minutes ago, and she has failed to return. The children appear to be concerned about something. Can you please go check on her and explain that I am in a bit of a hurry to get home?"

Nanette followed Davis' directions and headed to the restroom. Even though he was irritated, he couldn't resist watching her hot little ass as she turned to walk away.

She noticed the "closed for cleaning" floor sign in front of the women's bathroom. She wondered why someone would clean the bathroom during the busiest time of the day. She moved the sign aside and went in. She looked in the first empty stall and saw nothing, but when she looked into the handicapped stall, she was filled with horror. She quickly found her manager; he went through the same motions with the same reaction.

After several minutes, the two employees, both pasty white, returned to Davis' table. Davis stood to face them. "What is going on here?" Davis hissed at the manager, who had already put a sign on the lobby door leading to the restrooms that read, "Restrooms are closed due to a plumbing issue."

The manager's voice was shaky. "Sir," he yammered, "your wife...is not in the restroom."

"What do you mean she isn't in the restroom?" he spoke in a condescending tone through clenched teeth, "She has to be in there; where else could she be? She hasn't come back out here now, has she?" The exaggerated contortions he was making with his face turned him into a frightful looking man, and Nanette took a couple steps back.

The manager whispered, "Sir, your wife is no longer in the restroom, and there is evidence that there may have been some sort of struggle. We have contacted the Orlando Police Department; they will be here momentarily."

Davis felt like he had taken a hallucinogenic drug that caused his whole world to spin like he was in the middle of a tornado. He became lightheaded, and his face turned ashen.

"Sir, you don't look too good; maybe you better have a seat." The manager grasped his arm and guided Davis into the booth across from his stupefied children. Awkwardly, the manager said, "We will go in back and see if the OPD has arrived." Both of the employees wanted to get away from Davis before they witnessed a potential explosion.

Davis knew something had gone wrong; this was not the plan. The children stared at their empty plates to avoid making eye contact with their father and to avoid the invasive stares of other patrons.

Realizing the police were only moments away, Davis had the wherewithal to know he needed to get rid of the only real evidence that would make him look like a suspect. He slid the flip phone out of his pocket, palmed the phone, turned in his seat, and used the back of the booth to lift himself out of the tight quarters. All in one fell swoop, he dropped the cell phone into the plant behind their booth and stood up as a police officer, accompanied by the store manager, walked toward the table.

The kids watched helplessly in fear as their father and the police officer exchanged a few muffled words. Davis told the kids to stay put as he walked in the direction of the bathroom. Left alone at the table, the children huddled next to each other and choked down feelings of sickness that were rising in their throats. William and Willow's ghostly faces spoke volumes, as they waited for what seemed like hours.

Goth-girl kept her face buried in the Angry Birds game on her phone and smiled at the children's misery. If only she could get away with walking by and taunting the two brats, but there would be plenty of time for that. She couldn't get too cocky with her finely-tuned plan.

The sound of nearby sirens froze the children in their seats. The manager turned the sign on the door around to read "Closed." Police cars arrived in the alley behind the restaurant and around the side of the building. The children could see three police officers standing out on the sidewalk in front of the building. An elderly waitress was given the job of gathering the traumatized children and their belongings and shuffling them to the manager's office, where they sat paralyzed in fear for the next few minutes.

A female police officer quietly approached them and introduced herself as Sergeant Breanna Pickett. She said, "You two are completely safe with me. I am going to ask you a few questions about what you saw. Is that OK?"

The children nodded in silence.

As each child bravely gave the exact same account of what they saw, Officer Pickett took notes. They were trying hard to be tough because they didn't want their father to yell at them for acting like babies.

Pickett explained that they would be going with her for a while until the police found their mommy. "Meanwhile," Sergeant Pickett explained, "your daddy is going to help the police figure out what happened. I promise he will be right behind us." She expected an outburst of tears as the children left their father, but the two numb faces didn't even look over at their paternal figure as he stood in the hallway talking with police officers.

Sergeant Pickett led the stunned kids past the bathroom door, now covered with yellow police tape. Chills raced up and down their bodies, and their legs felt like rubber bands. Both secretly prayed they would see their mommy again. Neither could erase the image of her blood-stained green cotton shorts and white top stuffed in the toilet, or the blood on the metal frame of the door. Silent fear made both children mute. Their hands, wringing with clamminess, were intertwined as if they now had only each other.

Davis, stunned and confused, moved into the manager's office and sat, weak-kneed with local police as he listened to a barrage of questions about his missing wife. He just kept shaking his head, saying, "I don't understand; we are on vacation. This doesn't make any sense." Officer Jordan Daniel asked Davis if he had a picture of his wife in his wallet or on his phone.

Davis awkwardly replied, "No."

"Do you have a Facebook or other social media account that would have a picture of your wife?" Davis quickly explained that he kept his accounts professional by not including personal pictures of his wife and children.

"Please give me a physical description of your wife, sir, including what she was wearing this evening," Officer Daniel inquired.

Davis could not, for the life of him, remember what his wife had worn to dinner. He knew she was wearing a tank top and the cut-off jean shorts earlier in the day when they were arguing; he despised those shorts. He had to admit, however, that he thought she had a gray or white summer top on but wasn't quite sure what color shorts she had on or what style of shoes she wore to the restaurant. The officer gave the man across from him a judgmental look.

The officer continued, "Can you tell us what your wife's activities included today?"

Again, Davis struggled with his wife's timeline because he had been dealing with his own problems all day.

Daniel felt Davis' mental struggle. He tried to give the man the benefit of the doubt by understanding that his wife had just disappeared. The officer encouraged him to take a deep breath and start at the beginning of the day. He told him to give any and all events as they came to him, no matter how insignificant they might seem.

Davis started with the morning's events. He said, "I left the condo at 5:30 a.m. to go down to the fitness center. I worked out until 7:00, and then ran to the Starbucks around the corner to get a cup of coffee. I didn't think Ella and the kids would be awake, so I didn't want to disturb them."

Daniel looked at Davis' muscular stature and assumed the gym was part of his daily routine. He sarcastically wondered if he hit the tanning beds after the gym. He knew this kind of guy, and he wasn't a fan.

Davis continued, "I got back to the condo at 8:00, and Ella was fixing breakfast for the kids. I had some work to get done and needed peace and quiet, so they packed a cooler and headed down to the pool sometime around 9:00. I heard them come back in around the noon hour. She fixed all of us some lunch-- grilled cheese sandwiches and soup."

"Did you all eat lunch together, as a family?" the officer interrupted.

As Davis began to explain. "I am working on large-scale business investment," he quickly looked at his watch and muttered, "Fuck... Gianni!"

This caught the officer off guard, and he inquired about Davis' outburst. Heat climbed its way up to Davis' neck, as the officer asked him who Gianni was. In as little of an explanation as possible, Davis explained, "Gianni is a fellow investor, and he is supposed to meet with other investors tomorrow; we had planned a telephone meeting tonight at 9:30 to finalize our part of the plans."

Officer Daniel looked at his own watch in an exaggerated way and expressed, "Well, Mr. Masters, it is 9:42. Did he try to call you?" Masters found himself stuck for words as he tried to weave a web of lies that would not leave him stuck in the middle of a pile of his own shit.

Officer Daniel repeated, with emphasis, "Did he try to call you? You may check your phone if this meeting is so important."

"It is fine," Davis lied. "Let's please focus on finding my wife."

Davis knew the reality was that Gianni would have already tried to call him, most likely several times. He was glad he kept his flip phone on silent. His hand unconsciously went to his right pocket, and the recollection that he had the foresight to dump the phone sent a rush of relief through him. Davis was immediately conscientious of his now-fidgeting clammy hands on his lap. If he didn't get hold of Gianni soon, there was a considerable chance their deal would go south.

Daniel acknowledged that they had somehow gotten off track with his wife's timeline from earlier in the day. He looked back at the previous page in his notes and said, "Let's see, so you stopped at lunch. I had asked you if you ate lunch as a family." As he continued his notes, he scrawled, "Gianni" on the yellow pad.

Davis indicated that he ate lunch in the bedroom while he worked on projects and that his wife and kids ate lunch at the kitchen table. This admission brought another raised eyebrow and an inquisitive look by Officer Daniel.

Davis quickly continued, "After lunch, Ella ran some errands. I didn't know she had left until I went to the kitchen to get some water. William told me she left strict instructions for them to read and not disturb me. Like I said, I have this big business deal." He again nervously looked at his watch.

"What errands did your wife run, Mr. Masters, and what time did she return?" the officer prompted.

"I know she went to the grocery store and to the Redbox to exchange movies, but I don't know what other errands she ran."

Daniel asked, "Would she have paid with cash or a bank card?"

"I don't know for sure. I assume Ella used our debit card for any purchases. I know that is the only way Redbox works, so she definitely used a card for that transaction. I can check our online bank account if I need to."

"Mr. Masters, we might need a record of all transactions from the past week." He knew he could not demand anything of Davis since he was only gathering information, so he chose his words carefully.

Davis questioned, "Why do you need transactions from a whole week ago?"

Daniel explained, "Often times in a missing person case, financial, computer, and telephone records provide the most telling story of what happened to the person. Granted, this may be a random kidnapping, but over ninety percent of all abductions take place by someone close to the victim or at least knowledgeable about the person. We also need to consider the possibility that she left by her own volition."

Davis argued, "She would never just up and leave the kids and me. Plus, we don't even live here, much less know anyone in Orlando. We are on fucking vacation!" His voice rose, "That makes no fucking sense."

Daniel inwardly questioned whether or not Davis Masters was somehow behind his wife's disappearance, and he couldn't hold back the snide remark, "Why is that, Mr. Masters? Because you are such an attentive, loving husband? Is THAT why she would never leave you, sir?" The officer bit back the additional words he wanted to spew at Davis. Instead, he made several notes as he continued questioning the man about his wife's behaviors and actions over the past several weeks. Davis felt more like a suspect with each question asked.

He said, "Officer, do I need to get an attorney before I answer any more questions?"

Daniel knew that it was all over if Davis brought in an attorney. With a gentler tone, he replied, "Sir, I'm sorry if my words have, in any way, made you feel like you have any reason to obtain an attorney. You are by no means being questioned as a person of interest. We are simply trying to gather as much information as quickly as possible to bring your wife safely back to you and the kids. Please accept my apology if I have been too blunt. The first twenty-four hours are critical in these situations, and sometimes I get so wrapped up in the investigation that I forget I am dealing with a concerned husband." Daniel backed off, and both men settled down.

At 10:00 p.m. Officer Daniel told Davis his shift would be ending soon and that he needed to finish up his paperwork from the day's events. He asked Davis if he minded accompanying him to the police station, where Officer Patricia Irvine would be taking over the case for the night.

Davis was relieved when he heard a woman's name. He was able to use his charm more productively to disarm women. Men, he assumed, were intimidated by his physical prowess and cut-throat business sense.

In a reassuring tone, Daniel said, "Mr. Masters, officers will remain at the restaurant throughout the night to look for further clues into your wife's disappearance, but we may need to check out your rental car since Ella used it for her errands today. We might find something that will help us determine a motive for her disappearance." The officer knew he didn't really need Davis' permission to check the car but wanted to keep him from thinking he had a need for a lawyer for as long as possible.

Davis knew there was nothing in the car that could possibly incriminate him of anything, so he said, "Yes, please,

Officer, do whatever you need to do to get my wife back to me safe and sound."

"That's our objective here, Mr. Masters. We appreciate all of the help you are giving us." Daniel's words did not parallel his thoughts.

Officer Daniel led Davis out the back door of the restaurant and into the back of his squad car. Orlando Police Department officers took pictures of the crime scene and gathered the evidence in the women's bathroom, which included a small purse and a set of clothes that had been stuffed into the toilet. They checked the men's restroom and secured the perimeter of the building. Since there was evidence of blood, they assumed Ella had not left the restaurant willingly.

Officer Rick Thompson checked the contents of the small purse; it contained a pack of gum, Burt's Bees chapstick, a glass rollerball bottle labeled BREATHE, and a leather wallet. The wallet had Ella Master's Illinois driver's license, debit card, credit card, forty-seven dollars in cash, and school pictures of her children. A folded Post-it was tucked between the plastic cards and photographs. Thompson unfolded it and read the five words aloud, "I WANT TO HELP YOU!"

"Why," he wondered, "does Ella need help." He further questioned, "Why do you have so little in your purse, but feel this note is important enough to keep?" The note was not faded, which led Thompson to believe it was not in there for keepsake purposes.

"Talk to me, Ella," he said, as he looked at her driver's license picture. "Who wants to help you, and WHY?" He took pictures of each item, bagged the items and handed them off to crime scene investigators.

Without giving specific details about Ella's disappearance, Thompson informed the employees and patrons that police were looking into a situation that had occurred at the restaurant. He asked restaurant staff members to please find empty booths out in the lobby.

He opened the door between the hallway and the dining area and said, "Folks, if I may have your attention, please. We have a situation at hand that is going to require that you all be interviewed before you can leave the restaurant. We will interview families with small children first and progress as quickly as possible to get everyone out in an expedited manner. Please refrain from using your mobile cellular devices until you leave the building, so that valuable information is not compromised."

Immediately, a buzz of conversation filled the room as families speculated what might have happened. Teenagers secretly started tweeting, #lockdown at Gastone's Pizzeria... something bad has happened. Police everywhere, and we can't leave. #Freeprizza."

Officer Thompson called his first family of five back to a makeshift desk in the kitchen and began his line of questioning.

"I need each of you to please state your name, telephone number, and address, and then tell me what time you arrived and any observations you made about other patrons or employees."

He took copious notes as each family member filled in the details of his or her dining experience, including observations throughout the dinner.

Most of the comments by the interviewees were generic, but several people mentioned the couple with two children at the booth at the north end of the restaurant. They discussed some version of the man acting irritated, leaving the restaurant for several minutes, and returning still annoyed. One couple mentioned the wife going, presumably, to the restroom. Several recalled that the man raised his voice at the children, who seemed really upset about something. Thompson drew lines from one note to another as if he were connecting the dots to solve a puzzle. Patrons discussed conversations they overheard from other tables as they engaged in their own dialogue, but none of this additional information was consistent enough to seem relevant.

The homely looking girl in the corner booth continued to bury her face in her Angry Birds game. She wore ripped blue jeans, old-school Converse tennis shoes, a black sleeveless zip-up hoodie, Goth-looking gloves with the fingertips cut off, and a striped stocking cap. She ate the last bite of her pizza as the final scene of the movie she had ingeniously created unfolded. It was her turn to be interviewed. She had seen it all. There was the agitation of a man who apparently didn't want to be sitting in a pizza joint with his family, his ogling of the young waitress, his wife who was trying to keep the kids occupied, and his trip outside. She had watched Mommy Dearest disappear, as well as the prized reactions of her terrified children, obnoxious impatience of her husband, and nervous responses by restaurant workers. It was the perfect scene, and it was all her extraordinary work. *I am a genius*, she thought.

Of course, she only thought all of this. When it was her turn to be interviewed, she said very little. She gave her name, address and phone number, in between chomping her gum and blowing bubbles, which grated on Thompson's nerves.

"I'm just a local girl, grabbing some grub and getting out of the summer heat," she told him.

The smart-ass in him wanted to say, "Maybe you would not be so hot if you didn't wear a stocking cap and gloves in the middle of summer in Florida," but he knew these local skateboarders had to keep up their 'I hate the world' hard-ass images.

Her accounts of the evening were less descriptive than the other patrons. She explained that she had her earbuds in and was playing Angry Birds on her phone while she ate her pizza. When Officer Thompson asked her if she noticed any families that stood out in the restaurant, she responded, "Dude, this place is full of yuppy families on vacation all summer. I do my best to block them and all their rich bullshit out when I'm just trying to get something to eat and chill out."

Most of Officer Thompson's questions were answered with grunts, shoulder shrugs, and one-word answers. *This girl is less-than-appealing and even less helpful*, he thought; thus, the interview was short.

As with the other patrons, Thompson handed the girl his business card and told her to call the number on it if she thought of any other details that might be important. Thompson was sure the girl would not have additional information.

June, or Brandi Conrad according to the stolen Florida issued driver's license, walked out of the kitchen and back through the door to the dining area of the restaurant. She was relieved to see that there was only one officer in the dining area, and he was talking to the employees. She returned to her booth that had not yet been cleared, slurped the last of her Coca-Cola, threw a twenty-dollar bill on the table, and headed toward the front door. She walked very close to the begonia located near the Masters' booth, reached in, grabbed the cell phone out of the dirt, shoved it in her pocket, and continued walking right out the front door, just like the other patrons who had patiently endured their interviews.

She walked the winding streets until she arrived at the laundromat, a mile and a half from Gastone's Pizzeria, where the tan Honda Civic was waiting for her. She wanted to make sure she hadn't been followed, so she carefully wound her way through side streets and backyards. She hopped in the front passenger seat, looked back at the figure slumped against the back door, and said, "Let's get the hell out of here!"

"What took you so fucking long?" barked the man in the back seat, with a teasing tone.

"I had to finish my dinner, Donny." the girl laughed, as she reached over and gave the driver a peck on the cheek.

"Thanks, Jax," she whispered as she licked his ear. "I promise I will pay you very well for your efforts."

Jax gave her a long kiss, and, from the back seat, Donny watched their tongues dance in and out of each other's mouths.

"I will hold you to that promise just as soon as we get this long-ass drive behind us and get our trophy wife into her new home."

Watching the two lovers grope at each other in the front seat made Donny want to have his way with Ella even more. He knew he was under strict orders not to touch the goods, but he might just have to see about those strict orders. *After all*, he thought as he caressed his dirty fingers up and down Ella's thighs, *Rules are made to be broken.*

The car made its way to the Florida Turnpike, and Ella's heavy breathing indicated that the magic pill had done its job. At some point, she awoke with a migraine, caused by the tight bandana that now covered her eyes, but she was given another drink of water and passed out again. As she drifted in and out of sleep, she occasionally heard the whispers of the other occupants in the car, but she was too out of it to comprehend, or even care about anything that was being said. When she woke up enough to try to talk, her dry mouth begged for water. After every drink, she passed out again. This pattern continued for what might have been hours or days. She couldn't process her thoughts enough to know how long she had been in the backseat of the stale, vomit-smelling car.

Jax could not help but watch his rearview mirror nervously as the car made its way up Highway 75, but local authorities were busy looking for Ella in Orlando, and each passing mile made him breathe a little easier. The thirty-year-old had spent most of his teens and twenties skirting the edge of societal rules. He drank too much whiskey, smoked some weed, and got a bit mouthy on occasion, but he had a clean rap sheet, and, aside from this little adventure, he had never committed any real crimes. He had been working as an independent courier for the past two years for companies who needed faster service than UPS or the snail mail postal system. He had met June a year earlier when he delivered items to the country club where she was a waitress. He was immediately hooked when she flashed him her flirtatious smile. June had an uncanny ability to look super sweet one minute and like a total rebel the next, but deep down, he knew she was a good girl; she drank very little, had never smoked cigarettes or weed, and had never received so much as a speeding ticket. Jax melted every time she looked at him with her big brown eyes. She had him wrapped around her little finger, and he would do anything for his girl.

Donny, on the other hand, had not cleaned up his act, and his brushes with the law had landed him in jail a few too many times. The last time he went to court, the judge told him if he saw him again, he would go away for a very long time. Donny knew the reason Jax had recruited him was that he wouldn't rat Jax or June out to the cops.

As the distance between Ella Masters and her family grew, local authorities frantically searched for clues into her disappearance. The lieutenant in charge decided not to tell Davis about the unknown mass they found in the toilet underneath his wife's clothes.

After all of the restaurant patrons were gone, the detectives began interviewing restaurant employees, who made few meaningful contributions to the case. They all gave essentially the same story. The cooks indicated they never see the customers, and the wait staff said they were too busy keeping up with the summertime crowds to notice much.

Nanette, the young waitress who waited on the Master's table, recalled through the nervous chomping of several of the free mints the restaurant provided to customers, "Well, the dad sat on one side of the booth and the mom and two kids sat on the other side. He seemed irritated during most of the dinner. See, the deep-dish pizzas take a lot longer to cook, and I think he was pissed off or something that they ordered that."

Officer Dane Curtis inquired, "Can you describe this pissed off behavior?"

Nanette continued, "Well, the mom and kids were playing guessing games and having fun, but he didn't even talk to them or play along. He just sat across the table on his phone, watching his phone throughout most of the dinner. He barely touched his pizza when it did come."

Officer Curtis continued, "Did he go to the restroom or anywhere else at any time?" Nanette recalled his leaving the pizza place for maybe ten minutes or so, "I think he might have gone out for a smoke, but I don't know if he used the bathroom at all. We get swamped in here during the summer, so, like, I don't pay much real attention to the customers. I just remember him because he seemed really irritated with the whole family dinner thing." She paused for effect and continued, "But not too irritated to check me up and down a few times." As Nanette spoke the last words, she unconsciously sat up a little taller and fussed with her hair as if to validate the stranger's interest in her.

Officer Curtis continued to cover his yellow notepad with black ink scrawls. As he finished up the interview, he gave Nanette his business card and asked her to contact him if she thought of anything else, no matter how insignificant she thought it might be.

Nanette shook the police officer's hand and walked out of her manager's office. She felt a guilty pang in her gut over leaving out one tidbit of information, but she quickly justified it in her mind. *I need this job if I want to keep my apartment, and if manager Jim found out, I would get canned.*

She pictured sneaking out the back door to grab a few quick drags off Nick, the cook's, cigarette. Jim despised smoking, and he gave strict orders that waiters and waitresses were not allowed to take smoke breaks while they were serving customers. Nanette had heard his lecture on smoking multiple times. "Customers don't want to get wafts of cigarette stench from your hands, clothes, and breath as you serve their pizzas. That is a disgusting turn-off." To escape the scrutinizing eye of Jim, Nanette had slipped around the back side of the building;

it was then that she saw the man's face lit up by his flip phone as he smoked a cigarette and texted under the night sky. When she returned to his family's table, he had not yet returned, but an iPhone vibrated at his spot at the table, and his wife didn't answer it. Nanette assumed the phone was his, but a lot of business people had two cell phones, so it didn't seem that unusual. She also justified that if the police searched him, they would find two cell phones, and they would be none the wiser that she withheld information. This quelled the guilt over her not being completely honest, but it did make her wonder if the man might have something to do with his wife's disappearance.

Officer Curtis interviewed Jim, the manager, next. "Was the back door closed and locked all evening?"

Jim could not confirm that. He explained that although the sign stated, "This door MUST remain closed at all times," sometimes the cooks propped it open when they burned something and needed to get the smell out the back door instead of into the dining area.

"Sir, did you put the portable sign in front of the bathroom door that read, "Closed for cleaning?"

The manager shook his head, "I don't know who put the sign there, but I didn't do it. We would never clean the bathrooms during our rush times. I only noticed the sign when Nanette and I went back to check on the man's wife."

"How many of the signs do you have and where are they kept?"

"We have two, one for each bathroom, and we just keep them back in the corner outside the women's bathroom."

"So, anyone could have grabbed it and put it in front of the women's bathroom door, correct?"

"Yes, I guess so."

Officer Curtis said, "We will need to see surveillance from all of the security cameras."

Jim hemmed and hawed for a moment before reluctantly admitting that the security cameras splattered all over the restaurant were entirely useless because they were only for show. He explained that he put them up to deter customers from dining-and-dashing and employees from giving away free food, doing nasty things to the food, or stealing food or money.

Officer Curtis shook his head in frustration. He had heard this explanation one too many times when they desperately needed video surveillance to help solve a crime.

Several other employee interviews brought no enlightenment or resolve to the case of the missing Illinois woman. Law enforcement officials were uncertain if a crime was involved or if she left on her own accord. The evidence in the bathroom didn't look good for the latter, but they saw all kinds of things in the summertime in Florida, and there was no concrete evidence to rule out any possible scenarios since none of the employees said they saw anything.

4

Davis Masters' drive to the police station was a quiet one; he replayed the images of the evening's events over and over like a bad video loop. Officer Daniel apologized that Davis had to sit in the back seat of the squad car. "Police protocol, ya know. Civilians aren't allowed to sit in the front seat." Davis didn't argue the point, but he knew this excuse was a bunch of horse shit because he saw police officers toting their kids all over town in the front seats of their squad cars.

Daniel reminded Davis as they walked into the Orlando Police Station, "You are not being questioned as a person of interest, but we need your help putting the details of today's events together."

Daniel led Davis to a stark white room with a white metal table and matching chair, where he silently waited for the new officer on duty. He was taken away by her looks as Officer Patricia Irvine introduced herself. She extended a consoling handshake to Davis and expressed her concern over his unfortunate situation. She was tall, tan, and muscular, with thick blonde hair that was twisted up into a ponytail. Her blue eyes, that seared into anyone who looked directly into them, were the color of an ocean wave. She took a few minutes to look over the copy of the notes Officer Jordan Daniel had left with her. Davis interrupted her reading as he stared intently into her eyes and said, in a charismatic but vulnerable tone, "Officer Irvine, may I call you Patricia, or is it Pati?"

She looked disdainfully up from her notes in a curt tone and said, "Only my family calls me Pati. You, Mr. Masters, will call me Officer Irvine, nothing more, nothing less. Do we have a clear understanding, Mr. Masters?" She held on to "Mr." long enough to indicate she was not buying anything this arrogant asshole was selling. She couldn't believe the man was coming on to her while she was investigating his wife's disappearance.

He regrouped as he realized, too late, that he had pulled the wrong tactic out of his bag of tricks. This chick was a balls-to-the-wall kind of cop, who wanted to let everyone know she wasn't about to be pushed around. Or maybe, he thought, Officer Irvine was the type that wasn't into men. *If the latter was true, what a shame*, he thought. *She was too pretty to be a dike, but that seemed to be the vogue thing these days*. Either way, he knew his charm and good looks were going to get him nowhere with this bitch.

Irvine spent a few minutes looking over Daniel's notes before addressing Davis. After she felt like she had a sufficient understanding of Ella's earlier activities, she asked Davis to begin by explaining what happened between the time his wife arrived home from her errands and the time she disappeared from the restaurant.

He explained that she came home and got the kids settled into a movie, while she took a bath. Davis lied, "She needs a lot of 'me' time-- if you know what I mean. She doesn't like to take the kids on errands with her, and, well, she enjoys her private time." Davis was hoping to paint a picture that took the negative attention off of him and placed it on his missing wife. As innocently as he could sound, he questioned aloud, without looking at the police officer, "Do you think maybe she ran off on us?" He hung his defeated head for effect. Deep down, he knew that was not the answer to her disappearance; she loved her kids too much to leave them with him, but he didn't mind invoking that question in the minds of the police. He was willing to create any motive that didn't lead back to him because he knew fingers would start pointing his way soon enough.

Irvine took his words as a rhetorical question and didn't bother with a response. She was exhausted by him after only a few minutes, and she was disgusted by the persona of the man across the table. She asked him to please continue with the details of the evening.

Davis continued, "Ella took the kids down for a swim in the outdoor pool and then we all got ready and went to dinner." He decided there was no need to add the details about their fight. He knew admitting they had engaged in an argument earlier in the day would not bode well for the police.

He finished his statement by explaining that they got into the car at around 6:00 and drove to Gastone's Pizzeria. "We had to wait an hour to get a table, and it took nearly that long to get our pizza. I have to admit; I was more than a little irritated about the slow service." Davis thought he better throw that out in case the accounts of workers or patrons included this fact. "We had just finished our pizza when our family's nightmare began," Davis concluded. He shook his head in disbelief and pressed his fingertips into his scalp, as the thoughts of the evening rambled around in his head.

Officer Irvine said, "I read in the notes that you were supposed to make a phone call at 9:30. Was it a business or personal call?"

"A business call," he responded.

"I see. Can you tell me a little bit about your line of work, sir?"

Davis explained, "I am a bit of an entrepreneur, but my biggest business endeavor is partnering with other like-minded men in buying less than desirable commercial buildings and turning them into profitable real estate investments."

Irvine was not impressed, but she nodded her head as if she cared.

"Mr. Masters, what is the name of your business, and where is it located?"

Masters responded "IMAGE, Inc. My home base is in Springfield, Illinois, but I do most of my business in Chicago."

Irvine asked, inquisitively, "Is that an acronym for something, Mr. Masters?"

"Yes, ma'am, it stands for Investment Management and Gold Enterprises, but the bottom line," Masters explained, "is that I named my company IMAGE because it really is all about the image."

"I see" she responded in a less-than-impressed tone.

She changed her line of questioning because she didn't want to give him the opportunity to turn the interview into a brag session. "Does your wife work outside the home, Mr. Masters?"

"She is a free-lance photographer."

"What kind of photographer is she?"

Davis replied, "She does a little bit of everything, but mostly children. She loves children, and her clients love her. She has some clients who get their pictures taken every month."

"I see. Do you have contacts for all of your wife's clients?"

"I am sure all that information is on her computer."

Irvine asked, "Did she bring her computer with her?"

Davis said, "No, which was surprising. She usually takes that computer everywhere she goes. It is like another child to her. When I asked her about it, she said, 'I decided I want to unplug from electronics for a week.'"

After a pause, he said, "She spends quite a bit of time editing her portraits and creating specialty prints for her clients."

"Is that her only client-base?" Irvine asked.

"She does a lot of landscape and architectural photography, but that is mostly for her enjoyment. She sells a few prints here and there, but it is more of a passion than an income generator. A few local businesses have hired her to create images for them, but she has avoided that market for the most part. As I said, she prefers people photography."

Irvine nodded in understanding.

Davis continued, without being prompted, "She can create her own schedule, which gives her the flexibility she needs to manage all of the kids' activities."

Again, Irvine nodded and jotted down additional notes.

"Can you tell me about your wife's family? Does she have siblings, and are her parents still alive."

Davis explained, "Ella's father lives in Springfield, but he has dementia. She has a twin sister, Emilie, who lives in Chicago, but they don't see each other much." He provided a bit more information about Ella's father and sister and then added, reluctantly, "Her mother passed away in a car accident a couple of years ago."

Irvine asked a few more questions and said, "Thank you for the information, Mr. Masters. I know this is extremely hard for you. I am going to excuse myself to see if there are any updates on your wife's disappearance. I will be back in a few minutes. Can I bring you back a bottle of water or something?"

"A water would be great. Thanks."

As Officer Irvine left the room, she thought about Davis' company name. She knew that for this man, IMAGE was everything. What she didn't realize was the measures he would take to keep that image up. *If business deals weren't going well and money was an issue, might he take desperate measures to ensure his image didn't falter,* she wondered. She felt a tinge of guilt over jumping to stereotypical conclusions that the husband did it, but this guy gave her the creeps.

Davis was once again left alone in the stark white room. He focused on who he had made mad enough to do something like this. He had yet to wonder if his children were doing OK.

Sergeant Pickett led William and Willow to the "Bright Future Children's Center," which was currently unoccupied. William wondered about the name of the room, given the fact that it was in a police station. The children looked around at the books, games, television, and Xbox 360, but none of the items looked appealing. Sgt. Pickett told them she needed to take care of some quick business. The worried looks on their faces screamed, "Please don't leave us!" She assured the children that she would be right in the next room for a few minutes. What William and Willow didn't know was that the two-way mirror on the wall opposite of them would provide a glimpse of their behaviors, without the influence of adults lurking over them.

Officer Irvine joined Pickett and filled her in on Davis' interview. They watched the children for the next twenty minutes, as the lifeless siblings sat on the couch huddled close together. The older brother was doing his best to comfort his little sister. The nonverbal communication between the two spoke of a close relationship, but what silenced them? What kept their young voices from working?

Irvine verbalized what the two both questioned. "Most kids would be screaming or freaking out right now, but these two are just quiet. Do you think their mom often leaves, so they don't get all that rattled, or do you suppose they are in shock?" Twenty-three minutes into the observation, Willow held her thumb up to her big brother. He pressed his thumb to hers, and they gave each other gentle smiles that turned to tears. The two officers looked at each other quizzically and noted the behavior.

Officer Irvine said, "I will run to the evidence room to get a forensic update and be right back."

Johnny, the lab guy, gave her a quick update. He said, "We have her phone, but it is locked. If her husband can give us the code, maybe we can get some information from it."

Instead of asking Davis about the code to his wife's phone, Irvine took Sgt. Pickett the evidence bag and asked, "Do you think the kids might know the code to their mom's phone? I'm guessing we have a better shot with them than we do Davis." Pickett agreed and said she would give it a try.

Pickett returned to the children's center. She didn't reveal that she had seen their secret signal. She said, with a bit of a fib, "Your father is still helping the police, but he doesn't know the code to your mommy's cell phone. Do either of you happen to

know the code? We want to see if she has received any phone
calls that might help us figure things out."

William said, "Yes, the code is 1329."

Both children knew the code because they always took
pictures and videos of all of their activities, using their mom's
phone. Although they had begged and pleaded, she had not
caved to the societal pressures to get them their own cell phones.
They were not surprised that their father did not know the code;
it was a combination of their birthdays, and he never seemed to
remember their birthdays.

With the newly obtained information, Sergeant Pickett
tapped in the four-digit code through the clear plastic and
unlocked the phone. She felt a tinge of guilt as she rummaged
through the electronic corridors of Ella's life. Her first chore was
to look at the recent calls and texts. Ella's call log only showed
records for the day of her disappearance; all previous data was
deleted. Officer Pickett saw two calls from a 3-1-2 area code
earlier in the day that lasted seven minutes and sixteen minutes
respectively. There were seven missed calls from a blocked
telephone beginning at 6:17 p.m. and ending at 8:16 p.m. There
were several outgoing phone calls to a contact labeled "Daddy,"
throughout the day, a call to Gastone's Pizzeria at 5:13, and calls
to two other local eateries earlier in the day. The duration of the
calls to her father were all under one minute. Pickett guessed this
meant Ella had reached her father's answering machine.

"Why, Mrs. Masters, were you trying so hard to contact
your father?" the sergeant found herself saying aloud. She
scribbled notes on her yellow notepad detailing the numbers and
times of all of the calls. The fact that Ella had deleted her call
log history up to today nagged at Pickett.

It was now 1:15 a.m. Florida time, which meant it was
after midnight in Illinois, so she didn't call Ella's father, who
Davis had told police had early stages of dementia. Sergeant
Pickett decided to dial the 3-1-2 number. She knew this was a
Chicago number, and thought there might be a remote chance

that the phone number belonged to Ella's sister, Emilie. Pickett had searched Ella's contacts and did not see an entry with her sister's name. She found it odd that Ella's only sibling wouldn't be considered valuable enough to hold a spot in the corridors of her phone.

Pickett knew it was late, and she was well aware that she would have to explain her actions to Lieutenant Ward later, but she pressed the unknown contact anyway. Her gut told her that this call would provide valuable information that she wouldn't get by using the station phone. She was just about to hang up when she heard a groggy female voice on the other end of the phone. "What, Ella? You finally want to talk now that I'm trying to sleep. I tried to talk earlier, and you didn't have time. Well, it is late, and now I don't have time, so this better be important!"

Pickett couldn't find her words; the pause was long enough for the phone to go "click."

"Damn," Pickett muttered. She quickly dialed the same number from her Orlando Police Department issued cell phone. It did not take the female voice as long to answer this time. In a bitchy tone, she said, "Who is this and what do you think you are doing calling me at fucking midnight?"

As quickly as the officer could get the words out, she said, "Is this Emilie Randolph? My name is officer Breanna Pickett with the Orlando Police Department."

Emilie sprang up out of bed and said, "Who did you say this is?"

Pickett replied through stuttering words, "M-M-Ma'am, I am very sorry to wake you, but, um, we have a bit of a situation here in Florida. Your sister disappeared from a local restaurant earlier this evening."

A stunned Emilie replied, "I just got a call from Ella's phone, but the person didn't say anything. Oh my God, what is going on?"

A guilty Pickett quickly admitted, "I'm sorry ma'am, I used her phone to call you. You see, the children gave me the code to Ella's phone since Davis didn't know it. When I checked Ella's call log on her iPhone, I saw the 3-1-2 area code with no name attached. Besides a few calls to a contact labeled 'Daddy,' a couple of incidental calls to restaurants, and several missed calls from a blocked number, this unlabeled number was the only other number in the call log. I took a wild guess that the number belonged to you, so I used her phone to call it."

Emilie's face reddened, and tears stung her eyes at the realization that her twin sister did not even have her contact labeled in her cell phone. Before she could get the words past the lump in her throat, Sergeant Pickett continued, "I am sorry; I know this is not police protocol, but quite honestly, I have been watching her poor children go through hell tonight, wondering where their mommy is. I have a little girl of my own, so watching them is breaking my heart."

"Oh my God, the children!" was all Emilie could get out.

"The children are fine…well, physically anyway. They are holding up pretty well considering the circumstances, but I think they might need all the family they can have right now. They explained that you and Ella are twins but that you have no other siblings. Is that correct, Emilie?"

"Yes," Emilie replied. "So, where the hell is her bastard of a husband right now? I sure as hell hope he is locked up and they are questioning him."

Sergeant Pickett was thrown off by the crass response. She had expected more questions about the children. Without thinking, Pickett said, "Well, Emilie, tell me how you REALLY feel about Mr. Masters." Pickett regretted the words before they slipped past her tongue, but they were like water flowing down a mountain; she couldn't stop them once they formed in her mouth. She had pegged Davis for a pompous asshole from the moment she met him; Emilie's comment solidified that impression, confirming her and Irvine's speculations that he might have had something to do with his wife's disappearance.

"I apologize, Emilie; that was an inappropriate comment. I was just surprised to hear such a strong comment about your brother-in-law." As Pickett continued to fumble awkwardly for words, Emilie let her off the hook by continuing her berating of Davis.

"He may be my sister's husband, but I do not consider that son-of-a-bitch my brother-in-law. I knew it was only a matter of time before something like this happened. He never loved her, and he doesn't love those kids; all he wants is our daddy's money. I'm telling you, you better be looking at him carefully; he has his filthy fingers in this somehow."

Officer Pickett listened to Ella's sister disparage Davis, and she found herself secretly agreeing with Emilie. She scribbled notes as fast as her fingers could move.

Finished with her tirade, she said in a more somber tone, "I will get on the first plane possible; I will get there as fast as I can. The children must be horrified. Oh, and, Officer Pickett, can you do me a favor? Please don't tell Davis I am coming. I would love to surprise him." The tone of her voice indicated that this was not a term of endearment.

Pickett returned to the room where the children felt they were being held as prisoners. They were beyond exhausted, but they could not will themselves to fall asleep on the hard couch. The officer told them she had contacted their Aunt Emilie and that they would be seeing her soon. The children gave each other a confused look that didn't get past Officer Pickett. They couldn't remember the last time they had seen their aunt.

Officer Pickett asked the young children about their aunt. William said, "Aunt Emilie is my mom's twin sister, but they don't really look much alike anymore. Mom has brown hair, and Aunt Emilie dyes her hair blonde. They dress a lot different, too."

"How so?" inquired Pickett.

Willow took over the explanation, "Mom just likes normal, like hiking clothes, but Aunt Emilie has like a million pairs of shoes and fancy clothes and dresses; she even travels all over the world to get new clothes."

Since Officer Pickett had the kids talking, she decided to probe a bit further. She asked the pair if they saw their Aunt Emilie very often. William explained, "Mom and Aunt Emilie had an argument a while back, and we haven't seen her since." Somehow, he thought these words painted his mom in a negative light, so he quickly added, "And she lives far away and travels a lot."

William questioned how the police knew where to find their Aunt Emilie. He wondered if she would stay with them. He knew their mom was the only person who could take care of them, and she had disappeared, but where had she gone? His stomach turned.

Willow wished their Nana was still alive or that their Papa could remember things better. "Did she leave us? Does she not love us anymore," Willow wondered, "but why was there blood in the bathroom, and why were her clothes there?"

The children were holding it together by a frayed string, but Officer Picket could tell they were on the brink of an emotional freak-out. She assured them that their daddy was nearly finished helping the police and that they would be able to leave soon.

An ominous silence filled the space in the room. William finally cleared his throat and broke the silence. Through a quivering lower lip, his broken voice squeaked out "Ma'am, do you know what happened to our mom? Something bad must have happened; she would never just leave us like this." That acknowledgment opened the floodgates, and William and Willow began crying uncontrollably for the first time since their nightmare began. Officer Pickett scooped the children into her arms and held them tightly in a futile attempt to console them. An image of her daughter snuggled in her bed flashed through her mind, and she imagined her little girl's reaction if her mommy disappeared. Pickett shuddered and squeezed the children a bit tighter, as much for her comfort as for theirs. She wanted to take William and Willow to her house and tuck them into bed with her daughter and keep them safe from their nightmare. Instead, she spoke empty words filled with empty promises of bringing their mommy safely back to them. She knew they were smart kids; she only hoped she could miraculously fulfill her promise.

5

Emilie absorbed Sergeant Pickett's words as she dialed the number she knew by heart. A groggy, Gianni, said, "Emilie, what is going on? Why are you calling me so late?"

Unable to hold back her tears, Emilie breathlessly sobbed, "Something has happened to Ella; she has disappeared."

"Whoa, calm down, Emilie, I can barely understand you. Stop crying and speak slowly; tell me what is going on." It was easy to dish out the advice, but as the words left his mouth, he had a difficult time following his own orders.

Emilie blurted, "I don't know what could have gone wrong," in an accusatory tone that questioned whether or not Gianni had a role in her sister's disappearance. "Gianni, what has happened here? I thought you had everything under control. I thought you said within a couple of days you would take Davis down and expose the financial mess he has made of his and my sister's lives. How did my sister end up disappearing, and Davis is apparently just fine?" The panic in her voice was uncharacteristic of Emilie, and it was disconcerting.

"Please, Emilie, stop yelling and tell me everything you know." Through tears, Emilie explained what the Orlando police officer told her. Fear gripped Gianni's throat as he processed what she said.

Gianni recalled the events of the previous day as he knew them. He told Emilie, "I was supposed to have a phone conference with Davis at 9:30 p.m., but he did not call, nor did he answer the phone when I attempted to contact him. I became concerned when Davis did not make communication because I had given him an ultimatum that if he could not secure the funds by 9:30 p.m., there was nothing else I could do, and the deal was over for good." Gianni had not told her he had sent his best friend, Stephano, to Florida to ensure Ella's safety as they set the "Shake and Take Down" action into motion. He didn't want her to be unnecessarily suspicious of his actions.

Emilie filled Gianni in on her phone calls with both her sister and Davis. She said, "I have never heard Davis grovel as much as he did on the phone with me today. He was clearly in desperation mode, and he was pulling out all the stops. I finally hung up on him because he kept repeating the same banal pleas about how the money would be multiplied tenfold within the year if I consented to let him borrow from the family trust. He told me he could convince Ella to make the financial move, but Davis knew he couldn't move forward without my clearance. You don't know how bad I wanted to ask him why he didn't have quite the same conscience when he took money from the account on other occasions. I called Ella within thirty minutes of my conversation with him to give her a heads up that Davis was in serious financial trouble and that he had contacted me for money, but she said she was on vacation and she would look into the situation when they got home. Oh, God, Gianni, what have we done?"

Gianni took over the conversation with a guilty tone, "I made this most recent deal so impossible that Davis would have to take great risks to get the necessary money. I knew those risks would include contacting you or finding another way of accessing your father's money or engaging in other illegal activity to obtain the money. I was ready to turn him in the second he made one illegal move, but there is no way I thought he would do something to Ella or put her in harm's way to save his own ass."

"What makes you think Davis is behind her disappearance?"

Gianni responded, "Davis might try to get rid of Ella to set up a situation where ransom money is demanded." He added,

"On the message that he left on my voicemail today, he asked if I could put our investors off for another week. He said he thought he could find a way to get the money by then. I assume he contacted you as a last resort and you told him no, so where else would he get the money? He has already burned every financial bridge he had. It makes sense, doesn't it?" He hesitated, momentarily, before verbalizing his worst fear. "Emilie, here is another scenario I just thought of: what if Davis has made other people mad or owes someone a lot of money. What if this is someone's way of getting back at him, and Ella is the pawn?"

Emilie's temples pulsed as the possible scenarios bounced through her head. She wasn't comfortable with the speed at which Gianni devised a story that placed all the blame on Davis. She wanted to trust him, but he had been working so closely with Davis lately that it scared her. She knew what Gianni was telling her about trying to financially bury the man she despised, but what if this was a trap in which she, and now Ella, had fallen. What if he and Davis were secretly in on a plan to get both of the twins' family money?

"Gianni, I need you to come clean with me! Have you done something with my sister?"

Appalled that she would insinuate such an accusation, Gianni said, "Emilie, you know I have always had your sister's best interest at heart. I wouldn't have given Davis Masters the time of day had it not been for Ella. He is an asshole and a horrible businessman. I have strewn him along for the past two years just to catch him in his own web of lies. I know you and I had our plan, but I wouldn't implement it without your knowledge or input, especially since you are integral to the plan."

Emilie unconsciously rubbed her fingers through her short brown, curly hair.

Gianni added, "My pushing of Davis might be the very thing that has put the only woman I have ever loved in jeopardy. I don't know what has happened to Ella, and I am scared to death."

Emilie was relieved that he couldn't see her cringe when he said the words. An awkward silent moment passed through the virtual phone lines. She couldn't comprehend how a man like Gianni could find her sister so much more attractive than she. As hard as she had tried to create chemistry with the man, he just didn't feel for her the way he felt for her twin. A very awkward one-night-stand induced by one-too-many glasses of wine proved it, and it led to months of no communication and finally to a sort of "We fucked up, now let's move on with just a friendship" kind of friendship. The encounter left Emilie even more perplexed about what her plain Jane sister had that she didn't possess. Most of the time it wasn't awkward, but right now it was.

Gianni knew he had been just another challenge for Emilie Randolph, and he had regretted it ever since. He felt the woman's discomfort, but at this moment it wasn't about Emilie, which he knew in itself was difficult for her because Emilie preferred everything to be about her. That was the self-centered world in which she lived; it was a world he didn't really care for.

Emilie broke the tense silence and the regrettable memories they were each re-living. "Where do we go from here? Gianni, what do we do?"

Gianni did not have an immediate solution to this monumental problem. He had wondered why Davis hadn't picked up the phone when he called hours earlier; now, he knew. Gianni also knew there was a good chance his phone would ring at any moment if the police had obtained Davis' cell phone. He knew he had some fast talking to do if that happened.

"Give me a chance to get my wits about me and figure out our next steps. We need to make sure Davis doesn't somehow frame either or both of us for Ella's disappearance. I won't put anything past him at this time."

Emilie had not thought about Davis framing her until Gianni said the words; now her worry reached a new level. She said, "I'm flying to Florida first thing tomorrow morning."

Taking a glimpse of herself in the mirror across the room, she added, "I think Davis will be amazed when he sees me walk into the police station."

Gianni had not seen Emilie's new hair style and color, so the double meaning of her remark went over his head. He said, "Call me after you leave the police station and update me on anything you find out about Ella. I will see what I can find out on my end. And Emilie, we need to find your sister. If something happens to her, and somehow I was in any way responsible for her getting hurt or...." He couldn't bring himself to finish his sentence. "Well, let's just find your sister...unharmed!"

He disconnected the call and turned on the television, hoping to catch something on the news. After flipping through several channels, he realized that in the vastness of political events and world issues, one missing woman meant little. To him, however, she meant everything. Would he ever have a chance to tell her everything he had to tell her?

He opened his MacBook Pro and quickly typed in, "Missing woman Orlando Florida." Within seconds, a headline on WESH 2 News read, "Female disappears from a local pizza place." Gianni read the short blurb, "A woman vacationing with her family in Orlando, Florida, disappeared from Gastone's Pizzeria at around 8:30 p.m. The restaurant was immediately closed, and all patrons and employees are being questioned. According to eyewitnesses, the woman was at the restaurant with her husband and two young children. At this time, police are not sharing any details about the case, but according to restaurant employees, foul play is suspected."

Sickness filled Gianni's heart, and the handsome Italian man began to cry. He had put many wheels into motion within the past week in an attempt to keep Ella Masters safe, and now the woman, who didn't know he had been secretly stalking her and loving her for years, had disappeared. Fear for her safety and concern for his involvement with her husband's shady side made his head spin. He could be closely tied to Davis Masters, and on this night, that was not good. He would have a great deal of explaining to do, and most of it would leave him looking guilty.

His first instinct was to call Stephano Esposito. Stephano had been Gianni's best friend growing up in Terni, Italy. They had been the brothers each had not had in his biological family. When Gianni moved to Rome, Stephano joined him in the big city, and they were inseparable to the point that Stephano followed his best friend to the states within a year of his leaving Italy to work for him. The occasional women who had floated in and out of their lives knew they couldn't compete with the brotherly bond of the men, and they eventually tired of being the third wheel and moved on, usually with no hard feelings because both men had a charisma that made it impossible to incite anger.

He hesitated before hitting the call button. He realized he was possibly only moments away from being interviewed in the missing person's case of Ella Masters, and he knew there was already a call recorded on the system from Ella's sister, Emilie. If he contacted Stephano right away, he knew it would put a target on both of their backs. As much as he needed to talk to Stephano, he reluctantly put the phone back in his pocket. He would go to his office first thing in the morning and call him from the multi-system office phones.

Gianni got down on his knees for the first time in his adult life, clenched his hands together in prayer, and begged God to keep Ella safe, and then he cried himself into a restless sleep.

He arose early, showered, made a cup of espresso, and walked the seven blocks to his swank Chicago office. He dialed Stephano's number. Before Stephano could get out, "Hey brother, what's going on?" Gianni's desperate voice cried, "Something has gone awry, Stephano. Something bad has happened to Ella. Tell me what interaction you had with her. When was the last time you saw her? Did you talk to her yet?"

Stephano said, "Whoa, brother! Slow down and start at the beginning."

Gianni did not slow down. "Emilie spoke with Ella yesterday at around 5:30. Ella told her that the family was going to dinner. They went to Gastone's Pizzeria, and that is where she disappeared. She went to the bathroom and just disappeared! How can this be? How could something like this have happened? I thought you had it all under control. I thought you were going to protect her." Panic caused Gianni's voice to raise an octave. "Did you have any contact with her yet?"

A blur of confusion stormed its way through Stephano's head. He envisioned Ella standing in front of him at the Redbox movie kiosk, and he recalled slipping the note between her two DVDs. "Had Davis found the note?" Stephano wondered. "Had his action cause a domino effect that put the love of his best friend's life in jeopardy?" As Stephano processed Gianni's words, a tunneled roar filled his head through the silent phone.

Gianni was teetering between panic and accusation. The two men had been best friends since they were four years old, and their bond was stronger than most friendships. It stung at Stephano's heart to think his friend might be questioning his involvement in Ella's disappearance.

Stephano explained his interaction with Ella at the Redbox, leaving out the part about her being very flustered. "She was in front of me in line, and when she turned to leave she bumped into me and dropped her videos. I picked them up and handed them back to her. I had written a simple note on a Post-it that said, 'I want to help you.' I stuck the note between the movies. I didn't know how Davis would react when today's fictitious business deal fell through, so I wanted to let her know she had someone looking out for her. I got paranoid about the whole plan blowing up as the afternoon and evening progressed, so I tried calling her cell phone several times throughout the evening, blocking my call so it couldn't be traced. She didn't answer any of my phone calls. I just wanted to warn her to watch out for Davis because he might get violent. I was going to go to the condominium today when I knew Davis would be gone, to give her a heads-up warning about Davis' bad financial deals."

Gianni, frustrated with Stephano's lengthy explanation, interrupted his best friend, "Do you know if she saw the note?"

"She got in her car with the movies, looked at them, and then scanned the parking lot, so I assume she did. But what if it fell in the car somewhere and Davis found it later? What if she showed it to Davis? Do you think?" He stopped the flow of words, but Gianni finished his thought.

"If Davis found the note, it may have sent him over the edge. I think he did something to Ella. If he has hurt her, it is all my fault. I know Emilie and I were pushing him to the edge, but neither of us thought he would go to this extreme. Oh, my God, I won't be able to live with myself if something happens to my sweet Ella."

Stephano made futile attempts to assuage Gianni...and himself. "I will keep as close an eye on Davis as I can, but I don't think I will be the only one doing so; I need to keep enough distance that I don't gather my own unwanted attention."

As they hung up, Stephano wondered where the Post-it Note had gone. He knew his fingerprints were all over it, forcing his thoughts back to the only run-in he had encountered with the law. During a routine stop for a minor moving violation, the Chicago police officer had asked Stephano for his visa. When he produced his expired visa, explaining that the updated card was still in the envelope in a drawer at his apartment, the officer didn't respond favorably. He was handcuffed, stuffed in the back of a police car and taken to jail. Although it was cleared up within an hour when Gianni took the updated documents to the police station, Stephano had already been booked and fingerprinted. The police insisted there would be no record of his detainment, but he couldn't help but fear the incident might come back to haunt him. Had they truly expunged his information or were his prints still hanging around in some system? He knew Gianni was most likely thinking the same thing, but neither man verbalized his thoughts.

6

With each passing mile, Jax's breathing relaxed, and his white-knuckled hands eased up on the steering wheel. The Honda Civic rolled up Highway 75, away from the hustle and bustle of Orlando and the local pizza joint that was now crawling with cops. Jax looked over and smiled a tender smile at June. They had been through a lot, and he loved his girl. Like June, Jax was smart, but he had not been school-motivated. His blonde hair curled around his face, and his gentle blue eyes warmed June's heart. The two were best friends and lovers, and someday, when this whole thing was behind them, he knew he would get down on his knee and ask his girl to marry him.

June opened the glove compartment, took out a pair of rubber gloves and carefully put them on. Jax looked at her aghast. "June, what in the hell are you going to do?"

June pulled Davis' cell phone out of her pocket and waved it in front of Jax's face. "Score!" she yipped. "Mr. Masters thought he was sly dumping his phone before the shit hit the fan, and I'm sure he thinks the phone is still safe and sound. After all, who would think about looking for evidence in a plant? I am so genius that I can't even handle it! Now, let's see why Mr. Davis Masters needed two phones!"

She grabbed a pen and a used bank envelope out of the console and opened up the flip phone. She took copious notes as she listened to all of Davis' voicemails. She wrote down the phone numbers associated with each voice mail and made additional notes on the envelope.

She went through his call log and wrote down all of the outgoing and incoming phone numbers. She highlighted the numbers that had already been connected to a voicemail and circled the rest of the numbers.

Finally, she moved to his texts. "Wow, Davis, you are QUITE a busy man! I am finding out even more about you than I already knew, Mr. Masters! You have played right into my game, and you didn't even know it!"

June was giddy that her plans were coming together so beautifully. Davis made it so easy for her to nail him to the wall, and he was about to pay dearly for being the dickhead he was.

She used her phone to painstakingly take pictures of all of his screens. She had several hours stuck in the car, so she didn't mind the monotonous chore. She ravaged through the console and glove compartment to find more scraps of paper to scribble additional information. Donny's eyes kept a careful watch on his friends in the front seat as his hands made their way under Ella's shirt and up and down her thighs. Ella lay slumped against the door in the back seat, unaware of it all.

June opened her notebook that was already full of notes, and she spent the next several hours meticulously adding the new information in sequential order. She wrote furiously and calculated the detailed plans of the demise of Mr. Davis Masters and IMAGE, Inc. She wondered how high and mighty he was feeling right about now.

Back at the Orlando Police Station, Davis sat alone in the interview room. It felt like a jail cell, and he was beginning to unravel. In a raised voice, he said, to nobody in particular, "How in the hell could my wife have disappeared from a fucking pizza place with people everywhere?"

The messages that he had given his wife and children about not showing emotions or letting people see your fear were all thrown out the window. As shitty as he felt his family life was most of the time, he still needed his wife! This wasn't part of his plan! The timing was all off! *Who the fuck had messed this timing up?*

He anxiously thought. *This wasn't part of my fucking plan! I need my wife! This is all wrong!* The words screamed through his head.

He thought of the number of times he had promised Natalia in the past several months that he was close to getting out. But Davis knew he was going nowhere until Ella's daddy was dead. Sure, he had concocted many scenarios to get rid of his wife, but he knew he wouldn't go through with them because he didn't want to be stuck raising the kids by himself. In his ideal plan, he would have Charles Randolph's money before something like this happened; then he could ship the kids off to boarding schools and let someone else raise them.

This was too soon, he thought. *The timing is all off!* A life tending to every need of the children, without Ella's help, passed before his fear-stricken face. He imagined the all-nighters he would spend in the next few weeks trying to console the children. He didn't know the first thing about fixing a meal, giving medications, or getting the kids ready for school, much less comforting a crying kid!

Fuck, where are the kids? he wondered. It was the first time all night that he had thought about the children.

The uncontrolled panic Davis felt enraged him, mostly because he didn't panic! He was calm, cool and collected, even when he saw a business deal slipping through his fingers. This, however, was different. In a split second, he realized the negative ramifications of this event. His head was swimming with the conversations in which he had engaged over the past year regarding the eventual fate of his wife; this scenario had not been part of those conversations.

Detective Luke Rogers entered the stark room and handed Davis a bottle of water. He extended his hand as he introduced himself.

"Mr. Masters, first, let me say I am truly sorry you are experiencing this nightmare. I have a wonderful wife, and if anything ever happened to her, I can't imagine what I would do."

Davis lowered his head, closed his eyes and dug his fingers into his temples. "I just can't figure out what went wrong. We are supposed to be on vacation."

"I know, sir, and we have a whole team working on this to put the pieces together."

Davis replied, "I appreciate your efforts."

Rogers explained that since there was evidence of blood at the scene, it was being treated as a crime scene instead of a typical missing person.

"Sir, we are bringing in additional law enforcement personnel to bring your wife back to you."

Davis once again thanked Detective Rogers.

"Would you mind emptying out your pockets for me, Mr. Masters? You are not in any sort of trouble, sir. This is normal protocol."

Davis willingly did as the officer requested. The contents that lay on the table from his pockets included his wallet, a pack of Pall Mall cigarettes, an engraved lighter, an iPhone, and some loose change. The detective seemed satisfied with what he saw, and Davis was allowed to put the items back into his pocket.

"Thank you," Detective Rogers said, "sometimes people have small pocket knives or other self-protection items in their pockets, and, well, we can't have them making their way through the station. Hell, nowadays, we have people even trying to bring in guns. Again… appreciate your cooperation. I will remind you that you are here of your own free will, and you are free to leave anytime you like, but like I said, we appreciate you working with us."

Davis finally asked Detective Rogers about the kids. He mustered up a concerned look and said, "They must be worried sick. They are like magnets with their mom."

Rogers reassured Davis, "Sgt. Pickett is taking excellent care of the children. She said that they are holding up better than most kids she has seen in this situation."

"Well, I have raised my children to be tough. I have told them that crying is a sign of weakness and it will get them nothing but beat up. I have tried to toughen the kids up because this is a tough world, and only the strong survive. I know sometimes their mom thought I was too tough on them, but she babied those kids way too much. We had to balance each other out."

Rogers listened as Mr. Masters defended his parenting skills. He thought two things. First, the kids were eleven and eight, not really old enough to be told to toughen up. Second, he was already talking about his wife in the past tense.

Rogers took out his legal pad. "Davis, I apologize in advance that I may be asking questions for which you have already provided answers to other law enforcement officers, but I want to go over the details of today with a fine-toothed comb, so I don't miss even the smallest details."

Davis nodded in understanding.

When he was finished summarizing Davis' own words, he asked, "Is there anything else you have thought of since you spoke with Officer Irvine that you think might be important?"

A weary Davis shook his head no, and said, "I have told you everything I can think of. If you have everything from me, I would like to take my kids and get back to the condo."

Rogers explained that because they were treating the investigation as an abduction and that there was evidence of foul play, they would have to keep the rental car, but that the company had been contacted and they had sent another vehicle for Davis to use.

Rogers said, "It is a BMW instead of a Mercedes. I hope that won't be a problem."

Davis thanked the detective as he took the keys from him.

At 2:00 a.m., a haggard-looking Davis summoned the kids from the children's center, walked out of the police station, and drove back to the condo. The physically and emotionally drained trio made their way inside. Davis turned on the television, ordered The Lego Movie from the hotel list, went to his room and shut the door, all without saying a word.

William quickly set up Willow's make-shift bed and ruffled her curly hair to take the edge off of the moment. "Sissy, I am right here for you," William said. "You and I are going to be just fine! I am old enough to take care of you! Do you understand me?"

Tears streamed down Willow's face as she buried her head in her big brother's chest. The two fell asleep cuddled up on the sleeper sofa that they were too exhausted to pull out. They had not bathed, put on pajamas, or brushed their teeth before they fell into a restless sleep.

7

Emilie waited for the American Airlines boarding gates to open in the nearly empty terminal of the Chicago O'Hare Airport; she finally took a few deep breaths. The earliest available flight was not until 6:30 a.m. Her perfectly manicured nails clicked on her phone screen as she posted Instagram pictures from earlier in the evening. She had looked so put together in her little black dress and 2-inch stilettos as she drank and danced the night away; now, she was anything but put together. She replayed the earlier conversation she had with the lady officer in Florida. She had listened numbly as the female voice on the other end of the line gave brief details about her sister's disappearance. Her legs had turned to rubber as the officer said, "I think you need to get here as soon as you can. The children look as though they are holding themselves together by a weathered thread, and I think they could use a familiar nurturing female."

I don't know the first thing about nurturing children, she thought. It had been just over two years ago since she had seen them; it was Valentine's Day to be exact. She wondered how big they had gotten during her two-year absence from their lives.

Her memories flooded back to the special birthday dinner she shared with her identical twin sister. She pictured Ella's beaming smile as they sat across the table from each other, sipping red wine and laughing at the kids' antics. She recalled the abrupt turn the evening took when Davis showed up drunk and smelling of cheap perfume, ninety minutes after they finished dinner.

At that moment, Emilie saw her sister's life for what it was, and years of hatred spewed out of Emilie's mouth as she told Davis precisely what she thought of him. She recalled the ordeal, and her hand instinctively drew to her cheek. Davis had slapped her so hard that it sent her glass of wine soaring through the air and crashing onto the ceramic tile floor. She left without even gathering her belongings, vowing to never step foot in her sister's home as long as Davis was part of Ella's life.

After that night, conversations between Ella and Emilie had been short and strained, consisting only of discussions about their father, and, of course, Emilie's accusations that Davis was pilfering money from their family. Neither sister ever mentioned that night again. Emilie's stomach turned at the realization of what her sister must have had to endure at the hands of the monster she called her husband.

Emilie pulled the compact mirror out of the Louis Vuitton purse, which perfectly matched her carry-on bag. She stared into the mirror, barely recognizing herself with short brown hair. She had donned long, straight, blonde highlighted hair for most of her adult life, so the transformation to a brunette still caught her off guard when she caught a glimpse of her reflection in the mirror. She felt like she was staring her sister in the eye. She thought it would be a great joke for Davis to see her looking just like his wife when Gianni brought his lies to public view, but now that Ella had disappeared, she felt sick about her decision.

"There is nothing I can do about it now," she regretfully said to her reflection in the mirror.

Ella had opted for the soccer-mom look. Her curly brown hair hung at the nape of her neck, and she wore very little make-up. Most of the time she wore yoga pants and flip flops or hiking pants and hiking boots that did nothing to flatter her slight, muscular shape; at least she had managed to keep her attractive figure after the birth of two children; she had that going for her.

Just eight hours earlier, Emilie had been the center of attention in her Prada dress that left just enough to the imaginations of her suitors who gawked at her all evening as she sashayed around the party. Several men commented that her new hair style made her even more seductive, and she realized her new look didn't seem to affect her sex appeal.

Now, she was dressed in black yoga pants, a loose-fitting gray razor tank top, and a new pair of gray Nike running shoes. She carried a hooded sweatshirt for the chilly plane ride. Her party makeup had been replaced with natural, tinted face lotion.

Emilie pressed her thumb and forefinger into the bridge of her nose as tears escaped her closed eyes. She felt ultimately responsible for her sister's disappearance. She and Gianni had come at Davis from both sides to put a financial squeeze on him that would leave him squealing like a pig.

She thought about their most recent plan to catch Davis in the act of pilfering their family's money. It involved Emilie transforming her physical appearance to look like Ella, kidnapping her sister and putting her somewhere safe so Emilie could impersonate her twin in order to get into Davis' home and bank accounts. The idea seemed foolproof as they sipped wine and laughed about how much fun it would be to fuck with Davis, but it wasn't supposed to happen for three more months.

Emilie stared at herself in the mirror and wondered how she could be so intelligent yet get involved in such an awful plan. She couldn't wrap her brain around what had gone awry, and she couldn't help but wonder if Gianni had moved forward with their plan without informing or including her. Emilie realized she might be walking into her own trap.

Her erratic thoughts were a Cirque du Soleil performance-climbing, falling, rolling, and flipping through her mind. She recalled her perfect childhood, her profound hatred of Davis, her emptiness over the loss of the relationship with her only sibling, her mother's death, and her daddy's slipping memory. She attempted to play out every possible scenario as she pictured the police interview and the inevitable awkward family reunion she was about to encounter.

"I need a strong drink," she concluded, but she knew nothing was open at the airport at 5:30 a.m.

8

Mommy would never have allowed us to go to bed without brushing our teeth, Willow thought as she groggily woke from her fog of a night's sleep. The funky staleness of the previous night's horror caked her teeth. Her first instinct was to cry when she awoke and realized her mommy was still gone, but she knew that she had to be tough. She knew William was doing his best to take care of her, but it just wasn't the same as her mommy.

Their father came out of his room, freshly showered and cleaned up. He told the children, "Shower and get dressed. I will run out and get you some breakfast."

William showered first, and then he drew a bath for his sister. Once he left the bathroom, she took off her clothes, carefully stepped into the bathtub, and submerged herself entire body under water in an attempt to wash away the evil of the previous night.

Willow put on the clothes William laid out for her. The children sat trance-like as William brushed out her curly, wet hair. Willow's head moved backward when her brother caught a snag, but she didn't complain; she knew he was trying hard.

She quietly said, "William, where do you think our mommy is?"

William held back his tears and said, "Sissy, Mommy will come back to us; she loves us so much, and she will come back soon."

They had both been cleaned up and ready to go for forty minutes, but their father had not returned. Willow's tummy began gurgling from nerves and hunger. William felt a panic. *What if something happened to Dad,* he thought. William tried to repress the fear that bubbled up through his body, but he could hear the thumping of his nervous heart as his anxiety grew over the possibility. He listened to the buzz of the door key just as he was contemplating calling 9-1-1.

His father's hands were full of juice boxes, yogurts, packaged muffins, and two bananas. In a gruff, rushed voice, Davis barked, "You will have to eat your breakfast at the police station. Gather whatever activities you need to keep busy while I speak to the police. Come on, let's get going."

William wanted to confront his father and ask him why he left them alone for so long, but he knew better. He could tell by the tone of his father's voice that his questions would not go over well. The children snapped into action under their father's orders.

Davis dropped the children off with Sgt. Pickett, who had agreed to come in on her day off to make sure she was there for the kids. Pickett took the kids to the children's center, and Detective Rogers led Davis to the same stark white room he had spent several hours in the previous night. Detective Rogers noted that Davis looked extraordinarily good for a man whose wife had disappeared. Rogers' partner, Detective Nathan Austin, introduced himself and began with an update on the investigation, which was not much. He and Rogers had already determined by flipping a coin that he would play good cop and Rogers would play bad cop if the interview went south. They knew they had to do the interview dance to obtain as much information as they could before Davis lawyered up. Rogers had handled him with kid gloves the previous night, so he would feel no reason to bring in an attorney, but today they would push a little further, and things might get sticky.

Detective Austin began, "Mr. Masters, as you must know, with any missing person's case, especially when foul play is suspected, we must look at the people closest to the person to rule out those individuals. We are in no way implying that you are a person of interest, but we will ask some questions that may get personal. We need to paint a picture of your wife's disappearance to find any possible links. Please don't think any information is unimportant because often it is the smallest details that lead us to solve the disappearance. Do you understand, sir?"

Masters nodded.

"First of all, when was the last time you and your wife argued?"

Davis replied that they bickered over small stuff all of the time, but that he usually gave in, to avoid arguments.

"OK, Mr. Masters, what was the last thing you bickered over?"

Davis responded, "We had a little spat last night, but it wasn't anything major."

"What was the spat over," Austin asked.

"I didn't want to go to a pizza place for dinner, especially Gastone's Pizzeria because it takes so long to get a pizza at that place, but she and the kids insisted, so pizza it was. It's times like those that I realize she is going to put the kids' wishes before mine, so I have learned to pick my battles over the years." Davis decided to leave out their argument over sex earlier the same day.

Detective Rogers thought to himself, *What an asshole! This guy has a beautiful wife and two great kids, and all he can focus on is that he doesn't get to pick where they eat dinner.*

He sensed jealousy of the children that bordered on hatred. Detective Rogers used his gut instinct to take the questioning in a different direction.

"Mr. Masters, are you the children's father?"

Davis looked stunned. He had mentally prepared himself for questions about their trip, the day his wife disappeared, how often they fought, even their sex life, but this question threw him, and the look on his face revealed that he was caught completely off guard.

Austin gave Rogers a look that said, "That was out of left field!"

"What the hell kind of question is that? Of course, they are my children! Why the hell are you asking that question?"

Noting that he had hit a nerve, Rogers clarified, "I was checking to see if this was a second marriage for either of you, you know, a blended family. I apologize for upsetting you."

Davis realized his face had grown warm. He tried to brush over his hot-tempered response.

Rogers pushed Davis' buttons just a bit further, by asking, "Did you want children, Mr. Masters?"

Masters was still rebounding from the unexpected shock of the first question. He wondered what the cops could have found out in only a few hours that could lead them to this question. He tried to compose himself before he answered the question. The pause was too long. The awkward silence that filled the room during the thirty seconds it took him to answer the question was almost painful. When Davis finally found his voice, what came out was even more awkward. Memories of anger and confusion bubbled up in his throat as he tried to speak, causing a high-pitched response to squeak out of his mouth.

"It wasn't that I didn't want kids; it was just that we weren't having any luck getting pregnant before William was born, so it became a huge source of angst and conflict. Once he came along, Ella's whole world was consumed by him. Then, when Willow came along, it was as if Ella didn't need me anymore. She spent all of her time engrossed in the children, and my primary role in the relationship was to make money to keep them in all of their activities. I admit that having kids completely changed our relationship, but she was always a great mom."

Interesting, thought Detective Rogers. *Here he goes again, speaking of his wife in the past tense.*

As if Davis could read his mind, he corrected, "She is a great mom! She does so much for those kids, and she loves them so much. She would never up and leave them. She must be worried sick about how they are doing in her absence." He chuckled a fake, awkward laugh as he said, "She is probably scared as hell that I am taking care of them! I mean, just this morning, I had no clue what to get them for breakfast."

Rogers and Austin did not laugh.

He nervously continued to chuckle, "She has always taken care of the meals, the homework, and the day-to-day activities. I have to be honest; I don't know the first thing about taking care of kids."

Once again, the detectives remained stone-faced.

"So, Mr. Masters, what I hear you saying is that you haven't been a big part of your kids' lives?" Detective Rogers's words took on a judgmental tone.

Davis responded, "Ella is a bit controlling when it comes to the kids' care. No matter how hard I try, I can't seem to do things well enough to her liking, but we each have our roles in the relationship, and it works for our family. My role is to make money, and she keeps the household in order."

The detective decided not to push this topic further, but both detectives made several notes on their legal pads.

Rogers took the questions back to the previous night at the restaurant. He asked Davis if he left the restaurant at any time during the family dinner.

Pissed, but trying to be more cooperative, Davis responded with an affirmative "I have answered this question about twenty times. I stepped just outside the front door to smoke a quick cigarette."

Detective Rogers explained that Gastone's Pizzeria had a surveillance camera on the front of the building. He knew this was a bit of a stretch since the manager had already established that none of the surveillance cameras were operational, but Davis wasn't privy to the information.

Without missing a beat or answering the question, Davis retorted, "So, there is a video camera on the front of the building, but conveniently there isn't one on the back side of the building?"

Rogers wondered to himself, "How does he know there is no surveillance camera in the back?" as he made a note of the comment. None of the authorities had mentioned that there was not a surveillance camera on the back door. Rogers knew this was Davis' way of deflecting from the question, but the detective wasn't taking the bait.

Rogers continued, "We saw you exit the building at 7:49 p.m. And re-enter the building at 8:07 p.m. Your wife disappeared from the restaurant approximately twenty minutes later."

Once again, this information was not exact, but Davis didn't know that. His waitress had given a general time of about 8:00 that Davis had left the restaurant, and she said he was gone about fifteen minutes. Rogers gave specific times to make Davis think they had obtained the exact times of his actions from the video surveillance tapes. The officers knew they might be in trouble if they needed to produce the videos in court, but it was a chance they were willing to take to catch Davis in a lie.

Davis tried not to focus on the surveillance camera information as he re-emphasized that he merely stepped out to smoke a cigarette and returned to the table a few minutes later.

Guessing Davis' real actions, Rogers explained that video surveillance showed the man walking out the front door, looking around and then quickly going around the corner, out of the sight of the surveillance camera. Rogers figured since he was making it up as he went along, he would add details that made Davis look like a guilty man.

Davis took the bait. "Ella hates my smoking, so I walked around the corner, so she didn't see me out the front windows of the restaurant."

Rogers responded, "So, Mr. Masters, first you said you stayed in front of the building. Now you are telling us you went around to the side of the building, so your wife didn't see you. Is that correct?"

"Yes. I didn't mention it last night because I didn't think it was relevant."

Detective Austin took over, "Mr. Masters, every tiny detail, whether you think it is relevant or not, is important in a case like this. How about if you err on the side of giving us too much information, and we will decide if it is relevant or not, ok?"

Davis nodded in understanding.

Austin continued, "Officers found two identical Pall Mall cigarette butts right next to each other. Did you share a cigarette with someone, or did you smoke two cigarettes in the short time you were around the corner of the building?"

Davis' mind flooded back to his text conversation with Natalia that he now acknowledged was longer than it should have been. He responded, "No, sir, I smoked two cigarettes. It's my one vice. I keep trying to kick the habit because Ella really hates smoking. The pizza was taking forever, and the restaurant was so loud; I needed to get some fresh air and clear my head."

Detective Austin thought to himself, *One vice, my ass.* Aloud, he added that officers had gathered some interesting evidence that would help them better understand possible motives behind his wife's disappearance. When Davis asked for details about the evidence, Austin responded, "I apologize, Mr. Masters, but we are not at liberty to share this information because we don't want to jeopardize the integrity of the investigation."

Davis exploded, "Integrity of the investigation? What the fuck? We are talking about MY fucking wife here! I should be able to have every bit of this fucking interesting information you say you have!"

Detective Austin calmly asked Davis to settle down. He continued, "We will share as much information with you as we can when we can share it, but as you know, the first twenty-four hours in a missing person's case are the most critical. We cannot jeopardize the case by sharing information that might lead us to Ella."

Rogers decided to push the issue even further, hoping it wouldn't lead to Davis' refusal to talk. He said, "We have to be honest with you, Mr. Masters, in missing person cases involving a spouse, we can't rule out the other spouse."

"You think I did something with my wife. I was sitting across the fucking table from her the entire evening! How could I have done something to or with her?"

Outwardly, he was defiant, but inwardly Davis thought about the extra cell phone he had dumped into the potted plant the previous night. *If there were security cameras outside, did they also have them inside, or are these officers just messing with me, knowing they have set the cheese for the mouse trap they want me to walk right into?*

Now, Davis hoped, someone would water the plant so that the phone would be ruined and all of the evidence on it unrecoverable. But he had no control over that happening, and it worried him. He knew there was no way he could retrieve the phone since the restaurant would be crawling with cops. The lies had rolled off Davis' tongue very easily the previous night, but if the police found the flip phone, the information on the phone would reveal all of his secrets, and it would not bode well for his story; it might, instead, make him the prime suspect.

Rogers said, "The Orlando Police Department cannot rule out anyone who might be responsible for Ella's disappearance, but that the more cooperative you are, the sooner we can rule you out as a suspect."

Davis gritted his teeth and with a dull growl said, "I am NOT responsible for my wife's disappearance!"

Rogers replied, "It will be up to our excellent team to make that determination, but the more forthcoming you are with your affairs, the more quickly we can move past you and look for other leads."

Davis did not like this cocky son-of-a-bitch! He wanted to reach across the table and slug the bastard, but he kept his clenched fists underneath the table.

"What the fuck do you mean, affairs? I am not having an affair!" Davis retorted.

Rogers quietly relished the sight of seeing Davis so pissed off. "My apologies, Mr. Masters, I only meant affairs in the loosest of terms, you know, as in matters-- business affairs, personal matters."

Rogers knew exactly what he was doing, and he loved the subtle control he had over this cocky asshole, who he imagined always had the upper hand. He had Masters right where he wanted him. His job was to push all the right buttons to find out if Davis' need for control might have led to Ella's disappearance. Rogers was going to play this card for as long as he could to make this guy squirm, but not so much that he lawyered up.

Davis' blood pressure rose to a boil as he firmly restated, "I am NOT fucking having an affair, and I am NOT responsible for my wife's disappearance! The more time you sit here trying to concoct a story that doesn't exist, the longer the bad guy has to hurt my wife. Now, if you have some relevant questions to ask me, you need to do so quickly, because, in thirty minutes, I am walking out of this interview room unless you are going to arrest me, which, in that case, I will call my attorney!"

Rogers questioned, with a rhetorical tone, "Mr. Masters, do you always have such a hot temper?"

Officer Austin interceded before Davis could respond. "Mr. Masters, I will go ahead and share with you that we have potential evidence that has raised some concern about your wife."

He didn't want to provide too much information to Davis, so his wording was calculated and cautious. "We are not at liberty to reveal the evidence because we can't jeopardize the case, but we would like to request a DNA sample from you. Now, of course, you can refuse, and yes, you are always welcome to obtain legal counsel, but I want to remind you that we all have the same goal and that is to find your wife."

"Why do you need my DNA sample if you don't think I am a suspect?"

Officer Austin went off his and Rogers' planned script. He quietly asked, "Davis, do you suspect that your wife might have been having an affair?" Davis responded with much too sharp of a tone, "She always has the kids, and there would have been no time for her to…" He realized the harshness of his voice, and he stopped talking. His mind turned to the many days and nights he left Ella and the kids while he was off managing his affairs.

Austin explained his answer. "Mr. Masters, I'm going to share a piece of evidence we obtained from the crime scene, but it is confidential information."

Austin hesitated momentarily, and with an apologetic tone said, "Sir,…we found a bloody mass in the toilet underneath your wife's clothes. We sent it to the lab, which can take up to a week to process, but officers on the scene question whether it might be an unborn fetus."

Davis' head spun. He could not fathom his wife being pregnant. She had a tiny frame, with nowhere to hide a pregnant belly. "

She had been unusually uptight lately," he told police, "but I assumed it was just her period.

One possibility that we cannot rule out is that your wife miscarried the fetus and freaked out.

"How do you fucking explain her clothes in the toilet?" Davis snapped. "She wouldn't walk out of a restaurant in an unfamiliar city with no fucking clothes on. Something terrible has happened, and I think you guys know more than you are telling me."

For the first time, the detectives looked into the eyes of a genuinely frightened man.

Austin agreed with Davis, "You are correct, sir; if she left willingly, someone brought her a change of clothes. We have to look at all possibilities, and we can't rule out your wife willingly leaving the restaurant with someone, especially since nobody heard or saw a struggle."

The thought sickened Davis. He thought, *Has she been as miserable in the marriage as I have been, and she beat me to the punch at getting out?* He concluded, "No way, she would never leave us." He wanted desperately to believe the latter.

He agreed to the DNA test because he knew there was no way his DNA could be in an unborn fetus. He, however, wasn't ready to tell the detectives why that was. This might just be the break he needed to take the heat off him, but the thought of his wife having an affair that led to pregnancy incited emotions he never knew he had.

Detective Rogers realized his partner had thrown a one-two sucker punch that knocked the wind out of Davis' sails. He asked Davis a few more questions about his wife's recent behaviors, and finally asked, "Do you know of anyone who would want to harm your wife?"

A much more subdued Davis Masters shook his head, "I don't think Ella has ever had an enemy." He put his elbows on the table and dropped his head into his hands.

Detective Austin said, "Mr. Masters, I think we have enough information for today."

Davis stood, and Austin extended his hand, "I apologize for the bluntness of our questions and the information we shared. I know this is tough for you and the children."

Davis shook the large man's hand and thanked Austin for being forthright with the information. He added, "I want to cooperate fully with the DNA testing."

Rogers extended his hand as well, "Thank you, Mr. Masters. You can provide the DNA sample in the lab down the hall. We will keep you informed as we get new information, Mr. Masters,"

Davis turned to walk out the door and walked right into his wife.

She said, "My you are looking good for having a missing wife!"

Shock covered his face. "What the fuck is going on here? Where have you fucking been? What the fuck?"

A wry smile fell over Emilie Randolph's face. "Davis, has it been so long that you don't even recognize your dear sister-in-law?"

"What the fuck?" was all Davis could manage to get out.

The officers watched the display between the two in bewilderment.

Detective Rogers interrupted the awkward moment, "Davis, try to settle down. What seems to be the problem here?"

All Davis could muster up was, "I want to know who the fuck is messing with me and why!"

Emilie looked innocently between Davis and the detectives as they struggled to figure out what had set Davis off. She masterfully concealed her delight in his reaction.

Detective Austin spoke, "Davis, we contacted Emilie last night. She was concerned for her sister, as well as you and the kids. She took the first flight available and got here as quickly as possible. We had an officer pick her up at the airport a little bit ago."

Davis could not believe his eyes, and Emilie knew it. She had anticipated the moment like no other, and she was in no hurry for it to end.

After several minutes of disbelief, Davis finally found words. "Why do you look like this, Emilie? Is this some sort of cruel, twisted joke that only you find amusing?"

Emilie calmly responded, "Davis, help me to understand what you mean?"

"You know exactly what I mean," he hissed. "You haven't wanted to look like Ella since you were thirteen, so why start now? Are you just trying to fuck with me? To mess with the kids?

You bitch! Do you know what this will do to the kids if they see you walk into the room?" He unleashed a fury of words on his sister-in-law that left the officers all with gaping mouths.

In response, Emilie said nothing.

Her demure silence sent Davis over the edge as he spiraled out of control. He spewed obscenities at her about being a high society Chicago bitch who thought she was God's gift to the world and who didn't have the time of day for her twin sister.

Rogers finally interceded. "Davis, I think we have asked you all the questions we need to at this point, and you wanted to get out of here over thirty minutes ago, right? Officer Pickett will take you to the children's center to pick up the kids."

Davis turned back as he was nearly out the door and spat, "I am still those kids' father, and I don't want that bitch near them. Do you understand?"

"We hear you loud and clear, Mr. Masters," Austin replied.

Davis was seething, but he needed Emilie to know that he had taken care of the phone he had used to communicate with her. He didn't want her to share information she didn't have to. He walked closely by Emilie and whispered, almost inaudibly, in her ear, "Dumped phone."

Without missing a beat, Emilie responded in a voice quiet enough to make the officers think she didn't want them to hear her but loudly enough to make sure they did, "No, Davis, Fuck you!"

When he was gone, Emilie innocently said, "Well, it didn't take Davis long to show you his true colors, did it? Welcome to my sister's world."

Rogers took a few moments to analyze what had just happened. He couldn't help but think that Emilie Randolph got what she wanted in life, and at that moment, it was to make Davis look like an ass and a lunatic; it had worked.

Pickett returned after seeing Davis and the children off. She explained to Emilie that Davis had not-so-subtly expressed his opinion of her. She suggested that it was probably a good idea that the children did not see their aunt for a while, at least until things got a little more straightened out. Emilie agreed with her.

Sgt. Pickett vacillated between finding pleasure in how much Emilie got under Davis' skin and realizing that Emilie had a side to her that Pickett wouldn't want to cross. Both thoughts were enlightening.

Officer Rogers asked Emilie to take a seat. He explained that she was not a person of interest but that the interview would be recorded. He started, "Please give us your full name."

Emilie responded, "Emilie Marie Randolph."

Detective Rogers initiated the interview. "Ms. Randolph, you live in Chicago, Illinois, correct?"

"Yes."

"What kind of work do you do in Chicago?"

Emilie replied, "I worked as a layout specialist at Runway Magazine for several years, but six months ago I started my own high-end women's clothing rental company, and it has really taken off."

Rogers thought about Emilie's relatively new Chicago business and pondered the expensive venture. He had only been around the woman for a short time, but he surmised that she did not take failure lightly. According to Sgt. Pickett, Emilie had been quick to accuse Davis of stealing money from her family on the phone the previous night. He wondered, *What if her business is not doing well, and she is the one stealing money from her father's account?* He jotted several notes, which made Emilie nervous as she strained her eyes to read his chicken scratch.

"Can you tell us a bit more about your business?"

Emilie began her practiced monologue about the business she was proud to have created.

"My company is called Emilease Gowns and Apparel."

Emilie smiled at the genius of her business name, hoping to get a positive reaction from her audience. "I came up with the idea a year ago while attending a gala event in Union Station. Men and women alike were dressed to the nines. I was freshening up in the restroom when I looked over to see a beautiful woman in a stunning dress. I noticed a sales tag peeping out from under her arm."

"I said, 'Excuse me, your dress is amazing!', and the woman thanked me for the compliment. A bit apprehensive, I said, 'I apologize for being so forthright, but it looks as though you forgot to cut the tag off; I can see it. Would you like for me to help you with that?' The woman became frazzled, refused my help, and carefully tucked the tag back down the side of her dress and hustled out of the restroom. When I returned to the party, I watched the other woman conscientiously checking her armpit to ensure the tag remained tucked. I had never witnessed such odd behavior before."

Emilie took a sip of water from the bottle Sgt. Pickett had placed in front of her and continued, "A few days later, I mentioned the situation to my friend Ellen, my partner in crime at the magazine. Ellen said, 'She was free-renting the dress!' She used the term casually, assuming that I and everyone else in the world knew what 'free-renting' meant. She asked me what kind of dress it was, and I told her it was definitely a Versace-- the one we had featured in our March edition. Ellen assured me that the woman was free-renting. I had never heard the term until that day. Have you heard of free-renting?"

Detective Rogers looked at Sgt. Pickett for some explanation, but all he got was a confused shrug of her shoulders.

"See, I'm not the only one who hadn't heard of it. Well, 'Free-renting' is when a person, usually a woman, saunters into a high-end store she could never afford, selects an expensive piece, charges the item, and wears it to an event. The next day, she returns it, and, in a haughty voice, says, 'My husband didn't like the style' or some other excuse from a list of reasons she has established. Men are even starting to do it."

Emilie had momentarily forgotten she was in a police station being interviewed about her missing sister. She continued, "When Ellen told me about this scam, I was amazed. I couldn't believe people would have the audacity to do something like this. I found out these people have several credit cards they take turns using, so their credit card companies don't come on to their tricks. Now the free-renting professionals, they are a little more sly and savvy, and they usually have a bit more money. What they do is buy a couple of smaller items-- a drastically reduced sale item-- socks, underwear, you know, small ticket items. That way, when they take the expensive item back, they aren't tagged in the system as a free-renter."

"Wait, really?" Sgt. Pickett couldn't help asking. "Retail stores actually TAG free-renters?"

"They sure do; it's a huge scam industry," Emilie responded. "They don't want to sell a dress with smelly armpits any more than a customer wants to buy it. Legitimate high-end buyers are not happy when they are at a party, and within thirty minutes, they start smelling because some other woman sweated the night away in the dress. It isn't like free-renters take the clothes to the dry cleaners once they wear them. Anyway, once the retailer tags a person, they keep the name in a database that generates a flag if the person returns to the store more than three times. Of course, there are so many high-end stores in Chicago that free-renters can get away with it for years. I'm surprised you guys don't know about it in your field."

Rogers responded, "I guess people in Orlando just steal the merchandise."

Emilie was in her own world; she barely acknowledged Rogers' response before continuing. "I can remember a lightbulb turning on in my mind the night Ellen told me about the scam, and I stayed up the whole night creating my new company, 'Emilease Gowns and Apparel.' My company slogan is, 'Look like a million bucks at your next event without showing your tags.' I borrowed money from Daddy to turn an old warehouse into my chic boutique. There is no flashy signage on the front of the store, and women are only able to come to the store by appointment. I used my knowledge of the fashion industry from my work with the magazine to create a website that is only accessible via a password-protected login, and access to my business is by invite only. I realize the importance of anonymity in this kind of business, and I pride myself on upholding that anonymity. Word of mouth is what brings customers to my store. My clients are mostly up-and-coming socialites in the Windy City, but my clientele extends to New York, San Francisco, and Los Angeles."

She took another sip of water, "I grow my inventory by attending runway shows all over the world and purchasing the items worn in the fashion shows at a significantly reduced price. It is a win-win situation. Designers can get some money out of the clothes that would otherwise wind up in their stock closet, and I provide a necessary service to women.

Rogers questioned the "necessary" part of the service, but both officers found the business venture intriguing. The passion with which Emilie shared her story enamored them, as they both found themselves sucked into her monologue, momentarily forgetting the real reason she was sitting in front of them.

Emilie finished, "My strong business sense helped Emilease Gowns and Apparel flourish quickly. I take thirty percent of all of my profits and put the remaining money into new purchases. I offer all sizes because, let's face it, not everyone is the size of a runway model. Another marketing strategy I use is the promise that if anyone else at the event has the same attire, my client will be fully refunded and will receive a $500.00 credit on future purchases."

"That is quite an interesting business, Emilie," Rogers remarked genuinely.

Sgt. Pickett nodded in agreement. To bring the interview back to Ella's disappearance without appearing rude, she asked. "How long have you lived in Chicago?"

"I moved there right after college. I have loved Chicago since I was a little girl, so I guess you can say the big city called me home when I got out of college. It is close enough to my family, but far enough away that I can still breathe. Springfield is too small for me."

Rogers smiled a disarming smile.

"Now, you and Ella are identical twins, correct?"

"Yes," was Emilie's only response.

"Do you and your sister have similar personalities…similar tastes also?" Rogers asked.

"Oh no! We have been like night and day since we were old enough to walk, talk, and think."

"You chose the fast-paced Chicago lifestyle, while your sister chose a much simpler family lifestyle, correct?"

"Yes," Emilie acknowledged.

"So, Emilie, why did Davis respond with such shock when he saw you. You said you two are like night and day, and yet Davis thought his wife had walked in the door. Help us to understand that interaction."

Sgt. Pickett said, "We asked Davis for a picture of Ella, but he indicated he did not have any.

Emilie scoffed, "That doesn't surprise me one bit."

Rogers added, "We did, however, find her purse, which had her wallet in it. I have to say, you look just like the picture on her driver's license."

Emilie felt her neck get hot as she explained, "Ella and I have had different fashion styles most of our lives, but I guess I look more like my sister now than I have in the past."

"What do you mean?" Pickett questioned.

With an innocent tone, she explained, "I recently changed my hair color and style. I can only presume by Davis' response that it is similar to Ella's. I haven't seen her for a while, so I guess it might be that 'twin telepathic' thing."

"So, Emilie, how long have you looked more like your sister, with your most recent haircut and style?" Pickett continued.

"Oh, I don't know," Emilie replied, evasively, "it hasn't been very long, I guess. I had been blonde for so long, and brunette seems to be the new 'in-thing,' so I decided to try it."

"Emilie," Rogers said, "We take it there is not much of a love-loss between you and Davis. Sgt. Pickett indicated that you did not speak favorably about him over the telephone, and, in fact, you accused him of somehow being responsible for your sister's disappearance. We heard Davis' words toward you when he saw you, and he also gave Sgt. Pickett an earful of choice words about you. "

"I am sorry for the words I spoke on the phone. You woke me out of a dead sleep, and, I said more than I should have. Davis and I have never, well, I guess you can say I have never been a fan."

Emilie went to the subtle work of masterfully throwing her brother-in-law under the bus. She knew she better do that before he did the same to her. She explained that she questioned Davis' marriage to her sister, and implied that it was only to gain access to their family money. She finished by saying, "I can't sit idly by and let him steal her inheritance."

"And your inheritance too, correct, Miss Randolph?" Detective Rogers questioningly clarified.

"Yes, mine too, and the children's, for that matter. My sister has already had to go to my parents for money several times because Davis does not make good financial decisions, and now that Momma is gone, and Daddy is sick…Well, let me just say that Davis is not the financial wizard he thinks he is."

"Miss Randolph, Davis does have a personal business, correct, called IMAGE Inc. Is that correct?"

Emilie sneered, "IMAGE Inc. may be the name of his company, but trust me, any image he thinks he has is a facade."

"Who is in charge of your father's estate should something happen to him?" the officer continued.

"Ella is since she lives closer to Daddy," Emilie replied.

Rogers started to ask the specifics of the estate but chose to redirect his questions to Emilie's relationship with her sister. He could find out the estate questions later, if necessary.

He asked, "When was the last time you spoke to your sister, and can you fill us in on what you discussed?"

Sgt. Pickett had already told Emilie that they had retrieved her sister's cell phone, so Emilie knew she had to be honest about the phone calls the previous day.

"I spoke with Ella twice yesterday."

"Who called whom, Emilie?"

Once again, Emilie knew they had this answer, but she played along with their question and answer game, giving them more than ample information.

"I called her early in the day. I had been looking over Daddy's financial records that morning. Even though she is primarily in charge of the estate, we both have access to all of his financial accounts. I noticed that someone had shuffled large amounts of money between the accounts. There were also funds that didn't quite add up to what they should have been. I assumed Davis was behind it because my sister doesn't spend money on anything. She was running errands when I first reached her, so we only spoke for a few minutes before she said she had to let me go. I called back later in the day, closer to, like, 5:00 p.m. Florida time. She was watching the kids play in the pool. I could tell she didn't want to talk to me about it, but I kept bitching at her that I knew Davis was stealing our daddy's money. She told me she would take care of it when she got home from vacation. That, you see, has always been Ella's biggest problem. She will do anything to avoid conflict. She lives with blinders on when it comes to her son-of-a-bitch husband, and now it is impacting my inheritance. If she wants to live in a shit-hole of a relationship, that's on her, but it isn't fair to the kids, and it certainly isn't fair to me. I told her I am finished with Davis' bull shit and that I have already secured an accountant and an attorney to check into the missing funds. That was our last conversation."

For dramatic effect, Emilie said, "Forgive my cursing, that man's deceptive ways get under my skin!"

Both detectives scribbled notes. "We also noticed that Ella tried to call your father several times but must have repeatedly gotten his voice mail. Would this have been normal for her to make so many attempts to contact him?" Rogers inquired.

"Yes, she is a Daddy's girl, and if she were upset over our conversation, she would likely call him to talk. She would never mention any of the concerns I have about his money, but she would seek comfort in his voice."

"Davis said a lot of nasty things to you before he left. You handled them with grace. I think I might have smacked him," Pickett baited Emilie. "Did any of his comments cut more deeply than others?"

"Not really," Emilie continued. "I live a different lifestyle than my sister, and I believe Davis is extremely jealous of that carefree lifestyle. He wishes he had the freedom I have, but he is very tied down with Ella and the kids, and let me say, he feels it."

Emilie chose her words carefully. She had to be careful to say just enough to pique the detectives' interest, but not so much that it looked as if she was trying to frame Davis for Ella's disappearance. She was also quite aware that her phone number was not only on Ella's phone log, but on Davis' burner; she knew Davis said he had dumped the phone, but she had no way of knowing if authorities had retrieved it or if he was indeed telling the truth.

Emilie was well-spoken and charming. Pickett found a pang of envy as all of the male officers in the station swooned over her, asking if she needed any more water or anything to eat. The Chicago woman was pretty, but the way Emilie carried herself made her irresistibly captivating. She imagined a blonde Emilie turning heads as she walked into a room in an elegant evening gown, wearing just the right amount of make-up and expensive perfume. No wonder the men around her were smitten. She assumed they imagined that, and so much more, as Emilie engaged each one in conversation, making him feel as though he was the only man on earth.

She is good, Pickett thought. The officer felt inferior as she looked down at her own unsexy body that still needed to shed fifteen pounds of baby fat three years after her daughter's birth. Her blue uniform did not lend to sex appeal; that was for sure.

But why had Emilie changed her appearance, Pickett wondered. She realized Davis' shock was not in seeing his sister-in-law but in thinking she was Ella. *Was it just to throw him off-guard or was there more to her physical changes?* Pickett couldn't wrap her head around the woman's intentions, but she knew she didn't buy the story about simply wanting a change in looks. *This was a calculating woman who had a reason for everything she did.*

Pickett replayed the phone conversation she had with Emilie. She recalled the bitchy tone of the woman on the other end of the phone. Pickett assumed she had awakened Emilie and realized anyone would be shocked if they received a phone call in the middle of the night saying her sister had disappeared. The woman who was sitting in front of her now, however, did not seem at all like the woman on the telephone, who had immediately blamed her brother-in-law for Ella's disappearance. Pickett knew there was more to this woman than the male officers could see behind their clouded glasses.

After an hour-and-a-half interview, the male officers privately bickered over who got to take Emilie back to her hotel. Sgt. Pickett said, "I'm going that way, so I will take her."

Emilie thanked the officers for their kindness but insisted on grabbing a cab. She knew she needed to make a stop at the local liquor store for a much-needed bottle of wine on the way back to the hotel, and she didn't care for the whole police department to know.

Back in her room, she organized her belongings, ordered a late lunch from room service, and drank a glass of wine. She tried to make sense of her sister's disappearance, but every option brought more questions. She drew a hot bath, sank down in the water, and finished the bottle of Merlot.

She mustered up the energy to drag her wine legs and naked body to the king-sized bed, and she passed out.

9

Detectives Austin and Rogers, along with street patrol officers, continued their investigation into the disappearance of Ella Masters by responding to hotline tips, most of them from crazies trying to make a quick buck that led nowhere. They knew the likelihood of finding Ella alive and unharmed decreased exponentially after the first twenty-four hours. They canvased restaurants and local businesses near Gastone's to see if they had any surveillance videos that might provide a lead. They waited for the crime lab to process the evidence they had obtained two days earlier. With little more than a few tipsters who recalled seeing a tan Honda Civic, with a Florida license plate, driving around the block of the restaurant a couple of times, Rogers and Austin had nothing.

They held their first press conference in which they shared that the Orlando Police Department had few leads in the case of the missing Illinois woman. The primary purpose of the press conferences was to trigger the memories of viewers who may have seen something the night of Ella Masters' disappearance. As Detective Rogers wrapped up the press conference, he urged, "Anyone who was in the vicinity of Gastone's Pizzeria on June 2nd between 5:00 and 9:00 p.m. and may have information regarding the disappearance of this woman, please contact the Orlando Police Department."

An image of Ella Masters was now plastered all over the local news stations, thanks, not to her husband, but to pictures her children had taken of her on her own cell phone, photos that showed a happy, vibrant mother of two; the children had been blurred out to protect their identity. Davis' absence in the pictures, the detectives thought, spoke volumes about the family dynamics.

Gianni Russo had tabbed the online links to all of the Orlando local news stations to get updates on Ella's disappearance. He stared blankly at the computer screen in his posh office. The first press release was vague and uninformative. It summoned Orlando locals and visitors to come forward with any information, no matter how insignificant it might seem.

He was emotionally sick, wondering where Ella was and what was really going on with the investigation. He wanted to place an additional call to Davis' private cell phone, but he knew he couldn't take the chance. If the police had the phone in their possession, they would easily trace his call. Even if they did not have the phone, Gianni was certain they were monitoring Davis' phone usage.

Instead, he called Stephano who was still in Orlando, Florida. His friend had little more information than Gianni had acquired from the internet. He asked, more for a sense of comfort from his good friend than for actual knowledge, "Do you think Davis told the police about me? Should I attempt to phone him? On the one hand, if I reach out to him, I risk having the police connect me to him so soon after Ella's disappearance. On the other hand, is it strange that I have not contacted Davis all of a sudden if he did, in fact, tell the police about me? Doesn't that make me look guilty? I can see the headlines now: 'Was bad deal with Big Chicago businessman the reason this woman disappeared?'"

As the two friends continued analyzing the situation, Gianni knew there was little chance his name would stay out of the investigation; he realized he needed to come up with a story, but he couldn't focus. For the first time, he felt as though the sketchy plan he had made with Emilie and Stephano was about to blow up in his face, and the carnage had Ella's name written all over it.

While Emilie slept off her bottle of wine and the Orlando Police Department continued their search, Ella lay blindfolded, hogtied and crumpled like a rag doll with her face pressed against the door in the backseat of the small car. She had awakened a little while earlier but lay motionless, trying to put the pieces of her abduction together.

She was suffocated by the weight of the man next to her, who, by his smell, was sleeping off large quantities of whiskey. His right hand was tucked between her thighs at her crotch, and the violation repulsed her empty stomach. She went into survival mode. Careful not to move, she tore the tips of her fingernails off and let them fall onto the seat cushion. She pulled out several strands of hair with her tightly bound hands and let them drop between the seat and the door. She gathered what little saliva she could from her dry mouth and let it drip onto the inside of the car door. She was bound and determined to leave as much DNA as possible. She acknowledged the frightening reality that with every mile that grew between her and her family, the less likely it was that she would see them again. She had read the stories, and she knew the statistics. She was not in a good place.

She attempted to create a timeline as the foggy details of her nightmare floated in and out of her head. Her family had been at Gastone's Pizzeria in Orlando, Florida on the evening she was abducted. She had no clue how long she had been in the car or in what direction they had driven. She smelled the stench of vomit on her shirt. She recalled drinking water, which must have had something in it to knock her out. At some point, she had been blindfolded and hogtied. There were two guys whom she guessed were both white men in their late twenties or early thirties. She had a hazy memory of another figure in the passenger seat at some point during the ride, and she vaguely remembered hearing a quiet female voice; otherwise, conversations were limited. They made a few stops during the trip; two of the stops, she guessed were for gas, because she remembered having a blanket put over her head and hearing the clanking of the metal on metal of the gas pump near her head. She had been taken out of the car on three occasions to go to the bathroom on the side of a road.

Her thoughts were interrupted by a quick right turn and an abrupt halt of the car that plastered her face more deeply into the door. The whir of the engine stopped, and Ella heard car doors open and close. She was sure her pounding heart was audible as she tried to gain control of her erratic breathing.

"This is your last stop," the male voice whispered as he licked her ear and cackled, "Now, it is time for us to get to know each other more intimately." The combination of stale cigarette and whiskey breath was nauseating. He rubbed his rank nicotine-laced finger across her dry lips, snaked the fingers of his left hand through her hair and slowly caressed his right hand up and down her body. Her thigh muscles involuntarily forced her knees together in a protective act.

"Bitch, you can try all you want to keep those legs together, but I am a whole lot bigger and stronger than you are."

His right hand momentarily left her body. Ella heard the snap of a switchblade knife and felt the cold metal at her throat; she froze. He slid the blade over her breasts, down her stomach and stopped at her crotch. He cackled and gripped her hair harder.

"Don't forget for one minute, who is in control here." He traveled the knife down her legs to her ankles. She heard the rope being cut, and her ankles were free. He did not free her wrists that were still bound tightly in front of her.

He retraced his knife back up her body to her throat and said, "We are going to get out of the car now and go into our new home."

Ella wondered where the others had gone. The man reached over her and opened the car door, catching her before she toppled to the ground, and guided her out of the car.

There were no noises that would help her decipher her location. Wherever she was, she guessed the temperature to be in the 70's; it was cooler than Florida, so she surmised they had left the state. Her mind had been jolted to the reality of her horror, but her legs had not yet caught up as she took her first couple of wobbly steps. The stranger led her about thirty steps through muddy terrain. As her flip-flops squished through mud, the top of her right flip-flop broke off; she stumbled and planted her face into the muddy ground. Ella's abductor grabbed her by her hair and pulled her to her feet, threatening her through gritted teeth. "If you so much as make a sound, I will stab you right in the heart!" The pressure of one hand pressing the blade of the knife into her side and the other nearly ripping her hair out influenced her decision not to scream at the top of her lungs, even though she knew that might be her only hope.

She heard a door open. The man led her up three concrete stairs and through a door. The door closed immediately behind her. The temperature was warmer. He shuffled her down a set of stairs. Ella heard the click-click sound and felt the slick feel of stick-on laminate flooring under her now-shoeless right foot. She tried to concentrate on the sounds inside the building and the number of steps. She heard a wooden door creak open, and the next thing she knew, the man shoved her head down so hard that it sent her crashing onto a cold cement floor. Her restrained hands prevented her from breaking her fall, and she could feel the trickle of blood down the side of her face. The man kicked her with his heavy work boots until she lay in a wadded heap. She heard the creak of a wooden door shut behind her and the click of a padlock. She was stuck... locked in some sort of container or closet. Terror ripped through her veins, and she retched what little food she had left in her stomach. Instinctively, she attempted to catch the vile mess with her bound hands, but it slid through her fingers onto her lap. The smell of the vomit continued to induce dry heaves as tears soaked the blindfold that still covered her eyes.

The sound of her own voice singing the made-up lullaby she had sung to her babies as she gently rocked them to sleep jolted Ella out of her physical misery and into an emotional hell.

Oh, precious little baby, I love you so much.
Your smile and your giggle, and your warm, soft touch
And I love the way your precious eyes, they smile up at me
As I hold you… and rock you… and sing you to sleep.

Fear paralyzed her! The lullaby stopped, and the male voice outside her new prison proclaimed, "Welcome home, my precious. I am going to allow you some private time to settle in, but I will be back in a few to… well…you will see."

She sat blindfolded and motionless in the damp, musty space. Her body ached from the blows she had taken. After several minutes, she reluctantly decided to take off her blindfold. She wiggled it up her forehead, and it fell to the ground.

Darkness enveloped her. She couldn't see three inches in front of her face. She sat, trembling, in her own vomit. She closed her eyes to make the nightmare go away.

Through gritted teeth, the man on the other side of the door growled, "Can you remember your children's sweet faces as you left them in the restaurant? Well, If I hear one peep out of you, your precious children will disappear just like you did-- only they won't be locked in a closet-- they will be buried six feet under… maybe in Starved Rock, their favorite place for a hike; that seems like a fitting resting place for them, don't you think? That way when, or should I say IF, you get out alive, you can visit them on your hikes." He added, "Ta Ta, for now, I need to get some rest. You better do the same; I am going to need you well rested for what I have planned for you."

The stranger tossed a water bottle and a granola bar through the small cut-out in the door and, in a more civil voice, said, "Drink some water to rinse out your mouth."

Her tongue was like sandpaper from dehydration, so she guzzled two quick drinks. Terror suffocated her. Trying desperately to stifle the guttural noises that were rising from her stomach up through her throat, Ella shook and whimpered uncontrollably like a cold, hungry puppy. This man knew her family, and he knew how to incite fear in her. She had no reason not to believe his threats. If these people were able to pluck her straight out of a busy restaurant, what would stop them from going after her children? She focused on her breathing and sipped a little more water. Her last thought, before she passed out on the hard concrete was, *Is anyone looking for me?*

10

An obnoxiously bright light shocked Ella out of her a drug-induced sleep. She took in the space like a feral cat looking for an escape route. She instinctively covered her sensitive eyes. She had no idea how many hours had passed, but Ella did not forget where she was. Her prison had been pitch black when she passed out. Now, it was lit like an interrogation room. A small wind-up alarm clock in the corner read 10:00, but she had no clue if it was morning or night, or if it was even correct.

Intermittently, she opened and closed her eyes to slowly adjust to the blinding light. As her eyes adapted to her new environment, palpable fear gripped her by the throat. She was sitting in the middle of an identical, but a much smaller version of her children's playhouse that she had created in the closet underneath the steps of her home. She opened and closed her eyes several times in an attempt to blink away the reality, but her efforts were ineffective.

Ella took in her prison with wild helplessness. On a homemade desk made from a bed serving tray were pens, pencils, colored pencils, glue, yarn, and construction paper. The glue bottle was labeled, "William Masters." Ella had meticulously written his name using a blue Sharpie nearly a year earlier when she and her children excitedly organized their school supplies. Placed carefully in a corner were Willow's pillow, one of William's Lego creations, and several more of her children's toys and books. Chills wound their way from the base of her back up her spine to every hair follicle in her head. An uncontrollable scream escaped her throat, but it was cut off staccato by the same booming voice she heard the previous night. He was on the other side of the door; she could hear his heavy breathing. A freight train of fear washed over her.

"Do you like your new home? It's kinda like Twinkies, huh?" He bellowed. "Get it? Your new home has a twin out there, and they look amazingly alike!"

Ella's head pounded with the reality of her surroundings and the man's words. This man knew her family; he even knew she had an identical twin. For God's sake, he had been in her home recently, and he had also somehow recorded her singing to her babies years ago. She couldn't muster the mental capacity to process it all.

Anguish overtook her. She looked around the room and picked up her children's special items. "Where are my babies?" Ella questioned aloud as she attempted to shake the reality of the horrific nightmare.

The whispered words of an unfamiliar female voice through some kind of intercom system made Ella jump. Her already aching head hit the low ceiling, radiating pain down her neck and spine.

"Well, good morning, sleepyhead. I see you have finally awakened from your dream-filled sleep; only, this isn't a dream, sweetheart, this is your cozy new home. I took great care in decorating it just the way you like, down to the purple walls, blue skies with puffy white clouds, and of course the white picket fence. I hope you like all the personal touches I added. It is like your children are right here with you!"

"Who are you, and what do you want with me?" Ella spoke in an angry tone.

In a sickeningly sweet voice, the stranger responded, "Listen here, Mommy Dearest, you are in no position to use that kind of tone with me. I am running the show here. You may think only men like your hubby, Davis, are strong enough to control you, but you would be surprised at the power I hold over you and your family. I'm the lady of the house from here on out, and you are living under my roof. Do you understand?"

"Yes," Ella quietly conceded, "but why?"

Her words were cut off.

"Once again, Ella, you need to use your manners. We haven't even been properly introduced, and you are already asking me personal questions. My name is June, and we are going to become besties. I spoke with Kristina, and she says she doesn't mind."

Ella stiffened at the sound of Kristina's name.

"Names are meaningful, don't you think? They make us who we are. But then, heck, you probably have been called by two names most of your life. I guess we have that in common."

Ella was too sick to respond.

"So, now we are on a level playing field," she laughed, knowing the sardonic nature of her last words.

The stranger continued, "You met Donny already. You need to watch that one. He thinks you are very pretty! Well, not as pretty as your sister, Emilie, but pretty enough. I will try to make sure he leaves you alone, but I can't be here all the time. After all, I am a productive member of society with a real job and all."

Donny cackled on the other side of the wooden door. Ella shuddered.

"As for my other colleague," she added, "He is my boyfriend, and unlike you, I don't share my man with other women. Anyway, you don't need to worry about Jax; you have more important matters to concern yourself with, like how your dick of a husband is taking care of your children."

June smiled at the tormented disfiguration of Ella's face her words caused, and she continued. "You ask why? Well, we have a plethora of reasons that involve your hubby, including lies, deception, and financial debt. Your husband FUCKED the WRONG people, and now he has to pay! The bottom line, however, is that your perfect family isn't as perfect as you look, so my colleagues and I think it is time to expose the truth, because, my love, only 'The truth shall set you free.'"

The stranger's words wrapped themselves around Ella and sucked the air out of her. Ella was sure her captor would not have shared their names if they had any intentions of setting her free.

As if she hadn't twisted the knife enough, June added, "The funny thing is we don't really want you; you are just in the way of what and WHO we really want, which is Davis. We know the only way to hurt him is to hit him in his pockets, and the only way to hit him in his pockets is to play you as his pawn. You see, we know things about Davis that you won't believe we know, but you will soon be enlightened about your husband's games. He may have won many battles, but I will be victorious in winning the war."

The calm female voice continued in a sing-song voice as if to provide additional explanation, "You see, sweetheart, I PERSONALLY know Davis doesn't love you or those two brats he considers nothing more than offspring, and deep down you know you don't really love him."

The word, personally, hung heavy on Ella, and questions swirled in her head. *Was this an affair gone bad? Was it a bad business deal? How many people were involved?*

As if June could read Ella's mind, she said, "Don't worry, Ella, it will all make perfect sense by the time our game is over. I know you are a smart cookie, but don't try to overthink this one. The more games we play, the more the puzzle will come together, and you will understand the truth. As I said, that truth might just set you free, but only if Davis plays the game without cheating; therein lies the problem. You see, Ella, I'm just a normal girl trying to get through life, but Davis has been a thorn in my side for too long, so we need to put an end to this behavior."

She said her last words with firm resolve, and it frightened Ella.

"Right now, though, sweetie, I need you to do me a favor. Donny is going to slide a piece of paper into your door slot. On my command, you will read the piece of paper aloud. Do you understand me?"

Before Ella could respond, she heard the sound of metal clanking as the piece of paper made its way through the door slot and fell to the floor.

Ella fumbled awkwardly to pick up the paper with her still-restrained hands. Her eyes scanned the note. "Hi Davis, I know you aren't expecting to hear from me, but I thought I would call and check on you. I can't imagine how you are managing with the kids, but I know Emilie will be glad to come to help out. I will have to see how you two work out your relationship before I decide if I am going to return home. It really is all in your hands. Give my love to the children."

Ella burst into tears, but she was startled back to her senses when the female voice screeched through the speaker, "Shut the fuck up, you whimpering baby! You are going to get yourself together, muster up a melodic voice, and read the note aloud. If you can't manage to do this, you will rot in this basement. Now, when I say, 'go' you better start reading."

Ella's head pounded, her face flushed, and her heart raced. She took three deep breaths, closed her eyes, and waited for the word, 'go.' She read the note aloud just as she was instructed, assumed this stranger was recording her speech, and wondered what Davis and the children would think when they heard her voice. Her heart broke at the thought of her children thinking she had willingly left them.

June said, "Thank you, Ella, that will be all for now; you need to get some rest," but Ella knew rest would not find her as long as Donny lingered outside her door.

She looked more closely at the pile of her children's school supplies. A brown leather journal peeked out from under the pile. A hair-raising sense of recognition engulfed her. It was her journal… but which one?

Ella hesitantly picked up the journal. It had the familiar yellow flower and the word 'Wanderlust" on the cover. She was sickened at the thought of strangers reading her deepest, darkest secrets.

"Do you like your journal, Ella?"

Ella jumped, and the journal flew out of her hands.

"You are so jumpy, silly!" the woman teased.

Ella's eyes darted around the room, and she saw the small eyeball camera mounted in the corner of her 4'x 8' cubicle. Instinctively, Ella covered the camera with her clasped hands.

In a sickening sweet but sadistic voice, June said, "Take your fucking hand off of the camera or I will march downstairs, shoot my pistol right through the door, blow off your pretty little face, drag your dead body to the woods, and let the wild animals eat every part of you!"

Ella instinctively removed her hands.

"I asked you if you like your journal? Go ahead and open it...Oh, wait a minute; how about if I have Donny take that rope off your wrists; there is no way you can give us the slip now; we have you safe and sound. "

The sound of the metal key clicking the lock open reverberated fear into Ella. As the door slowly eased open, she saw the switchblade knife and heard Donny's voice, "Here, kitty, kitty! Let me pet you, you sweet little thing."

June scolded Donny through the speaker, "Dammit, Donny, just cut the rope and lock her back up; you know the rules. I will tell you when it is your turn."

Donny roughly grabbed Ella's wrists and cut through the rope.

He whispered in a hushed tone, so June couldn't discern his words, "Bitch, the longer I have to wait for my turn, the less you are going to like it!!"

He closed and locked the wooden door. Ella realized the irony of the safety she felt as she sat, petrified, on this side of the locked door.

In a less-than-patient voice, June told Ella to open her journal.

Ella cautiously untied the leather tie and opened the journal. She realized with relief that is was neither of her journals.

"Gotcha, didn't I," June laughed a hearty laugh. "I knew that one would really get you; you thought it was your real journal…or your REAL journal, but it is neither silly; those are tucked away safe and sound.

The woman continued as if the two were old friends catching up on memories of days gone by. "You see, Ella, I placed this journal in the children's playhouse just before you left for Florida, knowing that Willow would think you had written it as one of your stupid teacher games. I thought you might like a sweet memory of your beautiful daughter to get you through the lonely nights."

The first page of the journal was filled with what Ella recognized as Willow's handwriting. At the top of the page, written in an adult's script that resembled her own, was, "I love my mommy because…" Underneath the statement, Willow had written:

- You make me yummy breakfasts
- You play school with us
- You make us chocolate chip cookies
- You take us hiking
- You come to all of my school stuff
- You sing us silly made-up mommy songs like the one that you made for me when I was little because I didn't like getting bath water on my head.

As if on cue, June sang through the speakers.

Rub, Rub, Rub,
Rub, a Dub, Dub,
Little Willow's taking a bath.

Jax bellowed in,"Dadada!" just like William and Willow had done so many times.

June continued, "I always try to talk to you, I try to make you laugh. Rub, Rub, Rub, a Dub, Dub. Little Willow's taking a bath."

Jax finished with an exuberant, "DADADA!"

As June continued to laugh, Jax said, "I have really been practicing hard to get that perfect! How did I do?"

Ella covered her ears and slammed the journal shut. Pain took her small and large intestines, tied them around her lungs and strangled the breath out of her. She put her face in her hands and sobbed. She knew the intimate recordings she had made of all of her children's songs had been hidden deep in their playhouse, along with her journal. If these people had the tapes, they had her hidden diary.

The woman laughed, "Did I mention that I ALWAYS found my hidden Christmas presents, too? I do have to admit, though, hidden cameras are a big help. I hope you don't think that is cheating."

As if she had an afterthought, she added, "Oh, and by the way, I'm sorry you didn't get to enjoy the rest of your vaca! See, I hadn't planned on playing the game so soon, but there was a bump in the road, so I had to move forward with my agenda. It would have been financially more convenient if you had stayed a little closer to home, but at least the police are on a wild goose chase in Orlando, Florida, right now. Eventually, they will get a CLUE, but they only have thirty-two days to do so."

She let her words hang in the air, and then she laughed again.

Without warning, the room went pitch black. Ella heard the rattle of the padlock, followed by Donny's creepy laugh, and she momentarily stopped breathing.

Through heavy breathing, Donny whispered, "Me and you-- we are going to have some fun getting to know each other."

June yelled down the steps, "Donny, behave yourself and get upstairs."

As his footsteps ascended the stairs, Ella let out the breath she had been holding. She fumbled through the dark, found her little girl's pillow, balled herself into the fetal position on the concrete floor and quietly wept.

11

Emilie ordered a pot of coffee and two boiled eggs from room service to combat the gymnastics performance in her stomach and the leftover haze of the previous night's bottle of wine. Helplessness clouded around her for the first time in her life. She had felt deep sorrow when her Momma passed away, but this was different; this was not an accident. She couldn't get the kids' faces out of her mind, and she couldn't shake the guilty pangs that somehow she might be partly to blame. And then there was the worry of her name coming up as a suspect in the investigation.

She and Gianni decided to limit contact for a while because of the likelihood that their phone records would be checked. She certainly couldn't contact Davis. Given their disdain for each other, that would raise a red flag. The lack of contact with both men caused paranoia to set in.

Questions flooded her head. *Did my refusal to help him out or Gianni's deadline ultimatum send him over the edge? Maybe I should have told him I would allow him to use some of daddy's money for his investment just to string him along? Would he have had time to plan Ella's abduction or disappearance, or had he already planned it as a backup plan? Did Ella confront Davis about pilfering daddy's money? If this abduction is financially motivated, why hasn't anyone presented a financial demand? Is Gianni not being honest?* She could not rule out any possibilities.

Exhausted from worry, Emilie turned her focus to work. She set up her makeshift home office and contacted Ellen, her only employee, to make sure she would be able to get out the week's clothing and accessories. Thanks to the internet, Emilie had access to all of her accounts, contacts, and layouts right at her fingertips, and the hotel had a business center she could use if she needed to copy or fax anything.

Emilie sipped her third cup of coffee as her thoughts vacillated between her growing business and fear over what had happened to Ella. The brutal truth was that just because her sister had disappeared didn't mean her clients quit going to functions that required high-end attire; they counted on her, and her business was too new to risk poor business practices. She was grateful that her friend, Ellen, had recently left the magazine to work for her. It was a win-win situation because Ellen was able to spend more time with her three children, and it lightened Emilie's workload.

Emilie pressed the second number down in her favorites, and Ellen answered on the first ring.

"Please give me some good news, Emilie."

"I wish I had some. Ella simply vanished; nobody saw anything suspicious, but the detectives did indicate they are treating it as a crime scene because of evidence left in the restroom."

"What kind of evidence?" Ellen winced as she asked the question.

"They told me they aren't at liberty to share that information yet because they don't want it to compromise the investigation. I have a bad feeling about this; I think it is going to get ugly."

"Have you seen the kids yet?"

"No, but I saw Davis, and, true to form, he was an ass."

"What a son-of-a-bitch," Ellen scoffed, "Too bad he isn't the one who disappeared!"

Emilie looked at her watch, "Speaking of 'son-of-a-bitch,' I need to get back to the station and face Davis and the kids. Are you okay to take care of things at the boutique? I have no clue how long I will be here."

"Emilie, you know I will do anything you need for as long as you need. Dave will totally help out with kid transportation to and from summer activities, and little Piper loves accompanying me to the boutique."

"What would I do without you, Ellen? You have been there for me through thick and thin. I will keep you updated as I get more information."

Emilie showered, threw on a running skirt and tank top, slipped on her flip-flops and checked herself in the mirror one final time. For the first time, she realized the timing of her new look maybe wasn't such a great idea. She loved the effect it had on Davis but cringed at the thought of the kids' reactions. She didn't want to cause them any more pain than they were already experiencing. She briefly considered finding a hair salon to change her hair color back to blonde, but she knew the police would question her motive if she did so now; she was stuck with the new color.

Emilie's stomach churned as she sat in the back seat of the musty cab she had called to take her to the Enterprise Car Rental. She handed the driver a twenty-dollar bill and told him to keep the change.

He smiled as he looked at the bill, "Thanks, pretty lady. Let me know if you need any more rides."

She looked from the building to the cabby, and with a bit of sarcasm said, "Ok, but I'm renting a car, so I think I should be good."

She stepped out of the cab into the shock of the Florida heat, and her sunglasses fogged. She entered the building and was hit with an equally shocking wave of cold air. She waited, impatiently, behind three other customers. When it was finally her turn, she quickly completed the paperwork, provided her license and credit card, took the keys to the silver Hyundai Sonata, found it in the lot, and drove to the police station. She called Sgt. Pickett on the way and asked if Davis and the children were there.

"Yes," Pickett responded, "and, after a little encouragement from me, Davis has agreed to allow you to see them. Just between us, I think he is at his wits-end with what to do with them."

Emilie admitted, "I have to be honest. I don't know if I can do much better. I don't know the first thing about taking care of children, especially the emotional stuff. Ella stole that gene from me when we were in the womb."

Pickett chuckled a little, "Emilie, you will be just fine. You will take to loving those kids like they are your own. They are great kids."

Emilie wiped away an unexpected tear.

"Emilie, I also took it upon myself to prepare the kids for your appearance. I want to make this as easy for them as I can."

Emilie winced as she recalled Davis' reaction. "Thanks, Sgt. Pickett, I really appreciate everything you have done for William and Willow. They don't deserve to be mixed up in adult games."

Pickett cringed. She didn't like the sound of the words.

Ten minutes later, Emilie cautiously stepped through the doorway of the children's center at the Orlando Police Department. Four wide eyes took in their aunt, and two gaping mouths produced nothing.

Emilie kneeled down, and William and Willow ran into her arms; both tried to process the fact that it wasn't their mom. She looked like her, but she definitely didn't feel like their mom. The trio wept as their entangled bodies heaved up and down in a heap on the floor.

A few minutes later, Davis entered the room after getting an update on the investigation. Watching his children wrapped up in their aunt's arms stung. He and the children had never exchanged affections, and to see the woman he hated so much hugging his children sent a rage through his blood that he could not hide. His face reddened as he said, "Hello, again, Emilie."

Davis and Emilie exchanged cold niceties. He barked at the kids, "Get your belongings together so we can get out of this miserable place." He directed the last words toward Emilie. The children nervously gathered their belongings.

Emilie gave them a final hug and said, "I will see you soon, ok. Keep your chins up." She wished she could take the words back before they escaped her mouth. How could she expect them to keep their chins up when their mom was gone? She really wasn't cut out for this kid thing.

Davis whisked the kids out of the room, but not before looking back and mouthing, "Bitch!"

Sgt. Pickett watched the interaction from the two-way mirror. Emilie sat on the couch and buried her face in her hands. Pickett exited the room she was in and walked back into the children's center. She gave a slight cough so as not to startle Emilie. She joined the woman on the couch, a woman who looked much less sure of herself than she had the previous day.

Pickett's update was short, as there were no new leads. Emilie asked, mostly out of concern, but partially to fish for information that might incriminate her, "How can there be no leads? Have you checked Davis' phone records or his activities while he has been here? Do you think this is a random crime?"

The officer explained, "I am not at liberty to discuss Davis' connection to the investigation, but most crimes of this nature are not random."

Emilie wanted to spill her guts and tell Sgt. Pickett, everything she knew about everything-- whatever it took to bring her only sister back home: instead, she sat quietly. Tears streamed down her face.

Pickett realized Emilie genuinely cared about her sister, and her heart broke for the vulnerable woman.

"I promise to keep you updated with any new information since I don't think Davis will do so."

The mid-day heat smacked Emilie in the face as she walked out of the police station. She fumbled in her purse for her sunglasses, partially to protect her eyes from the fireball, but mostly to conceal her red eyes. She cussed Florida, the sun, the leather seats, and anything else in her direct vicinity as she started the rental car and left the station.

Emilie returned to her hotel room, via the same liquor store for more wine. She held two different choices in each hand for several minutes, unable to make a decision. She made her way to the checkout, and the cashier scanned the two bottles of wine. Emilie's soul felt empty and afraid; she knew the wine was her only solution to sleep.

12

Ella lay awake on the cold concrete, and June's words darted through her head. Was she back in Springfield, or at least close? Was her family still in Florida looking for her.

Oh my God, she thought, *How are William and Willow surviving this hell? Who is taking care of them?*

The light switched on. Ella felt like she was the victim of an interrogation. Her kidnappers knew just how to taunt her. Her weak voice squeaked out, "Pleeeeaaaassseeee!" She didn't bother finishing the question she knew would not be answered.

June's spine-chilling voice laughed, "Ella, you and I are going to catch up on old times. Isn't that going to be fun?"

Ella questioned, "What do you mean catch up on old times? Do I know you?"

June responded, "Oh, Ella, you could say we go way back, but we aren't nearly as close as Davis and I are. The problem with Davis, though, is that he barely acknowledges my existence."

A brief silence filled the small space, followed by Willow's voice, "What game are we going to play today, Mommy?"

June answered the question as if she were the mommy, and it curdled Ella's sour stomach. " I love playing games with you, sweetie. Daddy loves playing games, too, but not kid-friendly games. In fact, if the walls of Daddy's house could talk, we would know that games have already been played."

In a Jekyll and Hyde voice changeover, June angrily said, "Davis may have the poker face, but we have the trump card."

Switching to a sickening-sweet voice, she directed, "Sweetie, take out your pretty new journal and let's start writing."

"We are going to play a game today called 'What's in a name?' Is that a good idea, Ella? So, here is how the game works. I give you different names, and you write down everything you know about that name. Let's start with an easy one, Ella. Tell me about your name."

Ella was confused as to where this game was going, but she knew it was going to be ugly. June was smart, and she was a mastermind at playing mind games. Ella wondered what had happened to her that made her seem so evil one minute and seem as though she might actually care the next.

"I'm waiting," spouted June.

Ella said, "I was named after my maternal grandmother. My family was from Georgia; it was customary, and almost expected, in the South to name children after their grandparents."

"Very good." June praised. "So, is it the same for your sister's name?"

Ella nodded, knowing June could see her.

"So, what about your children? Why didn't you name them after their grandparents? You know, your and Davis' parents?"

Ella knew she was entering a trap, but she answered the question as instructed. "Davis insisted on naming our child if he was a boy, so he chose William's name. When we found out our second child was a girl, he allowed me to name her."

"Hmmm!!! I see. Interesting," June replied intently.

"Now, let's take a minute to analyze my name, ok? What is my name, Ella?"

Hesitantly, Ella said, "June."

"Yes, but you don't know my full name, do you, Ella?"

Ella shook her head.

"I can't give away all of my secrets, but I will admit I am bitter that you got to take your husband's last name and I didn't."

"This is about an affair, isn't it?" Ella whispered as if she was afraid of the answer.

"Oh, Ella, this is about sooooo much more than an affair! This is about your husband not taking responsibility for his actions. I am very sorry for my sudden outbursts and my fluctuating moods. You see, Ella, I am a bit hormonal these days."

Was this woman pregnant? But what about her boyfriend? The thought that Davis had gotten another woman pregnant sickened Ella. She couldn't make sense of it, but her mind naturally jumped to the worst-case scenario.

"Enough about my plain name, let's move onto more heartfelt matters. Let's explore the name, Mommy. I know by the many hours I have watched you and your children frolic in your daily activities that their mommy is very special to them, and I know that has been passed down through the generations, well, at least with your family...Davis' family...not so much. So, I want you to write Momma in your journal and create a mind map around the word."

Ella's breath caught, but she did as June instructed. Writing the word "Momma" brought tears to her eyes. Her mom had only been gone two years, and a day didn't go by that she didn't miss her. She wrote, "great cook, sweet, gentle, loving." She stopped writing. A flash of intense emotional pain washed over her as she recalled the night she received the telephone call about the tragic car accident that crashed down on her family.

"I seemed to have struck a chord, dear. You look as if you've seen a ghost. You had a special relationship with your momma, and you have a strong bond with your own daughter. Well, welcome to my world, Ella. Now you know what it feels like to have that bond ripped right out of your heart; it sucks doesn't it!"

The room went black and dead silent. Ella was left to relive the memories of her momma's death.

13

William took the lettuce, veggies, bag of shredded cheese, and salad dressing out of the refrigerator and made salads for himself and Willow. He didn't bother making one for his father since his paternal figure seemed to be drinking his dinner these days. William pictured his mom's beaming smile when she walked through the door with her hands full of groceries and their movies. He was grateful she had gone to the grocery store that day; otherwise, he wasn't sure what he and Willow would do for food.

Davis sat alone in the bedroom where he and his wife had argued just two days earlier. The whir of the television provided background noise while cartoons played on the TV in the next room.

He read the headlines of the Orlando Sentinal in disbelief, "Still No Trace of Missing Illinois Mom." The article stated "The details are sketchy. The family was dining at Gastone's Pizzeria when Ella Masters disappeared. At this time there are no leads and no suspects." The article outlined the events of the disappearance, mentioned that foul play was suspected, and concluded, "Anyone with information is asked to contact the Criminal Investigations Unit of the Orlando Police Department at 407-244-1111."

The familiar words, "Missing wife and mother of two, Ella Masters" stole Davis' attention from the newspaper to the television. The report was primarily the same feed he had seen several times on various stations, including News 13, WFTV, WESH 2 News, and Fox 35. In all of the interviews, Detectives Nathan Austin and Luke Rogers provided the same information and answered the same questions as if they had spent weeks on the well-rehearsed script. Davis could tell they were enjoying the limelight. Detective Austin explained during each of the interviews, "Due to evidence left at the crime scene, the FBI will be taking over the case but will continue to work with local authorities."

Davis' head spun. He wanted to believe this was a random act of violence, as the police had initially suggested, but deep within the entrails of his gut, he knew it wasn't random. He also knew this wasn't about his wife; it was about him. He had pissed off a lot of people. The thought that someone would go to this extreme told him this was more than an ex-girlfriend, or an affair gone bad; this person or people meant business. He pondered the timing of the abduction. He racked his brain about the meeting that was supposed to take place the previous day. "Was Gianni behind this?" he questioned. Davis knew the man had power, but he had never seen an ugly side to him. He wondered whether Gianni had tried to get hold of him the past two days? He secretly prayed that restaurant employees or the police would not recover the phone he had dumped. He assumed it was dead by now. His mind sped in every direction. If Gianni had not attempted to call him, was it because he was guilty, because he was mad at Davis for not taking his important phone call, or because he had moved on to other investors? He recalled his first interactions with the man. Davis had read about him in multiple newspapers and business journals for the past decade, including a three-page article and full photo layout of his financial successes in Forbes magazine. Davis was like a little boy wanting to meet his favorite baseball player. He had been so enamored by the man to the point of obsession that he wormed his way through every social network he could in order to meet him. Davis dreamed of being half as successful as Gianni, and he knew if he could somehow wiggle his way into this guy's wheelhouse of opportunities, he could make some real cash.

Gianni Russo was a suave, handsome, Italian businessman who had an entourage of successful businessmen on his coat tail at all times. He had kind eyes, and he looked people in the eye when he spoke to them. He made each member of his audience in any venue feel as if he or she was the only person in the room. Unlike many successful businessmen, Mr. Russo was approachable. He listened to other investors' ideas with genuine interest, and he provided feedback and suggestions like a business therapist.

Davis finally met Gianni at an investing seminar in Chicago three years earlier. The two-day seminar cost $5,000 per person at Russo Enterprises. It was limited to 20 attendees, each with the guarantee that he or she would have the opportunity for a fifteen-minute consultation with the man himself, Mr. Gianni Russo. The attendees were each randomly given a number between one and twenty, and that determined the order of the consultations. Davis received the number twenty. He had mixed feelings about being last because he wondered if Mr. Russo would tire of hearing the same story. On the other hand, maybe Davis had an advantage being the last person because if Mr. Russo really liked him, the businessman might say "Let's go grab a beer and talk some more about our future." Neither extreme occurred.

Davis cringed as he recalled shaking the man's soft hands with his own nervous, clammy hands and fumbling for words to try to impress the one and only, Gianni Russo. When Davis finally settled his nerves enough to form a coherent sentence, the two engaged in an intense conversation over business philosophy and Davis' goals. When the subtle dinging of Gianni's cell phone indicated the consultation was over, Mr. Russo asked Davis if he had a business card. Without hesitation, Davis pulled a stack of business cards from the breast pocket of the expensive suit coat he had charged the previous month with a card his wife didn't know existed.

Gianni studied the card and said, "IMAGE, Inc., I like the name. A person can tell a lot about another person by the quality and look of his business card. I think you and I might be able to come together for a project or two." Davis left the short meeting feeling like a giddy school girl who had just been kissed for the first time, but he also wondered if Mr. Russo had collected nineteen other business cards and given the other attendees the same morsel of hope.

Six months after the seminar, Davis got a phone call from Russo. He was soft-spoken, but Davis knew he meant business. He had turned around several neighborhoods in Chicago in the past decade, and he had just purchased several buildings in a dilapidated area on Chicago's north side. Davis was star-struck as he heard the words, "Would you like to become an investor in the project?" Without hesitation and without considering the financial requirements, Davis responded, "Yes, Mr. Russo, it would be an honor to work with you, sir."

Russo laid out the timeline of the three-year project and explained the financial investment needs of all involved parties. Davis would need to provide $2.3 million by the summer of 2014. Russo shared that he had chosen the best candidates from the many seminars he held in order to bring a team of like-minded individuals together to turn around a Chicago neighborhood. Gianni explained that he would invest the lion's share of the money, but he wanted to use this opportunity to teach smaller investors the ropes of the trade. The businessman explained that all investors who contributed less than $3 million would be silent investors, but if Davis could come up with the capital to invest over $3 million, he would become a public investor. Russo emphasized that if Davis wasn't able to come through by the deadline, he needed to decline the offer from the beginning. Davis assured Gianni Russo that he was ready to commit to the investment.

Russo's response rang through his ears as if he was hearing it for the first time, "Our investment group is kind of like a baseball team; if you strike out, Davis, it affects the whole team, and it might cost us the game. That would not make me and my colleagues happy."

A new picture of the Italian man flashed before him. Instead of the suave gentleman he had come to know, he saw a picture of a mafia leader with gun-wielding mafia men by his side. Davis had never questioned a mafia involvement until this very moment; now, this was all he could imagine. The thought of his wife being in some warehouse, with a bunch of mafia men, doing God knows what to her, turned his stomach. He knew his time had run out with the investment opportunity, but he had never contemplated Gianni Russo causing harm to his family if he didn't provide his portion of the investment.

Davis had not shared the names of the other investors or the details of the project with his wife. He said only, "We will be set for life when my most recent deal comes to fruition." He liked keeping her in the dark with his business deals, because the fewer details he provided, the fewer questions she asked, and ultimately, the fewer lies he had to tell. Now, he wondered if Gianni and his men had abducted his wife.

Davis also had to face the harsh reality that he had engaged in risky business and gambling deals that had not panned out. He realized there was a possibility his wife's abduction could be about debts and paybacks. If this abduction were about debt, the only way his wife would be returned unharmed would be if he came up with the money he owed his debtors…and that would require a lot of money. His only source for the kind of cash he guessed it would take to get his wife back alive was Ella's father, and his sister-in-law had made it clear that he would not get any more of her family's money. He wondered if she would continue to take that stance if it meant she would never see her sister again.

This thought led to yet another paranoid idea. *Is Emilie behind this? Does she have enough connections to pull something like this off? Is this her way to take our family out of the inheritance equation?* He recalled the threatening words she had spoken to him two days earlier as he groveled over the phone for a loan from her father's bank account. The final words she spoke before she disconnected the call rang through his head. "I can promise you that, over my sister's dead body, you will never see another dime of my family's money." At the time she spoke the words, he threw them off as part of a hot-headed tantrum, but now, they played like a bad country song over and over in his head. He knew he couldn't tell the police any of this because it would only bring to light all of his financial problems and backfire on him.

For the first time in his life, Davis felt a fear he didn't realize was possible. The doorbell jolted him back to the present.

"Dad, do we want maid service?" William's cautious voice asked from the other side of the closed door.

"No, tell her just to leave fresh towels."

William looked around at the disheveled condominium and wished his father had said yes. When the maid was gone, William said to Willow, "How about you and I pick up this place; that will make Mom happy." His younger sister complied, and the two took to cleaning up dishes and picking up clothes. They left the towels for their father's bathroom on the floor next to his room; neither dared open his door.

14

News of the terrible event reached Ella's hometown in Springfield, Illinois within twenty-four hours of her disappearance. Neighbors, friends, and acquaintances were glued to FOX News and CNN to keep up with the latest breaking news in the case. Community members huddled around break room water coolers, prayed in churches, and sat in bars and coffee shops, speculating about what might have happened to the woman most barely knew, who had now been missing for three days.

June smiled as her eyes moved between the news broadcast and the TV monitor. She shook her head and bellowed into the makeshift speaker system, momentarily drowning out the newscast, "What a shame! A sweet mommy ripped from her children!" She watched Ella's face contort in horror as she was forced to listen to the newscasts through the speakers that provided her only connection to the outside world.

As the reporter switched to highlighting local summer festivals, June taunted Ella. "It looks like you have drawn quite a bit of attention in multiple states, and I bet your little brats' hearts are breaking. After all, it is just horrible to lose your mommy to such brutal violence, isn't it, sweetheart?"

Ella remained still, but her face turned pasty white as she endured her captor's words… and then the music rang through the speakers. The first song repeated the words, "last to know." June paused the music after the song finished and said, "Ella, I just didn't want you to be the last to know."

Cheating songs continued ringing through the speakers for the next several hours. Ella repeatedly pleaded for June to stop the music, but with each request, the volume increased. When she tried to cover her ears, she was scolded like a two-year-old about to touch a hot stove. She begged her captor to stop the torture, but she was a helpless victim in the hands of an evil woman.

The music stopped abruptly, and June said, "Ella, we have been roomies for three days now. Can you believe that? My doesn't time fly when we are having fun! So, I decided it would be nice to let all those fine folks in Florida, who are working so hard to find you, know you aren't even there anymore. Was that a good idea?"

Ella said nothing in response.

True to June's words, an envelope addressed to Detective Luke Rogers arrived at the Orlando Police Department later the same day; it had a Chicago postmark and no return address.

Rogers read the letter.

Detective Rogers,

What's blonde and white and is a favorite snack of you good men (and women) in blue? Hint-- it's a sweet treat, but it isn't a donut! Remember the movie, Die Hard?"

Rogers knew the reference was Twinkies.

He continued reading, "I am sorry your missing Ella case has left you with no leads. I know this type of thing doesn't bode well for a popular Florida vacation destination. I mean, come on, Orlando is the place for family fun… and a missing mommy doesn't scream, 'Come to Orlando for a great start to your summer,' right? So, I will give you a 'CLUE' in your game of 'Hide (Ella) Go Seek.' She has not been in Florida since thirty minutes after we borrowed her. It has been fun, however, watching y'all scramble. You and Detective Austin do an especially nice job with the press, sir. I'm sorry this case was too big for your local britches, but I know you will find satisfaction when the Feds can't solve the case either. After all, you guys are all full of a whole lot of... TESTOSTERONE! Don't get me wrong; I'm not envious; I have enough of my own."

-J-

"Shit," Rogers shouted, slamming the letter on the table. He was pissed at himself for opening the piece without gloves; now his prints might interfere with other fingerprints left on it. He took a picture of the letter, bagged it, and sent it to the crime lab before it could be compromised further. He emailed the image to himself, printed a copy of it for Austin, and faxed a copy to The Federal Bureau of Investigation, Tampa Division.

He assumed they were dealing with a man by the testosterone comment, which confirmed their overall profile of the abductor. He also knew the reference the riddler made to Twinkies was about more than just a jab at the police; it was a reference to Ella's twin, Emilie, who, up until recently, was a blonde, which also confirmed their beliefs that this was not a random act of violence. Ella's abduction had been planned, which made him question Davis' involvement even more.

Detective Rogers called Davis and Emilie down to the station to share the newest information. They arrived within five minutes of each other. He asked them if they could put their differences aside for the duration of the meeting, so the officers only had to explain the situation once. Both nodded in agreement.

Detective Austin began, "The good news is that we have received what we believe to be legitimate information indicating Ella is alive."

Davis and Emilie both exhaled a unified sigh of relief.

Rogers took over, "However, we also obtained information that leads us to believe she is no longer in Florida." He intentionally left out the part about the Twinkie riddle, but he did tell them they had received a letter with a Chicago postmark. Davis and Emilie's eyes widened when they heard the word Chicago. Since they both had strong Chicago ties, the detectives knew the comment would have that effect on them.

As if playing a game of tennis, Austin took over the conversation before either had a chance to ask questions about the letter. "We aren't at liberty to discuss the details of the message because we don't want to jeopardize the investigation. We have turned the case over to the Federal Bureau of Investigation because the abduction is now considered a multi-state matter. Since the case has been turned over to the FBI, and we have obtained all the information we need from the two of you, you are free to return to Illinois."

Davis and Emilie were speechless. Emilie looked grief-stricken. Austin made a genuine apology for not having been successful in finding her twin sister. In front of the detective, Emilie addressed Davis in a sweet tone. "I know you and I don't see eye to eye on most things, but let's put aside our differences for the sake of Ella and the kids. After all, William and Willow are going to need both of us, and they don't need the added stress of friction between us."

Davis knew her games well. *You are such a fake bitch*, he thought to himself. Aloud he said in an equally kind voice, "I absolutely agree, Emilie. I am going to need your help with the kids. Maybe you can stay at our place, so the kids can keep a sense of the security of our own home. I am certain you will find the guest bedroom accommodating."

He was playing her at her own game, and he had just taken the lead. If Emilie said yes, she would be stuck under the same roof as Davis, but if she said no, she would look like she wasn't concerned about the children. Thinking quickly, she responded, "Well, I will need to tend to Daddy's place, since Ella was the one who took care of it." She quickly added, "I mean, with it being up for sale and all, I need to make sure I am available to show it and maintain it. I can split my time between the two houses, and the kids are welcome to join me at Daddy's house. After all, they love that place."

Davis could not disagree with her. He knew the children would move into their mom's childhood home on Lake Springfield if they had the choice. He was actually relieved at Emilie's suggestion. He hated to admit it, but right now, he needed his sister-in-law. His blood still boiled, however, at the fact that she refused to lend him the money necessary for the Chicago project.

Maybe, he reasoned, *if she had allowed me to borrow the money, we wouldn't be sitting here.*

Emilie knew she had Davis right where she wanted him, and she loved the power it gave her. She was determined to find out what he did to cause her sister's disappearance, and the closer she was in proximity to him, the more she might be able to get to the bottom of it and get her sister home alive. Emilie asked to see Sgt. Pickett before she left to thank her for taking care of the children. Davis was pissed that he hadn't thought of that. He shook the detectives' hands, and in a desperate voice, pleaded that they do not give up on finding his wife. Detective Austin almost believed his sincerity for a moment.

Emilie took the next available flight back to Chicago to get her business in order, pack some clothes, and do some of her own investigative diggings. The fact that the letter to the police was postmarked in Chicago was unsettling. Davis had a lot of Chicago connections, and many of them were not good. Could her sister be in Chicago? Suddenly, the Windy City, that had become Emilie's playground, felt like unchartered land.

Davis booked an American Airlines flight for the next morning. He and the children spent the evening packing their belongings and their horrible memories of the trip. With the suitcases stacked neatly by the door and the children's backpacks leaning against them, William and Willow huddled together on the couch dressed and ready to leave. Both secretly wished it had been their father who disappeared; neither dared to speak the words. They numbly watched Nickelodeon and cried themselves to sleep for the third night in a row, while their father drank Scotch until he passed out in the next room.

15

Ella dozed in and out of fitful sleep. She was awakened by two voices over the speaker. One of the voices was June; the other was a male voice, but it wasn't Donny.

It must be Jax, she thought.

The two chanted,

"KNOCK KNOCK,

"WHO'S THERE?"

"Mother"

"Mother Who?"

"MOTHER, MAY I?"

"Mother, May I, Who?"

"Mother, May I play RED ROVER, RED ROVER, SEND ELLA ON OVER?"

June's laughter increased and then decreased as it was replaced by Willow's laughter. Ella squeezed her eyes shut and covered her ears. Her little girl's giggles grew until they had a tinny sound to them.

As Willow's giggles dissipated, Donny's whistling voice grew in volume and closed in on Ella's prison. "Hey, you sweet thing; you've got mail," he laughed. "Just remember that it would be quite silly for you to try to escape from your schoolhouse. After all, Smith and Wesson, here, and me...well...we have a bit of an advantage-- just in case your foggy brain forgot the bathroom scene and the long ride home."

His voice lowered to a whisper so he could not be heard through the speaker. "In fact, you and I will play some secret games when nobody else is in the house. I have been thinking about that a lot, since our intimate drive home. Ella, I like the way your body feels."

The sound of the key unlocking the lock and the door creaking open crippled Ella. She filled with panic over the realization that her horrific fear might come true.

Donny cracked open the door and with a scraggly smile said, "I've got a REAL special present for you, and I think you are going to like it; I think you will like it a lot."

She realized he was mimicking her favorite movie, Dumb and Dumber. She locked her gaze on his face; she recognized him, and fear consumed her. She momentarily closed her eyes and saw the beat-up truck in the next lane over. He was one of the two men who had taunted her just a few weeks earlier in Springfield; she was entirely sure. This once again made her think she was back in Springfield.

She took another visual snapshot of the evil man to burn his image in her head. She wanted to memorize every pock in his acne-scarred face, his dark, beady eyes, and his nose that looked like he had been in one too many bar fights. If, by some miracle, she got out alive, she wanted to be able to create a sketch of the monster who forced her away from her family and who, she feared, would do much more.

Donny placed a wrapped package on the floor and continued, "Anyway, that is for another day." He licked his lips and flicked his tongue in and out before he closed the door and clicked the lock. Ella hoped to hear his heavy boots make their way upstairs, but he sat down on the other side of the door. She could hear his heavy breathing and low moans, and it caused her own breath to become erratic.

Her mind traveled back to the encounter she had experienced with the two men in a truck less than a month earlier. A new kind of fear overtook her. It was a beautiful spring morning. Ella had dropped the kids off at school and was heading to a photo shoot. As she rolled to the stop light, she looked over at the vehicle in the next lane and smiled innocently.

This was a habit that she had tried to break because Davis told her many times, "One of these days, someone is going to take that pretty smile of yours the wrong way."

Ella remembered the sense of uneasiness she felt when the two men in the rusty, white, beat-up Ford creepily smiled back at her, both with yellow-stained, crooked, and missing teeth. As she quickly diverted her eyes back to the road ahead, she could still feel the heat of their eyes mentally undressing her. A quick glance back at them confirmed her fear as the passenger licked his lips, smiled, and lip-synced, "I wanna fuck you." The light turned green, and Ella quickly accelerated the gas, hoping to get through the next green light and lose the truck. The driver changed lanes and sped up, so the rusty bumper of his '88 Ford was kissing the bumper of her husband's Mercedes Benz.

Ella recalled scolding herself, "Dammit!! I shouldn't have taken his car. It is too flashy. I should have moved it and taken my SUV. If something happens to his car, he will flip out on me."

Ella watched the truck move closer to her car, and she saw the driver and passenger exchange wicked laughs. They were about to make a sport of her until they looked in the rearview mirror and saw flashing lights. She saw the driver's mouth form the word, "Shit," as the two men tossed empty beer cans into the back floorboard. Ella extended the distance between the two vehicles and watched the rickety truck move to the side of the road with the police car right behind it. She sighed a deep sense of relief mixed with satisfaction. Trying to erase the visual from her mind, she turned up the radio and began singing "Blowin' in the Wind," along with Bob Dylan. Now, however, the reality that Donny had been following her in Springfield sickened her.

June's voice broke her thoughts, "Don't open your present yet. Remember we were talking about playing games. Well, I want to explain a super exciting game we are going to play. It is kinda like baseball; If everyone plays well, you will get to home base, but if players get three strikes, well...you are out.

Players get strikes by being dishonest, not guessing a riddle correctly, not completing a task, or of course by cheating. We have a feeling Davis will struggle with this one." She laughed a wicked laugh and continued, "The game players are Davis, Emilie, and William; we decided Willow is too young to play big people games; plus, she might... oh, never mind; I won't make you worry about something that might not even happen?"

Ella flinched at June's casually spoken words. Before Ella could contemplate the underlying threats to her daughter, June continued. "We also sent the police a letter explaining the way the game will be played. After all, we want to make sure everyone understands the ground rules. Let's not burden you with all those silly details right now, though; instead, I want to watch you open your first present. I am so excited, I can hardly stand it."

Ella hesitantly opened the package to find a binder-style scrapbook with a plain hunter green cover. She cautiously turned the cover to see a two-page layout. The fancy lettering that made its way across both pages read, "Our Family Tree." Covering the pages from the left to the right were a series of pictures of weeping willow trees, beginning with a new sapling and moving in progression to larger trees and then finally to a dead one. Ella gasped, and her shaking voice quivered, "What does this mean?"

The woman laughed a haunting laugh and said, "We had such fun playing the name game yesterday, I thought we could continue it today. You see, right now, your daughter, Willow, is but a fresh, young sapling, and like all young saplings, she needs nourishment and care. You are the water and sunshine in her life. Without you, I worry about her. I hope nothing bad happens to her... but, let's not get ahead of ourselves."

Ella stared at the picture of the dead weeping willow tree. Every hair on her arms stood in attention. "Do whatever you want to me, but I am begging you, please don't harm my babies!" her desperate high-pitched voice implored.

June's response was simple and to the point, "Those two brats of yours are just too perfect. We don't want them growing up with the fairy tale life their mommy had, now do we? See where it landed you?"

She continued, "But enough about your kids, Ella. Let's focus on us. I have been planning our visit for a very long time, and I have made you many gifts. I also have LOTS of stories to share. I think you will like them! I hope you do, anyway. At the very least, you will be enlightened."

"The first story I am going to tell you is about how long I have known you. Oh, my goodness, it seems like forever. I have to say, I haven't always been happy with you, but I have been working hard on my anger issues. The problem is that you are so perfect; you have been since you were a kid. I guess that's how it is when you are a silver spoon kid. I understand why Davis continues to choose you over me, but I would be lying if I said I don't resent you. Part of me is bitter that I have been deprived of the opportunity to share a beautiful home with Davis; instead, he has forced me to live in poverty for longer than I like to acknowledge. He throws a little money my way every couple of weeks, but it is only for services rendered."

Ella winced. *Is this woman a prostitute?*

Satisfied with the reaction, June continued, "I admit I have become a bit obsessed with you and your home. You keep it nice and neat, and you are an excellent cook. I have only been lucky enough to get a few leftovers, but even your leftovers are good. I keep thinking one day I might be as good at playing homemaker as you are, so I watch you often to learn all of your tricks, just in case Davis finally chooses me. I will tell you, though, things are a little rough there right now. William is doing his best to man up and keep things together, but he is struggling a bit.

Before Ella could respond, June ended the conversation, "Well, we will chat a little later. I need to go see how Davis is doing today."

Ella could not help but wonder if this woman was going to meet Davis right now. Maybe she would lay in his arms and console him or innocently ask if there are any updates. It sickened her.

The lights clicked off, and darkness once again engulfed her.

Ella's hours vacillated between pure darkness and painfully bright lights. During the dark, Ella lay haunted by the demons of her experience. During the light, when she wasn't enduring the torment of June's taunts or demands, she continued adding notes to the pages in the back of the journal. She added, "fifteen steps, money, Emilie, William, Willow, three people? more money, husband, games." She drew more trees, the sky, sun, and even trails, and placed additional words in the rays of the sun. She wrote the words "Fucked the wrong person," noting that June hadn't said, "Fucked WITH the wrong person."

Oh my God, what has Davis done, she contemplated.

Writing the details of her prison probably wouldn't help her, she thought, but at least it would give the police information if they found her dead. Cold chills and goosebumps covered her body at the realization that these people were monitoring her every move.

Ella had not showered since her arrival to her hell-hole. She had wet wipes for daily cleanups and a box of baking soda, which she used as shampoo and deodorant. Her toilet was a five-gallon bucket with a makeshift seat. A bag of cat litter was propped up against the wall next to her toilet. She had held off as long as possible before using it, first because she knew there was a camera on her at all times and second, she knew once she used it, the smell would fill up her tiny home. She was correct. The stench of her own urine and feces filled the closet. She sprinkled the cat litter into the toilet, but it did little to quell the odor. She took the dress off of one of Willow's dolls that had been placed in the closet before her. She wrapped it around her face in a futile attempt to dull the putrid stench. She unstitched a small portion of the seam in the back of the doll and pulled out tiny bits of stuffing. She put the filling in each of her nostrils. It helped.

Alone in her 4'x8' cubicle, Ella reasoned, *OK, I have lived in a tent smaller than this for over a month. I was able to shower or wash up in streams, though, and I had water-always plenty of water. I had food that kept me nourished, and I had been prepared; I am not prepared for this!* Her heart raced as claustrophobia rushed over her and sucked the breath out of her. She couldn't breathe; she couldn't scream. Panic overtook her. Her body began to shake uncontrollably.

A calm, soothing voice came over the speaker. She knew the familiar voice like a child knows his favorite nursery rhyme; it was the audio recording of her anxiety relief book. The calm female voice recording she had listened to hundreds of times to deal with the stress of her marriage, gently spoke, "Take a deep slow inhale through your nose. Hold it for five counts and now gently release any anxiety you feel." For the next thirty minutes, Ella followed the directives, and a temporary calm lay its gentle hand on her. As the recording stopped, she was keenly aware that this was but a temporary reprieve before another verbal onslaught.

She was correct! The next barrage of torture was with the boisterous giggles of Ella and her children as they played their familiar games in their closet playhouse. The realization that these people had a recording device underneath the steps paralyzed her. After five minutes, the sounds ended abruptly, and June's voice broke through. "First of all. Davis is hanging in there, but I think he is looking forward to Emilie's arrival. I mean, he didn't tell me that in so many words, but I know him well enough to read between the lines. Anywhooo, I am ready to chat some more if you are up to it. I want to share with you the thoughts and efforts that have gone into this game. That way, you will know I'm not just some crackpot. Well, I am not cracked, but I am more than a bit broken; we can thank your hubby for that."

Ella tried to interrupt June to ask how Davis had hurt her, but June screamed, "This is MY story time, so shut your fucking pie hole!"

Ella recoiled. She held Willow's tiny pillow to her chest and braced herself for the unknown.

June belted, "Now if you interrupt me again, you will have hell to pay, do you understand me?"

Ella nodded, knowing the woman was watching her every move.

"Very good," June replied as if she were praising a new puppy for peeing outside. In a Jekyll and Hyde moment, June's voice turned to calm. "I'm sorry, Ella, for raising my voice, but sometimes you try my patience. Anyway, by now you are wondering how I would know so much about your life, right, Dearie? Well, with all of my visits with you and the children, I know more about you, sweetie, than anyone else. We have spent so much quality time together. I feel like we are closer than you and Emilie. June laughed uncontrollably, and chills raced up and down Ella's body.

"I bet the children are missing their school time with Mommy. I can't tell you how SICK and TIRED I got of your 'Let's play school' game in your classroom cubby under the stairs, with its pencil chairs and painted walls and all. And while I'm venting, the puffy white clouds on the blue-sky ceiling, the purple walls, and the white picket fence were a little over the top; they are so cliché, don't you think?"

For the next few minutes, Ella heard only a hum through the speakers as June continued her taunts. Her mind escaped to the last time she and the children had played school. She recalled the call with her sister that had gone better than those in the previous few months. Davis had gone to the office for the day, so she had the whole day with William and Willow without the stress of her husband, and she looked forward to some uninterrupted time with them. They agreed they would play school in the morning and then pack their backpacks for an afternoon hike and lunch. She involuntarily smiled as she recalled the kids' squeals with delight at her fake British accent, "Good Morning, children, my name is Mrs. Cruxtable. Let's take out our math books." They completed their pretend math lessons and nestled into their bean bags to listen to the magic of their mom's voice as she read Harry Potter, changing her voice to match the personality of each character.

The words "kill your sweet little Willow if you don't fucking listen to me" gripped her by the throat as the hum through the speaker once again became June's voice.

"What had she missed June saying while she momentarily escaped?" she fretted.

June continued as if recalling the same day, "Your house was opened up on that perfectly crisp spring Saturday morning. Your back door was open, but the screen door was locked. As you and the children delighted in your game of school, I quietly sliced the screen door right at the seam by the lock, swiftly unlocked the door and made my way directly to your bedroom. This wasn't the first time I had been there, so I knew exactly where I was going. It was a huge risk, but I knew I could do what I needed to do in fifteen minutes. I was certain you would be in the basement with the children for at least another hour, but I worried that Davis might return home from the office early. Based on conversations he and I had earlier in the week, I didn't think he would return early that day, but I couldn't risk the chance. I had to get in and out quickly."

June's words, "conversations he and I had" hung in the air like nerve gas. June now had Ella's full attention.

June continued matter-of-factly, "I knew If I got caught, my organized plan would be ruined-- not to mention the financial and legal ramifications that would follow. Then there is the fact that I would have had a lot of 'splainin' to do with Davis, you know, kind of like Lucy and Desi. Well, it would NOT have been a good situation. I quickly replaced the ceramic figurine in your bedroom with the original version I had switched out the previous month; you know, the white angel with the floral head wreath-the one your mom bought you? Now, I had just what I needed: voice recordings from the past thirty days. Oh, I already had plenty of audiotapes from your schoolhouse. After all, this was only one of many visits I made to your beautiful home. You really ought to think about investing in a security system, you know," June chuckled.

She continued, "Then, just to mess with you, I opened up your dresser drawers and stuffed a pair of your underwear, your favorite old hiking t-shirt, and a pair of yoga pants into my Nike stringed backpack. I have to admit, the idea of you looking high and low for that hideous t-shirt made me chuckle to myself. I love messing with people's minds, and you had become my new favorite target."

"Anyway, I swiftly left the bedroom, tiptoed down the stairs, slipped through the kitchen and out the door, all while you and your brats were tucked away in your playhouse in the basement. As I carefully closed the door, I reached my hand through the cut screen to lock the screen door, took out my super glue, and made a make-shift repair on the seam of the screen. It wasn't perfect, but I had done it several times before and you obviously hadn't noticed it, or you would have replaced the screen. I figured that if you did notice it, you would attribute it to your beloved yellow lab, Beau. I checked my watch. I had successfully done everything I needed to do in 13 minutes, two minutes less than I had allotted. I remember thinking, *I should do this for a living!* I put on my sunglasses, tucked my hair up into my helmet, got on my bike, and slowly rolled through the neighborhood. Ridge View is indeed a lovely place to live, Ella. Luckily for me, it isn't the gated community Davis wanted to live in; it was one of the few battles you won. Aren't you glad you did?" June laughed.

Freezing sweat dripped past Ella's temples, and goosebumps covered her body, as she attempted to grasp the fact that this woman had been in her home on multiple occasions. It was too much to fathom. Her brain was so close to exploding that she thought she might begin seizing at any moment.

Her meek voice squeaked out through her dry mouth and chapped lips, "How long have you been stalking my family?"

"Ella, I have been around so long that I tend to think of it more as 'our' family. I mean, come on, we have shared the same bed for heaven's sake."

Ella shuddered.

"I gave up the best years of my life for your husband; those are years I can never get back; yet, he has thrown me away like an old pair of dirty gym shoes and moved on to others. I guess I just can't let go that easily. You know, all this chit chat is making me less-than-amenable, so I am going to stop before I say, or do, something I might come to regret."

June's voice was gone, and Ella was left miserably alone in her thoughts. "What kind of monsters lock up an innocent person, like a caged animal, in a musty, wet, bug-infested basement full of mold, rotten wood, and wet carpet?" She languished as her world turned to black.

16

While Ella endured emotional torture in her prison, her motherless children accompanied their dumb-struck father on the Friday morning flight back home from what was supposed to be the start of their summer vacation. They had arrived at the airport at 9:00 a.m., but the flight did not take off until 11:30 a.m. Awkward tension could be felt by each family member as they sat in the airport waiting to board American Airlines Flight 403 back to Springfield. William realized just how little he and his sister knew the man they called Father.

Willow had periodic quiet meltdowns, and William tried to console her. They were both anxious and exhausted. Their mom's absence seemed more final than it had the previous two days, and the kids felt they were somehow letting her down by leaving Florida.

They landed at The Abraham Lincoln Capital Airport at 6:02 p.m. and found their mom's car in the parking lot right where they had left it one week earlier. The heat of the closed car and the smell of their mom's essential oils added to their misery. Davis stopped at the Arby's drive-through on the way home because he knew they had little food in the refrigerator.

Willow secretly hoped her mommy would open the door when they pulled up to the house and say, "Gotcha! That was a good trick, huh!" Instead, the only greeting the trio got was a stifling warm house. The kids dragged their suitcases to their rooms and tried to make themselves invisible.

A Chegg textbook rental box was sitting on the front porch within an hour after the exhausted trio returned home from Florida. Davis had gotten the mail when they first got home, and the box was not there. He had not heard a FedEx or UPS truck, but the package had been delivered within the hour. Upon further inspection of the box, he realized it had no mailing label, but instead, a handwritten label with William's name and address on it. He looked around the premises and took the box into the house. The kids had gone up to their rooms, and Davis had no desire to interact with either of them. Even though the package was addressed to his son, he opened it.

Inside, a note rested on a pile of wrapped gifts; it read, "Welcome home, Family. We come bearing gifts. Inside each of these personally wrapped gifts, you will find personalized journals. You will need to respond to the journal prompts in your special 'diaries.' You will then carefully wrap each journal independently and place them all back in the box, and you will place the box back on the front porch by 3:00 p.m. on Wednesday, June 11th. We have hired a courier to pick up the box and deliver it to our Chicago headquarters. You are not allowed to look at or share the contents of other family members' diaries because that would be CHEATING, and HE WHO CHEATS…LOSES!!!!

Davis' jaw dropped as he looked at the four gifts, wrapped in white tissue paper; each package was designed differently with the names Daddy, Son, Daughter, and Sissy. "What the hell is going on here?" he said.

He needed some liquid courage before he could further explore the contents of the box. He mixed a Jack and Coke and chugged it down in one gulp, leaving only the clanking of ice in the bottom of the glass.

He carefully unwrapped the gift labeled Daddy. He was sick to his stomach, as his eyes passed over the cover of the journal. Snapshots of him and the various women with whom he had engaged in relationships, as well as pictures of Ella's mom, Eastern Illinois University, and an assortment of buildings that Davis recognized, covered the book. Nervous fury burned from his chest to his hands, causing his sweaty palms to stick to the pictures as he gripped the journal.

The ringing of the house phone made him jump, and he quickly shoved the items back into the Chegg Box. William answered the kitchen phone at the same time that Davis answered the phone in his office. "Hey William, can I talk to your father, please?" the unfamiliar voice remarked.

"William, I got it," Davis barked into the telephone.

"Ok, Father," William nervously responded, as he hung up the phone.

The male voice on the other end said, "Is that any way to talk to your child? Tisk, Tisk, Tisk, Davis. Before you fuck up anymore, let me explain; we are going to play a game of strike-out. As we told Ella, it has rules similar to baseball; the players in this game are you, William, and Emilie. If everyone plays well, your wife will come home safe and sound, but if any of you gets three strikes, well…she dies. You will get strikes by being dishonest, not guessing a riddle correctly, not completing a task, or of course by cheating. Essentially, Ella's life is in your family's hands. Now, you know the rules."

The baseball reference nagged at Davis; Gianni had made a similar baseball analogy during their first meeting over the Chicago investment. He had no time to analyze the comment before the caller continued.

"Unfortunately, we already had to assess you one strike. I know this might not seem fair since you didn't know the rules, but your lies were so blatant during the initial interviews that we can't simply turn our heads."

Jax paused long enough to make Davis wonder how the man knew what he had said to the police. Of course, Jax was making it up as he went along, but, based on Davis' history of lying, he figured there was a good chance his words spoke true.

He continued, "We should assess you a second strike for opening your son's mail. Did the box have your name on it? I think not. It isn't polite to open someone else's diary… I mean mail, now, is it? Anyway, lucky for you, I hadn't given you the ground rules of the game, so we will let this one slide. You still have nearly a month to get through the game without breaking the rules, so you better start being a bit more careful."

Davis looked frantically around the room and through the window. How did this guy know he had opened the box? Panic was the concrete block that kept his feet from moving.

"What do you want from me?" Davis yelled through clenched teeth. "Wh…"

His voice was cut off by the sound of a muffled scream followed by a gruff, "You hear your wife whining like a baby? It is YOUR fault! It is only going to get worse if you don't start following my directions! If you keep making mistakes like this one, our game won't make it anywhere close to thirty-two days, and the little Mrs. will be no more, leaving you out of reach of her daddy's money."

The man's voice grew in anger, "You expect everyone to respect your privacy, but you invade other people's property like you own the fucking world!"

"CLICK," and the caller was gone.

Davis threw the receiver against the wall and cursed a string of profanities. The incident left a hole in the drywall.

Willow's quiet voice stopped him short in his tirade. "Father, do you think Mommy will come home soon?" she said, as her tiny frame stood, shaking, in the doorway.

"Willow, I am not sure what is going on, but I know the police will do everything they can to bring your mother home safely."

Davis quickly closed the orange box and carried it up to his bedroom. He placed the box on the dresser, removed his journal from it, and hid it under his mattress. He shook his head. After years of lies and deception, would his world come down to a small journal? He feared the answer to his own question.

The presence of the journals prompted Davis to go to Ella's secret hiding place in the entrails of their bedroom closet to see if she had any recent entries. The journal was gone. "What the fuck? Why would she have changed her secret spot? Does she know I have read her journal? Did she take it to Florida with her and hide it somewhere in the condo?" Davis felt like a kid searching for the hidden cookie jar. He rummaged through the bedroom closet and drawers and then moved to the hallway closets, but it was nowhere to be found. Had she taken it somewhere else? Had she known she was going to leave? Davis felt more out of control with each new piece of information. He made a mental note to check the kids' bedrooms when they weren't around. He returned to his bedroom to try to get into his wife's mind.

"Ella, where did you move your journal, but more importantly WHY? What is in there that you didn't want me to see?"

The vibration of his cell phone in his pocket startled Davis out of his stupor, and the digitally distorted female voice sang,

Olly Olly oxen free,
You will play a game with me.
You won't tell the cops about our game,
or Ella you will never see!

Our game will last 32 days,
A significant number you will see.
It will end when freedom rings,
And you will finally acknowledge me.

CLICK! The caller was gone! Sweat beads dotted Davis' forehead. How did these people have his cell phone number? He wracked his brain to figure out the significance of the number 32. The words "When Freedom rings" reverberated in his head;

then it clicked…Independence Day… Fourth of July. He raced to his office and looked at the calendar off his desk. He flipped the page to July, placed his pointer finger on Friday, July 4th, counted back to Tuesday, July 1st, flipped the calendar page back to June and continued counting backward thirty-two days, Bingo! He was correct; it was June 2nd… the day Ella disappeared.

Alarm bells rang in his head. "This is not a fluke," he stammered, " This is calculated beyond belief." This new reality knocked him off the cocky pedestal on which he had been living for years, and now he needed to figure out very quickly who was behind this torment.

The rattling of his iPhone, as it danced its way across his smooth, cherry desk, made Davis nearly piss his pants. He saw the blocked call. The cockiness was out of his voice when he answered this time, and it was replaced by a shaky, less confident one.

"Please tell me what you want from me!"

Jax knew Davis was finally beginning to understand the gravity of the situation.

In a voice Davis recognized from the call made to the house phone a short time earlier, the man chanted:

Olly Olly oxen free,
I said you'd play a game with me!
The game is based on truth and lies
Let's place bets on how honest you will be!

You'll share your deceptions
And the truth will come out
And everyone will know
What you're really about

If you continue to deceive
As you have done ALL your life

The truth will be revealed
and I'll kill your wife.

That will leave you all alone
To take care of those two brats,
And you won't have Daddy's dough
RATS, RATS, RATS!

Click! This time, it was before Davis could respond--partially because the caller didn't give him a chance to do so, and partially because the golf ball sized lump that had wedged itself in his throat prevented anything from coming out, even if he could have thought of something to say.

His knees buckled, and he sank into his leather chair. On a notepad that rested on the cherry side-table, he wrote "lies, $, game, truth, bets." He needed to remember what the man had said. This had to be someone to whom he owed money. As of late, his gambling had gotten a bit out of control because he was desperately trying to accumulate the financial resources he needed to ensure his partnership in the Chicago project. Ella's bitch of a sister was also filling his wife's head with accusations about Davis stealing money from their father. This caused Ella to look more closely at her father's finances, so Davis was not able to pilfer money from the accounts as he had done previously.

He wearily walked to his liquor cabinet and picked up a highball glass. He opened the freezer, took out an ice cube tray, and dropped three ice cubes into the glass. He grabbed the Jack Daniels and filled half the glass. He opened a sixteen-ounce bottle of Coke and gave the whiskey a splash. He sucked the drink down in one long gulp. He glanced over and saw that the green message button on the answering machine was lit up. He clicked play. The glass he was about to refill fell to the carpet with a dull thud, and ice cubes danced their way across the hardwood floor.

In a soft, quiet voice, he heard, "Hi, Davis, I know you aren't expecting to hear from me, but I thought I would call and check on you. I can't imagine how you are managing with the kids, but…" The message cut off with that irritating beep that occurred when the caller paused a moment too long. It was Ella.

The color drained from his face into his stomach, and combined with the strong Jack and Coke, Davis felt like he was going to throw up. He sat down before his legs gave away, grasped at his head and grabbed a handful of hair. He was losing it! He looked up just in time to see two little feet turn from the corner of the hallway. He yelled in a much-too-harsh voice, "Get in here!"

Willow, petrified and shaking, peeked around the corner at her father. She said in a muffled cry, "I thought I heard Mommy talking to you." Davis motioned for her to come over to the chair.

Willow hesitated just long enough for it to be noticeable, and when she did enter the room, it was with great caution. She smelled the liquor on her father's breath, and memories of what he had done to her mommy on more than one occasion when he smelled like this, froze her in her steps. She recoiled when he reached for her.

Anger flashed in his eyes as he realized Willow was a Minnie-me of her mother. Willow felt his hatred burn through her tiny body, and her eyes quickly turned to the floor. Father and daughter stood awkwardly staring at the answering machine. Davis lied and said, "That was a message from your Aunt Emilie. She has offered to come and help take care of you and William for a few weeks.

Willow quietly said, "That might be a good idea." She grasped her mommy's t-shirt next to her face and used it to keep the tears from drenching her own shirt. Head hung low, she shuffled out of the living room and up to her bedroom. Davis made himself another, much stronger Jack and Coke and picked up the phone. He needed to call Emilie to find out how soon she could get there, but if he didn't call her now when he had the liquid courage to do so, he knew it wouldn't happen. He hated having to admit to her, of all people, that he couldn't do this thing called parenting without some help.

17

"What game are we going to play today, Mommy?" sounded through the speaker, as the click, click, click of high heels and the thump, thump, thump of a man's boots drew closer to the closet. Ella cringed. Hunger pangs consumed her stomach, but fear of what might happen to her in this basement closet overrode her hunger.

"I have a riddle for you, Ella," June said:
I can be chopped, but I'm not a carrot.
I have rings, but I'm not an onion.
I can be climbed, but I'm not a mountain.
I'm made of wood, but I'm not a table.
I have a trunk, but I'm not a car.
What am I?
After a pause, Ella whispered, "A tree."

"Very good, Ella," June's voice murmured in a bitter voice. "You saw the progression of your sweet Willow tree yesterday, and I imagine it upset you a little. Well, I am MORE than a bit upset about your family tree, but let's get to the details about your roots."

June shoved four more scrapbook pages through the slot and instructed her to add them to her binder. "You see, the roots of the tree are the foundation, but your foundation, or should I say Davis' roots, aren't what they seem. So we need to get to the 'root' of the problem."

"Please just tell me why you are doing this to me."

June's response was simple. "Davis has a debt to pay, and you are the only way for us to get his attention. You see, he has ignored this debt for too long, and he keeps making the same mistakes. He needs to learn his lesson once and for all."

Ella responded, "I will give you the money he owes you! Just tell me how much, and I will get it for you."

The woman responded, "Ella, this time your daddy's money can't get your family out of the pickle Davis has gotten you into."

"You don't have to believe anything I say, but only the truth will set you free," June explained.

June slid four more pages through the slot. The first two-page layout revealed a picture of a loblolly pine tree, ripped down the middle so that the tree split apart and separated. Ella had spent a great deal of time in the woods, and she knew her trees. In the top of the tree, there was a snapshot of a dapper young man around seventeen or eighteen, posing with his arm around a pretty, young brunette. There was a large X across the entire image. A ripped and faded picture of a little boy, about seven years old, in front of a trailer, was placed in the middle of the tree trunk. He looked like William, and if it hadn't been for the cracked and tattered effects of the picture, Ella might have thought it was her sweet boy. The clothes were mismatched, and the boy was barefoot. On the right side of the tree were three pictures. They included a Polaroid of a slightly older version of the same boy with a scowl on his face, as a woman kissed him on the cheek. Right next to the picture was another image, presumably of the same woman. She was older and much more wrinkled. She sat, smoking a cigarette, in a precarious metal lawn chair in front of the same trailer. A picture of a seemingly well-to-do couple posing at the Master's Golf Tournament in Augusta, Georgia was placed on the upper right-hand side of the page.

On the left side of the tree, drawing lay only two pictures. The first was another couple, both donning Master's Golf Tournament shirts in the same spot as the older couple in the image on the opposite side of the tree. The other photo on that side of the tree was a family picture, presumably taken for a church directory; it revealed the perfect family; a man, a beautiful woman, but not the same woman as the picture with the X over it, and two adorable little boys, who also hauntingly resembled William. The writing that snaked around the edges of the scrapbook page said, "We never quite know the roots of any given tree. We can see the trunk, the branches, and the leaves, but it is the roots that determine the true strength of the tree. If the roots are bad, the tree is bad, and when the roots give out, the tree MUST GO!"

Ella could only guess the pictures were connected to her husband. Davis had told her he was an only child and that both of his parents were killed in a house fire when he was in high school. He explained that he did not have any pictures or other keepsakes. She had no reason not to believe him, so none of this made sense. How could she be looking at a childhood picture of her husband, and what did it mean?

The next two-page layout had several pictures, including a postcard of The Master's golf course and stick-figure drawings of broken families that were meant to tell some sort of story. On the corresponding page was a typed, one-page story, titled, "The Making of a Monster: The true creation of Mr. Davis Masters." Ella's mind raced as she tried to take in the pictures from the two previous scrapbook pages.

June said, " Ella, you and your children have had so much fun with your stupid little tape recorder and microphone, so I decided to let you use it to read this story to your sissy. After all, we both know she is always trying to dig up dirt on your hubby."

Her voice turned nasty, "Now, turn the fucking tape recorder on and read the story! Your sister is going to receive this gift soon and very soon."

The scolding voice and the sound of the word "sister," brought her out of her thoughts. Ella quickly followed June's instructions and began reading the unfamiliar story.

Her voice quivered, "Once upon a time there was a young man named Davis Love Brown, who grew up on the proverbial 'wrong side of the tracks.' He had no opportunity, or reason, for that matter, to cross paths with a beautiful young lady born into a privileged family on the right side of the tracks. If only Davis' mother, Alice Johnson, would have gotten pregnant under different circumstances, his life might have turned out totally different...better, but Davis' eighteen-year-old father, Tommy Brown, got the hell out of Dodge as soon as sixteen-year-old Alice got pregnant."

Ella's voice caught, and bile made its way up her esophagus and into her raw throat. She swallowed hard to force the bitter taste back down.

"Keep reading," June demanded.

Ella continued, "Davis Love Brown arrived on December 23, 1964, weighing in at only 4 lbs. 8 oz. He was his mommy's little souvenir from the Master's Tournament, but his mommy was left alone and destitute, rejected by her family, and broken-hearted. Poor little Davis grew up a bastard child because his daddy dumped his mommy, married a beautiful woman, and fathered two perfect little boys.

Ella's heart momentarily broke for her husband. She thought about her own son, William, and how a traumatic event like this would affect him.

"Fucking READ! June scolded.

"At a young age, Davis questioned his mom about his name. When he was eight years old, his mother finally explained the sketchy details of his early years. The fatherless boy spent most of his young life explaining and defending his first name. Most people called him David because they were certain Davis was a spelling error. Classmates jeered at him because of his name, and teachers mispronounced it. He was often referred to as the "hothead" of the class because he got so pissed off about his name. His name was also a reminder of the mother fucker that left his mom knocked up with nowhere to turn and forced to make ends meet just to put food in his belly and thrift store clothes on his back.''

Ella paused long enough to catch her breath, "During middle school, Davis decided he was going to be a successful businessman, but not with a lame last name like Brown. 'After all, he often told his classmates, 'no rich man I know has a dumbass name like Brown.' So, at the age of 18, Davis scraped enough money together from his odd jobs to hire a local attorney to file name-change paperwork on his behalf. He became Davis Masters. Of course, the information had to run in the local paper for six weeks, so he couldn't entirely escape his past."

Ella was stunned! She couldn't wrap her head around this story. She felt a mixture of sorrow, pity, and confusion. She should have been outraged at her husband for lying to her, but she mostly felt pity. *Poor Davis*, she thought, as she gently caressed the unhappy face of the little boy in the picture. She couldn't understand how her captors would have known details about an event that happened fifty years earlier, but they seemed to have a kind of control over her life that she could not grasp.

June said, in a softer voice, "I know this is a lot to take in, dear. Just take some deep yoga breaths and allow yourself to process the whole scenario. See, I thought it was time you knew about Davis' childhood...the real one, not the lie he has told you all these years. You might be wondering how I know all of this. Well, you see, Davis and I have a much closer relationship than the two of you will ever experience, so he has shared a lot of things with me. In fact, we are so deeply connected that.... Oh...you probably don't want to hear those details."

Ella's pity for her husband turned to anger. How could Davis be intimately involved with a woman who sounded half his age? The momentary sadness she had felt for her husband, as she took in the pictures of a broken little boy, turned to bitterness over the thought of what her own children must be experiencing right now. She spoke loudly. "If this is all about you wanting my husband, then quite frankly, you can have the son-of-a-bitch. I just want my babies to have their mommy back."

"If only it were that simple," June's calm voice responded, "Now, kindly slip that cassette out through your mail slot so I can get it to your sissy."

Strong male hands momentarily gripped Ella's fingers, sending chills up her arms.

"Oh, and by the way," June chuckled, "Davis' mommy and daddy are both still very much alive. It's such a pity that sweet Grandma has had to watch her grandchildren grow up from a distance. She has even seen several of William's baseball games. She knew she would be safe in doing that because Davis doesn't have time for mundane activities like his kids' activities; he is too busy juggling all of his women."

The woman sang, "Olly Olly oxen free, be careful of fruit from a poisonous tree!" The click, click click of June's heels ascended the steps.

Ella held her breath and waited, but she did not hear the thump, thump, thump of the man's boots she so desperately needed to hear. Was it Donny? Was he still lingering on the other side of the door? Was it his turn? Could she really hear his heavy breathing, or was it her imagination? Fear, once again, gripped Ella.

Thirty minutes of terror passed before Ella heard what she needed to hear. She slowly steadied her breath and relaxed her muscles as the thump, thump, thump of his boots made their way up the steps.

Donny grabbed several bottles of beer out of the refrigerator and joined Jax and June in front of the television for the extensive news coverage that showed the police on their wild goose chase of the woman they had in their possession. They laughed as each recounted his or her version of the abduction, and the pile of empty beer bottles grew.

"We pulled it off," Donny said, "the abduction of the year."

Jax joined in the revelry, "We drove Ella back to Springfield and secured her in her new home, all while authorities were focusing on looking for her in Florida. We are genius!" he stated, triumphantly.

June laughed along with the two men, but deep down she wasn't laughing. She knew the guys didn't have the same stake in this as she did; they were just having a good time. This wasn't a game for her; it was payback, and she knew a lot of people would end up hurt. She hadn't yet filled the guys in on all of her plans. She needed to wait to do that until they were in too far to turn back because she knew they would never go along with such a cruel ruse.

Now, she thought, *the fun begins in making Davis and Emilie both look guilty.* She smiled a wry smile, peered into the bottom of her empty beer bottle and said, "You boys think you can keep an eye on that wildcat downstairs, while I will run out and get some more cold ones? Let me rephrase that; Jax, you watch over little Momma. Donny, don't even think about going downstairs! I can't trust you to keep your hands off of her."

Donny winked at June and said, "You're the boss!"

The three laughed, but Jax and June were well aware of Donny's previous sexual assault charges, so there was a serious undertone to their orders. They knew he was a risk factor, but they also knew this made him a safe accomplice because he wouldn't run to the police if something went wrong. Jax and June knew they had to watch him carefully and not give him an opportunity to be alone with Ella. They wanted to scare her, but deep down, they didn't want Donny to get hold of her.

18

Emilie flitted around the clothes racks with a nervous energy Ellen had never before witnessed. It was like she was under the influence of drugs and could not control her manic behavior. She ranted about Davis' total incompetence as a parent as she rearranged perfectly organized shelves.

"You know it killed him to have to call me and ask how soon I could come. I mean, come on, they JUST got home today, and he already can't handle parenting. He is a worthless piece of shit!"

She continued reorganizing accessories that she had already meticulously displayed five minutes earlier, and she obliviously moved dresses from one rack to another.

"Now, remember, Alana is coming in on Wednesday at 9:00 a.m., but she has to be done by 10:30 to get across town for her luncheon. I scheduled Vivian for 10:45, and Kay for 1:00 p.m. That should leave you an hour for lunch."

The longer Emilie talked, the faster her words rattled out of her mouth, and Ellen scribbled notes as quickly as her hand could move. Finally, she put her hand up, and said, "Emilie, I've got this. This place is the last thing you should be thinking about. Emiliease Gowns and I will be right here when you get back. I will call you if I have any issues, but really, go be with your family and let me handle this place."

Emilie broke down, and Ellen wrapped her in her arms. "Things are going to be OK, Emilie. I just know they are."

Emilie cried, "I don't even know how something like this happens. I mean, you see these reports on the news or on the internet, but it is always somebody else's family."

Ellen continued to console her friend, but her words felt empty.

Emilie gave her a final squeeze that indicated her outburst was over and said, "Thanks, Ellen, I know I have already said this, but I have no clue what I would do without you."

"Emilie, you would do the same thing for me. That's why I love you."

Emilie squeezed her one more time and asked, "Do you mind if I use your cell phone? I left mine out in the car." Ellen handed Emilie her phone and got back to work folding clothes. She watched Emilie slip into the back office.

Emilie dialed Gianni's number. She hoped he would answer since the number was not a familiar one. She had decided not to use her phone since she knew the police might be checking her phone records.

Gianni could hardly speak. He had always been a calm, cool, and collected guy who was the envy of other men. Now, he sounded broken. As Emilie told Gianni about Davis whispering, "dumped phone," she relived the sense of relief she felt knowing he had the insight to ditch his throw-away phone that was his only connection to her and Gianni. The two of them breathed a collective sigh of relief, but they both wondered if the police may have somehow obtained the phone. Together, they pondered the possibilities of Ella's disappearance, but nothing made sense. They agreed it was not a random act and that somehow Davis had to be behind it. They each secretly questioned whether the other knew more than was being said.

They wanted to devise a plan, but they had no clue where to begin. Each knew their first priority was finding Ella, but they didn't know how to do so without bringing up any of their personal baggage. If their names arose in the wrong light, they might look guiltier than Davis.

Emilie said, "I need to get Ellen's phone back to her; somebody keeps beeping in on it. We will need to have limited communication for a while, but I will do my best to get hold of you if I find anything out. I just wanted to make sure you knew what has happened so far, especially the part about Davis' phone."

Gianni replied, "I am not thrilled about the fact that you will be spending time at Davis' house, but I know you have no other choice." To lighten the mood, he added, "as ill-equipped as you are to take care of children, you are the best they have right now."

"Thanks for your vote of confidence," she smirked, "But you are absolutely correct. Those poor children." Her closing words were spoken with the lightness of Gianni's comment, but the heavy undertones weighed both of them down as they ended the conversation.

Ellen heard the buzz, buzz, buzz of a phone vibrating. She walked around the shop trying to find the source of the buzzing. The sound led her to the counter, where she saw Emilie's purse on the floor. By the time she went to pick the bag up to take it to her friend, the buzzing had stopped.

Ellen was holding Emilie's purse as Emilie exited the office. They exchanged an awkward look.

"Your purse was buzzing," Ellen said, half apologetically and half quizzically.

"Oh my God, I thought I left it in the car. Thank goodness you saw it. I might have reached Springfield before I realized I didn't have it. That would have been bad."

The two exchanged purse for phone and gave each other a departing hug. Emilie fought rush hour traffic out of town. The four-hour trip to Springfield seemed like ten. As strained as her relationship with her sister had been over the past couple of years, the thought of something happening to her was unbearable. The many fights they had over their parents' money no longer mattered, as long as her sister came home safely, and Davis was no longer part of the equation.

The hum of the radio drowned out the silence of the car, but Emilie heard nothing through the cacophony of noise that rang through her head as she imagined her sister's plight.

Four hours later, she pulled into the driveway of the house she hadn't seen in two years. Just as she turned the ignition off, her cell phone buzzed. She looked down at the screen that read, "blocked."

"Hello," Emilie answered, hesitantly.

The female voice on the other end said, "Hi, Sissy, I'm so glad you arrived safely," Click, the call ended.

Emilie wheeled around in her seat and surveyed her surroundings. Fear climbed its way into her extremities and made it impossible for her to lift her rubber legs out of the car.

Davis opened the front door, a scowl on his face, and motioned her to come in. Emilie didn't move. After several minutes, Davis walked toward the car; when he got close enough to make out his sister-in-law's face, he realized all of the color had run out of it.

"What the hell is wrong with you? You look like shit!"

Emilie wanted to scream, cry, or cuss him out, but when she opened her mouth, she was mute.

Davis almost felt sorry for her.

After several minutes, Emilie regained some of the strength in her legs and found her voice. She said, "I just got a phone call...I mean right when I pulled up in the driveway. The woman said she was glad that I had arrived safely. Davis, what the hell is going on here?"

It was Davis' turn to panic. His eyes darted wildly to the houses, cars, and trees around his home, as he looked for signs of someone watching him. "Let's get inside," he urged through a nervous, raspy voice. He was oblivious to the tiny frame of a woman perched up high in the neighbor's red oak tree.

June smiled as she sat perched and well-hidden in the neighbor's tree. She snapped several photos of Davis grabbing Emilie's hand and the two rushing toward the front, not even bothering to grab Emilie's belongings. The children's weary faces peered at them through the glass of the front door as Davis and Emilie scuttled across the driveway.

June returned home, empty-handed an hour-and-a-half later. Jax asked in a joking manner, "Where have you been, but more importantly, where is my beer?"

"Shit," June said, "I forgot the beer. Sorry, baby, I got sidetracked."

Jax pulled her close to him and said, "You went to their house, didn't you?"

She nodded but could not get out the words to explain why she continued to be consumed by the man who had caused her so much pain. Deep down, June knew Jax didn't need an explanation. He hated Davis for what he had done to his girl, and he wanted to see the man go down in flames as much as June did; his only worry was that she would go too far and get caught before the truth came out about Davis. It was a tightrope that June was walking on, and he didn't want the woman he loved so much to fall. The reality was that if the police found out about June's involvement in Ella Randolph's disappearance, she would see jail time, but if Davis found out she was connected to his wife's disappearance before the police did, he would have no hesitation to make her another one of his expenditures.

Moments passed as June found comfort in her lover's muscular arms and chest. She knew Jax had the physical wherewithal to hurt Davis, and all she had to do was ask. June, however, made it clear from the beginning that she didn't want to let Davis off the hook that easily; she wanted him to suffer emotionally and financially-- just as he had made her suffer.

June broke the momentary silence. "I need to print a couple of quick pictures, and then I will go tell Ella how everything is going on the home front."

"Well, stalker," Jax teasingly scoffed, "I guess I will go to bed since I don't have any more beer. Donny gave up on you an hour ago and went out to get his own."

June hugged Jax. "I don't know why you put up with me, but I'm sure glad you do. When this is all over, I promise I will make it up to you."

"Oh, I am making a list!" Jax replied, as he swatted her on the butt. "Now, make that basement visit a quick one and come to bed soon so we can get an early start on that list."

June turned and seductively bit her lower lip as she popped the memory card into the printer, "Is that a threat or a promise?"

Jax's eyes lit up as he winked, "Baby, I only make promises to you."

"Well then, I will make my visit a quick one." June winked back and watched four pictures make their way out of the printer. She glanced at the images of the children's confused faces pressed on the glass of the front door as they watch their father and Aunt Emilie skip across the driveway arm in arm. The time stamp on the pictures read "2014/06/08." As she descended the stairs, she turned her thoughts from Ella to Jax and smiled a giddy teenage girl kind of smile. She knew Jax was the real deal; she couldn't believe she had found such a fantastic man, given all of the garbage she had brought into the relationship and the emotional roller coaster rides on which she continued to take him.

Ella heard the footsteps and braced herself for the unknown.

"Knock knock. Is anyone home?"

Ella remained silent.

"Not feeling up for a visit, Ella? I thought maybe you might want to hear about the visit I made to your house tonight, but since you lack the politeness to welcome me into your home, I guess I will head on to bed. I just thought you would want to know about your sister's arrival, though, and the smashing reunion she and Davis are having. In fact, I took a few family photos to ease your pain."

June's words confirmed her location; she was back in Springfield.

"Are my babies OK?" Ella whispered in a barely audible voice through the door. "Did you see my babies?"

June's heart broke momentarily at the helplessness that filled Ella's voice, but she recovered quickly and said, "Oh, William and Willow are managing just fine. Their faces glowed as they excitedly waited for Emilie to get out of the car. She took so long because she was on the phone with me; in fact, Davis finally came out and asked what was taking her so long. I was trying to figure out who was the most excited to see her, Davis or the kids. So, yes, I would say they are doing fine."

June passed the pictures through the small slot in the door. Ella's eyes stung as she took in the four images, but she refused to let this woman see her cry.

"If one didn't know better, she would think that was you flitting across the driveway with Davis. I guess that makes sense, though, seeing that you are identical twins and all."

It was dark outside, but Ella could still see that Emilie's hair was no longer blonde. Had the date not been stamped on the picture, Ella wouldn't have believed it was real.

"Davis certainly didn't take long to replace you with your sister. They had quite the reunion right in your driveway, with your children's precious faces plastered against the glass of the front storm door watching their every move. I only wonder if the FBI will be as understanding as the children are."

Ella couldn't respond, not that June was looking for a response.

"Yes, by the amount of luggage your sister brought, it looks like she plans on staying a while. It was quite a touching reunion, although it hasn't been nearly as long as you think."

Before Ella could ask for an explanation she wasn't sure she wanted to hear, June said, "Well, while your sweetie is entertaining your sissy, my sweetie is waiting for me in bed. As much as I would like to continue our girl time, he asked that I come to bed soon; he is doing everything he can to help take my mind off of your husband. Night, Night, Ella."

June paused long enough to allow Ella to catch her breath before she brought in the one-two punch, "Tomorrow morning, sweetie, we are going to do something about that hair of yours. We can't have you looking too much like yours, sissy. We will teach her a lesson for trying to become you. I will bring my scissors with the morning coffee, okay, sweetheart." With those words, June was gone.

Ella was left with the unfathomable vision of her sister tucking her children into bed and then sitting on the back patio sipping wine with her husband. Her nutrition and sleep-deprived mind struggled to process the pictures, but she couldn't keep herself from visualizing the worst. She caressed her hair, partially as a self-soothing mechanism and partly because she realized it would be gone by morning.

19

Within an hour of her arrival, Emilie tucked the kids into bed. She said, "I know I am no replacement for your mom, but I will do whatever I can do to help you through whatever is going on."

Innocently, Willow asked, "What happened to your long blonde hair? Why do you look so much like our mommy now? You have never looked like our mommy. I don't think I like it very much."

Emilie was without words; she couldn't formulate an answer that was remotely reasonable. All she could say was, "I am sorry," as she kissed her forehead and left the room.

Davis poured two glasses of red wine to ease the pain of the inevitable barrage of questions and accusations he knew he was about to receive. In a whispered hush, Emilie began, "What in the hell is going on here, Davis? What have you done to or with my sister?"

Davis responded, "Emilie, I would like to ask you the same question. I have no clue what happened, and I have to be honest; I am scared to death. Whoever has her seems to know a lot about all of us. I received a box within minutes of returning home Friday. It did not have a mailing label on it; it just appeared on the front porch. It wasn't there when we got home, but fifteen minutes later it was; it was like someone was waiting for me."

"What was in it?" she questioned.

"You won't believe it unless I show you. I hid it in my bedroom."

"Is this some sort of sick ploy to get me into your bedroom?" she hissed. "Maybe you can get rid of me too, and then you will get all of Daddy's money?"

Davis stood impatiently, and said, "Please, just come to take a look for yourself."

Emilie stood to follow him, but uttered, "I don't trust you as far as I can throw you, Davis."

William looked over and saw Willow sleeping in the matching twin bed that was usually reserved for his overnight guests. He quietly crept out of bed. At the top of the stairs, he strained to hear the conversation that he knew would be heated and accusatory. It was only a matter of time before his father and aunt brought out the boxing gloves; it happened every time they were in a room together for more than an hour, and he dreaded it. Instead, he heard only his father's last sentence, "Do you seriously think I am going to do something with you when my children are in the house?"

Emilie responded with a laugh that young William couldn't judge, "Davis, we do have a history. Get a couple drinks in you, and who knows what you will do?"

Realizing the whispers were making their way up the steps, William quickly slipped back into his room, got into bed facing the door, and put the blanket over his head, leaving only a sliver of an opening over his eyes.

From the low light of the hallway, he saw his father and his aunt, wine glasses in hand, as they ambled to his parents' bedroom. His father carried the remaining bottle of wine in his other hand. He heard the bedroom door shut, and then he heard nothing more than muffled voices. Tears streamed down his face. For the first time, he wondered if the two of them made his mom disappear.

The following morning, Emilie strolled out of the guest bedroom to get a much-needed cup of coffee. She was still in the same clothes from the day before. She tousled William's already mussed hair as they met in the hallway.

"You hanging in there?"

William responded with a cold glare.

"Hey, little dude, what's the matter?" she sputtered before she realized how ridiculous the question was.

"Nothing," was all he muttered as he moved past her and closed the bathroom door behind him.

His reaction hurt Emilie. "He seemed fine with me last night," she thought. Obliviously, she wondered if he had experienced a bad dream. Maybe, she thought, her presence was a harsh reminder that his mom was gone.

As she brewed a pot of coffee, she thought about the night before, and the exchange that had occurred after she and Davis slipped into his bedroom. Davis had given her the journal, wrapped in tissue paper, with the name, Sissy, on it. He explained that the instructions specifically indicated family members could not share their journals, and he assured her that he had not looked at the contents of her journal. He told her about the three-strike rule, leaving out the fact that he had already received one strike. His concerned words played through her mind, "We are up against some bad actors, Emilie. I have no clue how many, who they are, or why they are coming after our family!"

Emilie did not believe Davis, but she saw a fear in him she had never seen before. She didn't care about him, but she needed to keep him in good enough graces to get him to slip up or do something that would lead her to her sister.

Emilie retreated to the guest bedroom, nervously sipped her coffee, and cautiously opened up the wrapped journal like she was opening up a crocheted sweater from Aunt Edna. The front of the journal was covered in pictures-- not just any pictures, but pictures she and her family had pored over year-after-year as they sat around the fireplace at Christmas time, teasing each other about clothing and hairstyles of days gone by.

The melancholy moment turned into a pit in her stomach that grew in diameter as she took in the images. Davis' face had been carefully carved out of every picture. The instructions on the bottom of the page read, "Turn Over…"

Emilie followed the written instructions; When she turned the journal over to the back cover, she stared into several variations of Davis' arrogant face that were missing from the front cover; each one had a huge red X through it.

Emilie's immediate thoughts turned to Gianni. "Was he behind this?" she wondered. "Was he so obsessed with Ella that he would do something like this?" She shook her head as if to clear the rocks that now rattled in it. "He can't be behind this."

The message at the bottom was confusingly simple, "Davis picked the wrong family!"

Emilie reluctantly opened up the journal. A loose-leaf piece of paper and an envelope with several pictures fell to the floor. She picked the items up, opened the letter, and began reading.

Dear Emilie,

We know you prefer your high and mighty Chicago lifestyle, and we are sorry you have had to crimp that style to come to take care of little sister's brats, but we think that's the least you can do for poor Ella. After all, you have taken so much away from your sister; it's about time you make it up to her, don't you think? Take a look inside the envelope, Emilie, and I think you will know what we mean.

-J-

Emilie removed the rest of the pictures from the envelope and flipped through them like a deck of cards. Her jaw dropped lower with the observation of each image. She stared at a blonde version of her current self, talking and laughing with

Davis, as they walked along Lakeshore Avenue or sat in various Chicago restaurants. The pictures would be impossible to explain to her twin sister, especially given the volatile nature of the conversations she and Ella had endured over what Emilie referred to as Ella's deadbeat husband.

She continued reading, "By the way, Ella received the doubles of these sweet images, and if you don't follow the rules of our game, the police will end up with the third set; that is, unless, of course, they have already received them. I guess you could always call them and ask. Is that a good idea?"

"How could someone have taken all of these pictures," Emilie questioned, as she studied the incriminating evidence one more time. It was at this moment that she knew she was right in the middle of a horrible nightmare. What started as a conspiracy to catch her son-of-a-bitch brother-in-law stealing her family money had gone very wrong. Was this Davis' way of setting a trap to catch her? She knew that no matter how hard she tried to convince her sister of the truth, pictures were worth a thousand words.

Emilie continued reluctantly shuffling through the pictures. She cringed. The images of her and Davis were enough to incriminate Emilie, but the photos of her and Gianni, the true love of Ella's life, would be the final twist of the knife in Ella's broken heart.

With shaking hands, Emilie set the pictures aside and examined the first two pages of her journal; they were vanilla. The first one read, "Tell Ella how much you love her." The second page asked Emilie to write about how the kids were doing. The third page seemed normal in that it instructed her to update her sister on their father's health. At the bottom of that page, however, was a message that said, "You really should check your daddy's meds-- STAT!" Things aren't always what they seem. Below the message was a small cut-out of a website URL about causes of dementia. Emilie took a picture of it and rubbed her aching temples.

She slowly turned the page. Her mouth turned to cotton as she read, "My dear sister, Ella, I have not always been the best sister in the world. You have only loved two men, and I have had relationships with both of them. I must finally tell you the truth in hopes that it will set us both free!"

Directly under the heading was written: "Here, Emilie, is where you write the truth!." Sick guilt coursed through her veins as she anguished over what she knew she would have to write. She had lied to the police multiple times, and putting the truth down on paper would bring those lies crumbling down all around her.

Her hands shook as she turned the page. The sentence at the top read, "Just in case you didn't tell the WHOLE story...Rock-a-bye-bye baby!" The journal slid out of Emilie's drenched hands and fell to the ground; she shrank into a pile next to it. Her only thought was, *How can I reveal a lifetime of mistakes in two days?* Lying in a heap on the soft carpet, Emilie cradled the journal as fear of the truth pounded through her head. She reluctantly turned to the next page; it was blank, thank God!

Emilie carefully placed the journal in the dresser drawer. She knew she couldn't put off her writing for long, but she needed a shower first; she had to scrub her sins away before she could put them on paper. Emilie caught a glimpse of herself in a hallway mirror on her way to gather her belongings from her car. She had aged ten years.

Davis' face, red and sweaty from his morning run, silently mirrored her thoughts, as they passed each other at the front door. Neither spoke. Emilie returned to the kitchen to help with the kids. She and Davis engaged in awkward niceties as they made their way around the kitchen. Both were secretly glad William was old enough to take care of most of his and Willow's needs because neither adult knew the first thing about taking care of kids. William glared at both of them.

After breakfast, Emilie retreated to the privacy of the ensuite bathroom of the guest bedroom, took off her stale clothes, and stepped into the shower. Standing under the hot water, she angrily scrubbed at her raw skin, but no amount of scrubbing could rub away the guilt. She slithered down into the tub and rocked as the scolding water streamed down her back.

She dragged herself out of the shower and dried off,. She wondered how she would find the strength to make her fingers put down the words she knew she had to admit. She sat down at the white desk where she and her sister had spent countless hours doing homework as children, and she began to put pen to paper. Seeing her words on paper, Emilie realized that if the journal ended up in the wrong hands, she would become a prime suspect. Whoever was behind her sister's disappearance knew Emilie's deepest, darkest secrets, and now they would be in print for anyone to see. She shivered and rubbed her hands up and down her arms to get rid of her goosebumps.

Emilie picked up her journal and placed it back in the drawer. She rolled up in a tiny ball in the queen-sized bed and cried herself to sleep.

20

With Emilie retreating to her room, Davis knew he could no longer ignore the Chegg box he had carefully hidden in his bedroom. The note in the box explicitly stated that the police were NOT to be told about the journals. This was the only thing keeping him from flipping out.

He sat the children down and uneasily said, "William and Willow, your mommy is fine, but she wants you both to write to her for the next couple of days. It is like when you play school, and she gives you journal topics. You will write in the journals like you normally do." He tried to calm his shaking voice.

Willow wasn't old enough to put the puzzle pieces together, but William was still convinced his father was somehow involved in his mom's disappearance. He realized his growing hate for the man who stood in front of him, and asked in a tone that was a bit too accusatory, "Did you get a journal, too?"

Reluctantly, Davis said, "Yes, and so did Aunt Emilie. We need to mail them back to your mom in two days."

"Where is our mom?" Willow cautiously asked, afraid her father would yell at her for her inquiry.

Davis saw the terrified look on his daughter's face and the look of scorn in William's eyes. *Was he really that harsh?* he wondered. *Were his kids that afraid of him?*

"I don't know where she is, but she will definitely get the journals we mail to her, so spend a lot of time on them. You want your mom to know how much you love and miss her, right?"

William spouted back, "Do YOU miss her?" before he could stop himself.

Shocked, Davis responded, "Of course, I miss her." He wanted to backhand the little son-of-a-bitch, but he knew he was in no position to discipline William like he knew the boy needed. William knew it also. He was smart enough to know how far he could push his father. He had never confronted him like he had in the past couple of days, but he knew if his dad laid a hand on him or Willow, he could tell the police. Even though Sgt. Pickett was in Florida, she had given William her cell phone number and said, "If you need anything, day or night, you call my cell phone, and I will get hold of someone in Springfield for you." William trusted the lady he had only known for a few days much more than the white-knuckled stranger in front of him who was shooting daggers at him and wanting to sock him.

The kids quietly unwrapped their packages to reveal beautifully decorated covers. Their mouths fell open as they looked at a collage of pictures of them, each with their mom.

"Did Mommy make these for us," Willow naively asked.

Before his father could reply, William said, "She sure did! Now, let's you and I go down to our schoolhouse and get our homework done so mean Mrs. Cruxtable doesn't make us eat spider juice for dinner!"

Crocodile tears hung on the lower lashes of Willow's big blue eyes as she said with a pouted, quivering lip, "but Mrs. Cruxtable isn't here to feed us dinner."

William took his sister by the hand and said, "I know, she isn't here right now, but she will be back soon. I promise."

Davis watched the two as they descended the stairs to escape into their schoolhouse closet; he realized he had never even seen the inside of it. He thought it was ridiculous that they had a big, beautiful home, but his wife and children spent much of their time in a tiny closet in the basement. He shook his head and questioned to himself, *How did I get myself into this life?*

William was the first to enter the playhouse. He flipped on the light switch and ducked to avoid knocking his head, as he took a step inside. He gasped when he saw the pile of nearly deflated, brightly-colored balloons. Willow was on his heels before he could redirect her out of the playhouse.

"What are those?" Willow asked, feeling nervous, but not knowing why.

William gathered the wad of balloons up quickly, so Willow wouldn't see the messages.

He said, apologetically, "Mom must have put them in here before we went on vacation."

"What does Bon something mean?" I saw Bon something…"

William snapped at his little sister, "Let's not worry about the balloons, OK? And don't mention them to anyone else. Do you understand me?"

Willow's eyes stung with tears at the tone of her brother's words. He had never raised his voice at her.

William embraced his sister and lied, "It is all going to be fine. Mom will be home before you know it."

Inside he wondered why his mother would put balloons in their playhouse that read, "Bon Voyage" and "Miss You" with the word, "DON'T" written in black permanent marker on top of the message. A tear trickled down his cheek. He didn't want to stay in the playhouse, but he didn't want to be anywhere near his father, so he stuffed the balloons in the corner. He looked around for his scissors to pop the balloons, but the supply box his mother kept them in was not in its usual place. Upon further inspection of the playhouse, William realized several of their toys and personal items were not there. Sickness filled his gut as he pondered the possibility that their mom had left them and had taken some of their belongings to remind her of them.

Willow asked William, "Where is my special pillow?"

In a gentler tone, he replied, "Maybe Mom put it in the laundry." He knew that also was most likely a lie. He quickly added, "How about we take our journals up to my room and write in them?" Lowering his voice, he admitted, "This place doesn't feel right without Mom."

Willow nodded in agreement.

William made a mental note to return to the playhouse when Willow wasn't around, to see what else was missing and to get rid of the balloons. The words, "Bon Voyage" and "DON'T MISS YOU!" repulsed him. He didn't understand how their mom could do this to them.

Davis did not hear the children go into William's room. He was engrossed in his own misery. He made himself a Bloody Mary, carried the drink up to his bedroom, closed and locked the door, and took his journal out from under the mattress to begin the inevitable. His first journal entry needed something a little stronger than a Bloody Mary, so he went to the makeshift bar he had created in his bathroom and made himself a neat bourbon. He sat on his king-sized bed, put the glass to his nose and inhaled the herbal aroma. Davis parted his lips on the edge of the glass and sipped the aged bourbon. The sweet, smooth liquor slid down his throat, followed by the sting of the after-burn. He held the rocky tumbler up and toasted the air. "Here is to one fucked up life!"

He opened up the letter that stuck out the top of the journal; it was specific.

"Davis, you have until 3:00 on June 11th to complete all five journal entries. The longer you put off the inevitable, the less time you will have to complete the task, and if you don't complete the task, don't get the package sent off, or heaven forbid LIE in ANY of your journal entries, you will get your second strike. You know, three strikes and you are out. Well, let me rephrase that: Ella will be out. You, on the other hand, will be IN…prison. We have everything in place to make that happen. After all, we are professionals; no amateur could make a person simply disappear in a restaurant full of people, right? You have to trust us on this because you have no other choice."

Davis closed his eyes and tried to wrap his head around the scrapbook and the letter. He forced himself to continue reading.

"Oh, and Davis, just so you know, I have already shared your childhood story with Ella. She actually felt pity for you…until I told her how intimately close the two of us are. I have pictures that reveal the truth, just in case you do not provide the correct information. Remember, visuals don't lie! AND your stories need to match Emilie's stories WITHOUT THE TWO OF YOU COMPARING NOTES! After all, you and Emilie have already shared more than Ella knows! ONLY your truth will set her free, Davis! I know the truth, and therefore, I will know if you are lying!"

The letter was signed, "Sincerely, Summer Love."

Davis noted the inconsistent use of pronouns in the letter. At times the writer used I, and at other times, we. He felt like there had to be multiple people involved. The question was, *Who are these people?*

He glanced back over the pictures that covered the homemade journal. He got up, poured another bourbon, sat back down, took a deep breath, and opened the journal. He quickly and painfully perused each heading to find out just how bad things were. They were bad!

The bold words on the first page read,

"MY LIFE HAS BEEN ONE BIG FAT LIE!"

April 1988-

Olly Olly oxen free,
You had a very special tree!
But Ella doesn't know the story,
So tell it to her to set her free.

Olly Olly oxen free,
You spent so much time under that tree.
You should have studied the books, not her,
Then maybe you would have a degree.

"Fuck!" Davis yelled.

The journal was titled, "The Tree and My Carefree College Days." The directions were clear, "Tell your wife about her college days...and yours!" With shaking hands, Davis read the next two lines.

"Ella, I have known you for _____ years. Here is how I met you." (Fill in the correct number of years, Davis, and don't get the number wrong; otherwise, STRIKE TWO!).

Davis was already in a conundrum; how far did these people go back? If they knew things about him as far back as college then what else did they know about his life? He felt like this was a trick question, and he wasn't sure how to answer it.

His thoughts spun out of control, so he turned to the next page, hoping he would gain some clarification. Fear leaped through him and then stopped right at the door of his heart. The page was titled, "Operation." It had a cut-out picture of the popular children's game next to the word. Davis read the sentence under the title, "Just like in the popular children's game, if you pick the wrong operation, Ella will be 'zzzzzzappped'!"

His worst fear came to fruition with the words on the third page: "Riddle Me This! Riddle Me That, Who's Afraid of a Little Black Cat?" The color drained out of his face.

Written in small letters at the bottom of the page were the words, "If this riddle is not quite enough to jog your memory, let me help you out a bit more, 'What's red and tan and goes off-road?'"

Davis didn't need the memory jogger to understand the meaning of the riddle, and fear gripped him by the nuts. Only Frank knew about this. "Shit, is Frank behind this? Did I call him a moron asshole one too many times?"

He read the note that was taped to the page.

"You know I know what you know, so write a letter to Ella explaining precisely what I am talking about, and I mean EVERY detail. I hate to keep repeating myself, but your family's lives are in your hands. I have only one question, Davis, were your actions a result of the bitterness you felt toward your mother all these years because she is such a loser? I'm just wondering!"

Crimson started on his neck and rose up his face. "What the fuck? Nobody fucking knows my mother, not even Frank!" Davis had an immediate picture of his shriveled mother smoking a cigarette as she sat in a tattered lawn chair in front of the run-down, roach-infested trailer he was forced to call home for way too many years. It had been twenty years since he had gone back to that place, but he could still smell the stench of thick stagnant water that bubbled up through the unusable bathtub.

Davis was afraid to turn the page, but he couldn't imagine anything worse. The fourth page had the title of the famous Beatle's song, "You Never Give Me Your Money," with the instructions, "Davis, tell Ella who wouldn't give you money." Again, he knew the gist of this title.

He turned the page. In large bold letters was the message, "Only Your Truth Shall Set Her Free!"

He did not have to think hard to answer the riddles, but the thought of putting his responses in writing paralyzed his fingers to the point that he was physically unable to pick up the red pen that was attached by Velcro to the journal.

Davis knew if he completed the journal entries honestly, it would probably land him in prison, but if he didn't, he would most likely end up dead because the kidnapper would kill his wife, leaving him without any hopes of getting the money necessary to keep the collectors from killing him. This was a double-edged sword that could either keep him alive or bring him and his wife to their deaths. He desperately needed to figure out which of his debtors was ruthless enough to do this to his family.

With a gulp of his drink and shaking hands, Davis began writing. He started on the first page, knowing he would need a whole lot more liquor before he could muster up the courage for the other pages. He wasn't going to fall for their tricks, so he wrote the truth.

"Ella, I have known of you for thirty-three years. Here is how I met you."

Dear Ella,

I have to tell you the truth, once and for all. Our meeting on the hiking trail at Fox Ridge State Park was not exactly by chance. As you know by now, I'm not really that big of an outdoorsman, but I had no other way of getting into your good graces. See, the truth is that I had, well, sort of, known you since high school. I guess you could say we didn't run in the same circle, but I knew who you were. I saw you at the Long View Country Club, and I was smitten by you. I knew you had a twin sister, but I thought she acted like a bitch. You, on the other hand, were kind to everyone. I quit going to Long View, and I lost track of you once you went away to college; in fact, I didn't even know where you were.

When I started going to Eastern Illinois University and saw you sitting on the quad, I thought, I just have to get to know that girl. You didn't seem to have a boyfriend or even many female friends, so I wasn't sure how I could possibly introduce myself. I was too shy to come up and start talking to you.

You seemed to like the outdoors, so I took up hiking. You happened to be on the trail one Saturday when I was going for a morning hike. It seemed like a natural time for me to introduce myself.

Love,
Davis

Davis knew this admission was not technically a lie, but not exactly the truth either. He HAD quit going to the country club, but it was because he got fired for punching out one of the cooks, who made fun of his name. He did start going to Eastern Illinois University; he just wasn't enrolled as a student. He had also not lost track of Ella, but that was just a little white lie. He continued filling his drink glass and writing.

William and Willow sprawled out on William's bed and looked at the covers of their personalized journals. They knew all of the places, times, and events of the pictures. As they looked at images of them hiking the various trails in Springfield as well as Starved Rock State Park and other trails in Illinois, they wondered who could have been close enough to take the pictures. William hoped that Willow was not old enough to figure this out, and Willow knew her big brother was doing his best to protect her from the truth, so neither brought up the elephant in the room that was haunting each of them-- the unspoken truth that someone had taken the pictures.

Each quietly set into writing responses to the first painful journal question, "Tell me how your father is doing in my absence." Rocks filled their tummies as they provided the details of their father's behavior and actions since she left them.

William wrote, "Mom, I know you wouldn't just leave us. I found the balloons in our playhouse, and they don't make sense. I am worried. I am taking good care of Willow, but she is having a tough time. I am trying to make sure she eats good and keeps her hair brushed."

He realized he was not answering the prompt, so he put a large X over the writing and started a new paragraph. "Dad, well, he mostly stays in his room and drinks a lot. He leaves us alone a lot, but I am taking good care of Willow. We miss you.

Please come back home soon. We will work everything out--whatever everything is."

It was signed, "Love, Your Son."

Sitting next to her brother, Willow finished her last sentence. She didn't mention her father once. She only begged her mommy to please come home soon so she could take care of her. Willow's tears warped the page.

The children agreed to complete one more page, knowing they had to put the journals back in the box within two days. They kept their responses private because their father had told them they were not to share the contents of their journals with each other or with him or Aunt Emilie.

Written across the top of the next page was, "Recall your favorite Mommy-Time activity."

William wrote several paragraphs about the times they spent at his Papa's lake house and about all the hikes they took. He finished the journal by saying, "I like our hikes because it's just me and you and Willow, and sometimes Beau. I like it when it is just us; it feels right."

Willow wrote sentences about their school house and the hiking adventures they had taken. She decorated the page with drawings of trees. At the bottom of the page, she drew a picture of the schoolhouse. Beside the drawing, she wrote, "This is in case you forgot what our special schoolhouse looks like!"

Willow's belly gurgled, and William realized it was past lunchtime. "Let's go get you something to eat, Little Bit."

Willow was thankful for her brother.

21

A week had passed since Ella Master's disappearance, and the only lead the Florida Police Department and the FBI, Tampa Division had was a report by two witnesses that a tan Honda Civic with Florida plates circled the block around the restaurant a couple of times at around the time of Ella's disappearance. They indicated a man was driving the vehicle, but they didn't see anyone else in the car. One of the witnesses provided a license plate number, which came up as a stolen plate. Interviews with restaurant employees and patrons offered little detail, except the opinion that Davis was an ass, and they knew they couldn't arrest a person solely for being an ass.

The only other evidence the OPD had received was a letter that indicated Ella was no longer in Florida. Since the letter was postmarked Chicago, Illinois, and Ella was from Springfield, Illinois, the FBI Tampa Division had contacted the Springfield Division to join the case.

Springfield agents Drew Scott and Brad Gibbons were assigned to the case, and they started their investigation before Davis had even returned home.

Brad Gibbons was a seasoned agent who had seen it all during his tenure. He had a wife, Amber, and three amazing kids. Elise was 14, Van was 13, and Hunter was 11. He couldn't help thinking about the case from his own kids' perspective. They relied on him and Amber for everything, and they would be devastated if something like this happened in their family. Amber was a saint. She let him talk about work when he wanted to, but she didn't ask questions or bring up his job when she could tell he was in one of his moods. He appreciated his wife. He decided maybe he should say that more often to her.

Agent Scott was relatively new. He had been on local police forces before the Bureau, but he had only been with the Bureau for four years. He was not married, but he had a beautiful one-year-old baby girl, Reese. He often explained parenthood by saying, "She is the piece of me I hadn't realized was missing." He had been burned a few times in love, so he had sworn it off. He justified his choice to remain single by claiming he needed to devote all of his time to his career and his daughter. His partner, Agent Gibbons, knew this was a cover-up to avoid getting hurt.

Scott and Gibbons had balked at holding a press conference since they had very little information they wanted to share with the public, but their Supervisory Special Agent, Walter Winkler, insisted on it.

During the press conference, the agents explained that the investigation into the missing Springfield woman was ongoing. Scott stated, "We continue to work closely with agents in the Tampa Division, and they are keeping in close communication with the Orlando Police Department. We have very few leads at this time, but we continue to interview persons of interest, and we are confident others will come forward with information about the missing woman."

What the agents did not disclose was that they were looking into Davis Masters' personal and financial dealings. Although they had not yet interviewed Gianni Russo, they interviewed one of the other developers, Justin Riley, who was heading up the Chicago waterfront restaurant project. After a short interview, they realized Masters was just a small fish in the project, and it was unlikely that there was a connection between this business transaction and Ella's disappearance. Riley did, however, reveal that Davis was not able to follow through with his financial commitment to the Chicago project, so they had to take him off the team. He explained that Davis had struggled for months to provide his investment money, so they had to give him a deadline.

"When was that deadline?" Gibbons had asked.

Riley asked, "May I put you on hold for a moment?"

"Sure."

Moments later, Riley picked the phone back up and said, "It looks like we gave him until Tuesday, June 3rd to come up with the rest of the money."

Austin inquired, "What happens to the money he has already invested since he is no longer on the team?"

Riley explained, "All investors sign several disclaimers that protect all parties. The money Davis has already invested will be turned into investment shares once the project is finished, but that won't amount to much, since, in the scope of the whole project, his contributions were minimal."

The agents also were exploring Emilie Randolph's new business venture. They knew company start-ups were expensive, and Chicago real estate was not cheap, but was Emilie Randolph selfish and driven enough to take her sister out of the financial equation, so she would have more financial resources to grow her business? Preliminary investigations indicated that Emilease Gowns and Apparel was on the up-and-up, but they kept her on their radar.

22

William's cold silence sent the clear message to Emilie that he resented her presence in their house. Although his aunt tried to approach him several times to ask him what was wrong, he found ways to avoid or ignore her. He couldn't fathom where his mom had gone, but he couldn't get the thoughts of his dad and Aunt Emilie out of his mind. He caressed his fingers across the embossed phone number of Sgt. Pickett's business card. She had told him he could call if he needed anything.

He kept hearing the argument he and Willow had overheard the day their mom disappeared; the words repeated themselves through his head. When he listened to his dad's words during the fight, he didn't think much about it, because his dad said mean things to his mom, Willow, and him all of the time. Now, however, the words haunted him, "I am f- ing sick of this life, and I am sick of you! If only…" He felt like he needed to tell someone. He stuffed the business card in his front pocket and waited for Abe's mom to pick him and Willow up to play at their house for the afternoon.

While the rest of the kids were out in the backyard running through the sprinkler. William snuck into the house where Kristina was preparing snacks. Hesitantly, he asked, "Do you think I might be able to use your cell phone? It might be long distance. Does it cost on your cell phone to call long distance?"

Kristina quizzically asked who he needed to call. In a polite voice, he said, "I would prefer not to share that information with you, ma'am, but I promise it is for a good cause."

She smiled at William's maturity level and handed him her cell phone.

William dialed Sgt. Pickett's number and scrambled into the empty living room before Kristina could hear him address the person on the other end of the line.

"Orlando Police Department, how can I direct your call?"

William whispered, "Can I please talk to Sgt. Pickett."

The dispatcher said, "Hold one moment, please."

Within seconds, William heard the familiar voice.

"Good afternoon, this is Sgt. Pickett."

Williams emotions vacillated between comfort in hearing her voice and worry over whether or not he was making a mistake by calling her.

"I want to tell you a couple things that might not matter, but if they do and I don't share them with you, and something terrible happens to my mom, I don't know what I will do. I will feel like it is all my fault."

Pickett listened as William repeated the words he and Willow had heard his father spew just hours before their mom disappeared.

Hesitantly, he recounted the details of Emilie's first night at their house in Springfield, including the interaction in the driveway and their trip to the bedroom with a bottle of wine. "I just don't think it is appropriate that my father and Aunt Emilie were sharing a bottle of wine when my mom is who-knows-where."

"William, it is courageous of you to call me with this information. You did the right thing. You are an amazing young man, and your mom would be proud of you. How is Willow doing?"

"This is really hard on her, but she is closer to Aunt Emilie than I am, so that seems to help her a little."

"William, I know you are angry at your aunt, and I am not saying you shouldn't be, but I think it is good that she is there to help take care of you and your sister."

William retorted, "Willow needs Aunt Emilie, but I am just fine on my own. I am old enough to take care of myself, and I am doing a pretty good job of taking care of Willow. Aunt Emilie doesn't know the first thing about taking care of kids anyway, so she isn't as much help as she thinks she is. The only good thing about her is that she takes us to Papa's house, so we can still see him."

Pickett reassured William, "You are taking good care of your sister, and she really needs you to be there for her right now. How about you keep doing what you are doing and give us a chance to figure out what's going on with your dad and aunt. Is that fair?"

"That's fair," William agreed.

William returned to the kitchen and handed Kristina her cell phone back.

"Thank you, Kristina. You don't know how much I appreciate it."

"Anytime, William," she responded.

He headed toward the French doors to join the kids outside, avoiding eye contact with Kristina.

His hand was on the handle when he heard, "Hey, William…"

He reluctantly turned around.

"Yes, ma'am?"

"You know you can talk to me about anything. I won't share the information with anyone."

He choked back tears.

"Thanks, Kristina. I'm good, but I appreciate you helping out with Willow and me."

Pickett contacted Agent Scott with William's information, and Scott filled her in on the updates of the investigation in Springfield. Neither of the two verbalized the unspoken realization that most missing persons' cases that weren't solved within the first forty-eight hours didn't usually turn out well.

Pickett said, "Agent Scott, my heart is breaking for those kids. If you would have seen them the night of the disappearance. Well, it is a night I will never forget. They were both trying to be so strong, but they broke my heart. Please let me know if you get any breaks in this case."

Scott agreed to keep in contact with Sgt. Pickett as the case proceeded. He closed the conversation with, "In fact, when we bring this woman home, maybe we can fly you up to Springfield for the family reunion."

"I would like that," Pickett admitted.

The gold envelope was addressed to Agent Drew Scott, Federal Bureau of Investigations, Springfield Division, 800 S. Cunningham Ave, Springfield, Il. 62703. The return address stopped Agent Scott in his tracks: "Ella Masters, Somewhere, Il. 32847." He studied the words, Somewhere, Il. "Was she in Illinois?" he questioned. The zip code didn't make sense because all Illinois zip codes started with a six. He looked at his database to determine which state zip codes started with a three; it included Florida, the state where Ella had disappeared. He filled in the rest of the numbers, but a legitimate location did not come up. Scott put on rubber gloves, opened the envelope, and carefully removed the piece. A sticky not on the top of the paper read:

Agent Scott,

We just love to play games, and we know the Masters family plays plenty of games. That being said, we are going to help you along with your investigation by giving you a few clues, via favorite childhood games. Everything you need to find your missing Momma is contained in this letter. You big tough FBI agents think you are so smart. Let's see if any of you are smart enough to win this game. Here are a few clues.

Dear 'Game' Players,

You have been invited to play a game with us. We are 'SORRY' to make you 'GO FISH' and jump through 'HOOPS' for the truth as we play 'KEEP AWAY' with Ella in this 'GAME OF LIFE.' We promise this is no traditional game of 'COPS AND ROBBERS' or 'DUCK, DUCK, GOOSE,' but we will let you know if you are 'HOT AND COLD.' You might choose to roll the 'DICE' because you think we are playing 'BLIND MAN'S BLUFF.' So, 'STINKY PIGS,' it is your turn to try to 'GUESS WHO' is behind this 'OPERATION,' with only a few 'CLUES.'

You see, it seems as though the 'RICH DAD' would prefer no CASHFLOW FOR KIDS,' because he has had way 'TOO MANY MONKEYS.' He would have preferred a life of 'PERFECTION' in which he was numero 'UNO' and had a financial 'MONOPOLY.' Daddy, however, is short on cash and long on lies.

Now, Mr. FBI agents, don't 'COUNT YOUR CHICKENS' before they hatch in this 'TWISTERED' game. We are just trying to give you a 'HEADS UP SEVEN UP.' We wish we could let 'SLEEPING LIONS' sleep, but because Davis has been a cheater in the game of 'LIFE,' we can't merely turn our heads.

Now, If y'all don't cooperate, you might find that 'GRANDMOTHER'S FOOTSTEPS' will lead to another 'GHOST IN THE GRAVEYARD,' but if everyone plays the game correctly, THE TRUTH SHALL SET HER FREE! Now, you may have to do some research to remember all of the childhood games y'all played, but if you carefully analyze this letter, you should find all of the 'CLUES' to see how 'LOW' Davis has 'LIMBO'D.' If y'all do just like 'SIMON SAYS,' Ella's life might not 'TOPPLE' over, but there will be real 'TROUBLE' if you try to 'LEAP FROG' over the truth. Your 'MEMORY' will serve many of you well, but others will be 'BOGGLED' as to how we know so much.

Sincerely,
'OLD MAID'

Agent Scott had no clue what the letter meant, but he had a feeling it provided more questions than answers. He took a picture of it with his cell phone and carefully placed it back in the envelope, bagged it, and sent it to the lab. Reading the letter had been the easy part; now he and his team needed to figure out what the hell it meant. They decided they would hold off on sharing any part of the letter with Davis.

Unbeknownst to the FBI agents, Davis received a modified version of the same letter the very same day, only his was addressed, "Dear Mr. Masters" and had specific instructions NOT to tell the police about the letter. It left out any reference to the FBI but retained all of the details Davis knew pointed to him.

As Davis read the letter, panic bubbled through his blood. The words, "DICE," "GRANDMOTHER'S FOOTSTEPS" and "GHOST IN THE GRAVEYARD" shouted at him.

Davis' phone buzzed and "blocked number" appeared on his screen.

"Olly, Olly, Oxen Free. You took my music away from me."

Click, and the caller was gone.

Davis worst fears were confirmed, and he knew what he had to do.

23

It was late at night when Davis lured the children down to their playhouse closet by telling them their mother had left them special presents way back in the rear part of the closet. William silently questioned his father's actions, but the hopeful look on Willow's face caused him to acquiesce to his father's words. When they both made their way to the back of the closet, Davis closed the door, placed a chair under the doorknob, put a pile of clothes just outside the closet, and lit the clothes with a match. He blew the match out and dropped it into his pocket, casually walked upstairs through the kitchen and out the back door, got in his car, and drove away. William watched smoke seep under the door as he tried to kick through it with his bare feet. Willow covered her mouth and nose with her teddy bear, but it was to no avail. The smoke overtook the children, and they passed out. The flames made their way through the wooden door and burned both children beyond recognition.

Ella woke from her nightmare with a start. Sweat drenched her t-shirt. The dream was so real she could not convince herself otherwise. Her face contorted with the horror of the dream.

June took a sip of her coffee. The corners of her mouth turned upward in a wry smile as she watched Ella through the monitor. "Did you have a bad dream, sweetie?" June taunted. As if this monster had a direct connection to Ella's mind, she added with false bravado, "My heavens, I hope nothing bad happened to your children or your daddy in your dream! Maybe I can come to help you take your mind off your nightmare."

Cold chills covered Ella's already sweaty body at the sound of June's footsteps descending the stairs, followed by the glean of a pair of scissors that made their way through the door slot and clinked to the concrete floor. Her fingers instinctively made their way through her hair. She had not doubted that June would make good on her promise.

"Let's see, sweetheart, what kind of haircut should we get today? I think we want to go short for the warm summer months, don't you think?"

After a pause, June said, "What? Cat got your tongue? I guess since you don't seem to have an opinion on the matter, I have to make all the decisions. Let's start by taking off two inches all around and see how we like that."

Ella reluctantly complied as she watched two-inch bunches of her dirty brunette curls fall to the floor. She placed the scissors on the floor, hoping her action would end the torture.

June laughed, "Oh, Ella, we aren't quite finished. Let's go a half-inch now or better yet a quarter inch, and I don't mean I want you to take off another quarter inch. I mean leave a quarter of an inch of hair all around. I hear it is going to be a scorching summer."

Ella reluctantly picked the scissors back up, closed her eyes, and continued cutting her hair off at the base of her head. The cold metal of the scissors grazed her scalp as the rest of her curls fell to the floor.

"That is so much better, Ella; now, everyone will be able to tell you and Emilie apart again." June's gloved hand pushed a small paper sack through the door. "Scoop up your locks of love and place them in the bag. I am certain your family will be glad to receive a little memento from you. Oh, I need those scissors back, too. I don't want you getting too depressed and harming yourself."

Tears fell onto the pile of hair in front of her, but she followed June's directions. She scooped the pile of hair up and placed it in the bag. She looked at her dirty fingernail beds. She deposited the scissors through the slot first and then the bag of hair. June grabbed her fingers through rubber-gloved hands and squeezed and twisted them so hard that Ella yelped like a small puppy that had been kicked across the room.

June released her hand and reminded Ella, "Just remember who is in charge here, little Momma."

Ella withdrew her stinging left hand back through the slot and watched two of her fingers turn a dark shade of purple and begin to swell. This monster had just broken two of her fingers. She heard June walk into a nearby room, turn the washing machine on, and begin singing at the top of her lungs as if this last bit of torture was a regular part of her daily chores.

Ella's left hand lay throbbing in her lap as her right hand made its way over her nearly bald head. She assured herself, "It's just hair; it will grow back," but the thought of her family receiving a pile of her hair sickened her, and she was overcome by grief.

She closed her eyes and tried to meditate away her fears and the physical pain that was now radiating through her entire hand, but thoughts of her children and her father found their way through the crevices of her psyche. *Who is taking care of my babies? Is Emilie around? Are the police watching Davis?*

Ella snapped herself out of the downward spiral of negative thoughts, knowing this would only cause more anguish. She forced herself to focus on problem-solving instead of wallowing in her physical and emotional hell.

She took several deep breaths and began processing everything she knew about her location. Based on June's words and the pictures she had seen, Ella speculated she was being held captive in her own hometown, Springfield, but she wondered what part of town. She listened to the pounding of tires on pavement, and to police, ambulance, and fire truck sirens on a regular basis, so she conjectured she was on a relatively busy street, not far from a hospital and police station. The incessant train horns at all times of day rattled her nerves. She knew she had to be near several major crossroads because the horns blared for several minutes many times each day. She figured out daytime versus night-time, based on the level of traffic she heard as the hustle and bustle of the community moved right along, just outside her prison walls, oblivious to the prisoner in their own backyard.

Ella was relieved June had not broken the fingers of her writing hand. Her growing list of things for which she was thankful became more warped as the hours and days went by. She was like an abused child who was grateful when the abuser only blacked one of her eyes rather than both. She took out her journal, turned to the back, and added to her list the details she could guess about her location.

- Urban
- Noisy street
- Hospital, fire station, and police station nearby (sirens at all times)
- Barking dogs
- Occasional gunshots

Then, as if it was the most natural thing to do, she turned the paper to a fresh page and wrote:

My Dearest C,

There are three of them, and they are toying with me. My every breath, my every move in my oppressive, claustro-phobic prison is being watched through a video monitor, as if I am a zoo animal on display. I don't know why they have taken me. I don't know what they plan on doing to me. Do you remember so many years ago when you told me I was one tough girl? Well, I am not feeling tough now. I feel helpless. I have let my children down; I don't know who is taking care of them or if I will ever see them again. From what I can judge, this is about Davis; he has made them very mad, and I am their revenge. They are using me to get back at him. The guys are the muscle, but it seems like the girl is running the show. I think she is the one who wants the revenge. They have not told me about their plans for me, but it is not good. If I never see my children again, I don't know how they will survive. You probably have your own beautiful family. I know I am crazy for continuing to write to you, but I have to reach for any positive I can find; if that means writing to a man I haven't seen in nearly thirty years, I guess you can call me crazy. I am crazy!" she scribbled, *"They are making me crazy..."*

Ella scribbled so hard that the pen tore through the paper. She ripped the paper out of the journal, threw down the journal, wadded the paper up, and threw it as hard as she could at the eye of the video; it bounced off the camera and hit her in the face.

Ella laughed a psycho kind of laugh. She knew she was losing it; her captors, especially June, were accomplishing what they had set out to do- make her go certifiably crazy. She resignedly said, "I can't control what they do to me, but I can control my own mind." With that, she decided to take a different strategy. She turned to business mode. She picked her journal up with a new focused fervor and began a new page of notes.

"Alright," she reasoned, "William is mature enough to help with Willow. If they don't make it to all of their activities, it is OK, as long as they are fed and kept safe. He will make sure he keeps Willow safe."

"Let's see," she continued as if she were leading an organizational planning meeting. "Beau was boarded at The Holidog Inn. Certainly, William would have told his father he needed to pick up Beau, but, worst case scenario, Beau is safe and being fed at the boarding facility. Homefront In-Home Healthcare will certainly continue to take care of Daddy and make sure he gets additional meals if Emilie does not come to help out," she tried to reassure herself.

Pangs of hurt thumped at her heart as she thought of her daddy. He had been her solid rock all of her life, so when she heard the doctor say the nasty phrase, early stages of dementia, while her father visited with the nurses out at their station, her heart broke. Of course, Emilie was unable to make the appointment because she was off in Paris buying new clothes, so Ella had to absorb the news all alone.

She knew her father was in his last year of independent living at the beautiful lake house, where he and her momma had raised their twin daughters. Signs of dementia had crept up behind him, and they started to steal bits and pieces of his memory, forcing him to reluctantly retire from his successful career in the medical field.

The sudden onset had shocked and confused Ella; it was as if he was fine one day, and the next day his memory and actions became jumbled. The doctors explained to Ella that there were still too few studies about the disease to categorize the various stages.

He continued managing reasonably well on his own, with only limited help. Ella had hired Homefront In-Home Healthcare to check in with him daily, and she and the kids took him dinner each night. Ella loved hearing his daily chant as the children burst through his back door, "I think I hear my two favorite little people in the whole wide world!"

Ella was brought back to reality by the return of footsteps followed by June's words. Her breathing became shallow, and her heart palpitations doubled in speed. She gripped her journal as if it were her only connection to the outside world; it had become her prized possession.

June chanted, "I'm baaaaaaack" in a tormenting tone. "You are going to write your hubby a note-- not just any note, but a very specific note to go along with your beautiful locks of hair."

Ella realized June had taken over the operation. The guys were still around, but they only brought food or other items occasionally. She wondered if this was where the woman asked for ransom money. *Would Davis give it to her*, she wondered.

June slid a piece of pink stationery through the slot and dictated the words that Ella wrote on the pink paper. Ella hesitated when she was instructed to sign the letter, "Your Loving Wife." Davis would know the awkward words were not his wife's. She would never have signed a letter like that. Nevertheless, she folded the letter and slid it through the door slot.

June sang her way up the stairs, "Olly Olly Oxen Free. I think you should know that Allie makes three."

Who is Allie? Ella was left to wonder. *Is she Davis' lover? Has he had two affairs before her, and now her affair makes three? Was June bitter because he left her for this Allie woman?* She added the words to her growing list of notes right before the lights clicked off and her world again turned to darkness.

24

Davis took in a deep breath and exhaled loudly as he watched Emilie's car pulled out of the driveway. He was relieved to have some much-needed time alone to collect himself. He quickly went for the mail, a chore he still wasn't used to since Ella had picked up the mail every day since they were married. With darting, paranoid movements, he looked around to ensure he wasn't being watched before retreating inside with the stack of mail. He stood at the kitchen counter and flipped through the pieces of mostly junk mail; two envelopes jumped out at him. The first was handwritten to Davis in what appeared to be red lipstick. His heart sped up as he hesitantly opened the envelope. Guilty fear ran through his veins at the thought of the multiple affairs in which he had engaged, momentarily paralyzing his shaking hands. His legs felt like concrete. He gathered his nerve and opened the folded pink stationery and read:

Dear Davis,

I am alive, but not for long. These people are telling me we have three weeks to solve several riddles about your life, or they will kill me. I want to see my babies again. PLEASE help me get back to them. Don't share any of this with the police, but PLEASE play their game!

Your loving wife,
Ella

As Davis read and re-read the note, he scrutinized every word. It was Ella's handwriting; at least it looked like Ella's handwriting.

"Could she still be alive or is someone really messing with me?" He shook his rattled brain back to the other mail he held in his trembling hands. He grabbed the counter to steady himself.

He regained his strength and took the stack of mail up to his bedroom. He looked at his typed name and the lack of a return address on the envelope of the second piece of suspicious mail; it had a Chicago postmark.

Davis reluctantly opened the letter, and read, "Remember to be completely honest about your game of 'OPERATION' when you complete your journal. This will be one of the first bits of information Ella receives. After all, she needs to know that you like games."

Davis' heart collided with his chest cavity as it pounded out of control. He knew exactly what the note meant. When he saw the word operation, he knew the reference.

He recalled the fateful morning, March 1, 2001, like it was yesterday. He had awakened with a pounding headache from late night drinking with his buddies when Ella's shrieking voice screamed, "We are pregnant!" Through his hangover fog, Davis' thought, *We aren't shit! I'm shooting blanks!*

Ella had bound into the room and jumped onto the bed. "Can you believe it? This is unreal! Everyone told us we should just relax, and it would happen-- and it did! Davis' mind raced to the business trips he had taken over the past several months that left his beautiful wife home alone. *Was she having an affair? Who was the mother fucker? He would kill him.*

Pressing her thumb to each of her fingers, Ella exalted, "We celebrated the New Year by creating a child!" This comment jolted Davis into reality. New Year's Eve, 2000 had been a drunken blur for him! He recalled reluctantly taking Ella to his New Year's Eve office party, even though it put a kink in his style with the ladies. His wife had little in common with the other women at the events, and she always wanted to leave early. He preferred keeping her close enough to his professional life to make her feel like she was part of that world, but far enough away that she didn't find out what really went on, including the women, sex, shady business deals, gambling, and money stashing activities that occurred on a daily basis. He also recalled the uncharacteristically wild sex they had when they returned home.

He was jolted out of his memory by a sickening revelation. Natalia had been hounding him lately about leaving his family and starting a new family with her. He had told her about his vasectomy in hopes that it would dissuade her, but she said, "We can get that silly thing reversed. I'm still young and VERY fertile!"

"Is Natalia behind this?" he uttered aloud.

On several occasions, as he and Natalia lay enveloped in each other's arms in her silk sheets, Davis had promised the much-younger woman that he would leave Ella. He knew, however, that he had no intentions of ever marrying Natalia or for God's sake reversing any vasectomy.

Is Natalia ruthless enough to take things into her own hands? he contemplated. He knew the woman had a dark side; it's what attracted him to her, but was she darker than he knew? It was time he made a surprise visit to her apartment.

Davis had purchased six throw-away phones during Radio Shack's 'Going Out of Business Sale' back in February. He had activated one when he returned from Florida, so he could stay in contact with Natalia, but they had talked only briefly twice because he was afraid the police would somehow find out. Now, he had no choice. He had to know if she was involved in his wife's disappearance.

He was relieved that Emilie had taken the kids to see their papa, against William's objection, who proclaimed, "Aunt Emilie is NOT our mom, and she needs to stop acting like she is!" He couldn't figure the boy out. William had seemed fine when

Emilie first arrived, but he developed a chip on his shoulder the following day that hadn't gone away.

Davis slipped into the driver's seat of his Mercedes Benz and started the car. He could still see Natalia's message as they exchanged intimate texts in the alley outside Gastone's Pizzeria the night his wife disappeared, and her words took on a new context, "You have NO idea how I am going to rock your world and turn it upside down!!??!"

Davis knew he was taking a chance because he assumed the cops were watching him, but he couldn't get a sense about his suspicions about Natalia only from the texts they had exchanged; he needed to see her in person.

As he reached the end of his driveway, the afternoon sun shone through his windshield, bringing his attention to a bright orange piece of paper, folded just one time, on the dashboard. He reluctantly opened the paper and read,

> Hickory Dickory Dock,
> You've done bad things with your _____.
> Write down the names of ALL your dames.
> Don't leave any off or she'll burn up in flames!

Below the rhyme, were ten lines. Below the lines, were specific instructions: "When you finish the list, put it in an empty can, put the can in a grocery sack, drive the sack to the bridge at Lincoln Park, and set it next to the garbage can; then drive away. You have until midnight tonight to make the delivery. We will know exactly when you drop it off, and we will wait until we see you drive away. No funny games, now, Dearie! We are watching you carefully, so don't do anything crazy or Ella will die."

"Dearie" rang through his ears. Natalia mockingly called him "Dearie" every time she chided him for leaving her to go back home to play what she called 'The Happy Little Family' game. This validated his thoughts that somehow, she was part of the game, but he knew she wasn't smart enough to be the mastermind behind something this big. Had she finally gotten sick of waiting for him and partnered up with one of his guys to make his life a living hell. Davis had no question that whoever was doing this to him meant business. He pulled the car back up the driveway, went into the house. He wanted to make the delivery during broad daylight, so he didn't become the next victim.

He sat on his bed, a neat bourbon in his hand, and followed the instructions. A watermelon-sized pit welled up in his stomach. He had not been faithful to his wife, but to write the names down of all the women with whom he had affairs was disconcerting-- mainly because he was afraid he might not remember all of them.

He started with the most recent women and worked his way backward. Natalia, Remington, Beth... Damn, this was hard! Torn between disgust in himself and fear that he would leave someone off the list, he continued wracking his brain and added Sensenya, Brandy, Stephanie, Collette, Tiffany, and Amy. That was it; he was sure. That was a list of all of the women with whom he had affairs while he was dating or married to Ella, but there was one empty line remaining. It didn't make sense; as painful as it was to write the names down, it wasn't like he was deliberately leaving someone off. "At this point, how could one more name hurt him?" he justified. The empty line haunted him as he put the orange piece of paper in a Pringles can that he had retrieved from the garbage. His shaking hands placed the can in a blue grocery sack, and he put the bag in the trunk of his car.

He drove to Lincoln Park. As instructed, he put the bag next to the garbage can by the bridge. He looked around. He saw nothing or nobody; yet, his bones chilled. He knew he was being watched. He drove away, carefully looking in his rearview mirror until he was out of the park.

Twenty minutes later, his iPhone rang, and "blocked" lit up the screen. The gruff male voice scolded, "Strike TWO, Davis, STRIKE TWO!" You did NOT list ALL of the women you have been with! One more strike and your pretty wife DIES!"

Davis' dry, desperate voice replied, "That's all of them, I swear!"

The voice on the other end sniggered, "Sometimes we choose to erase memories of our past. I should give you three strikes right now just for being so fucking stupid. Maybe we should get this over quickly and put your whole family out of its misery?"

Davis' groveling pleas sounded pathetic as he begged the stranger on the other end to have mercy on his family.

The caller scoffed, "Mercy? You want mercy? When will you learn, asshole, that you have to give to receive? I don't believe you know the definition of mercy."

"CLICK!" The conversation was over.

Davis drove back home, ignoring the several texts he received from Natalia. He didn't have the energy for her right now. He knew he needed all the emotional strength he could find because he had less than twenty-four hours to finish the journal entries. His eyes remained fixed on his rearview mirror. He wondered who was lurking in plain sight. He knew that they had him by the balls because they knew he couldn't take any of the information to the police.

Musty smells filled his nostrils when he opened the back door. He took in the piles of dirty dishes on the counter and in the sink. He opened the refrigerator to get a Coke for his bourbon, and the stench of a smorgasbord of spoiled food cleared his nostrils. He grabbed a can of Coke and slammed the door shut. He mixed his drink and called Ninja Cleaning Services.

"Ninja Cleaning Services, where we clean, so you don't have to. This is Lacy. How can I help you?"

Davis hemmed and hawed for several seconds. "Uh, yes, Lacy, this is Davis Masters..." A long pause settled into the phone.

"Yes, Mr. Masters," Lacy awkwardly replied, "how can I help you, sir?"

Lacy had never gotten a great vibe from the man on the other end of the phone, and she wasn't sure how she should proceed.

"Lacy, I am sure you have heard the news..."

Another awkward silence.

"Is there any way one of your crews can squeeze my house in this week? Things are getting a little out of control with..." his voice trailed off.

"Sir, our regular crews are all booked up for the next three weeks, but I can check with our back-up crew and see if they are available. Does that work?"

"Yes, if you can do that, I would appreciate it."

He was already dragging the garbage can to the refrigerator and dumping expired food into it before he ended the call.

Within twenty minutes, Lacy called back and informed Davis that a three-person crew she used occasionally was available to come to clean his house on Thursday.

Davis explained that he would not be around, but that he would hide a key in the planter next to the front door by 8:00 a.m., and he would leave a check on the kitchen counter.

Hesitantly, Lacy asked, "Sir, will anyone be home? And what about your dog? Will he be kenneled or loose?"

"No, nobody will be here," he replied through tight lips. As if further explanation was necessary, he added, "The children will be with Ella's sister at their papa's house, and I have not yet gotten the dog from the boarding kennel."

Lacy regretted asking the question and quickly tried to regroup. "Great, Mr. Masters, our team will be there on Thursday at 9:00 a.m."

Davis made another pan around the room and absently said, "It might take them the whole day."

He hung up the phone and made a mental note to have Emilie keep the kids at their papa's house on Thursday. He also needed to find out where Ella boarded Beau. He was afraid to know how much that bill would be. He was feeling the financial impact of no longer having access to his father-in-law's money. They used the same bank, so in the past, it had been easy to maneuver money around electronically, but one of Emilie's first stops, when she returned to Springfield, was a visit to the bank to eliminate all electronic access to her father's accounts. Davis only realized this when he attempted to make an online transfer of $1,000.00 from Mr. Randolph's account to his family's account three days earlier. Instead of the "Transfer Complete" message he usually received, the following message popped up on the screen: "This account has been electronically frozen. All transactions must be made in person."

He cursed his sister-in-law's actions again as he recalled the moment. He rifled through the kitchen drawer looking for Beau's boarding information. He found a glossy business card with an image of two perfectly groomed dogs. "Holidog Inn," he scoffed. What a stupid fucking name. He called the Chatham kennel to make arrangements to pick Beau up from the kennel.

The nasal voice on the other end of the phone suggested, "Sir, we can keep the dog for an extended period for a small additional fee if that is better for your family."

"We don't need you to keep our dog. We are perfectly capable of keeping our own animal."

"I'm sorry, sir. No problem. You can pick him up at your convenience." she said, apologetically.

Davis disconnected the call without so much as a good-bye.

"What a jerk," the young assistant mumbled under her breath.

Davis fired a text off to Emilie, "Can you pick Beau up from Holidog Inn in Chatham and take him to your father's house for a few days?" He figured if she picked the dog up, she would also pay the bill. It was the perfect solution.

Emilie cursed under her breath and immediately apologized to Willow for her inappropriate language.

She fired a text back, "Well, I am taking care of your kids; I might as well take care of the dog, too."

She hoped Willow did not see her words. She didn't want her niece to think she was a burden to her aunt. She turned right at the Chatham exit and headed to Holidog Inn.

Willow cautiously said, "Where are we going, Aunt Emilie?"

She tapped her niece on the nose and said, "We are going to get Beau and bring him to Papa's house. How about that?"

A look of relief and comfort washed over Willow's face. "That's a really good idea, Aunt Emilie. Thank you. Does this mean we can stay at Papa's again tonight?"

"It sure does! Do you think we should pick William up from practice and let him stay, too?" Emilie teased.

"Yes, most definitely. He will be happy to see Beau."

Instinctively, the little girl reached over and held her aunt's hand.

Emilie choked back tears.

The car pulled into Holidog Inn. "Let's go get that dog of yours."

Emilie paid the bill, while the veterinarian tech went to get Beau. There was an uncomfortable silence while Emilie and Willow waited. Emilie knew the techs had heard the news, but nobody mentioned Ella.

Willow led Beau to the back seat, climbed in next to him, and buried her face into his fur. She was glad to be taking him to her papa's house.

25

Emilie dropped the kids off at their house the following morning, so she could take her father to his doctor appointments. At precisely 3:00 p.m., Davis put the Chegg box, full of each family member's journals, on the front porch. Bile made its way up his esophagus, and he tasted vomit as it crept into his mouth. He swallowed hard. He had been instructed to take the family to an early dinner at Cracker Barrel. William and Willow welcomed the early meal because they had not eaten lunch. Emilie had agreed to meet them at the restaurant. Davis and the kids left the house, and he watched his rearview mirror as they pulled out of their cul de sac. The ride to Cracker Barrel was quiet. Davis took in all of the cars in the massive parking lot. There were plates from a variety of states, given the summer travel season. He squinted to notice anyone who looked out of place or for someone sitting idly in a car. He couldn't help but question every person who rocked in the chairs on the front porch of the family-style restaurant.

The instructions in the Chegg box had been clear, and like clockwork, thirteen minutes after the family's departure, Jax got the text from Donny, "I'm enjoying a caramel frappe' at McDonald's and... 'the eagle has landed.'"

The kids played checkers while they waited for their food to arrive. Davis and Emilie sat in awkward silence; he felt like he was sitting across from his wife, as he glared at her identical twin. He had never liked Emilie; now, he despised her. Davis couldn't help but recall that his last interaction with his wife was in a similar situation. "I wish this place served alcohol," he said, to no one in particular.

Seeing their mounds of dumplings arrive, the children returned to the table. The kids clasped each other's hands, bowed their heads, and William said a barely audible prayer. An older couple sitting at the next table smiled at the children and scowled in disgust at Davis and Emilie. Emilie lowered her head in embarrassment, and Davis glared back as if to intimidate the couple that had to be well into their seventies.

Davis picked at his ribeye steak. His gut was like a rock. He nervously looked around the crowded room and wondered who was watching his family. It was early, and the average age in the restaurant was sixty. He had never realized how many people, even old people, sat with their faces in their cell phones when they were out to eat. He had been guilty of doing so, but now, he was too busy scrutinizing every patron and worker, wondering which of them had his wife. He questioned how many times someone had taken advantage of his lack of awareness, to stalk and photograph him.

They finished their meal in silence. The waitress asked, "Is this on one check?"

Davis' hesitation pissed Emilie off because she knew his game.

"Yes, one bill is fine," she said with a smile to the waitress followed by a jeer at Davis, who did not meet her eyes.

Davis excused himself to use the restroom, and Emilie and the kids discussed their evening plans while they waited for her father's to-go meal. When Davis did not return to the table, Emilie and the kids decided he must be waiting for them in the restaurant store. The kids milled around the store while Emilie waited in line to pay the bill.

When Davis still did not emerge from the bathroom after ten minutes, a familiarly eerie feeling washed over the three of them. Emilie called his phone. Davis answered on the third ring.

"What is taking you so long in the bathroom?" Emilie hissed in a whispering voice.

"Bathroom? What are you talking about? I am out of the bathroom."

Emilie scanned the country store. "Then, where are you? I don't see you anywhere."

"I left. I am nearly home. I thought you knew that."

Fury rose through Emilie's slight frame, "No, Asshole, we have been standing here waiting for you, and as you can imagine, the kids...Oh, never mind, ASSHOLE! You wouldn't get it." And, she hung up the phone.

William and Willow looked at their aunt with a knowing look. For once, William agreed with his aunt; his father WAS an asshole. The three walked out of the restaurant, got in the car, and drove to their Papa's house. Emilie seethed in silence the whole way to the lake.

Jax had driven his white courier van into the sleepy cul de sac twenty minutes after the Masters family left their house. He was dressed in a black hoody, black jeans, and black tennis shoes. His van was legitimate, but, if someone questioned him, he was prepared to explain that some unknown guy in Chicago had paid him cash to pick up and deliver the box. He had chosen a fictitious name with a legitimate address in the most violent Chicago neighborhood because he was pretty sure the police wouldn't risk their lives to go there. He hopped out of the van, grabbed the box, and left Davis' house-- all within four minutes.

Jax and Donny returned home at the same time to find June aimlessly staring at the computer monitor. Her hardened face broke into a smile as she grabbed the Chegg box from Jax. "Now, Ella's fun REALLY begins!" she said with a bitter smile. "Tomorrow, Ella's world will be irreversibly turned upside down, and she will finally understand what it is like to not be able to trust family."

She took the sealed box to her makeshift command center, and carefully opened it like a Christmas present she had been anticipating for a year. She only had a few minutes before she had to leave for work, so she went straight to Davis' journal. She flipped through the pages and scanned the paragraphs that would ultimately bring him to his demise, but not before they crushed his wife to the core.

The men each grabbed a beer and headed to the living room. June playfully punched Donny in the arm and gave Jax a kiss goodbye, "Thanks, guys, for doing fine work today. As she hustled out the door to catch her night shift, Donny teased, "I get no respect around here! Can't I even get a peck on the cheek?"

June teased back, "You are lucky I even gave you a love punch," and the door swung closed behind her.

The two men drank beer, watched the Cubs beat the Cardinals, and played cards to pass the evening away. At ten o'clock, they flipped on News Channel 20, while they waited for June to return from work. The story of the missing Springfield woman was losing steam amidst stories about the recession, Barack Obama's battle with health care reform, same-sex marriage debates, the San Antonio Spurs win over the Miami Heat, and new information on the mission Malaysian airliner that had disappeared without a trace in March. At the end of the news clip, just before the sports news, however, was a short segment on the missing Springfield woman.

Jax went to the room where June had her equipment set up, turned on the speaker to Ella's prison, and said, "I thought you might like an update on your missing person status."

Ella listened to the words of local reporters who provided little information on the missing woman, Ella Masters. She heard the anchorman report, "Authorities still have few leads, but new information indicates the woman may no longer be in Florida. Authorities in Florida and Illinois are working diligently on the case to bring the wife and mother of two safely home."

June returned home at 11:00 p.m., sipped a beer as she watched the monitor for a while, and she and Jax hit the sack by 11:30. Donny was too wired to sleep; he couldn't get Ella's body off his mind. He grabbed the movie he had picked up from the Redbox on his way home from McDonald's and quietly slipped downstairs to Ella's closet.

Her heart pounded loudly with each step; she knew it was one of the two men. She heard Donny's voice. "I bought a Redbox movie you might like to watch." "He slid the movie through the opening.

Ella immediately recognized the title; it was the same as the one she had chosen for her children the day of her disappearance. She questioned herself. Had she brought this whole thing on? She should have told Davis about her strange interaction. She tried hard to recall the details of the incident. Was the guy who was behind her in line part of their group, or did he know about them and was trying to protect her? Donny must have been watching her at the Redbox. That was the only explanation she could fathom.

The man's creepy voice jolted Ella out of her memory. He began, "Ella, I was so close to you as you carefully selected your movies on the last day you saw your little angels. You were all high and mighty in your rented Mercedes Benz, but look at you now-- you are just like the rest of the world-- a pile of shit!" Ella listened to the increased heavy breathing on the other side of the locked door; she recalled the odd Redbox incident.

"Yes, Ella, I have been watching your every move for a VERY long time! In fact, you got me and my buddy in big trouble a little while back. I didn't really appreciate it; that one might just cost you!"

His seductive tone frightened her, and Ella knew she had correctly recognized him earlier in the week.

Donny spoke into the small slot in the door, "We will talk more about this, bitch-- just not today! I will be back when we can have a little more private time without June and Jax watching us on that silly camera. We wouldn't want them to be privy to our thralls of passion, now, would we?"

A mixture of relief and panic coursed through Ella's veins as she heard Donny retreat back upstairs.

Across town, Davis, unaware that his wife was no more than fifteen miles away, cussed the local news team for watering down an event that had turned his world upside down. He clicked off the television, shut the lights off and staggered upstairs. The house felt empty. He poured his third bourbon and Coke and retired to his room. He passed out with the empty tumbler still in his hand.

26

Eleven days into Ella's disappearance, Agent Scott held up the newest piece of mail to Agent Gibbons. The return address, written in multi-colored crayon, was the same as the other pieces he had received. Scott read the poem.

We've been playing Olly Olly oxen free,
But Y'all can't seem to catch me.
We have three more weeks
Of our fun and games,
And then you might see what's in a name.
But if anyone gets 3 strikes in a row,
Poor, sweet Ella will have to go.
Davis has already received two strikes,
But he hasn't been forthright.
His reasons are many for not showing you.
Many secrets he is holding tight.
We'll see those who stand and face the truth,
And those who are just too weak.
As we continue our games of riddles and such
And continue our hide-and-go-seek!

Within an hour of receiving the letter, the agents received the final report on the bloody mass found in the toilet at the crime scene, accompanied by an apology and over-explanation of why it took four days longer than it should have, citing employees taking summer vacations and cuts in staff due to the horrible economy. Agent Scott mumbled obscenities about the incompetence of other law enforcement agencies and then read the report, which indicated the bloody mass was an unborn fetus, with a gestational growth of four months. It didn't make sense. He called Gibbons into his office.

"Here's the deal; the mass was tested for both Davis' and Ella's DNA, right?"

Gibbons nodded.

"Well, it has Davis' DNA, but not Ella's. The fetus is not Ella's!"

Gibbons sat, stunned for several minutes, processing the latest revelation. Finally, he pondered; "Ok, so Davis knocks some other chick up, and she wants to get back at him, so she abducts his wife, and leaves an unborn fetus, which would clearly have her DNA all over it. This makes absolutely NO sense. Why would she implicate herself?"

Scott took over, "Well, it looks like we need a list of the women with whom Davis has had affairs. We may have our work cut out for us to get through that list, but at least now, we have a possible motive."

Gibbons added, "But we can't assume Davis isn't behind it. Maybe he found out his lover was pregnant, killed her, and paid someone to off his wife and make it look like the other woman did it."

"True," Scott conceded. "Maybe we need to look at recent missing person reports in Illinois or Florida that might trigger a red flag?"

"How about we pay our friend, Davis, a visit first to see if we can narrow that search."

Gibbons made the call while Scott drove. They wanted to catch Davis unprepared for a visit.

"Good morning, Mr. Masters, this is Agent Brad Gibbons."

A pause and then a hesitant, "Hello, Agent Gibbons."

"Mr. Masters, we are in the area and thought we might be able to stop by and discuss the investigation; would that be OK, sir?"

"Do I need my attorney present? If so, then today won't work. He is out of town until tomorrow."

The agents raised their eyebrows in unison and gave each other an all-too-familiar look that said, "Why does an innocent man ask if he needs his attorney present?"

"We don't think that will be necessary. We received the DNA results, and we have a few questions regarding those results. As always, if you don't feel comfortable with the interview, you can ask us to leave until your attorney can be present."

Davis exhaled the nervous breath he didn't realize he had been holding more loudly than he intended.

"Mr. Masters, are you OK?"

"Yes, yes, sir. Fine, it is fine for you to stop by," Davis replied as he stopped pouring the bourbon into the glass tumbler.

"Great, sir, we will be there in a few minutes. Are the children or Emilie there?"

"No, they are at their papa's house for the weekend."

Part of him felt guilty. He didn't want them to think he was a lousy father, but he was glad the kids were gone.

He quickly added, "They begged to spend the weekend at the lake. I think they have plans to invite friends over to go out on the boat and swim. They love that place so much."

His rambling over-explanation was greeted with an uneasy silence, so he stopped talking.

"We will be there shortly," was all Agent Gibbons said.

Davis looked around the house. He was grateful Ninja Cleaners had been able to come the previous day. He put the bourbon bottle and bourbon-filled glass back in the liquor cabinet, wishing he had time for one quick slug, but not wanting to have liquor on his breath when the FBI agents arrived. He started up the stairs to brush his teeth and run a comb through his hair when the doorbell rang.

"Damn!" Davis muttered, "Fuck!" He saw the two figures through the frosted window panes of the front door. "They could have given me a few more minutes to get myself together."

He ran his fingers through his hair, slapped his cheeks a couple of times, and hustled to the front door.

"Good afternoon, gentlemen, please come in." He was aware Gibbons and Scott were taking in his unkempt appearance, and it made him feel uncomfortable. He prided himself in his looks, and, under normal circumstances, he wouldn't so much as even retrieve the newspaper off the front porch without being put-- together.

They stepped into the foyer. Agent Gibbons updated him on the generalities of the investigation and then cut to the point, "Davis, our real reason for stopping by is that we have had a break in the case, that, quite frankly, leaves us with more questions than answers. We are hoping you will be able to help us fill in some gaps."

Agent Gibbons' words froze Davis, and his mind whirred, *Was the DNA explanation for the visit a ruse to get them into my house without my attorney? Did Ella's captors give them the items in the Chegg Box? Do they have everything they need to carry me off in handcuffs?*

Gibbons hesitated long enough for Agent Scott to take over.

Scott spoke calmly. "Do you mind if we have a seat?"

Davis noticed the agents looking around the house as he led them to the living room.

"It looks like you've done a little cleaning up since the last time we were here."

"I called our cleaning service," he replied, a bit apologetically. "They sent a crew out yesterday."

"They did a nice job. What cleaning service do you use?" Scott asked, casually.

"It is a small company called Ninja Cleaning Services."

"I will have to keep them in mind. Being a bachelor, I could probably benefit from giving them a call." Scott was really thinking that he might want to give them a call to see if they saw anything suspicious when they were cleaning. He didn't want to write the name down immediately, but he tucked Ninja Cleaning Services in the back of his head.

"So, gentlemen, what brings you here?" Davis attempted to quell his right shaking hand with an equally shaking left hand. He wished he would have had just one swig of the bourbon.

Scott began, "The report came back today on the bloody mass that was found in the toilet." He paused for effect and watched sweat drip down the side of Davis' face.

"It seems as though the DNA sample of the mass matches your DNA."

Davis' whole body shuddered as his memory took him back to the days Ella announced her pregnancies with both of the kids. "How in the fuck can that be?" he muttered through clenched teeth and a shaking head. His response surprised even him.

"Mr. Masters, we need you to calm down, sir," Agent Gibbons stated.

"Calm down?" Davis questioned in a still too loud voice. "You are telling me that my wife miscarried our child in a toilet and then just disappeared. Well, I am telling you that there is NO FUCKING WAY she could have been pregnant with my child! And you expect me to remain calm?"

"No, Mr. Masters, we are not telling you that your wife miscarried your child."

"Then what in the fuck are you telling me?" he yelled.

"What we are telling you, Mr. Masters, is that the unborn fetus in the toilet DID HAVE your DNA, but it did not have Ella's. The only thing this evidence can mean is that it was your child, but not your wife's."

Without warning, Davis punched a giant hole in the wall and fired off, "There is no fucking way that can be the case."

"Mr. Masters, DNA tests do not lie. That fetus in the toilet was your unborn child," an impatient Gibbons responded bluntly.

Davis knew this couldn't be true. "Were these agents planting information to make him look guilty?" he wondered. He decided it was time to come clean with the procedures to catch them in their own trap.

Scornfully, he said, "Well then, given the fact that I have had not one, but TWO, do you hear me TWO vasectomies, I think your fucking DNA test might just be WRONG this time." He knew his words stunned the agents.

A visibly confused Gibbons unconsciously wriggled in his seat as if he could still feel the effects of his own vasectomy and said, "Why in the hell would any man have TWO vasectomies?"

Davis reluctantly explained," Well, you see, my father hadn't been a great role model, so I didn't want anything to do with being a father. I knew I didn't want kids, but it wasn't something Ella and I discussed much before we got married. We weren't married long before that was all Ella talked about; it consumed her life.

He paused, and for the first time felt shame over his actions so many years ago. "I decided to get a vasectomy. I figured my wife would be none the wiser and think it was just the way it was. The problem was that when I was looking for a doctor to perform the procedure, it was next to impossible to find someone who wasn't somehow connected to Ella's father. I finally found a doctor who agreed to perform the procedure in complete confidentiality. I had the vasectomy while Ella was on vacation with her parents and sister. You can imagine my surprise when my wife informed me two months later that she was pregnant. I was so pissed off that I went back to the doctor. He explained that there might have been sperm lingering in my reproductive system, which could have caused the pregnancy. Because I had the procedure without Ella's knowledge, there was no legal action I could take against the doctor who completed the procedure. I was fucked! But I have to tell you, part of me wondered about the possibility of William not being my kid."

Davis threw the statement out like tossing a fat worm into a lake, hoping the agents would bite on his comment.

They didn't take the bait. Scott and Gibbons sat quietly, waiting for Davis to continue.

He awkwardly continued, "The doctor assured me that it was a fluke accident and that no further action needed to be taken, but when William was a little over a year old, Ella informed me that she was pregnant again. I knew she was either having an affair or the doctor had fucked up."

As Davis continued to retell the situation, his voice began to rise with anger. "So, I went back to the doctor, and he ran a sperm-count test. Sure as hell, I wasn't shooting blanks. And, can you believe, all the son-of-a-bitch said was that he would repeat the procedure at no cost. Do you believe the fucking arrogant nerve of that man?" I told him, 'Do you know how much two kids cost? How can you say that any of this is at no cost?"

Davis recalled how the doctor had remained so calm. "He knew he had me by the nuts…literally…because he knew I had no legal recourse." He concluded, "I mean, what could I do? I couldn't go to another doctor or admit it to my wife, so he performed the operation again and provided a sperm sample six months later to convince me that it was safe to have all the sex I wanted without further worry. But I still had one kid and another on the way."

Scott said, "You mean you were stuck with one kid and another on the way?"

Davis' face turned red in anger, but before he could respond, Gibbons quickly interceded, "What is the doctor's name, Davis? We will need to contact him to corroborate your story."

Davis said, "Dr. Joseph Smith."

The color drained from Davis' face. Exhausted from the admission, Davis walked his wobbly legs over to the couch and plopped down.

Scott said, "Mr. Masters, we are still going to need a list of any women with whom you have had sexual intercourse during the past year. I mean, just in case the second vasectomy didn't really take."

Gibbons added, "Mr. Masters, we know this is difficult, but somehow your DNA was found in the mass of blood in that toilet."

Agent Scott knew his next remarks would ensure they would not obtain that list of women they came to get, but he couldn't resist giving Masters a swift emotional kick to the gut while he was down. "Mr. Masters, we also contacted your insurance company. It seems as though you took out a large life insurance policy on your wife just six months ago."

Scarlet started in his neck and made its way up to his forehead. "I took the same fucking insurance policy out on myself!" he screamed.

"Yes, we are aware of that, Mr. Masters, but with all due respect, sir, you aren't the one who has disappeared without a trace," Scott retorted.

Gibbons knew they were treading on thin ice with Davis not having his attorney present, so he spoke quickly, "Help us to understand why you would need a two-million-dollar policy on your wife. I know many people take out policies up to a million dollars, but very few people we know take out TWO MILLION dollar policies." He intentionally stretched out a repeated, "T-W-O M-I-L-L-I-O-N." He whistled and said, "That's a lot of money."

Davis searched for a logical answer, but he came up with nothing that sounded believable. Thinking quickly, he said, "I knew if something ever happened to Ella our children would never see her part of her father's inheritance because Emilie would find a loophole that left her with all of his money. I wanted to ensure that if something happened to either one of us, they would be able to continue living the lifestyle they are used to."

Gibbons and Scott gave each other the look they had perfected over the years-- the one that said, "This cat is full of shit!"

Davis read their reactions. Before either could say anything, he said, "I think you gentlemen need to leave now. If you need to talk to me anymore, it will be with my attorney, Erik Dubin, present." He did not see them to the door.

Instead, he grabbed the glass tumbler out of the liquor cabinet and chugged it down in one gulp. The fire made its way down his throat, providing a momentary calm to his shaking body. He poured another and went up to his bedroom. He reached in between his mattresses and pulled out the letter he had not shared with the police or FBI agents. He read the message with a new lens and tried to make sense of the note.

Davis,

Olly Olly oxen free,
Two plus one-- that equals three
Except in your case, it equals two
Because there's one you didn't pursue.

A true businessman follows through on all of his dealings. There is one individual in particular that you really 'screwed' over, and then you failed to see the dividends the deal yielded. I would say it was your loss, but I'm sure you would see it as much more of a liability than an asset...and just so you know, DNA NEVER LIES!"

Sincerely,
Summer Lovin'

Davis had racked his brain when he first got the letter, but all he had focused on was business deals he had and hadn't pursued. He had realized he was screwed if this game was about business deals, and he was supposed to put some crazy puzzle together regarding all of his business endeavors. He was like every other good investor; sometimes he screwed people over to close a deal.

Now, however, in light of the news Agents Scott and Gibbons brought today, he began to look at the note in a different light. *What if*, he thought, *someone is framing me by making it look like I have gotten someone pregnant? But how would they have gotten my DNA into the toilet?*

Davis picked up his phone to call his attorney when it began buzzing in his hand. The number was blocked, and the call was short. The muffled female voice sang, "Olly, Olly, Oxen Free, this month is the root of the game, you'll see!"

He threw the phone across the room. He didn't have the energy or the brain power to tackle another fucking riddle! The rest of the day and evening became a blur as he drank himself to sleep.

27

Fully rested from a great night's sleep, June grabbed a cup of coffee, went to her makeshift command center, where she had audio equipment, a television video monitor, printer, and the assortment of newspaper articles she had collected on the missing Illinois woman. She sipped her coffee and read the contents of the journal entries Davis, Emilie, and the children had so dutifully written. June was pleased with the raw honesty of them; she knew that if all else failed, she could mail them to the police, and Davis' words would land him in prison. She could dump Ella on a dark road in the middle of the night and go on with her life like the events of the past couple of weeks had never happened. June liked having options, but she wanted more from Davis. She wanted to see him hurt for what he had done to her.

June watched Ella as she slept fitfully in her stark prison. She thought back to the many sleepless nights she had endured during her childhood. Most nights she lay cold and hungry, in the corner of the small living room on a second-hand mattress with metal springs popping through the stained material, wondering if she would have food the next day, and wondering if her mom would bring another man home in the middle of the night. From the time June was old enough to recall her impoverished life, she remembered taking care of her mother, just like she imagined her mother had done for her mother. She loathed the cycle. She knew Ella and her children were innocent victims of her pissed-off rage at Davis for his part in perpetuating the cycle, but somebody had to pay for his sins of omission. As if on cue, pain seared through June's pelvis, and she instinctively grabbed her stomach. Tears filled her eyes and dripped into her half-empty coffee cup. She swatted them away, cleared the lump that had settled in her throat, and sang through the speaker, "Wake up, sleepyhead; it is time to get our day going. We have a lot of catching up to do."

Ella's eyes opened suddenly in a startle as if she had forgotten where she was.

June's slippers padded down the stairs, and she made her way to the wooden closet as memories of her own childhood continued to parade their way through her head. She slipped a granola bar and a fruit punch juice box through the slot and said, "Let's get a little something in your stomach. You are going to need some nutritious food in you because we have a lot of work to do today."

Ella opened the generic granola bar and juice box. They were far from nutritious, but she was starved, and she knew there was always a possibility it might be her only meal of the day.

She had made the mistake of not eating her breakfast only one time since her arrival because she was sick to her stomach. Thirty minutes after Donny delivered her untouched food, he slung a long list of curse words at her, including "ungrateful bitch," and demanded she put the food back through the slot. Her captors did not provide another meal the rest of the day. After that, she ate her meager rations immediately when they arrived. Her frail body needed every calorie it could get.

Ten minutes passed before June slipped the scrapbook pages through the slot. "Ella, we all have childhoods that form the big people we are. How about if we play show-and-tell with some of those childhood memories. Now, no peeking ahead; focus only on the top page. I will tell you when you can move to the next page."

The first of the new scrapbook pages was titled, "Ella's PERFECT Childhood." The pictures included snapshots of her and Emilie as toddlers in matching pink Easter dresses and bonnets and several images of smiling parents doting on their twin daughters. This story told a stunningly different tale than Davis' beginnings that Ella had learned about in the earlier scrapbook.

Once again, Ella was instructed to read the story aloud, as if she were reading to her children. "This is because," June explained, "your children will receive a copy of this audiotape."

Ella imagined the children hearing her voice, and she wondered if it would bring them pain or comfort. Once again, her momentary mind-drifting was cut off by the angry, impatient voice, "I'm getting VERY, VERY tired of having to scold you, Mrs. Masters! GET READING....NOW!!!!" Ella quickly began reading her own story.

"Ella's daddy, Charles Randolph, was a physician by profession but he was a philanthropist by heart. He grew up in the heart of Georgia, the son of a prominent Georgia cotton grower. He left Georgia and the racial disparity he could never quite understand, to attend The University of Illinois for undergraduate school. After four successful years at the University of Illinois, Charles Randolph applied for, and was accepted to, the prestigious Northwestern University Medical School. When he graduated with his medical degree in cardiovascular medicine on May 4th, 1958, his first plan of action was not to buy a fast, new car or big fancy home, but to marry his high school sweetheart, Adeline Kay Merriweather. She had remained in Georgia for nursing school and had been working the previous few years in a pediatric unit in their hometown. They celebrated the union of their marriage in an intimate ceremony on the veranda at Adeline's childhood home in Georgia on Saturday, May 18, 1959, as cotton fields danced in celebration in the background. The two left the following morning for a two-week honeymoon in Italy. They were able to thoroughly enjoy their honeymoon because Dr. Charles Roger Randolph had accepted an offer at St. John's Hospital in Springfield, Illinois, which would start exactly one week after they returned from Italy. They had not accumulated many belongings, so the move to their new bungalow in the Washington Park area of Springfield was not difficult. Adeline's parents had given them the trip to Italy for their wedding gift, and Charles' parents provided the money for the down payment on their first home. Both sets of parents were sad to see their children move so far away, but they were happy for the life they knew their charmed children had ahead of them. Once they settled in their quaint two-bedroom bungalow just a few houses away from Washington Park, Adeldine took a job in the pediatrics unit at the same hospital. They worked hard and quickly made friends at the hospital and in their new neighborhood. They spent all of their free time embracing the activities and events in Springfield, traveling, and discovering their new life together. Regarding a family plan, Charles and his wife were late bloomers in the area of parenting, and their family and new-found friends often reminded them of this. They had agreed that they wanted to get a solid footing and spend some time traveling before they brought a child into the world. It took them a couple of years to conceive, and the news that there was not one, but two babies, was both delightful and overwhelming."

"Daddy's little sweethearts were supposed to come on March 21st, but they were delivered by an emergency Cesarean section on February 14, 1966. Emilie was the first to be gently removed from the protection of her mother's womb, and Ella was scooped up next. Charles Randolph couldn't believe he had two beautiful, though fragile, identical baby girls. The man was the epitome of a proud daddy, and he would forever celebrate Valentine's Day with a new zeal. Of course, being from a strong southern Georgia family, his baby girls were named in honor of their maternal and paternal grandmothers. The day they were born was the happiest day of his life."

Ella stopped reading. She was overwhelmed by the words she was reading-- words only her family knew. Words her mother had carefully scribed in her detailed diaries. This woman had taken her mother's detailed words and created this story.

"Keep reading!" June barked.

Ella acquiesced. "As the new father watched his resting wife the first few hours after the difficult birth of his daughters, the worrisome thoughts of how he could tell the babies apart much less take care of their physical and emotional needs raced through his mind. He helplessly fretted over getting the two mixed up and raising them with the wrong names. A sweet nurse, named Sherrie, alleviated his fears when she patiently helped him change his first diaper. She showed him the pink bottom of Emilie, his first-born. At the crease between her tiny pink bottom and her right leg was a little birthmark. He couldn't believe his eyes. The brown pigment looked like a small heart. Sherrie agreed with his assessment. He felt instant relief! *OK* he thought, *Emilie has a birthmark on her right bottom. I will be able to tell the two apart!* Sherrie smiled a mischievous smile as she took off the wet diaper of his second baby, Ella. A worried look came over the face of an exhausted, very inexperienced new father. 'Do not tell me Ella has the same birthmark!' As sure as the sun rose, Ella had the EXACT birthmark, but it was on her left bottom. It was the exact same heart shape!"

"Tears streamed down the proud young daddy's face, as he said, 'My baby girls spent all this time in their momma's belly with their bottoms to each other, and they were born on Valentine's day, with matching heart birthmarks. It is as if they imprinted each other with a permanent sign of love, and NOTHING will ever separate them. My girls will be forever bound by love!'"

"Adeline resigned from her job in the pediatric unit to give all of her time and attention to her new baby girls. Within two years of the twins' arrival, the Randolph's quickly outgrew their two-bedroom bungalow. Randolph was doing extremely well at St. John's Hospital in cardiovascular medicine because of his forward-thinking progress with minimally invasive open-heart surgery. They purchased a beautiful home on Lake Springfield, complete with lawn and pool care. Adeline still insisted on cleaning her own house, in spite of the constant suggestions by her husband to hire out the housekeeping."

"Once Adeline survived the first two years of two separate sleeping and feeding schedules and the bumps and bruises of the toddler years, she spent the majority of her time arranging her daughters' activity schedules, including swim lessons, piano, music, dance, and flute lessons."

June stopped Ella, "Doesn't this just make you want to throw up! I mean, really, who has this kind of fairy-tale life? But, I digress. Keep reading."

Ella continued, "Family and tradition drove the activities of the Randolph family much more than money. Yes, financial security had made Ella's life more comfortable, but she didn't need money. Her daddy had instilled a sense of reasoning in Ella that kept her grounded. Ella's sister, Emilie, did not absorb that same line of thinking. While the other girls in her high society socialite circle were spending money as quickly as their daddies could hand it to them, Ella was reading, researching, and exploring nature as much as she could. She didn't fit in with most of the girls at her school because, while they were busy making sure they made an enormous footprint on the earth, Ella was researching how to save beautiful landscapes from being turned into concrete parking lots, outlet malls and shopping centers. Yes, Ella was too good to be true...or so she thought!"

The story stopped there, and June's voice took over. "This is just the beginning, Daddy's little sweetheart. I have lots more stories for you, but for now, you need to close your scrapbook. There is no looking until I tell you to reopen it. It is so neat that your momma spent years writing in her diary, and it is sweet that she passed her love for writing on to you. Of course, we already know you like writing twice as much as your momma did, don't you?"

Ella realized she was dealing with a brilliant woman. As the sound of June's slippers became faint, Ella analyzed her final words. June's statement confirmed that she had both of Ella's journals, but this scrapbook page revealed that she also had her mother's diaries-- diaries that were tucked away in a fireproof box in the guest bedroom closet of her parent's lake house. She shivered at the realization that one or all of these people had also been in her parents' home, and they had stolen the intimate details of her life.

A couple hours later, June returned. She said, "You were a good girl not snooping ahead at your gifts; that was pretty hard, I imagine." She giggled a child-like giggle and admitted, "I have always been a snooper; I have never been able to resist peeking at things I was not supposed to. Go ahead, sweetheart, and check out the next page of your memories."

The newest addition to Ella's scrapbook was a collage of newspaper clippings, artifacts, and pictures of many of her accolades throughout high school. These weren't random artifacts; they were HER artifacts, stolen from her keepsake box that was carefully stored in the beautiful hand-crafted walnut cabinet her daddy had made and proudly placed in their family room in the basement of her childhood home.

"How did you get these items?" Ella responded angrily.

"I am pretty sure you are in NO position to raise your voice at me, little Miss Perfect! I mean, look at these accolades-- you were quite successful at such a young age, but then you had to go and marry Davis and have your brat kids, and now all you do is play...Mommy Dearest."

What did this strange woman mean that I play Mommy Dearest? I have never been unkind to my children, and I have only given them the utmost love. Ella was becoming more convinced that this was a Davis affair gone wrong, and June blamed Ella and the children for it.

June shoved a Ziploc baggie with a peanut butter sandwich through the slot and said, "Here's your lunch."

Ella heard the soft creaks of the stairs as she whistled up them, "I will be back tomorrow for another story; once again, NO PEEKING!"

Relief that she would not have to endure June's torture anymore today washed over her, but curiosity over what the other pages included needled her. She guessed they would reveal additional high school or college experiences. They were inches away, but she knew if she looked, June would punish her more. She was at June's beck and call; June made all the rules in this game.

Ella had just dozed into an unsettled sleep when she heard nearby church bells clang eleven times and June's footsteps make their way down the stairs.

"Sorry to wake you, Ella," June whispered from the other side of the door as if she was a college room-mate who arrived home in the middle of the night after one too many beers. "But I'm just so excited about the next page that I can't wait until tomorrow. Go ahead, take a look at it."

It took Ella a moment to focus her eyes. When she looked at the newest scrapbook page, she was correct. In the center was a picture of her posing in her high school graduation cap and gown, a picture of herself hugging her maternal grandparents, and a posed portrait of the girls with their parents. In the final photo, the twins stood, like bookends, in matching caps and gowns with their grand-daddy, who held two large envelopes.

Ella recalled her grand-daddy's words as he handed them each a large envelope. "I gave your momma and daddy a trip to Italy for their wedding gift, and that turned out very well; so, I thought I would continue the tradition by sending the whole family back in celebration of your high school graduation. Additionally, I believe it is your duty to carry on the family tradition by celebrating graduations and weddings with trips to Italy."

Ella's heart sank with this memory. She remembered breaking her daddy's heart when she declined the trip to Italy for her own wedding gift. He insisted that they had all promised to carry on the tradition. Ella told her father that Davis didn't want to go to Italy for their honeymoon, but she asked that her daddy never bring it up because it had been a source of argument with the young couple. The truth was that Ella hadn't told Davis about the tradition. Her heart had never recovered from her high school celebration trip, and she didn't want to blur her memories on her honeymoon. Her daddy reluctantly honored her wishes, and her family never brought it up.

Her thoughts turned to the trip and to Cristiano. While her sister was busy shopping at all of the upscale stores, looking for the perfect Italian leather shoes and purses, Ella spent her time walking the back roads and alleyways shooting pictures of the quaint Italian streets with the Canon 35 mm camera she got for graduation. It was on one of those trips that she met the young Italian she came to know as Cristiano.

She was sitting quietly at an outside table at a cafe in Rome, taking a break from her photography excursion. She had shot four rolls of film of landscape, people, and trans-portation. Usually, she tried to give herself a specific assignment, but not today. She wanted to shoot whatever suited her fancy, without thinking about composition, lighting, or color balance. A beautiful Italian girl and a young man about her age sat across the way. The girl wore a simple white dress that exposed her sun-kissed shoulders. The young man was dressed to the nines in a suit. They sipped wine and laughed; both of them had dark silky hair and beautiful smiles. "Is this what love looked like," she wondered. The girl affectionately slapped the young man on the arm as they conversed back and forth. Ella found herself telling their story of young Italian love through her lens. She put the camera up to her eye and shot three quick frames. The young man rose, kissed the girl on her cheek, and strolled into the restaurant. Ella quickly pointed her camera in a different direction and continued snapping so as not to reveal that she had invaded their privacy. She felt embarrassed and a little ashamed that she had somehow intruded on their intimate moment. A few minutes later, however, she couldn't stop herself from finishing up her roll of film as the young lady sat alone waiting for the love of her life to return.

As she removed the used roll of film and inserted a fresh roll into her camera, a male voice in her ear made her drop the canister. "Is there a reason you are stalking my sister?" Ella's cheeks burned with embarrassment. The handsome young man's disarming charm quickly alleviated her fears that he was serious. Without an invitation, he took the seat next to Ella, poured a glass of water into the extra glass on the table, and said, "Don't you know it is a sin to sit alone at a cafe in the most romantic city in the world?"

Ella was speechless as she rolled over the word, "sister," in her head. Her embarrassment rose to a new level as she fumbled over her words, trying to explain that she was creating a photography portfolio of the Italian culture. The young man sat quietly with an earnest look on his face as Ella rambled her way into a bigger hole. Finally, she handed him the film canister and said, "Here, you can have it. I'm sorry I took your photograph without getting permission." He could no longer hold his composure, and he broke out into laughter. "Good afternoon, young Juliet, I am Romeo." Instinctively, Ella slapped him on the arm. "That was NOT funny. You took pleasure in watching me turn into a bumbling idiot! I thought REAL Italian men are supposed to be kind and sensitive. You are a FAKE!" At this, the young man laughed harder, and the act became contagious. Ella joined in his laughter.

Moments later, his sister sauntered over to the table, threw her napkin at her brother, and teasingly said, "So you left me for a foreigner. I tell you, little lady, you just CAN'T trust an Italian man; they are flippant in love. I'm certain he introduced himself as Romeo, too. He is so NOT creative!"

"Now I am the one caught and embarrassed, thanks to my lovely sister, Caterina. I tell you, with her around, I will NEVER find a girl. She lurks in my shadows and tells all of my secrets to keep my heartstrings dragging on the ground behind me." At this, brother and sister laughed together, and Ella once again felt like an awkward onlooker of an intimate family moment. She knew Italian families were close, but at that moment she felt a pang of jealousy that she and her sister, even though they were twins, did not have a tight-knit relationship like the one she was intimately involved in watching right now. As the voices of bantering siblings continued, she heard the young man say, "Well, Caterina, we must be boring her. She left us and went into her own little world. We have GOT to work on our act. We must be getting rusty." They both laughed again at their own humor. "Hello, miss. I am young Cristiano, and this is my lovely twin sister, Caterina. Do you have a name you would like to share with us?"

"Wait, you two are twins? I am a twin! I have an identical twin sister! Of course, it all makes sense now. The connection I was feeling across the cafe was not a romantic connection; it was a twin connection. Oh, I'm sorry, my name is Ella."

Without missing a beat, Cristiano said, "You don't have much experience in the world of romance, do you?"

As the heat once again lighted up her cheeks, Ella responded with a shy, "Not so much."

Caterina hit her brother again and said, "You could probably use a little brushing up in that area too, Romeo!" Cristiano's responsive laugh sent the trio into another outburst.

Ella felt so comfortable talking to this guy, and the immediate connection she felt to Caterina was unexplainable. The three sat at the cafe for two more hours sharing their life stories and comparing their twin experiences.

The banging on the closet door jolted Ella back to reality.

June screamed, "If you don't start following my instructions a little better, I will bury your two brats alive." She was shaken out of her short reprieve from her hell-hole.

June told her to look at the next two scrapbook pages; the pages were filled with memories of her Italy trip: pictures, ticket memorabilia, and other keepsakes that had also been stored in the same walnut cabinet.

June chanted, "Davis is not your first love or your real love, now is he? You have forsaken your real love and left him bitter and alone. He tried to reach out to you several times, but you denied him further access to your heart. You are such a tease, Bitch! You flirted your way into his heart and played him like your fiddle, and then you walked away, taking his whole heart with you, laughing all the way to the airplane. I wonder what he is up to these days?"

Ella felt the passion the two had experienced. He had loved her, and she had loved him, in a summertime in Verona kind of way. But they were young, and both had college to attend and careers to build. She remembered the day he met her at the airport to say goodbye. He teased, in his broken English, "You and I will be together again. If you try to hide from me in the Americas, I will find you!"

June interrupted Ella's memory, "You know, Ella, eventually you will have to come clean with your husband about lover boy because I will share your La verità with him…if the police don't beat me to it. See they are on to your sweet Italian man, but once you find out the things he has done, well, I don't know how sweet you will think he is. Oh, also, I almost forgot to tell you, Cristiano is acutely aware of what is going on. You could almost say, he is at the center of it all, right between Davis and Emilie."

With that, she left Ella to think about Cristiano and wonder how he might be connected to her disappearance.

Gianni woke with a start. Sweat covered his trembling body as he shook himself awake from the recurrent nightmare, in which Ella fell into his outstretched arms. As he wrapped her in his arms, he felt her damp shirt. He pulled his hand away and held it up. Scarlet liquid dripped down his fingers. He looked into Ella's dead eyes.

Gianni couldn't remember the last time he had slept more than two hours without the vision. He didn't want to look at the clock because he knew it was still too early to get up. His hands clutched his pillow, and he felt the folded piece of paper. He rolled over, pulled the chain on his bedside lamp, put on his reading glasses and propped himself up in bed. He gently unfolded the piece of paper and glided his fingers over the handwritten entry, careful not to further rip the edges that had been haphazardly torn out of a journal. He read the piece he had already memorized. His chest tightened, and his heart palpitated uncontrollably. Seeing the words on paper did not get more comfortable with each reading. The thought of Davis doing the things Ella had written about in her journal sickened him. He wanted to kill the bastard, but he was in between a rock and a hard place. Davis still had no clue who Gianni really was, and he needed to keep it that way for now. He lay awake for the next several hours and ran every possible scenario through his head.

He had just dozed off when the nearby church bells rang six times and his phone burred; he recognized the area code and knew it was Emilie. She had used her daddy's cell phone to call Gianni to keep him updated on the investigation. They decided this was the safest way to communicate but had agreed they would limit their calls.

"Any new leads?" Gianni rasped in a desperate voice.

"Nothing to speak of, but, if these people are legitimate, Ella should have received the journals that Davis, the kids and I had to complete."

"Did you tell her everything?" he barely murmured.

"Yes, I told her everything."

Emilie knew that her definition and Gianni's definition of everything were two different things, but telling him about the abortion wouldn't help the situation now.

"So, do you think she knows I am in the states by now?"

His words spoke volumes, and Emilie felt his mix of hope, fear, and regret. It made her heart ache.

"I don't know, Gianni. I honestly don't know what to think anymore. All I know is that as of right now, they seem to be focusing on Davis and not on us. I know we haven't really done anything wrong, but our actions may have caused Ella's abduction. The fact that we are withholding information is a problem, and I have to tell you, it is keeping me up at night. Part of me wonders if we should both just go to the police and tell them everything."

Gianni interrupted, "Emilie, you know we can't do that. It will put a huge target on us that doesn't need to be there, and that might take their focus off of Davis. You and I both know he is behind this, so why send the FBI on a hunt for the wrong dog.

"I agree. I agree, but Gianni, you aren't the one who has to look into those children's eyes every night, trying to answer questions about where their mommy went. And you sure as hell don't have to interact with that fucking loser of a husband she has."

"Shhhh…. Calm down, Emilie, the kids will hear you."

"Gianni, I am about to fucking lose it! I don't know how much longer I can do this! I've got Daddy and the kids to take care of. I have the police asking questions that I can't seem to answer, and I am trying to protect you…not to mention trying to run a brand new business from four hours away!"

"It won't be for much longer, Emilie," he said, grasping at any morsel of hope he could.

"I have to go, Gianni. It is time for Daddy's meds. I will call you in a couple of days.

Doubt filled Emilie as she mulled over Gianni's final statement. *How do you know it won't be for much longer, Gianni? What do you know that I don't know?*

Willow's voice interrupted her thoughts. "Aunt Emilie, is everything OK? I thought I heard you yelling."

"Oh, sweetie, I'm OK. Come give me a morning hug."

She scooped Willow up and carried her to the couch, where they spent the next half hour wrapped in each other's arms. Emilie was surprised by how much she liked the feeling. It caught her off guard, and her eyes filled with tears.

William reluctantly joined them on the couch, making sure he stayed at the opposite end. He didn't like seeing Willow snuggling with Emilie. He was still bitter about what he saw her first night at their house, and he wasn't about to let her forget it. His aunt felt his cold reaction, and she was baffled at how much it bothered her.

William said, "Hey, Willow, how about you go get your comb, and I will fix that mop of hair, and then I will get us some breakfast."

He mussed her hair, and Willow went to get her comb. They could have heard a pin drop, while they waited for Willow to return.

Emilie was grateful when her daddy called her from the other room.

Loneliness suffocated Ella. Her bony chest labored under the weight of the information with which she had been blind-sided. Questions about her husband, her sister, and her past all crashed around in her head like waves breaking up the shore. For the past two weeks, she thought her prison walls were limited to the confined space she had been locked in like a dog. Now, she knew her real prison was her mind. She felt like a vehicle careening out of control as it headed down the highway the wrong way into oncoming traffic. She had all this new information, but she couldn't prove or disprove it. She knew how death row inmates locked in solitary confinement must feel, and she understood for the first time how a person could go crazy.

Her thoughts vacillated from rational to irrational. *Did Davis only marry me for my family's money? Did I isolate him after I had the children? Is this somehow all my fault? What if my children never see me again?* The struggle to stay strong in hopes that she would one day be reunited with her children was more than she could handle. She broke down, but she was too dehydrated to produce tears.

As if on cue in a major movie production setting, June's voice cut in, "Ella, let's connect the dots today. Have you had time to make the connection between your true love, your favorite Chicago hang-out, and, possibly, your visit with us?"

Ella knew the connection her captor was making, and she immediately recalled the first time she saw the Chicago grocery store on West Madison Street in October of 2010. In large letters, the store name read, "Cristiano's." It had been a blast from the past-- a past that was forever seared into her mind. She had immediately taken out her phone and surfed the internet looking for the name Cristiano. She was hoping something would come up that would enlighten her as to the origins of the store. The first hit to come up was the definition from the Urban Dictionary, which stated, "Cristianos are honest, loyal, faithful, full of life and always true to their significant other. They are creative and handsome, and they know how to set goals."

A second internet hit showed the opening of the store in March of the same year by a developer by the name of Gianni Russo. When she clicked on the link, she saw a picture of a handsome Italian man in the middle of a group of men and women. The photo was taken outside the store as the man used an oversized pair of scissors to cut a blue ribbon, signifying the opening of the store. She recalled thinking it odd that the man had the same last name as her Cristiano, but she explained it away by acknowledging that Russo in Italy was like Smith in the United States. She saw a likeness to her first love, but she scoffed at her silliness over trying to see a face she hadn't seen for twenty-six years in a small black-and-white newspaper picture. She rationalized that most Italian men had similar characteristics.

Her mind floated to Cristiano. She wondered if he would ever know how much she had loved him…would always love him?

"Ella, you clearly know the 'Cristiano' connection, but do you know the La Verità Caffe connection?"

Ella nodded. She, indeed, also knew that connection, and she knew June was, once again, baiting her fish. La Verità Caffe was her favorite place to go in Chicago, although it broke her heart every time. Ella had often compared her visits to the cafe to that of watching the same sad movie over and over, knowing it was going to end the same way and wreck her emotional psyche.

June watched Ella retreat into her thoughts. The memory of the first time Ella had walked into La Verità Caffe reawakened in her mind. It was a quaint coffee shop at the lower level entrance of Cristiano's, and on the wall in the cafe was the quote, "A True Taste of Italy, a flavorful journey with every cup." The prominent image next to the quote was a retro Vespa scooter that looked like the one she had spent many hours on the back of in Rome. As her eyes caught another picture of a cafe in Rome that covered a four-feet by four-feet section of adjacent wall, she realized she had sat photographing the locals in that very cafe. It was such a surreal experience that she was left speechless for several minutes.

The young lady behind the counter gently repeated, "Can I get you something or are you just looking?"

"I'm sorry," Ella shook off her confusion, "could I have a hot green tea?"

She sat at the cafe bar quietly sipping her green tea and taking in the fresh aroma of the cafe as she fondly reminisced about days gone by. When her eyes locked on the massive image that covered one of the walls in another section of the cafe, she gasped loudly.

"Is everything OK, ma'am? Did you burn your mouth on the tea?" the barista questioned.

"No, I'm fine," an embarrassed Ella replied.

The only visible part of the scooter in the oversized image was the bottom half, but Ella knew the two sets of legs that were displayed on that scooter. Holy cow, those were her boots and his faded Levi's!

Ella recalled the moment like it was yesterday. Emilie had snatched the camera out of her twin's hand and said, "Let me be little Miss Photographer for a minute." She quickly took five or six pictures in an exaggerated, 'I'm a photographer' manner, as Ella begged her through giggles to quit wasting her film. Cristiano had turned toward her and said, "I think this is a perfectly good use of film," and Ella wrapped her arms a little tighter around him on the scooter.

She stood with her cup of tea and walked around the coffee shop, gazing at all of the black and white portraits. Now that she looked at them through a different lens, she realized EVERY picture in the cafe was most likely her work; many even included recognizable, but not identifiable, parts of her as a subject. What was going on? She didn't know if she was going to scream with joy or burst out in tears; her heart beat so fast she was sure she was going to have a heart attack.

As she looked up at the ceiling, even the combination of ceiling tiles with an open concept of exposed concrete beams seemed to be in the shape of a heart over the coffee bar. Did she see too much? Was she imagining all of this? The goosebumps that covered her arms did not match the cozy temperature of the cafe.

How can this be? Who owns this place, and how did he or she get the images? she pondered. *Of all of the cafe's in Chicago, what made me walk into this one? Was it the name, Cristiano's, gleaming shiny in the sunlight, that drew me in?* she mused.

It clicked. Ella recalled the last time she saw the handsome Italian young man, standing in his white linen shirt and faded blue jeans smiling his gorgeous smile as they said goodbye after two weeks of summer romance. As Ella walked away from him, she reached into her camera bag, tossed Cristiano the roll of film they had shot that day, and said, "This will make it impossible for you to forget me!" He snatched the canister with his right hand, kissed it, and blew her the kiss. In his native Italian language, he responded, "Non morirò finché non sarai mio." Ella had no clue what Cristiano had said, but it didn't matter. It was beautiful Italian language spoken by a handsome Italian man. He could have said he was going to chop her head off and she wouldn't have cared. She would forever have incredible memories of her high school graduation present.

When Ella called the headquarters for the coffee shop to inquire about the acquisition of the photos, the media director told her the images were purchased as a bundle from a stock photo company. She spent hours looking at online stock photos in an attempt to find the images, but the sites were inundated with thousands of pictures, and none of her searches yielded her photos. It had nagged at her, but Ella shrugged it off as thinking her Cristiano probably tossed the film canister and someone found it, or maybe he took them to be developed and never picked them up. She knew she would look like a fool if she tried to convince others that she had taken the photographs, and she would have to explain too much if she further investigated the issue. So, she let it go, but she visited what she called "her café" nearly every time she went to Chicago.

For years, Ella had diminished the extent of her feelings by laughing the experience off as foolish, young love, but few weeks went by when she didn't wonder where Cristiano had ended up. She knew very little about him, other than he was from what he described as a "very influential" family in Italy. He attended a university in Rome, but his family was from Sicily. She knew enough about Sicily to understand that "influential" had a good chance of meaning mafia-related, but she had only two weeks with this Italian beauty, and she wasn't going to ruin it wondering about his family roots.

Ella was ripped from her memories by blaring Italian music. She was now forced to wonder about Cristiano's family and the possibility that her sweet Italian was doing this to her. She recalled June's recurrent use of the word "roots." Ella had assumed her captor was talking about Davis' roots, but maybe she was referring to Cristiano's roots.

June continued, "Isn't it quite a coincidence that your sweet Cristiano paid tribute to you after all these years? Could it be that he never got over you? Have you heard the phrase, 'If I can't have you, nobody will?'"

Ella covered her ears at June's words. The realization that this woman was confirming what Ella had spent years questioning twisted her stomach into knots. She didn't have the emotional or physical strength to process such a horrific thing.

"I don't believe you!" she screamed. "Cristiano would never hurt me."

"Well, sweetie, we will just have to see about that. You will find out that he has hurt you far worse than hubby ever has, and we know from your journals how bad that is."

June whistled up the stairs.

28

Emilie took the kids back home on Sunday night, against their pleadings to stay one more day at their papa's. She made sure they had dinner and showers at her daddy's house because she knew they would be on their own once they got home. She felt guilty for making them go back home, but she explained that their father wanted to spend time with them also. The children knew that was a lie.

When they pulled into their driveway, Willow begged, "Can you please stay with us, too, Aunt Emilie?"

It broke Emilie's heart. She cupped Willow's innocent face in both hands and said, "Sweetheart, I need to take care of Papa, and you need to spend some time with your father."

Deep down, Emilie realized two things. First, Davis did not have the emotional ability to step up to the parental plate. Second, she could not spend any more time in the house with the man she abhorred.

"How about you go get Papa and bring him to our house," Willow's negotiations bordered on desperation.

"Papa needs his own bed and his own surroundings, honey."

Willow knew her aunt was right, but she thought she would try anyway.

William shot his aunt a scornful look and said, "Willow, you and I will be just fine tonight. We will make a tent in my room and pretend we are having a campout."

Emilie added, "It is already 8:30, and I will be back first thing in the morning, OK?"

She looked into Willow's eyes as if she needed her permission to leave.

"Fine." William declared, bitterly, "Go take care of Papa. I can take care of Willow."

Emilie's eyes burned with the stinging of William's tone. She waited for them to disappear into the front door before she broke down in tears. On her drive back to her daddy's house, she thought about Ella, and she felt guilty not knowing more about her sister's daily life. She knew her twin spent most of her time with the kids, but she wondered if she had any friends with whom she confided. She knew William would not share anything with her, so she made a mental note to see if she could find out about Ella's friends from Willow.

She returned to her daddy's house to find him sleeping in his recliner. She gently roused him and waited for him to get ready for bed. She felt a tinge of guilt when she gave him his night-time meds, knowing she had quit giving him the Aricept prescription for his early onset dementia. She justified her decision by convincing herself that nobody else would have to know. She tucked her father into bed and kissed him on the cheek.

"Good Night, Daddy."

Her father asked, "Emilie, where is my Ella?"

His words stung worse than William's angry tone.

"Daddy, I told you, Ella had to go out of town for a while, so I am taking care of you."

"But Ella is the one who takes care of me. She is the one who knows exactly how to take care of me. Can you please call her and ask her to come back, so she can take care of me...and the kids? Those kids need her. They really shouldn't be left in Davis' care, and, well, you don't have much experience with kids, so you probably need to call Ella and just tell her she needs to get back home and do her job." His voice was filled with anxiety, and Emilie could feel his heart rate increase.

Through trembling lips, Emilie said, "OK, Daddy, I will call her tomorrow, but it is late tonight. The kids are all settled in bed, and we need to get some sleep."

She went to the bathroom, took out the prescription bottle and brought the small white pill back to his bed.

"Here, Daddy. I forgot to give you one of your medications."

She handed him an Ativan pill and glass of water.

He took the pill and softly said, "See, Ella would never forget one of my medications." After a pause, he added, "But I know you are doing your best, Sissy."

Emilie left the room before her father saw the effects of his words. She knew they were a result of his dementia, but it didn't make them hurt any less. She took the half-full bottle of wine out of the closet, grabbed a Dixie cup from the bathroom, and filled the cup. She emptied and refilled the cup until the bottle was empty. She fell asleep in her clothes, praying for her niece's and nephew's safety across town, her father's health, but mostly for her sister…wherever she was.

Emilie awoke early and fixed her daddy's breakfast. Their previous night's conversation did not come up.

"I am going to go help with the kids for a while. Do you need anything before I leave?"

"No, dear, I am fine. Are you going to bring my two favorite little people in the whole wide world to see me today?"

She replied, "Let me see what activities they have, OK?"

"No activity is more important than seeing Dear Old Papa," he teased.

Emilie felt like he was becoming more sharp and quick-witted as the days passed, but she still questioned her decision about his prescription medications.

She hoped Davis was long gone by the time she arrived at the house. She was relieved when she didn't find him home. As usual, he had awakened early and had already left the house. Emilie didn't know when he would return. She felt as though he was trying to catch her doing something in his home because he often appeared out of nowhere and startled her.

She glanced into William's room to see the television still on and two sets of feet peeking out of the blanket tent the children had carefully constructed the night before. She tiptoed away so as not to wake them. They needed all the sleep they could get, and she needed a few moments to herself.

Emilie made a pot of coffee and poured herself a cup. She sipped her coffee and looked around her sister's kitchen.

"Where did you go, Ella?" She whispered. "What secrets do you or Davis have, and who knows those secrets? Who do you confide in?"

She heard the pitter patter of Willow's bare feet on the wood floors as her niece made her way to the kitchen.

"Good morning, beautiful. I made you a pot of thick black coffee for breakfast." she teased.

Willow wrinkled her nose. "Yuck! I'm too little for coffee, Aunt Emilie."

"OHHHHH, sorry about that," she responded dramatically; maybe we better stick with juice, toast, and fruit. How about if we snuggle on the back porch while you have your breakfast."

"I guess."

Willow carried a piece of toast in one hand and her glass of juice in the other. She followed her aunt, who juggled the bowl of fruit and her coffee, to the back patio and joined her on the hanging wicker loveseat where she and her mommy spent many hours reading together and telling stories.

Emilie breathed in the fresh smell of Willow's curly locks. "You smell like a perfect lavender flower."

Willow knew it wasn't her mommy, but she needed to feel the security of a big person, so she relaxed her rigid muscles, nested into her aunt's arms, and ate her toast and fruit.

Emilie held her tightly. "I know this is hard for you and William; it is hard for all of us, but especially for you two. I am trying to do my best to take care of you guys, but you know I haven't had much experience with kids. If you need me to do something that I'm not doing right, just tell me, and I will do everything I can to do it right."

"OK," was Willow's only response.

"Can I ask you a question?" Emilie asked hesitantly.

"Yes," Willow replied just as cautiously.

Careful to speak in the present tense, Emilie questioned, "Does your mommy have friends she spends time with. I mean, I know she spends most of her time with you and William, but does she ever meet friends for dinner or girlfriend dates?"

"No, not really. I mean, she has Abe's mom, Kristina. They take us places together, and they visit while we are playing, but they don't do things without us. It's mostly just us and Mommy, though. I mean, besides spending lots of time with Papa. We spend lots of time at Papa's."

A guilty twang made its way through Emilie's body. Willow had no clue she had cut her aunt to the core with her innocent response. Emilie wished she had been there more for her parents, and for the first time, she felt incredibly selfish about the life she had chosen. She wondered if she would ever have the opportunity to tell her sister that or make things right with her family. Her success seemed so insignificant as she held her precious niece in her arms. They rocked together in total silence for several minutes. It felt good.

The harsh voice interrupted their tranquility. "What are you doing, Willow?" William barked.

Willow jumped, and the few remaining blueberries and grapes flew out of the bowl she was holding.

William immediately started scooping up the fruit and apologized to his sister, who now had crocodile tears pooling in her eyes. He realized by her startled reaction that he sounded like his father.

He sat in the small space that remained on the swing and drew her close to him. "Hey, little Missy. You are fine. No need to cry," he whispered. Willow began wailing inconsolably, "I want my mommy!"

William consoled his little sister, "Shhhh. I didn't mean to raise my voice. I am sorry." He glared at his aunt, who stared helplessly at the duo, tears streaming down her own cheeks.

Emilie wished she could get into William's head and find out what she had done to make him so angry with her. She mouthed, "Sorry," to William, who also began to tear up.

As Willow's sobs subsided, Emilie asked, "Can I make you some breakfast, William?"

"No, thank you, ma'am. I will make myself something in a little while," William responded curtly. "Willow, let's get that face of yours cleaned up and pick out a game to play."

The two left Emilie on the patio. She felt helpless and alone. It was her turn to have a meltdown. It took her several minutes to regain her composure before returning inside. She found Kristina's number in the kitchen drawer and punched it into her cell phone. She returned to the patio and whispered, "Hello, Kristina, this is Emilie, Ella's sister," as if she were doing something wrong.

The sound of Emilie's voice threw Kristina off. She sounded just like Ella.

"Hello, Emilie. How are the kids doing?"

"Well, actually, they aren't doing all that great. In fact, Willow just had another meltdown. Say, I was wondering if maybe you and I can grab a coffee or a cup of tea somewhere sometime soon. Willow told me you are Ella's only really close friend, so I thought maybe we could get together for a chat."

"Does Davis know you are calling me?"

"Definitely not, and I would like to keep it that way if that is OK with you."

"That would be best," Kristina responded. "How about if Mike takes the kids to the park after work today, and you and I can meet for tea, or maybe a glass of wine. Does that work for you?"

"That would be perfect, Kristina. I know my sister probably hasn't always had the most positive things to say about me, but I love her and the kids so much. I want to do everything I can to find her." Another guilt pang stabbed at her as she all but admitted she had not always been the best sister.

"Your sister loves you, too, Emilie. She was just in a tight spot trying to keep her marriage together and dealing with you always questioning Davis' actions. We can talk about it this afternoon, how about 4:30? Mike should be home by 4:00. He will swing by and get the kids, and we can meet at Wm. Van's. Do you know where that is?"

"Sure, that sounds good. That is the quaint coffee shop downtown, correct?"

"Yes, I will meet you there at 4:30."

Hesitantly, Emilie knocked on William's bedroom door.

"Come in," William said in an irritated voice.

Emilie hesitated long enough to hear Willow whisper, "Maybe you should be a little nicer to Aunt Emilie. I think she is trying her best."

"You are too little to know why I don't like her anymore. She can't be trusted, Willow. Do you understand? Don't tell her anything."

Tears again clouded Emilie's eyes. She thought back to when she first arrived. He had been fine that night, but the next morning he had started giving her the cold-shoulder treatment. It came to her like a wrecking ball. He must have still been awake when she and Davis carried wine glasses and a bottle of wine into the master bedroom. Sickness filled her. Of course, he was angry; with what he thought happened behind the closed doors of his mother's bedroom only days after she disappeared, he had every right to hate her. How could she ever make him think differently?

"I said COME IN," he snapped.

Emilie cracked the door and slowly opened it as if objects might be pummeled at her.

"Hey, you two, Abe's mom, Kristina called and asked if you might want to go to the park with Mike and the kids at 4:30 today."

"I didn't hear the house phone ring." William retorted, giving Willow a 'See what I'm talking about' look.

Emilie stammered over her words. "Well, I called her. I thought it might be good for you guys to get out of the house and be with your friends for a while."

"So you basically just lied to us AGAIN." He extended his last word to make his point and made eye contact with Willow again. "See, I told you. Now, do you see what I am talking about?"

Willow's cheeks flushed. She didn't know what was going on, but she didn't like it. It made her tummy feel icky.

"Hey, Willow, maybe you can go pick out a book for me to read with you, and I will come read it to you in a few minutes. I would like to talk to William if that is OK." She kept her eyes on Willow so to avoid eye contact with William. She wasn't going to give him the opportunity to decline her request.

Willow readily accepted the invitation to get away from the tense situation. Once she was out of his room, Emilie closed the door and said, "Can we talk about what is going on? I think I figured out why you are so upset with me, and I totally understand."

"Oh, I bet you do."

"William, what you think happened is nowhere near what happened, but I totally get why you think it did. I put myself in your shoes and realized I would have drawn the same conclusion. You have no reason to believe anything I say, but I promise you, it was not what it looked like."

"Ya, well, then why did you and my father disappear into MY MOM'S bedroom the VERY FIRST NIGHT YOU GOT HERE?" his voice began to rise.

Emilie whispered, "Please, can you hear me out? If you don't believe me after I am done talking, that is fine. You can continue being angry with me. I am going to share some things with you that I probably shouldn't share because you are too young to know them, but you are mature beyond your years, so I think you can handle what I am going to tell you."

She gave William the G-rated version of the reason she had not seen them for the past couple of years, including the fact that she didn't trust his father for reasons she didn't want to share with him. She finished with, "So, I knew I had to act nice in order to try to find out if he was behind your mom's disappearance. I am sorry to say this, but I do not like your father, and it is actually tough for me to even be around him. The first night I was here, I thought if he had a couple of drinks, he might slip up and tell me something that would help me find out what happened to your mom."

She looked directly into William's blue eyes, "I promise you on everything I love, what you think happened that night did NOT happen. I despise your father, and I will do everything I can to get your mom home safe and get the three of you away from him. I called Kristina because I know she and your mom talk some. I thought maybe your mom confided in her some things that might help me figure this all out. I promise that is why I called her. I am doing everything I can to find her!"

Tears streamed down William's face. He didn't want to believe her; he wanted to hate her. He wanted to have someone to whom he could direct his anger, and she had been an easy target. His real anger was for his father, but he couldn't show that because he knew his father wouldn't think twice about backhanding him if William treated him as he had treated his Aunt Emilie.

"I am sorry," William whispered, ashamedly. The two embraced. A gentle knocking on the door followed by Willow creaking open the door ended the embrace.

"Can I come back in? I was lonely."

"Of course," William responded. "Get over here and give us a hug." The three embraced tightly and cried openly.

Davis had not returned home by 4:00 p.m. when Mike picked up the kids. Emilie and William were both relieved that they didn't have to lie to Davis about where they were going. Willow was oblivious to it all.

Emilie parked on Seventh Street and fed the parking meter. She had never met Kristina, so she was a bit apprehensive as she ascended the stairs to the beautiful historic red brick home-turned-coffee-shop. William had shown Emilie a snapshot of Kristina, so when she saw the tall, slender woman with her hair pulled back into a simple ponytail, she guessed it was she.

Emilie was keenly aware that Kristina recognized her by the shocked look she gave her, followed by the drain of color in the woman's face. Emilie had forgotten not everyone was used to her looking just like Ella, and the first words out of her mouth were, "I am so sorry." She realized she had been doing a lot of that lately: apologizing for one thing or another.

Kristina gathered her wits and awkwardly hugged Emilie. "Sorry, you just caught me off guard. I had seen pictures of you, but you never...well...looked so much like Ella. I wasn't expecting that."

The words, "I'm so sorry," tumbled out of her mouth again before she could catch them.

"Please stop apologizing; it is OK. I am just glad to be able to meet you. I wish it were under different circumstance."

The two agreed they better begin with a cup of tea before dipping into wine. Emilie started by giving Kristina an update on the investigation and on Davis and the kids.

Kristina said, "My kids would be lost if something happened to me, but they have a great father who is super involved in their lives. I can't imagine what the kids would be doing right now if it weren't for you."

"Well, I don't know how much good I am. Ella got the mommy genes. It has been a rough week-and-a-half. William has had the toughest time. He and I started off bumpy, but we had a good conversation today that helped clear up a few things."

Kristina wrinkled her forehead and looked at Emilie quizzically, but Emilie just said, "Oh, it's nothing; we just had a little mix-up the first night I arrived. It's all good now." She didn't want to revisit the evening, nor did she want to give Kristina any reason to question her intention.

Emilie asked Kristina, "Can you tell me anything my sister might have said to you or shared with you that might shed light on what has happened to her?"

Kristina responded, "She didn't talk about Davis much, but her lack of discussion spoke volumes. I am always rambling on about what a great husband and father Mike is, and she doesn't say much; she simply does a lot of listening, so I have always taken her as a very private person. There was only one time I ever questioned her about something specific, and she got upset with me."

Emilie shot her a concerned look that begged her to continue. "See, no matter how hot it is in the summertime, sometimes she will wear a lightweight sweater or jacket. One day last summer, we were watching the kids play at Washington Park. It was just Ella and I because the other moms had a Junior League event; the two of us aren't Junior League-kind-of-gals if you know what I mean. Anyway, a bee flew into her zip-up jacket. She threw off the jacket to avoid getting stung. She wasn't afraid of bugs, snakes, or spiders, but she had a bee sting allergy, so it startled her. She successfully avoided a sting, but when I sat gaping at her bruised upper arms, she got flustered, immediately put her jacket back on, and quickly started talking about bees. Emilie, she looked like she had been used as a punching bag. She had knuckle marks and grip marks that were a mix of purple and deep red."

Emilie closed her eyes and shuddered.

"I calmly said, 'Ella, what in the hell happened to your arms?' I remember the sting of her response that told me to never ask that kind of personal question again. She said, 'Kristina, not all of us can have your perfect fucking life, so how about you worry about your own business and stay out of mine!' It was so out of her character that it stunned me. I had never even heard a curse word come out of her mouth before that day. I really like Ella, and the kids love to play together. I thought that would all be ruined if I pressed her for details or brought it up again; now I feel like I am partly to blame for what has happened to her. I should have forced the issue, but I didn't want to lose her friendship. Now…" her voice trailed off as she choked back tears.

"Kristina, none of this is your fault. Heck, I am her sister; I should have stepped in a long time ago, but I didn't. I guess I always figured she was the tough twin that handled anything that came her way. I reasoned that she would not stay in a relationship she didn't want to be in. I just don't understand what that asshole has over her that made her stay with him. I know he is good-looking, but physical appearance has never been important to Ella. Unfortunately, I am the one who got that gene. Now, I wish I was half the woman my sister is."

"I don't know what made her stay either. It was like they cohabitated and that was all. She and the kids had their own activities, and he never seemed to be part of them. I don't feel like I have been of much help to you."

Emilie asked, "Did you tell the police about your suspicion of abuse?"

"They essentially asked me the same things you did. I guess I was kind of Ella's only friend. I told them several of us often met to watch the kids play, but she kept most of her conversations on the surface. I did tell them about the bee incident but admitted that she completely shut me down. I told them I didn't see her for a couple weeks after that, but then she showed back up and acted like nothing had happened. The topic never came up again, and she continued to wear long sleeves much of the time."

Kristina shook her head and said, "I can still see those marks, and it haunts me at night. If Davis was capable of that, who knows what else he is capable of doing?"

Fury began to simmer in Emilie's gut. She said, "I don't know about you, but I think I will have a glass of wine." The two sipped a glass of Sauvignon Blanc in the nearly empty coffee shop and listened to the whoops and hollers of patrons playing yard games in the beer garden as it filled up with people winding down after a long day of work. Kristina shared additional stories about Ella and the kids. Emilie felt as though she was able to get back a little bit of the life she had missed with her sister in the past two years through Kristina's stories.

At 6:30, Emilie teased, "I think your perfect husband is probably wondering how long he will be stuck with my niece and nephew. I better get back to their house, so he can drop them off."

Kristina chuckled, and the two gave each other a much-less awkward goodbye hug. They agreed to keep in touch and joked that they would invite Ella to join them the next time. Each privately questioned the likelihood of this really happening.

Emilie drove to Davis' house. The fury that had slightly subsided as a result of the Sauvignon Blanc began to rise again up her esophagus and into her throat. She felt heat flush her cheeks, and she spouted a slew of curse words about her brother-in-law. She was relieved to see his Mercedes Benz was not in the driveway when she pulled up. She clicked the garage door opener she had taken out of Ella's car, and as the door rose, an empty garage caused Emilie to exhale loudly. She knew if she saw him now, it wouldn't be pretty.

With shaking hands, she wrote Davis a note, hustled upstairs to the kids' bedrooms, grabbed their overnight bags and stuffed them with a couple outfits and their favorite items, and returned to her car to wait for their return. Within fifteen minutes, Mike's Volvo pulled up, and the kids emerged from the car. Emilie gave Mike a "Thank You" wave and told the kids to hop into her car to go see Papa. When William gave her a questioning look, she gave him a subtle wink and said, "I already packed you a couple of outfits, and Papa is anxiously awaiting our sleepover."

Davis returned home an hour after Emilie and the kids left. He knew this because Emilie made sure she wrote the time of the note at the top of the paper. She indicated that since they hadn't seen Davis all day, they decided to go to their Papa's house overnight. She ended it with, "Based on your absence all day, I'm sure you won't even know we are gone." He crumpled the note in his hand, wishing it was her neck he had in his grip. He knew she had him by the balls because he didn't want the kids around, but he didn't want her thinking she was running the show. He also knew she would tell anyone she could that he was a dead-beat dad. He poured a Scotch on the rocks and pondered whether or not he should try to call Natalia. He decided against it. With Emilie having access to the house, he wouldn't put anything past her, including hiding a secret camera or audio recording device in the house.

His anger toward his sister-in-law increased with each additional drink. He stole down the dark hallway, slipped into his home office and felt his way in the darkness until his hands came in contact with the keys that were hidden in the secret compartment of the suit coat he kept hanging on the back of his door. Fumbling in the dark, he made his way to his filing cabinet and found the keyhole with his left fingers. He guided the key into the hole and released the lock. He reached to the back of the files and felt the cool metal object. He knew he was making a poor decision, but pent-up rage engulfed him. This whole mess was his sister-in-law's fault.

With his bottle of Scotch in hand, he went into the kids' bathroom and searched high and low for a recording device. He figured this was the least likely place for her to hide a device, so he thought this was the safest place for him to do what he needed to do. He wondered, through his wooziness, when he had become so paranoid. He knew the answer was that it was when his bitch sister-in-law arrived. Once he was certain she had not planted anything in the bathroom, he put the toilet seat lid down, took the cold metal object out of his pocket, activated it, and dialed Natalia's number. She didn't answer, so he dialed the number a second time. After several no-answers, he sent a text, "Can we meet somewhere to talk? I NEED to talk to you!" Still nothing.

Two more drinks and several additional unanswered calls and texts made Davis scream, "Fuck you, bitch! I don't need your cheap, nasty ass." He pummeled the empty Scotch bottle across the bathroom, and it shattered against the ceramic tiles. He spewed another slew of curse words as he cut his hand picking up the broken bottle. He found the first aid kit in the medicine cabinet and bandaged his bleeding hand through his drunken blurred vision. He used one of the hand towels to wipe up the blood on the floor and sink, tossed the towel into the garbage and staggered to his bedroom. His world went dark, as he passed out, fully clothed, on his king-sized bed.

29

The agents sipped their morning coffee and looked at the large whiteboard full of names, dates, locations, riddles, and games. Arrows and lines were drawn in an attempt to connect the missing pieces, but Drew and Brad were stumped. It had been over two weeks since Ella Masters' disappearance, and the agents knew time was not their friend. The longer Ella was away from her family, the less likely it was that she would be returned safely. They split up the investigative angles to expedite the gathering of information. While Agent Drew Scott investigated Emilie and Gianni, Agent Brad Gibbons looked into Davis' family background.

Gibbons read the reports from the initial interview with the Orlando Police Department, where Davis indicated his parents had both died in a Springfield house fire when he was a teenager. He decided not to ask Davis about his parents.

Instead, Gibbons contacted the Sangamon County Records division. He found no record of Davis' birth in Sangamon County, but he did find a name change request when Davis was eighteen. The request included a copy of Davis' original birth certificate, indicating that Davis Love Brown was born in Fayette County, the son of Alice Johnson and Thomas Brown.

"Why, Mr. Masters, would you change your name?" Gibbons wondered.

Gibbons spent the day researching the names of Davis' parents, which wasn't particularly easy since their names were so common. He started with death records and old newspaper articles from 1981-1982, but he found no information of a house fire taking the lives of Davis' parents or death records matching their names.

"Why would Davis lie about his parents, and why would he change his name?" he questioned Scott as they compared notes on the case.

Scott said, "It looks like we need to find Alice Johnson and Mr. Thomas Brown; maybe they are the missing links to this case. The two obviously were not married when Davis was born. Thirty years ago, that might have been scandalous. Alice most likely has a different last name now, and Thomas Brown is such a common name, so we have our work cut out for us."

Gibbons poured a fresh cup of coffee and began digging. Since Davis said he grew up in Springfield, Brad decided to start there. His initial database search on Thomas Brown yielded a few possibilities, but follow-up leads left Gibbons empty-handed.

Alice Johnson was another story. Gibbons found a likely match. The woman lived on the North side of Springfield, and she was around the right age. Gibbons filled Scott in on the information, and the two agreed that it would be better for him to take a female agent to visit Ms. Johnson.

Agent Tracy White accompanied Gibbons to the run-down trailer park. They pulled into the poorly-graveled driveway of the dilapidated trailer, spent a couple minutes going over their game plan, and slowly emerged from the car. White wished she had worn flats as she wobbled her way through mud and rocks.

Through heavy curtains, Alice Johnson watched the man and woman, both in navy suits, make their way to her door. *Were they here to take her trailer-the only thing she had left in life?* she wondered.

The broken screen door hung precariously on its hinges. Agent White carefully knocked, and Alice apprehensively opened the door. "Can I help you?" she said in a wary voice, as she covered her mouth with one hand to hide her missing teeth and exposed gums. She made an attempt to fix her disheveled hair with her other hand, all while trying to keep her housecoat gathered.

Agent White flashed her badge and said, "Good afternoon, ma'am, I am Agent Tracy White, and this is Agent Brad Gibbons. Are you Alice Johnson?"

White saw the panic on the feeble woman's face when she heard the word agent. Alice had gray, thinning hair and loose transparent skin that revealed deep-purple veins and wrinkles; she had lived a hard life, and her small mouth was pursed as if she was ready to bitterly defend her very being.

Quietly, Alice said, "What do you two want with me? I ain't done nothing wrong."

Gibbons felt for the old woman, and he was glad he decided to bring White along.

White said, "You are right, ma'am. You have done nothing wrong. We are wondering if we can talk to you a little about your son, Davis."

Gibbons and White waited cautiously for a confused Johnson to say, "I don't have a son, Davis," but the woman only hung her head as she stepped aside, allowing the agents to enter her trailer.

The room was dark, and smoke hung like a cloud in the air. The windows were covered with tightly-drawn, heavy, nicotine-stained drapes. Several plates and bowls, with dried food, were scattered amongst National Enquirer magazines on the coffee table and end tables. A scrawny tabby cat slinked in and out of White's legs as the agents sat on a soiled, brown couch. Both declined Alice's offer of a glass of water.

How could this be Davis' mother? Gibbons wondered. *Davis lives in an upscale house on the West side of town while his mother lives in this squalor?*

As if she had read his mind, Alice apologized for the state of her trailer as she scooped up some of the dishes and shuffled magazines, "I wasn't expecting company," she said in embarrassment. "I don't get much company."

"Oh, it's no problem," White quickly said, "We are sorry we didn't call first, but we weren't sure if we had the right person."

"You have the right person," Johnson admitted, shaking her head sadly as if she wished she hadn't been the right person."

"Ms. Johnson, we are here because your daughter-in-law has gone missing. Are you aware of that, ma'am?"

Alice closed her eyes and nodded slightly, but she said nothing.

"We have a few questions about your son, Davis."

Again, Alice nodded, as if she were expecting this.

White asked for permission, "Ms. Johnson, may I call you Alice?"

Alice quietly said, "Yes."

She dropped her head, and a tear fell onto her lap. Without looking up, she said, "Davis was a troubled kid. He never adjusted to not having a daddy. I tried my hardest to give him the best life possible, but nothing I could ever do was good enough. He resented me for getting pregnant at such a young age, and he resented me for him not having a daddy. When he was old enough to understand, I told him just enough of the details of his father to pacify his need to know, but I knew Tommy had moved on; he married a beautiful woman and had two more adorable little boys, and he wanted nothing to do with Davis or me."

"Alice, could you share that story with us? Maybe it will help us to understand Davis a little more." White asked.

Reluctantly, Alice spoke, "Both of our families worked the Masters Tournament, in Augusta, Georgia each year, and our fathers developed a good friendship. As the years passed, my friendship with Tommy grew, and it turned into puppy love."

Alice's cheeks turned pink with embarrassment, as she continued. "Our puppy love turned into a strong attraction, and the months between our yearly reunion were riddled with the angst of missing each other. But when our eyes met each spring, the world was once again right. We talked about growing old together and making it a family tradition to bring our children to the tournament every year."

White felt like she was listening to some teen romance novel.

"The beginning of the end started in April of 1964. Our favorite golfer, Davis M. Love, Jr., played in the final round of the 28th Master's Tournament. The next day, Love's wife, Helen, gave birth to a baby boy, Davis Love III. Riding high on the energy of the tournament and the effects of stolen beers, Tommy and I slipped away to the shade of a large oak tree. He held me in his arm and kissed me like I was the only girl in the world. He whispered, 'Let's make this a spring break to remember.' I knew he was going to be leaving for college in the fall and it might be the last time he came with his parents to the Master's, so I gave in to his seductions."

It was White's turn to blush with embarrassment as she and Gibbons listened to Alice Johnson reminisce.

Alice continued, "In June, when I realized I was pregnant, I was actually excited at the thought of being with Tommy Brown forever. He made me feel like I was the only girl in the world, even though we only saw each other one week each year. He had graduated from high school, had a part-time job, and was enrolled for fall classes at the University of Illinois. But I knew he would find a way to take care of me and our child, and that we would spend forever together, just like we had talked about for hours, as we lay underneath the star-filled Georgia skies. I knew my parents would be unhappy, but I assumed that after they saw the baby, they would change their minds. After all, they had always really liked and respected Tommy.

A pit welled up in White's stomach as the agents continued listening.

"I was only partially wrong. Yes, my parents were beyond upset; that part I was right about. They called me every name imaginable and told me I was an absolute disgrace to our family."

She hesitated as her voice caught and she used her shirt sleeve to angrily wipe away tears. The part I got all wrong was Tommy's reaction. I called him on the phone to break the news, in hopes that he would gently instruct me to pack my belongings while he drove the one-hundred-mile distance to pick me up. I had rehearsed the conversation numerous times in my head, and it always ended with his soothing words, 'SHHHHH, it is all going to be fine; I will take care of you and our baby.' Instead, Tommy's words stung like a swarm of wasps when I finally got up the nerve to call him. 'You are going to get a fucking abortion! I have my whole life ahead of me, and I am not throwing it away because some punk kid doesn't know how to take fucking birth control pills.' I didn't see Tommy again after that night."

She wearily continued, "My parents and Tommy wanted me to get an abortion, but I couldn't take the life of my unborn child. So, my parents shipped me off to live with my aunt and uncle on a farm out in the middle of nowhere. They provided minimal monetary support for me until I was eighteen, and then I was kicked out of their house and thrown out on the streets, left to raise Davis alone. My parents, Tommy, or Tommy's family never saw Davis, and I never saw them or Tommy after that. Both of my parents have passed on, and Tommy moved up to Chicago with his perfect new family."

Alice's voice contained a combination of bitter scorn and regret.

White repeated the question that Alice had yet to answer, "Alice, when is the last time you talked to, or saw, Davis?"

"I haven't talked to Davis in nearly twenty years. Right after William was born, I tried to see my new grandbaby, but when I called Davis, he screamed at me and told me I better never call his number again. So, I didn't. I had already messed up his life enough. I didn't want to cause him any more pain, especially now that he finally had a family of his own."

White's heart broke for Alice, and she dreaded the next question she was about to ask.

"Alice, do you know why Davis would have told Ella that you and his father died in a house fire?"

Alice cringed, and tears streamed down her face. She said, "I guess he just wanted to erase his past and start a new life." After a brief pause, she said, "I don't want to seem disrespectful, but if you kind folks don't have any more questions, I think I would like to be alone now."

Gibbons and White rose, apologetically nodding in unison.

Gibbons spoke for the first time. "Ms. Johnson, here are our business cards. If you think of anything later that might help us bring your daughter-in-law home safely, you can contact either one of us."

Alice took the cards, turned toward the bedroom, and said in a voice barely above a whisper, "If you don't mind, I am going to go rest for a while; do you mind seeing yourselves out?"

On the way back to the bureau, Gibbons and White concluded the only thing their visit accomplished was to further break the heart of this feeble woman, who was aged beyond her years. They did, however, find out that Davis' father was still very much alive, and, coincidentally, living in Chicago.

Before Gibbons continued his research on Thomas Brown of Chicago, he called Emilie.

Gibbons asked Emilie where she was. When she responded that she was at her daddy's house, he knew Davis was not around.

"Emilie, did Davis or Ella ever share anything about Davis' childhood with your family?"

"Davis told us that his parents died in a tragic house fire when he was seventeen and that they left him a small insurance policy that allowed him to finish high school and go to college."

"Did your sister ever talk about going to their graves?"

"No, she said Davis had a strained relationship with his parents before the fire, and he harbored guilt over the fact that he had stayed at a friend's house the night the fire broke out, so he wasn't there to help his parents get out."

"Really?" Agent Gibbons pondered in an exaggerative manner.

"Oh my God," Emilie gasped. "Do you think Davis had something to do with his parent's deaths?"

"No, Emilie, I am certain he didn't have anything to do with his parent's deaths."

The agent allowed Emilie to breathe a sigh of relief before saying, "Because Davis' parents are VERY much alive."

He paused, as he let the effects of his words sink in.

"What in the hell are you talking about?" Emilie gasped.

Gibbons realized he had shocked the woman. "I can't go into further details at this time, and I would appreciate it if you keep this conversation just between the two of us until I finish my investigation. I just wanted to make sure you didn't know about his past."

"No," Emilie said contemplatively, as though she was trying to process a lifetime of lies.

"Let me just say, Emilie, that Davis is not the man your family thinks he is."

"Sir, do you have any reason to believe I am unsafe with Davis?"

"No, Emilie, Davis knows he has a lot of eyes on him, and two missing sisters would not bode well for him...or for whoever has your sister. I have already told you more than I should have, but I was hoping you might have information about his parents that would expedite our investigation. I will give you more information when I am able to do so. Remem-ber, this is not information we want Davis to know we have just yet."

"I won't say a word to him, sir."

"Thanks again, Emilie. We are doing our best to get your sister back to your family."

Guilt hung in the air around Emilie as the investigator hung up. She did not know about Davis' parents, but she did know more about the man than she had shared with the agents.

Gibbons pored over his notes and added the information he gained from listening to Alice Johnson's story. *Could there be a connection with Davis' dad, if the man lived in Chicago? Or maybe his two half-brothers? Had Davis been in contact with them or done something to them that would warrant revenge?* It was definitely an angle Gibbons would spend the next several days exploring. One thing the encounter confirmed was that Davis was a bigger ass than he had initially thought.

When he returned to the bureau, Scott called Gibbons into his office to get an update and show him the newest piece of mail. He saw the familiar return address; it was the same as the other Ella Master's mail clues. Both men went through the ritual of putting on rubber gloves, and Scott did the honors of opening the piece.

Written in crayon, in what looked like a child's writing, was the poem,

I Have Many Names

I'm as small as an ant, as big as a whale.
I'll approach like a breeze but can come like a gale.
By some, I get hit, but all have shown fear.
I'll dance to the music, though I can't hear.
Of names I have many, of names I have one.
I'm as slow as a snail, but from me, you can't run.
What am I?   (Author Unknown)

Scott handed the paper to Gibbons and admitted, "I am horrible at riddles!"

Gibbons looked over the front and back of the paper, and he re-read the words. He wondered why the line, "Of names

I have many," was highlighted. After less than a minute, he said, as if he were the master riddle solver, "I've got you on this one, buddy. The answer is a shadow."

Scott said, "How did you figure it out so quickly?"

Gibbons turned the paper over; in the lower back corner, upside down, was the small answer: Davis' shadow.

He chided, "Dude, you are slipping! You better pour yourself a cup of Joe to get your brain firing on a few more cylinders!"

"So, Agent Smart Ass, is our clue in the title of the riddle, the riddle itself, or the answer?"

Gibbons was already analyzing the piece, "OK, the answer specifically says Davis' shadow, instead of a shadow, but the sender highlighted the line, 'Of names I have many,' so we are obviously supposed to be drawn to those words. The question is who has many names, and who is afraid of Davis' shadow or going to make Davis afraid of his own shadow?"

Scott interrupted Gibbons' thinking process, "Did you find anything out from your visit to Davis' mother today that might fit with the riddle?"

Gibbons filled his partner in on the interview, looking over his notes to make sure he didn't forget anything. "Essentially, the interview confirmed that Davis is an asshole and a liar, which we already knew. I did, however, find out that his father is still alive and living a successful life in Chicago with a wife and two grown sons."

Scott's brow raised at the Chicago connection. "Interesting. The mail is coming from Chicago. You don't think Davis' old man is somehow involved, do you?"

Gibbons let out a frustrated breath and said, "I honestly don't know what to think most of the time with this case. I feel like this guy is handing us clues on a silver platter, and we are too freaking stupid to figure them out. Alice does not know where Mr. Brown lives in Chicago-- just that he lives somewhere in

Chicago. With the name, Thomas Brown, it is going to be like finding a nun in a whore house."

Scott responded, with a wry grin, "Well, you better brush up on your hymns and keep your belt buckle tight because we have a nun to find."

30

June watched the broken woman on the television monitor and laughed to herself about how many years she had been secretly observing her prey. Now, Ella was nearly unrecognizable. Her short, chopped hair clung matted to her greasy scalp. Her clothes hung on the emaciated figure that, only weeks ago, had been lean and strong. Her bare feet still showed remnants of mud from her transport from the car to the house, even though Ella had tried to scrape it off. Dirt caked her fingernails. Her eyes were dull, and her face had turned ashen.

A mixture of anger and sadness worked their way through June's veins. Her eyes stung as she blinked quickly to avoid the tears that were hanging by a thread on her lower lashes. She took out her charcoal pencil set and sketch pad and began doodling. She drew Ella's prison, complete with the children's toys and games. She sketched a perfect image of the new Ella, huddled in the corner. Teardrops splattered the drawing; they were not tears of sadness over what she was doing to Ella, but from sorrow over the life Davis had stolen from her.

June knew she needed to snap out of her funk, and what better way than to drive the knife into Ella a little bit more.

June clicked on the speaker, cleared the tears from her throat and began, "I have been watching you for an hour now, Ella. I just love watching people. I have to admit, I have been a people-watcher from the time I was a small child. I have spent hours in coffee shops, restaurants, and parks hiding behind books or magazines and soaking up conversations of the people around me. Yep, I have traveled around the world, engaged in family outings, and endured the heartbreak of many relationships-- all by living vicariously through other people's conversations."

She paused long enough for Ella to look into the eye of the camera as if to encourage her to continue.

"I love trying to figure people out behind their fake facades. I learned at a young age that the way people dress, carry themselves, and talk greatly affect their interactions with others. Pretty people get all the attention. You are, or should I say, were, a pretty person. Not so much anymore, though. Anyway, the first time I witnessed this phenomenon was when I was five. I can still see Katie. She was a perfect specimen of a little girl on her first day of kindergarten; I swear she had been plucked straight out of a magazine. She had an angelic face with big green eyes that matched her chiffon dress. Mrs. Mefford uncoiled Katie's fingers from the hand of her even more perfect mommy as she coaxed little Katie to come into the classroom. One crocodile tear danced its way down her cheek like in the movies. I stood only fifteen feet from this seemingly wax figure that I feared would melt if she released any more tears. I remember looking down at my own outfit that I had carefully chosen for my special day: my yard sale pants were a bit too short, my wrinkled dingy t-shirt, and my tennis shoes that had lost their shoelaces long ago. I had never seen perfection like this, and I was in awe, but what came next was even more spectacular. Mrs. Mefford swooned over the little girl, as she spoke comforting words and gently pried her fingers out of her mommy's hands. I remember trying to muster up tears, so the teacher would come and hold my hand too, but when I looked down at my dirty fingernails, I quickly stuffed them into my pockets."

"The doting over perfect Katie started that day, and I watched teacher after teacher, year after year, exhibit the same behavior over the Katies of the world. I loved Mrs. Mefford because she treated all of her students as if they were all as special as Katie, but by the time I finished first grade, I realized I wasn't a Katie, and if there were any doubt in my mind, Mrs.

Sorenson, my second-grade teacher, solidified it. It was at that young age that I learned that pretty people have more comfortable lives. Her anger rose the more she reminisced about her childhood. She needed to blow off some steam. She descended the staircase, knowing she was about to do irreversible damage."

"Ella, today we are going to play a game called two truths and a lie. Have you ever played this game before?"

Ella nodded cautiously.

"Good, here are your three choices; you have to decide which is a lie. Now, remember, two of them are truths, and one is a lie, dear. Which statement is a lie?"

Ella felt like she was standing at the top of Mount Everest, waiting to be pushed off.

"Here we go."

1. Davis has known you since high school.
2. Davis has had not one but TWO vasectomies.
3. Davis murdered your mother.

Ella gasped at the words of the third statement, but the thought of any of the answers being true was unfathomable.

She knew this woman wasn't going to give her time to contemplate her words; she quickly thought about each statement. Given the fact that she had been inundated with so much information about Davis, she realized the first one could be true. She thought back to the reactions Davis had when she told him about each of her pregnancies, and she realized this one could also be true. She forced herself to believe her husband had nothing to do with her mom's death. As bad as the first two were, she couldn't imagine he was heinous enough to murder his own mother-in-law. She would never be able to recover from hearing the man she had shared a bed with for over fifteen years was responsible for her mother's death.

With a voice like sandpaper, Ella squeaked out, "Number three." She couldn't bring herself to say the words.

With a sick feeling in her gut, she waited for June's answer, knowing the woman on the other side of the wall relished her misery. To Ella's relief, June responded, "Good girl, Ella, Davis did not kill your momma!"

Ella released an audible sigh.

Then June dropped her bombshell. "Let me qualify my answer, sweetie. Davis didn't actually kill your momma...," she paused and let her words settle in the air of Ella's hell-hole. She enjoyed the physical reaction it provoked.

She continued. "Davis is not a big enough man to do something like that himself..." Her words once again fell away to silence.

It was as if Ella had taken a shotgun blast to the head and the percussion was concussing through her brain. She grabbed her head in agony over June's words.

"I seem to have upset you, my friend. Can I call you my friend? After all, we have spent so much time together we are almost like family! Do you remember the question I asked you when we first became besties?"

She knew June had asked her something, but she couldn't think. She was in a state of emotional fight or flight. Her eyes darted around her tiny prison as she processed June's words.

"It's OK if you can't remember, sweetie. I will remind you. I asked you what we have in common. But, let's forget about your naive mommy for a moment. I don't want to overwhelm you, after all."

June carefully slid the scrapbook page through the door. "Add this to your scrapbook, Dearie, but feel free to look closely at the pictures first before you read the letter your hubby has written to you."

Ella's newest scrapbook page was covered with several pictures of her under her favorite tree on the North Quad at Eastern Illinois University where she spent much of her time studying and writing letters to her sister and parents. There were also a few pictures of her standing in her usual phone booth in Old Main.

Memories of her college days flooded back as she took in the pictures. She wasn't the typical college student who partied her way through college; instead, she enjoyed hiking, camping, and studying photojournalism. By her final year at Eastern Illinois University, she had successfully avoided the dating scene- - a goal she had set the moment her foot stepped on the university lawn her freshman year. The caption at the top of the page read, "I spy a creepy guy watching your every move."

Two of the pictures were close-ups of her, but several were farther away and included other students enjoying a relaxing day on the quad. She studied the pictures and realized that one male figure was in all of them. He was wearing different sweatshirts, t-shirts, and hats, but he had blue jeans and the same red Converse high tops in all of the pictures. Who was this man? Was it just a coincidence? The images covered the span of her four years in college, so how did this same guy end up in all of the snapshots, and how in the hell did someone get all of these pictures?" she questioned.

June demanded, "Read the letter aloud."

Reluctantly, Ella read her husband's writing.

Dear Ella,

I have to be honest with you; our meeting at Fox Ridge State Park wasn't by chance. I had noticed you before, and I thought you were so beautiful, but I was afraid you wouldn't be interested in me. You hung out by the same tree several times each week, and I also spent much of my time on the quad. I saw you reading several hiking books when you weren't studying. I was a desperate man in love with a beautiful woman, so I took up hiking, ran into you on the trails, and I introduced myself to
you. Can you blame a guy for being in love?

Love,
Davis

June's voice took over after Ella finished reading. "You see, sweetie, Davis knew all of this information because he had been stalking you for quite some time. Your husband had become an expert at being an invisible observer of you, Ella. He didn't consider himself a stalker; he was simply inquisitive. He knew your schedule and favorite tree, so he always made sure he arrived before you did and sat strategically under a nearby tree facing the opposite direction. Look at the pictures closely, Ella."

She gave Ella a moment to process what she said before continuing, "He even knew your favorite pay phone in Old Main, and he heard many of the telephone conversations you had with your parents and your twin sissy."

June added the frightening details of Davis' stalkings. "Davis always brought along a couple of business marketing textbooks and a notepad. He switched books out at the beginning of each semester just in case you happened to be watching him too. He always had the textbook open, and he furiously took notes. He turned pages every few minutes and continued writing. His notes, however, had nothing to do with business marketing… and everything to do with you. He knew your class schedule, favorite restaurant, foods, and activities."

Ella looked at the pictures again. Davis was in every photo, disguised by various hats, jackets, glasses, and hoodies. He hid behind newspapers, magazines, or books.

"Ella, all the man wanted to do was meet you, but you had your head buried in your books or maps of your next hiking trip. You didn't give him the time of day, so he had to find another way to meet you. That's when he took up hiking; he HATED hiking, but you didn't know it, and it worked!"

"The problem with his admission, however," June continued, "is that I specifically instructed him to say how long he has known you, and he didn't provide the truth. I have to give him credit, though; he didn't exactly lie, but he wasn't forthcoming. You see, Davis had been keeping his eye on you a number of years before you were ever at Eastern Illinois University. Can you believe that? Kinda creepy, huh!?"

As if June were telling a childhood girlfriend the latest gossip, she rambled on in an excited voice, "See, he worked at Long View Country Club as a dishwasher during his high school years. You remember your high and mighty country club, right? Well, He caught bits of information about you by asking wait staff questions about the "socialite snobs," but he never had a chance to meet you. So, when you ended up staying relatively close to home for college, Davis was able to keep track of you. It was not by chance that you ended up at the same university at the same time, even though you were two years younger than Davis."

June paused for effect before adding, "And he wasn't even really a student at EIU."

Ella shook her head. This didn't make sense. *Did this woman say Davis wasn't a student at EIU?* She recalled Davis saying he had no desire to walk in the School of Business graduation ceremony, but she knew plenty of students who didn't go through their graduation ceremonies; it wasn't that uncommon.

"So, Ella, that's the story of how you two met. Crazy, huh? The even crazier thing is that you seem to have that effect on men. Why, because you are a pretty person…or were, anyway. You have a way of attracting stalkers, and you are so fucking oblivious that you have no idea they are always nearby."

Ella cringed at the thought of Davis watching her like a mountain lion watches its prey, and she further shuddered at the realization that June had also been stalking her, but what other men was this woman talking about. This new revelation momentarily took her mind off of the startling mention of her momma, but only momentarily.

June saw Ella's shift in demeanor and sighed, "Oh, I'm sorry. You must be back to thinking about your mommy. I'll tell you what, we have had a long day; how about if we keep the other stories for tomorrow. In fact, I have something that might lift your spirits. See, your hubby, sissy, and brats all wanted to give you presents. Isn't that exciting, Ella! I will be right back, so don't go anywhere, OK!"

June laughed a hearty laugh, "I just crack myself up. Do you get it? Don't go anywhere?" She continued to chuckle as she ascended the stairs.

Moments later, she returned with her laptop in hand, so she could see Ella's expression on the monitor as she opened up her gifts. She slipped a tissue-wrapped item through the slot.

"You look as though you might need a little pick-me-up after this newest revelation about your hubby, so I brought you a gift."

Ella assumed June was baiting her, only to rip her heart out again. She felt like she was part of a catch-and-release pond. June hooked her, reeled her in, battered her, and let her go-- only to hook her again.

"Well, go ahead, Silly, open it up."

The tissue paper had colorful drawings of trees, flowers, a swing set, a dog, and stick figures of a mommy and two kids. Ella's tears fell as she caressed the stick figure children.

June felt a pang of hurt for the woman but quickly recovered. In a stern voice, she said, "I said, go ahead and open it!"

Ella carefully removed the tape, without damaging the pictures, to reveal a small journal covered in pictures of her and William. It was the first time she had seen her son in ten days, and the raw emotion turned her tears into uncontrollable sobs.

June's own unexpected tears dripped onto the keyboard of her laptop as she sat on the other side of the locked door and watched Ella's breakdown on the computer screen. Both women sat, traumatized, for several minutes. Luckily, Ella wasn't able to see June's reaction.

June muttered in anger at herself, "Fucking hormones!" She finally stood, and without saying a word, went back upstairs.

Ella lay on her towel and held her treasured gift close to her heart; she didn't have the strength to read it. She cried herself into a turbulent sleep.

Jax returned home from his errands to find his girl-friend lying in the fetal position and crying on the couch. His heart stopped when he saw her. He feared someone had found out about their game.

"Hey, Baby, what's the matter?" he asked carefully.

"Nothing," June lied. "I think it is just hormones. My body is all fucked up!"

Quickly diverting the attention away from herself, she opened the laptop and said, "Let's see what our little lady is up to."

"Poor Ella is having a nightmare," Jax said, as they watched her writhe in her sleep.

"Maybe we should wake her," June said mischievously.

June pressed the play button and blared music through the speakers. Ella tossed and turned frantically until the music finally woke her from the nightmare in which William was chasing his little sister at Starved Rock State Park. No matter how loudly their mother screamed "Stop," both children continued to bound closer and closer to the edge of a steep cliff, giggling the whole time. They disappeared over the side of the cliff, just as Ella awoke, drenched in sweat. It took her several minutes to realize it was only a nightmare. It took her several more minutes to comprehend the words of the song that played repeatedly.

Ella listened to the song "There Goes My Life" by Kenny Chesney, as it rang through the speaker. She was not into country music, but the words were easy to understand. The words echoed a young man's negative feelings about an accidental pregnancy. At the beginning of the song, the singer sang 'there goes my life,' as an indication that his life was ruined because of an unwanted child, but by the end of the song, the same phrase referred to his beautiful children running out the door to play in the yard.

"Ella, I know you think your hubby doesn't like to play children's games, but that is not the case. In fact, his favorite children's game is OPERATION. He has written you a letter that will enlighten you a bit."

Soft footsteps descended the stairs. As if on cue, June slipped the newest scrapbook page through the door. There were several pictures on the page. One of the images was a doctor's office. Ella read the names on the sign in front of the building,

Patsy K. Sidener, M.D.
Joseph M. Smith, M.D.
Sherry L. Dimon, N.P.

There were several images of the children's game, "Operation," one of which had an arrow pointing to the groin area. Finally, Ella studied the picture and bio of Dr. Joseph Smith. Below the images was the letter Davis had been instructed to write to his wife about his game of "OPERATION."

June said, "Somehow, Davis doesn't quite see things the way Kenny Chesney does. Go ahead and read the letter, Sweetie,…ALOUD!"

With a shaky voice, Ella read:

Dear Ella,

I know things have been hard for you, and this is only going to make matters worse. I know the truth will hurt you, but I know if I do not tell you the truth, they will kill you. I had a terrible childhood, so I didn't want children. I knew if I shared that with you, you would not marry me. I got a vasectomy while you were on vacation with your family, but then you ended up pregnant, not once but twice. It was all a big fiasco! I saw how happy you were, but deep down I wondered if the children were mine. I felt like I couldn't connect with the children because I just wasn't sure. I am so sorry, my love. If you come back safely, we will begin to build a new life together as a family, one in which there are no more secrets.

Love,
Davis

Ella sat paralyzed with disbelief. Her skin crawled at the realization that she had been married to this man all these years. She tried to do the math, but she couldn't think straight. What WAS clear was the WHY behind the reason Davis had very little to do with William and virtually nothing to do with Willow. He had always blamed it on the fact that he couldn't relate to a girl, but the way he looked at her with disgust most of the time made perfect sense now. All these years, he didn't think sweet little Willow was his child, and he showed it. But, how was Willow not his child? There couldn't be any way she was NOT his. Ella tried to shake away the fog, but she couldn't wrap herself around the conundrum.

June said, "Goodness, Ella, seeing what a prize you have in a husband makes me REAL glad he didn't pick me! Maybe we still better leave the story about your momma for another day."

Ella's face contorted with horror.

"Ella, that is not a becoming look, dear," Jax piped through the speaker. "No wonder Davis had so many affairs." He laughed. Ella covered her ears.

She wanted to curl back up into a ball and make everything go away, but she knew the minute she closed her eyes her nightmares would return. She opened up William's journal and read her son's sweet entries. She felt a mix of heartache and tenderness in his words. She wondered where he and Willow were right now. She closed her eyes and imagined them safe and secure in their beds at Papa's house. She wished she were with them.

31

Agent Scott's office phone rang. He answered, "Agent Drew Scott, how can I help you?"

The husky voice whispered, "Olly, Olly Oxen Free, you might want to check out La Verità Caffe." The call ended.

"Damn," Scott said. He knew it was the same voice who had made the other calls, and the guy knew to keep the call short, so it couldn't be traced.

Scott googled La Verità Caffe. "Bingo!" He said aloud. The first hit showed La Verità Caffe, a popular coffee shop attached to a grocery named Cristiano's, on West Madison Street in Chicago. There were several articles on the up-and-coming area where the store and coffee shop were located. Scott sifted through the website information about the store.

One article in particular, "Chicago Business Mogul No Slum Lord," caught his eye. He read the piece.

"Gianni Russo has only been in Chicago a few short years, but he is already turning the city right side up. He has a vision, and he sees it come to fruition, one city block at a time. Gianni seeks out areas of Chicago that have been taken over by drug dealers, gang bangers, and homeless people. With the help of investors, he buys up one city block at a time, demolishes the buildings, and rebuilds them, turning them into posh apartments, hip stores, and unique eateries. Russo's most recent success story has been the block immediately north of Greek Town, which was his most successful venture yet."

Scott studied the picture of Cristiano's grocery store, with La Verità Caffe located at the base of the store. "Brilliant man," he thought, "and Davis was hoping to get in on the action, but he couldn't do it without capital, but why would someone want us to check him out?" Scott was pissed at his team for not looking more deeply into Gianni Russo. They had completed a cursory criminal check on the man, and he was squeaky clean. He admitted to himself that they had been so focused on Davis that they had become blind to other leads.

He took copious notes, as he read the rest of the article and then dialed Gibbons' extension. "I think we have a nibble," he said. "Do you have a few minutes?"

Scott printed the article, while he waited for Gibbons to fill his coffee cup and settle into the chair on the other side of his desk. "OK, so, Davis was supposed to be meeting this Gianni guy in Florida, right?

"Yes," Gibbons said.

"Well, I just got a phone call from our guy. He said, 'Olly, Olly Oxen Free, you might want to check out La Verità Caffe.' So I did, and guess what?"

He handed Gibbons the print out of the article. "I think it is about time we have a little conversation with Gianni Russo."

Gibbons said what Scott was thinking, "It's a nice day for a drive to Chicago, don't you think?"

As Agent Gibbons drove, Scott continued to research Gianni Russo. "This guy has been influential in turning some pretty bad areas around in the city, and he seems to be a pillar of the Chicago community. So why, then, does our mystery man think we need to check out La Verità Caffe?"

The men weaved through the busy streets of Chicago, found a parking spot in a lot around the corner from Cristiano's, and walked the short distance to the store. When they stepped into La Verità Caffe, the splash of bold red color provided a welcoming vibe, and the smell of fresh-brewed coffee was inviting. The two men each ordered the dark roast and carried their coffees to a corner booth. It was an upscale coffee shop with massive black and white photos of young couples on scooters or sitting in outdoor cafes in Italy. They drank their coffee and called Mr. Gianni Russo at the office number listed on the internet.

The female voice answered after only one ring, "Revitalize Chicago, Inc., where we are revitalizing Chicago, one block at a time; this is Kathy, how may I direct your call?"

"Good afternoon, Kathy, is Gianni Russo available by chance?"

"I'm sorry, Mr. Russo is in a meeting; may I take a message or ask in what regard you are calling?" she spouted as if she repeated the sentence multiple times each day.

"Yes, Kathy, this is Federal Bureau of Investigations Special Agent Drew Scott. We understand he is behind the development of La Verità Caffe. It is imperative that we speak with him as soon as possible. We are dealing with a time-sensitive matter."

Kathy repeated his words, "Agent Drew Scott with the Federal Bureau of Investigations, regarding La Verità Caffe-time-sensitive. Got it, Agent Scott. I will have Mr. Russo contact you as soon as he gets out of his meeting."

"We are only in Chicago for the day, and, as I said, it is a time-sensitive matter, so the sooner he can call us back, the better."

Kathy responded in a well-rehearsed voice, "Of course, Mr. Scott; Mr. Russo is very prompt at returning phone calls, but I will make certain I put this note at the top of his pile."

Scott said, "Thank you, Kathy," and hung up the phone.

The agents finished their coffee and decided to drive across town in case Russo was able to see them soon. Halfway in route to Revitalize Chicago, Inc., Scott's phone buzzed.

"Agent Drew Scott, how can I help you?"

The suave voice on the other end of the phone said, "Good afternoon, Agent Scott, my name is Gianni Russo. I am returning your call."

"Yes, Mr. Russo, thank you for getting back to me so promptly. My partner and I are in Chicago only for today, and we would like to know if you have time for a few questions."

Gianni hesitantly said, "May I ask what the questions are regarding?"

Scott hesitated, "Mr. Russo, we are very nearby your office. Would you mind if we stop by, sir?"

Russo repeated, "May I ask what this is in regard to?" as if Scott had not heard him the first time.

Scott reluctantly said, "We have a few questions to ask you about a business associate of yours."

Russo replied, "Sir, I have many business associates. Which associate are you asking me about?"

The color drained out of his face, and his stomach turned when he heard the name "Davis Masters," but his voice inflection remained unchanged.

"I have forty-five minutes before my next meeting. Do you know where my office is located?"

"Yes, Mr. Russo, we are actually only five minutes away."

Russo was relieved he had a few moments to compose himself before the agents arrived. He wet his face with a cold paper towel and attempted to wash and dry his uncharacteristically clammy hands.

The inevitable moment he had been dreading for nearly two weeks found its way to Chicago.

Kathy greeted the agents and asked, "Can I get you two some water or coffee?"

"No, thank you, we stopped by La Verità Caffe and enjoyed a cup of coffee there."

"Isn't that place great," she said innocently, "Out of all of Mr. Russo's accomplishments, that block is his baby. He even named the store after himself."

Kathy saw the quizzical looks on the faces of the two men and quickly explained, "Oh, Cristiano is his middle name."

"Thank you, Kathy, for giving these nice gentlemen a briefing on my business," Gianni said in a playfully scolding way, which caused Kathy's cheeks to turn pink.

"Sorry, Mr. Russo, we just got to talking."

Gianni smiled at the young girl and said, teasingly, "You are never without words, Kathy, that's why I keep you around."

Gibbons was surprised that he handled the way Kathy provided so much information with patience and easy joking. He thought, "A guy who had something to hide would not have responded that way."

Gianni invited the agents into his office. "What brings you to Chicago, and more specifically to my office?"

Agent Scott said, "How do you know we aren't from Chicago?"

Gianni said, "Well, Chatty Kathy out there is more than just a talker; she also takes impeccable notes, and she wrote down that you two REALLY needed to see me today because you are only in Chicago for the day." He presented the detailed note to the two agents, and they chuckled at the note.

Scott began, "We know your time is valuable, Mr. Russo, so we will keep our questions short."

Gianni said, in the same teasing tone he had used with Kathy, "Should I get my attorney in here? He's just down the hall; I provide free office space for him, just in case I need him on short notice." He chuckled at his own joke.

Scott couldn't tell if Gianni Russo was unconcerned or nervous. He responded, "I don't think you will have a need for your attorney just yet."

Gibbons began, "Can you tell us about your relationship with Davis Masters?"

Russo knew this question was inevitable, so he had mentally prepared for it.

Russo said, "Mr. Masters was interested in partnering with me on a city build on Chicago's east side, but our deal did not come to fruition."

"Can you tell us what happened to the deal?" said Gibbons.

"It was simple; Mr. Masters could not provide the necessary capital by the required deadline, so I had to move on to other investors. I had several people in the deal who were ready to move forward, and we couldn't wait any longer for one small investor."

"So, if you don't mind my asking, have you moved forward with the project?"

Russo's face lit up as if he was talking about his newest baby, "Yes, sir, demolition of the interior buildings has already taken place; they are clearing the mess up as we speak."

"Excellent," Scott said, "I did some research on your company. You are making some remarkable positive changes in the city. I saw some of the before and after pictures of the Madison and Halstead blocks, and you have done excellent work, sir."

Russo modestly said, "Thank you, as you can see I have a passion for positive urban growth."

Scott continued, "How long have you known Davis Masters?"

Russo pondered, as if he were doing the math in his head, "I can't say for sure, but it has been a couple years now, I guess."

"How did the two of you meet?" Gibbons asked.

Russo knew he was about to enter a slippery slope. He had run his business and his personal life with full transparency, except in the case of Davis Masters. His honesty had always served him well, so he didn't like being in a position of needing to lie.

He answered the question with carefully chosen words, "We knew several of the same people, and when he found out about my company and the fact that I am always looking for investors, he practically threw himself at my feet. He wanted to be part of the movement."

"And did he become part of any of your projects?" Gibbons questioned.

"No, sir, he always seemed to be about a half beat behind other investors."

"So what happened, Mr. Russo?"

Gianni explained, "Well, Agent Gibbons, I am a busy man, and I have a lot of people who want to latch onto my proverbial coat tail and ride the wave with me. They think they are going to get rich fast, but this is not about making a quick buck; it is about changing a community. If we happen to make money along the way, great, but the day it becomes only about making money is the day it will quit working. Davis wanted the quick rewards of the program, but he did not have the capital to invest. He kept saying he was just a few days and then a few weeks from getting me his investment money, but he never came through. So, I gave him an ultimatum. I told him I needed a million dollars to keep him on my investment team. This was higher than the $750,000 I usually require, and I thought the amount was outside his reach, but I didn't know how else to let him go. He was like a darned puppy dog that is just there, at your feet, every time you turn around. Again, I have a lot of people who want to be part of the movement, but I need people who have the financial means to be genuine contributors. "

Scott interrupted, "Mr. Russo, can you tell me the date of your supposed ultimatum?"

Russo looked at his large desk calendar, "Yes, sir, my deadline was June 3rd."

Scott asked for clarity, "Do you mean June 3rd of this year, 2014?"

"Yes, sir," Russo replied.

Scott knew what Masters had said about the 9:30 phone meeting that was supposed to take place on June 2nd and the supposed June 3rd deadline, but he wanted to see if their stories jived all the way.

"Mr. Russo, can you explain the agreement you had regarding the deadline?"

Russo looked at his calendar again and said, "Davis and I were supposed to have a 9:30 phone conference on Tuesday, June 2nd. I had a follow-up private meeting with our administrative members of the investment team on June 3rd to finalize the list of junior members on the project and their financial contributions."

"9:30 a.m. or 9:30 p.m., sir?" said Gibbons.

"9:30 p.m., sir," Russo confirmed.

"You said, 'supposed,' what do you mean, supposed?"

Russo explained, "He was supposed to call me at 9:30 p.m. on June 2nd, but he didn't call. I tried to call him at 9:35, but he didn't answer his phone."

Scott and Gibbons gave each other a look that did not get by Russo.

Most people would recoil at the questionable look, but Gianni Russo addressed it, leaving the agents a bit uncomfortable, "What about my comment did you not like, gentlemen?"

Scott asked, "What number did you dial when you called him at 9:35?"

Russo said, "I don't have it memorized, but it is the only number I have for him."

"Do you still have the number on your phone?" Gibbons asked.

"I may actually still have the call in my call log."

He searched through his call log, but he had too many outgoing calls, so they did not go that far back.

"Wait, I may have an old voicemail from him. He was pretty desperate to get hold of me that week."

Gianni looked through his voicemail messages.

"I'm pretty sure this one is from him."

Russo pressed play, and the three men heard Davis say, "Gianni, I really need to talk to you. I have hit a couple roadblocks, so I may need a little more time to come up with my investment."

To the agents, Russo said, "I have had more phone calls from him over the past year than you two can imagine. Like I said, he always seemed to be just short of making a big investment."

Agent Scott wrote down the number and the message, word for word.

"Mr. Russo, has Mr. Masters attempted to contact you at any time since Tuesday, June 2nd?"

Gianni replied, "No."

"Mr. Russo, are you aware that the reason Davis Masters did not call you on Tuesday, June 2nd was because his wife disappeared from the restaurant where they were dining."

With a visibly changed demeanor, he quietly said, "I heard about his wife through mutual acquaintances."

Scott asked, "Did you know his wife, sir?"

The questions were getting more personal, and more difficult for Gianni to answer.

He answered, "Mr. Master's never introduced his wife to me. He kept her and his children separate from his business affairs."

I have one final question, "Why do you think I got a phone call that led me to La Verità Caffe…and ultimately to you, and why did the person mention La Verità Caffe and not one of your many other Revitalize Chicago locations you have converted?"

"I can only guess that maybe it is because everyone knows that location is my personal favorite…as Kathy already mentioned."

The agents weren't sure they bought his answer, but it was all they had to go on for the moment. They thanked Mr. Russo for his time, and he saw them to the door. As they drove out of the city, they agreed that Chicago was a decent place to visit, but they were glad to be heading back to Springfield.

Once he was certain the investigators were far away, he told Kathy to hold all of his calls. He locked himself in his office and cried like a baby. His secretary wished the walls were a little thicker. She had always prided herself in working for such a morally upright man in a city filled with many business scum bags. Now, she wondered if her boss had something to hide.

She left him a note, "Mr. Russo, I am leaving for the day. If you need anything, give me a call." She gathered her belongings and quietly slipped out of the office.

Cristiano heard the door close and felt relief at being alone. He hoped his secretary had not heard his cries.

32

Ella's predictable days and nights crept along as slowly as the freight trains that had become the background music of her world. Her one consistent meal of the day was a generic granola bar and a juice box, accompanied by a riddle or scrapbook page. If she didn't respond the way June thought she should, that would be her only meal of the day.

Her shriveling muscles were cramped from her confinement in the small closet. The wet-wipe baths no longer took away the funk of her filthy body. She used the dress of Willow's doll to scrub at her teeth, but her breath tasted stale from weeks of not brushing or flossing. Flies buzzed around the open five-gallon bucket that was half full of pungent urine, diarrhea, and vomit.

Audio messages and songs about cheating husbands and broken families bellowed through the speaker several times each day, tormenting Ella and causing her to pull out her short strands of hair, one piece at a time.

Her red-rimmed eyes burned from crying and from a lack of sleep. Her body desperately needed rest, but her captors intentionally messed with her sleep. A precariously dangling light with a bulb that was much too bright for the tight, enclosed quarters, remained on for hours, messing with the part of her brain that needed darkness to sleep, and then she would be forced to endure total darkness for hours on end. There was no middle ground. Ella knew what it must have felt like to be the subject of interrogation or a prisoner in a war camp.

Over the speaker, the song "Memories" began to play, and a scrapbook page was slipped through the slot in the door.

Ella saw a black and white, side profile picture of what was meant to look like her, as she sat on a concrete bench on the Chicago River with Cristiano, only, she knew it wasn't her.

Below the image, was a letter. She recognized the handwriting.

Dear Ella,

I know that you and I have had some tough times the past few years, and what I am going to tell you may ruin any chance of mending our relationship. I know, however, that if I don't provide the whole truth, I risk the chance of never seeing you again. Sister, you are the other half that makes me whole. I know we have chosen different paths, but I admire the person and the mother you have become. I could never live up to the amazing woman you are."

Ella stopped reading in disbelief that her sister would actually write something like this. *Had someone else written the letter?* she wondered. "But how would they write exactly like her sister?" Emilie had always held herself up just a little higher in social status than her twin sister, so the words on the page felt just like that...words on a page, with no heartfelt emotion behind them.

June barked, "Continue reading the letter aloud!

Ella acquiesced,

"I made a mistake, Ella-- a big mistake. I ran into an old friend of yours in Chicago a few years ago at a party of a mutual acquaintance. Neither of us could believe we saw the other so far away from our original meeting place. I knew by the look in his eyes when he saw me across the room that he was a man who was still very much in love."

Ella's stomach made its way up into her constrained throat. She forced the vomit back down and willed the words to continue out of her mouth.

"Over late-night coffee, he admitted that he hoped it was you standing across the room, but realized it was more likely me because the place wasn't your kind of venue. We caught up on our lives, but the majority of our conversation was about you. We crossed paths several times over the next few months; each time he asked about you."

"It was the week after our terrible birthday fight over Davis two years ago. I was hurt and pissed, and part of me wanted to hurt you back. I called Cristiano up and told him I wanted to talk to him about you. We met for drinks, and I told him about our fight and about how Davis was tearing our family apart but that you refused to acknowledge it. One drink led to way too many, and he walked me back to my place."

Ella wanted to stop reading. She knew where it was going, and she couldn't take any more heartbreak. Had her sister been having a relationship with the only man she had ever loved, just to get even?

"Read it, dammit!" June bellowed.

Ella read, "We both regretted the moment as soon as it was over. He felt as if he had cheated, and I felt hollow because I knew he was only trying to find you in me. We avoided each other at parties after that."

"A couple of months later, I realized I was pregnant, and I could not face the fact that I had done this to you, my twin sister, when I knew how much you had cared for Cristiano. I couldn't risk the chance of you finding out who the father was, and I knew Cristiano would never agree to an abortion. I planned a long weekend in St. Louis and made the situation go away. I know you will never be able to forgive me for the hurt I have caused you. For that, I will never forgive myself."

Your other half,
Emilie

June's voice interrupted Ella's thoughts, "That is right, sweet Ella, your sissy is not only in a relationship with your hubby, but it turns out she hooked up with your lover boy. Yep, Cristiano has been living in Chicago for the past ten years, and he knows exactly where you are at all times. In fact, he has become close chums with both your sister AND your husband in order to keep an even closer eye on you. How is that for a coincidence?"

Ella could not wrap her head around the information. Was this some sort of cruel joke? Was she a pawn in someone's dangerous game?

June broke the silence, "You see, Ella, Cristiano's first name is Gianni."

The sound of the name, Gianni, rolled through her mouth like spoiled milk.

June observed Ella's recognition and subsequent anguish; she dug the verbal knife in a bit further. "Yes, sweetie, the same Gianni that owns that great grocery store and coffee shop in Chicago that you love to frequent. You know, the one with all of your pictures in it. THAT Gianni is your high school lover boy, Gianni Cristiano Russo."

She paused for effect before dealing the final blow, "and the man your husband has been working with on this Chicago business deal that has consumed his time and...."

The uncontrollable shake of her knobby knees clicking together reverberated through Ella's body. She recalled all the times she thought she was going crazy thinking she had seen signs of Cristiano in Chicago, even convincing herself that she had seen the man, himself, on a couple of occasions.

But how are Cristiano and Emilie connected to Davis? she questioned. The words had barely formed in her scrambled thoughts when she figured out the missing piece to complete her terrifying puzzle. She recalled Davis telling her months ago when they were deciding where to spend their first week of summer vacation, that he wanted to go to Florida because there was plenty to keep her and the children busy, while he engaged in several business opportunities with an investor he had hooked up with three years earlier. He explained that they had met in Chicago and that the man had a keen sense of investment knowledge. He further explained that the man had personally been responsible for turning around several Chicago neighborhoods from drug, gang, and prostitute havens to upscale neighborhoods that drew young entrepreneurs. The man, he had told her, created an investment team, bought up slum areas, cleaned up the location, and renovated the old buildings or built high-end residential and commercial buildings.

When Ella questioned her husband about the people who lived in the areas, Davis responded, "This guy has people who are able to persuade the drug dealers, prostitutes, gang bangers, and homeless to move along to another location."

Ella thought about her gentle Italian and couldn't imagine him having an unkind bone in him, but it had been thirty years since she had seen the man, and people can change in thirty years. "After all," she thought, "look how much Davis changed the first year we were married."

She pondered the inevitable, "If Cristiano has the resources to get rid of bad guys..." She couldn't will herself to go there.

June broke the silence, "And you thought you knew these two men. I am trying to provide you with options to think about to help you figure out who might be behind this fun game we are playing. I will tell you what, you get a good night's sleep, and we will chat some more tomorrow."

Ella's breath caught in her throat when she heard her little girl's voice. "What game are we going to play today, Mommy?" Her kidnapper knew precisely how to torture her! The sound halted, and the room went dark.

Ella knew she had another long night alone in her black dungeon, with nothing but time to ponder this new information. Sleep did not find her until what she guessed was the wee hours of the next morning. Her only presumption that it was morning was the Amtrak train whistle several minutes after the dong, dong, dong, dong, dong, dong of the nearby church tower. She had taken the 6:20 a.m. train to Chicago on several occasions, so she guessed the passing of each day by the consistent sounds. Each time she heard them, she scraped a new notch in the wall. Today's mark was number sixteen. June had told her she would be held in her prison for thirty-two days. She didn't know what was magical about thirty-two days, but the thought of being only halfway through her hell was more than she could handle. Ella knew she didn't have sixteen more days in her. Sadness and fear engulfed her, and she leaned over the disgusting bucket and retched.

A cheerful, "Good Morning, Sunshine," startled her. June announced with a false apology, "Your little playhouse has gotten very dirty, but I am so busy cleaning your big house that I just don't have time for your tiny house. You see, I am multi-talented, and I have to have several jobs to keep a roof over your head and maintain all this fancy equipment to make sure you behave."

She paused for effect as she allowed Ella to picture the faces of the four women who had cleaned her house for the past two years.

"I know you thought it was ridiculous to have a cleaning service clean your house every week, so you cut us back to once a month. But, good news for us; Davis doesn't seem to be managing the home quite as well as you did, so he called and asked us if we could come back every two weeks."

June lied, "He specifically requested me, and I have to tell ya' it is nice to feel like I am back in such a comfortable setting. I had especially missed your bedroom."

Ella cringed at the mention of her bedroom. "Did Davis have a fling with one of the cleaning ladies?" She shook her head to shake off the ridiculous idea.

June continued, "I know as well as anyone that with Davis, everything has to be just so, but he has to take on extra duties with those brats of yours, so something has to give. I guess you can say he is a bit flustered. You know his phrase, 'Everything has a place, and that means that everything should be in its place!'" She made the statement matter-of-factly as if this were just one of many things she knew about Ella's husband.

Ella thought back to the many times he blew his stack when the children left their toys out. The worst nemesis were William's Legos and K'Nex pieces. It infuriated him that Ella didn't get rid of the toys years ago. On more than one occasion, Davis had told his wife, within earshot of their son, that William should have stopped playing with these immature toys years ago. Ella responded by explaining that William may one day be a great architect as a result of "playing with these toys." Davis dismissed this idea and reiterated the fact that she was making a pansy-ass out of their son.

Ella recalled spending the first Monday of each month getting ready for Ninja Cleaners to come the following day. She made arrangements to volunteer at the children's school while the women cleaned her house. It embarrassed her to have someone else do her work, and she felt that it was demeaning to the women to have her sitting around while they cleaned under her feet.

"Oh, and by the way, remember how I said I just can't help snooping? Well, I guess I was a little snoopy when I cleaned your house. That's how I found not one, but BOTH of your diaries. It seems as though Davis found the fake one you planted, but you hid your true feelings very well. Even I would have missed it, had I not had the help of my little camera. What is hilarious is that Davis is still going crazy scouring the house for your diary. It is so funny watching the man who prides himself on controlling his entire world, spiral so far out of control. Oh, yes, I STILL have cameras in your home, and I am amazed at what goes on behind closed doors when Momma is away."

June closed with, "We still have several days to reminisce about your diary entries; won't that be fun, Ella?"

Silence filled the small room. Ella hummed her children's lullaby in an attempt to soothe herself, and she cried herself to sleep.

June listened to Ella sing to her imaginary children and buried her head in her hands, fearful she would never experience the mother and child relationship she had watched between Ella and her children over the years.

Although Ella's entire body begged for rest, she did not sleep long; her mind wouldn't allow it. When she opened her eyes, she had to put Willow's pillow over her head to shield her eyes from the bright light. She rolled off her towel and onto her knees. She moved into child's pose to stretch her lower back before crawling over to her makeshift toilet to pee.

She was in mid-stream when June's voice came through the speaker, "Ella, you need to decide why we have taken you. If you can figure that out, you will earn an automatic "Get out of Jail Free" card. Now, sweetie, you have several possibilities, so let's have a brainstorming session. Is that a good idea?"

Ella made a feeble attempt to cover herself, but she no longer had the energy to be modest. She sat on the bucket and stared blankly at the eyeball of the camera. She finished urinating and pulled her underwear and yoga pants up over her raw, bony hips. The empty cardboard toilet paper roll lay next to the putrid toilet bucket. It no longer mattered. None of it mattered. She didn't care that she smelled like pee. Ella sat back on her dirty towel. She did not take her eyes off the camera; her gaze was cold and hollow.

June continued, "I suspect you have always thought people liked and respected you, correct? Well, let's assess the situation and see if that is really the case. Maybe you feel differently about your popularity now. But there is a difference between someone not liking you and wanting to hurt you, which takes your situation to a new level, do you agree?"

Ella nodded.

"OK, let's look at who has a reason to hurt you; there are several possibilities. Davis clearly has many reasons to make you go away, and he has pissed off just as many bad people who want to make you go away. You and your sissy have also had some rocky times as of late, mostly thanks to your hubby. Am I correct thus far?"

Ella closed her eyes and, again, nodded.

"But, we can't disregard your dark knight, Gianni Cristiano Russo, now, can we? He is the unknown factor. Did you spend some time thinking about him as you napped, sweetie?"

Ella's heart raced at the sound of his full name. The plethora of pictures she had received of the man she knew only as Cristiano, as he interacted with her husband and sister, squelched her naivety that he had no idea who Davis' wife was. The fact that he had been working so closely with her husband ripped her heart out. She felt betrayed by the only man she had ever loved.

June instructed Ella to go back through the artifacts she had gathered. As she perused her scrapbook, her memories flooded to Cristiano. The feeling of a knife through her heart took her breath away, as she pondered the possibility, and even likelihood, that Cristiano was behind her abduction.

33

The letter was once again addressed to Agent Drew Scott.

Mr. FBI Agents,

We are very disappointed in you. We threw you a bone with La Verità Caffe, and you stopped short of making a significant connection, you dumb asses. Soooooo, let us try again. What is the 'CONNECTION TO' La Verità Caffe? Here is a little more information to help you along, but we REALLY are tired of having to do your job for you."

Signed,
Of Names I Have Many

Underneath the words, a copy of a page torn out of a diary was taped to the paper. Scott awkwardly read the words as the men experienced the intimate and revealing truth about Davis and Ella Masters.

My Dearest C-

Last night was bad! I feel like I need to get out while I am still alive enough to get out, but I feel stuck-- like there really isn't a viable way out. I know it is ridiculous that I am pouring my heart out to you; it isn't like you will ever see these letters. Somehow, though, thinking that this letter might end up in your hands gives me hope. Call me a hopeless romantic, but you are my knight in shining armor...at least in my dreams...and my prayers.

We were in Chicago because Davis had a political fundraiser he said we had to attend. He was already upset with me because I was unable to get us a room at Trump Tower, so we had to stay at the Crowne Plaza. He drank more at the event than I had seen him drink in a long time. He had turned to whiskey early in the evening; that's when I realized I was going to have a long night. I sipped the same glass of wine all evening, knowing I needed all of my faculties if Davis were drinking like this.

Davis immediately went to the shower when we returned to the hotel. When I heard the shower water turn on, I stepped out on the balcony to get a breath of fresh air and to rid my nasal passages of the stench of alcohol and smoke that radiated from my drunk husband. I knew that this meant he was cleaning and sobering up a little because he planned on executing the plans he had not-so-quietly whispered into my ears several times throughout dinner, as the men in the group jealously laughed.

I stood on the five-foot by four-foot balcony and lost myself in the sights and sounds of Chicago nightlife. I stared obliviously out at the city at no particular object, thinking about my children…and about you. I found myself imagining you and your beautiful Italian wife, hand in hand, as you carried a small child to a local cafe for lunch.

Of course, I always prefer to have my children with me, but Davis purposely created trips that excluded the children. I knew it was not by accident. As I stood on the balcony thinking about William and Willow…and you, I was literally shaken back from my thoughts of them. I felt Davis' large hands squeezing my shoulders a little too hard. His words stunned me as much as his tight grip. 'You fucking like what you see? Are you getting off watching that guy? Is that scrawny body turning you on, you fucking whore?' Startled, I said, 'What are you even talking about?' Just then I saw the back side of a naked man walking through the balcony slider of an adjacent high-rise apartment tower.

'Did you get a good enough look?' Davis' slurred words spit into the side of my face. He grasped me by the hair and the nape of my neck. He firmly pushed my upper body, so my ribs were pressing the guardrail, cutting off my breath.

I tried to explain that I was thinking about the kids, but he just kept pressing me onto the railing.

'Honey, I swear I didn't even notice the man! I was off in my own world thinking about the children!' I breathlessly whispered, as my breath was being cut off. As he forced my head and shoulders further over the wrought-iron railing, my calves and then my thighs turned to noodles. The only thing holding me up was the grasp of Davis' forceful hands; the sight of the hard concrete fourteen floors below gave me the sensation of falling helplessly to my death. I struggled to catch my breath and not throw up the contents of my dinner, partially from my ribs being crushed into the railing and partially from the panic of being unable to escape my husband's massive hands. After what seemed like hours, Davis finally released his grip, called me a fucking whore a couple more times, and walked back through the slider. My legs gave away, and I wilted down to my bottom on the concrete base of the balcony. I leaned against the sturdy walls of the brick balcony dividers and threw up the contents of my lobster dinner.

I could hear Davis snoring in the bed just inside the room, but I did not have the strength to go back inside. My legs lay limp, like noodles that had been overcooked. The good news was that I escaped the sexual experience he had threatened as punishment for not getting a room at Trump Tower. The bad news was that I had two more days of this trip to survive, emotionally and physically.

As Davis slept off his hangover the next morning, I walked over to La Verità Caffe and bought two coffees. When I returned to the hotel room, the slider was open, but I could not will my legs to return to the balcony where Davis stood, so I sat on the bed and waited for him to come back into the room. I actually think I saw a slight look of remorse on his face as I handed him his plain black coffee. I knew that was the extent of any apology I would ever receive from him, but it did slightly ensure that he would be a bit gentler with me the rest of the trip.

One of these times, C., I fear that Davis is going to get too drunk or too mad to stop himself from going beyond his limits, and I might end up very hurt… or VERY dead.

-E-

The two agents stood quietly for several moments as if they were in attendance at a funeral visitation.

Finally, Agent Scott said, "Do you think she wanted out badly enough that she feigned her abduction and is sitting on some beach in Mexico, maybe with the 'C' fellow? Who is the intended recipient of the letter, or is it not really a letter, but actually a diary entry? Furthermore, why is Ella writing the most intimate details of her life to this man, and how did the letter end up in our hands?"

Gibbons looked back at the first sentence of the letter and questioned Scott, "What is connected to La Verità Caffe...Literally?"

Scott replied, "Cristiano's."

Gibbons nodded, "And what did chatty Kathy tell us Gianni's prized project was?... So much that he named it after himself?"

Scott made the connection, "Cristiano, which starts with a C."

"AND...who has many names?" Gibbons added.

Scott nodded in understanding, "Gianni Cristiano Russo."

As if he had found the missing border piece of a puzzle under the table leg, Scott added, "Think about the poem we got the other day. It was a name poem, and the answer was 'Davis' shadow.' Does this mean someone is hidden behind Davis or that Davis is overshadowing someone? And what about the reference 'but from me, you can't run?' Is someone not able to run from Davis, or more likely, is this person making sure Davis can't run from his shadow?

"That's exactly where I was going!" Gibbons replied, "If, indeed, this diary was written to C for Cristiano, why does everything keep coming back to Gianni Russo? Do you think he somehow got hold of Ella's diary?"

"I guess it is time we figure that out. Maybe Gianni Russo knows Ella Masters better than we think. Let's give Mr. Russo another call. "

Gianni Russo stared blankly at the breathtaking skyline through the large panoramic windows of his office. He felt his world closing in around him, and suddenly all of his business success seemed for naught. Kathy had taken the day off to attend an art festival, and he welcomed the quiet. He knew his secretary had been walking on eggshells around him for the past several days because he was in an uncharacteristically depressed mood.

His office phone rang. He saw the 2-1-7 area code and froze. He finally picked up the receiver after four rings.

"Revitalize Chicago, Inc. Mr. Russo speaking."

"Good day, Mr. Russo, This is Agent Drew Scott from Springfield, Illinois. I was expecting Kathy to answer."

Doing his best to repress his pounding heart, Russo replied, "Hello Agent Scott. Kathy took the day off, so I am manning the office." He paused nervously, "How is everything going with your investigation?"

"Well, Mr. Russo, that is what I am calling about. You were very helpful when we came to visit you, but since our visit, new evidence has caused us to look at old leads with a new set of eyes."

Gianni's hands began to visibly shake, and the receiver became slippery in his sweaty palms; he held his breath and waited nervously for Agent Scott's next words.

"Mr. Russo, looking back on our last interview, Gibbons and I realized we weren't specific enough."

Russo nodded slowly, knowing where the question was heading and feeling relieved the agents could not see the guilt on his face.

Scott continued, "When we asked you if you knew Ella Masters, you responded, 'Mr. Master's never introduced his wife to me. He kept her, and the children separate from his business affairs,' but you didn't really answer the question, sir, did you?"

Russo knew this was a rhetorical question, so instead of answering it, he took a deep breath, and asked, "Sir, do you know what La Verità means?"

"No clue, sir."

Russo continued, "La Verità is Italian for 'the truth.'" After a resigned pause, he said, "I guess it is La Verità time; it is 'Truth' time."

Scott and Gibbons listened to Gianni Russo as he told them the story that had been eating him alive for years. Gibbons explained that he and Ella had hit it off when she visited his home country after her senior year in high school. He told the officers that he is a twin and therefore they had a twin connection. Russo admitted that when she left Italy, she took his heart with her. He knew she lived in the state called Illinois in the United States, so he decided to move to that state with the hopes of maybe running into her.

As if apologizing, he said, "I know, I sound like a hopeless romantic, but that girl did a number on me."

Neither agent responded, so Gianni continued, "I knew of Chicago, so I thought that would be a good place to move. After attending university, I worked hard for several years in my family's vineyards. My family had done well in the vino business, so my papa set me up financially until I was able to make my own finances."

Both agents took scratched notes as they listened.

"The day my momma and papa and twin sister waved goodbye, as they watched me go through security, my papa said, 'Andate a trovare il tuo vero amore,' which means 'Go find your true love.' It was hard leaving my family, but I knew what I wanted, and I needed to at least see if it was possible."

Agent Scott wrote, "Motive!!!????" and slid the note to Gibbons.

Gianni continued, "To make a long story short, I located Emilie Randolph before I found Ella; it was easy because she was in Chicago and her name had not changed. I added her on Facebook, but my account was generic when I first moved to Chicago, so she wouldn't have even known that I lived there. She and I didn't have direct communication, nor did I post things on my Facebook, but I was able to see pictures of Ella and her family. I found out Ella's last name was Masters through Emilie's Facebook page, but when I searched for a Facebook account for Ella Masters, there was none. I did, however, find an account for her husband, Davis Masters. I wasn't impressed.

As if he could read the agents' minds, Gianni said, "I know this sounds like some sort of, how do you say it, stalker story, but it wasn't like that at all. I knew if Ella was happily married, then my path was not meant to cross her path again."

He continued, "Ironically, her husband, Davis, signed up for a seminar I run for individuals who are trying to forge their way into the urban development industry. He was looking to extend his investment opportunities to the Chicago area. In the meantime, I ran into Emilie Randolph at a Chicago function, and we developed an acquaintanceship."

Agent Gibbons raised one eyebrow at his partner.

Russo continued, "Emilie confirmed my initial opinion that Davis Masters is not a nice man, and Ella deserves so much better."

This brought another raised eyebrow, this one by Scott.

As if Russo had been given a dose of truth serum, he said, "I'm gonna come clean."

The man paused, and Scott held his breath for what he thought he might hear.

Russo inhaled and exhaled deeply and loudly. "I feel like Ella's disappearance might be my fault. See, I suspected that Davis was obtaining his funds by shady means, including stealing from Ella's parents. Emilie all but confirmed it; she tried several times to talk to her sister about it, but Ella never wanted to discuss it. A couple of years ago, they had a pretty big blow out over Davis, and the twins' relationship has been strained ever since. I know recently Emilie has confronted Ella on several occasions because Davis is pilfering her father's money. Emilie and I devised a plan to try to squeeze Davis out. I made him an investment offer that I knew he wouldn't have the financial means to support, without stealing a great deal of Ella's daddy's money or obtaining the money in some other illegal manner. Emilie and I knew he would only have the audacity to contact her if he was at his wit's end; that would tell us that Ella was not in his plan to steal her father's money. I gave Davis a deadline I knew he couldn't meet, but things went wrong…terribly wrong. I don't know if he had engaged in other bad deals to try to get the money, or if he planned on using his wife's disappearance to get some sort of ransom money, and the plan backfired."

Russo's ordinarily smooth voice became more agitated and panicky the more he spoke, "Agent Scott, Agent Gibbons, I would pay any amount of money…heck, I would give my life…I just need Ella to get back safely to her children. Like I said, if my actions precipitated harm to Ella, I will never be able to live with myself…and just so you know, I know Emilie seems a little like a high-society snob, but she loves her sister. She would never do anything to harm Ella; she was just trying to nail Davis. She and I fear we pushed Davis over the edge, and he took drastic measures to get the money."

Agent Scott genuinely thanked Russo for his honesty and said, "We are doing everything in our power to get Ella back to her children. It isn't like whoever has her isn't giving us clues; we just can't seem to put them all together."

He added, "Russo, can you let us know if Davis or anybody else attempts to contact you?"

Russo agreed, saying, "It is the least I can do."

Agent Gibbons was already dialing Davis number before Agent Scott hung up the phone.

"Hello," Davis' slurred words bellowed into the phone a little too loudly, causing Gibbons to instinctively take the phone away from his ear.

"Good afternoon, Davis. This is Agent Gibbons. I am calling you to let you know we have an update on your wife's disappearance if you have some time to meet with us today, that will be great."

Davis' voice caught as he slowly said, "OK, do I need my attorney?"

Gibbons thought it was a telling response and said, "That is your call, sir."

Davis slurred, "I think I better. Can you give me an hour?"

"Sure, Davis, we will meet you at your house in an hour, does that work?"

"Yes, that works," Davis stammered, already walking to the kitchen to make himself a strong pot of coffee.

Gibbons hung up the phone and said, "We need to break this guy down. He is one cocky son-of-a-bitch. I know he has to somehow be responsible for Ella's disappearance, and I sure as hell wasn't about to give him a heads-up about Gianni over the phone.

An hour later, the two FBI agents sat across from Davis and his attorney, Erik Dubin, at Davis' dining room table. Davis was clean-shaven and fresh out of the shower. He wore navy dress pants, a yellow Polo dress shirt, and a navy and yellow striped tie. He nervously chewed mint-flavored gum. His hand, the agents noticed, was bandaged.

Mr. Dubin wore a tailor-made suit that Scott decided cost one of his clients an afternoon in court. It was expensive, and the guy wanted the agents to know it. He and Davis looked like they could be brothers. They both had tan skin, but Dubin's was a bit more leather-like. They both had bright smiles, that were much too white, thanks to new-fangled teeth-whitening systems that had recently hit the market.

Scott nodded toward Davis' bandaged hand, "It looks like you had a mishap."

"It's nothing. I dropped a glass in the dishwasher, and when I reached in to pick up the pieces, one got me pretty good. It didn't need stitched, but it bled like a son-of-a-bitch."

Scott continued, not really interested in the man's injury, "It appears as though you are quite the busy man with a variety of interests, with very little time left at the end of the day for your family. Also, we know you have stretched your money, or should I say, your wife's money a bit further than you should have."

The agents did not make small talk. They got right to the point. They asked Davis if he had ever heard the name, Cristiano. Davis, looking confused, questioned, "Do you mean a person or a business? I know the name of the grocery store Cristiano's, in Chicago."

Scott said, "And how do you know that name, Mr. Masters?"

Davis felt like he was being lured into a trap, so he said, evasively, "I go to the store often when I am in Chicago. They have a lot of healthy, ready-made meals."

"I see," Scott responded, "and do you happen to know the developer behind that building?"

Davis said, "Gianni Russo developed that city block."

The agents looked at each other before Gibbons spoke. "Do you know why it is called Cristiano's?"

They could tell by the blank stare Davis gave them that he was clueless.

"Mr. Masters, let me get straight to the point. It seems as though you aren't the only one who knows Mr. Russo. We have evidence that...uhhhh... your wife was quite familiar with the gentleman as well."

"What are you talking about," Davis felt his face reddening. "I never even introduced Ella to Gianni; you MUST be mistaken! I kept my business life separate from my personal life."

"Well, Mr. Masters," Gibbons explained, "it seems as though your wife kept her personal life separate from your business life." The agent actually delighted in watching Davis loosen his tie and unbutton the top button of his dress shirt. He knew what a scumbag this guy was, and he reveled in watching him writhe over the thought of his wife being involved with another man. "You see, Davis, it seems as though Ella and Gianni go all the way back to high school."

Davis' face contorted with confusion. "But that can't be...," he caught himself.

"Why can't that be, Mr. Masters?" The investigator knew there was a hole in Davis' story, and he needed to find a way to get him to reveal that hole.

Davis caught himself and quickly regained his composure. "You see, Mr. Russo isn't even from the United States; he is from Italy." He sat back in his chair with a smug look on his newly composed face.

With an equally smug look and a smirk added for effect, Gibbons retorted, "Ahhhh, you mean Italy, the place where young girls fall in love with beautiful Italian boys? The same Italy where Ella and Emilie went for their senior graduation present from their parents? Do you mean THAT Italy?"

A flash of something the officers could not place, crossed Davis' face.

His attorney saw the look also and said, "Gentlemen, you need to stop toying with my client and get out with whatever evidence you say you have."

His attempted intervention was too late. Davis could no longer keep his composure. His feathers were beyond ruffled, "If that son-of-a-bitch has hurt my wife, I will..."

"You will what, Davis? Just what WILL you do?"

"What do you know about this guy?" Davis snapped.

The investigator snapped back, "Davis, we are the ones asking the questions here. It sounds as though you have had control over all of your puppets, your wife included, for many years. But here, my friend, we are in control. So, how about you get comfortable and tell us everything you know about this man."

Davis' attorney said, "That will be enough gentlemen. My client is finished talking."

Gibbons said, "That is fine, but just so you know, the longer your client chooses not to be forthright, the longer it will take us to find his wife. You both know the longer it takes us to find her, the more likely it is that she will be dead when we do find her."

He directed his attention to his partner, "Drew, let's go get that search warrant we talked about."

Davis Masters' ordinarily tan face turned pale.

As the two agents saw themselves to the front door, they heard Davis' attorney hiss, "Davis, you better come clean with me right now. I can't help you if you are keeping shit from me."

Agents Scott and Gibbons smiled. They knew they would receive a phone call within the hour.

Davis' attorney, called Agent Gibbons at 4:20 p.m. He apologized for his client's behavior and asked the agents to please take into consideration the emotional stress Mr. Masters was under. He added that Davis was not aware that his wife had a relationship with Gianni Russo and that he had never told her the man's name. He added, for good measure, that his client was more-than-willing to cooperate with the investigation and would be more restrained in future interviews.

34

Ella listened to the sounds of the relentless rain for hours and assumed it was once again night by the decrease of automobile traffic and the increase of sirens in the city that moved just outside her prison. The orchestrated tunes of two crickets chirping in opposite corners of another part of the basement played their own symphony; at times they made music together, and then one would silence itself and give the other the floor for a solo performance. Ella marveled at how they found the energy to keep the melodic tunes up for hours. She pictured their skinny legs moving back and forth like a bow slides on a violin. She looked at her own frail legs; her shriveled muscles hung loosely from the bones.

Water from the most recent rains seeped along the edges of the carpet, forcing Ella to move her precious items away from the walls, thus further closing in the walls of her prison.

Three water bugs joined her in her lonely box. She hated water bugs, but she could not bring herself to kill her new roommates. Symbolically, they represented life, or maybe the devaluation of such. Many a water bug faced its demise under the sole of a crushing shoe, often accompanied by shrieks of terror, sounds of disgust, or mumbled cursing, but these would escape a tragic end-- at least on this night.

Ella took a piece of paper, gently scooped up the large black bugs, one at a time, and placed them in the plastic cottage cheese container that had served as her dinner bowl. She sealed the lid to ensure they stayed where they were. The moment she clicked the cap closed, she felt a mix of remorse, disgust, and angst. She was no more valued than these bugs. She had been put in a container and locked away, sealed up tight, with no chance of getting out. For a split second, she thought about releasing the trio, with their antennae moving in hyper-motion as they scurried around the edges of the bowl, but she couldn't handle the thought of them crawling all over her through another sleepless night. She felt sad about her choice. Occasionally, she heard a quiet thud in the sealed plastic container, and she knew one of the bugs had landed on its back in a futile attempt to escape. She envisioned the little guy's legs moving frantically in an effort to resume an upright position in his new prison.

The musty smell of her damp towel on the concrete floor sickened her. She shivered at the situation of her living quarters. She had spent many nights in the outdoors in nothing more than her hammock. She had faced swarms of gnats and mosquitos big enough to carry her away, but she would trade a hundred of those experiences to breathe in the fresh air of freedom.

She carefully placed the cottage cheese container in a far corner, so she didn't have the constant visual of the same horrific act that was being done to her. She tried to push out the thought of her own possible demise under the crushing heel of the three strangers who had ultimate control of her fate. Had they put her in her own unpleasant container to keep her ultimately safe, as she had done with the water bugs, or were they just waiting to bring their crushing heel down on her life, leaving her children without their mommy?

She propped her small pillow up against the wall and made a futile attempt at getting some sleep. Just as she got settled, June's voice sounded on the other side of the wooden door. Fear gripped Ella, and she questioned how she didn't hear June come down the stairs.

"How could you go to sleep without story time, silly? Your new little friends might be lulled to sleep by tonight's story, too. What a tender act?"

The scoffing tone of June's voice indicated her lack of sincerity in her statement.

Ella reluctantly listened to the words from her own journal, and the memories of the night flooded back like a tsunami.

My Dearest C,

It was a bad fight-one of the worst ever. The kids had gone to Momma and Daddy's for the weekend because Davis had a fundraiser for one of his companies. I don't like attending these events because everyone is so full of themselves that it feels like the whole room might explode. But things were already tense in our marriage, and I knew if I didn't go, the scene would be ugly, especially since he didn't usually invite me to his events. At the fundraiser, liquid spirits flowed, and the crowd grew louder as the night progressed.

As always, I took the role of observer. I have an uncanny ability to be involved in one conversation and still know everything else that is going on around me. As I stood, talking to a group of wives I barely knew, I saw Davis walk by a little blonde with a dress that left nothing to the imagination. He brushed her arm, tugged at her elbow and walked out of the room. Within minutes, the blond with way too much eye makeup, walked out the same door, but not before I took my cell phone out of my small purse and snapped a picture of her. Blondie saw me bring the camera up to shoulder level, and she smiled a "fuck you" bitchy smile at me as I snapped the picture. She flipped her hair and walked out the same door that Davis had just exited.

I was in no position to follow them because I didn't know the homeowners, and I knew if I went looking, someone might see me. My anxiety was at its highest. All I could do was mingle with the group of women I barely knew and act as if everything was OK, while my insides were burning with hurt, envy, and mostly rage!

Twenty minutes later, Davis returned to the party through the front door, but Blondie had disappeared. Davis immediately approached the group in which I was attempting to mingle. In a boisterous voice, he said, "There's my little lady; I've been looking for you!" I know my response was inexcusable, but I couldn't stop the words from running out of my mouth. It must have been the four glasses of champagne I downed within the first twenty minutes. Not only was the response inexcusable, I knew it wouldn't be forgotten-- at least not that night. I immediately retorted, "I've been in the exact same spot as I was when you and Blondie walked out of the room twenty minutes ago." The deafening sound of silence permeated throughout the intimate group. Davis laughed the comment off, adding "Yes, dear, work doesn't stop for a cocktail party. Sensenya and I had to meet a group from Business Tech International to close a big deal on a new building project. I just made us more money, so you can keep driving your fancy Benz." He knows I hate driving a Mercedes Benz; it is so ostentatious. His smile burned through me, and the heat, combined with the champagne, made me feel like my legs might give out. Davis downed the rest of his Jack and Coke and said, "Now, how about we get on home and take advantage of the kids being at Grandpa's." I knew I was in trouble, and I was correct.

That night was, for me, the beginning of the end. Davis blew up and started screaming at me. Before I knew it, he had me pinned to the couch. He was nearly pulling my hair out of my head with his left hand while his right clenched fist was balled up just inches from my face. I saw my own brutal beating flash before my eyes. I know Davis is capable of hurting me beyond repair. The rage in his eyes told me he wanted to kill me. I knew I would never see my babies again.

I gave up. I remember my words as if I spoke them yesterday. "Go ahead and hit me, Davis!" Be the man you really are! Go ahead, FUCKING HIT ME!" He tightened his coiled fingers deeper into my hair and twisted. He brought his gnarled face as close as his fisted hand, and with the stench of alcohol on his breath through gritted teeth he said, "You disgust me, bitch! You aren't worth going to jail for!" He forced his tongue into my mouth and moved his clenched fist into the top of my dress and twisted my breasts until I whimpered like a puppy that had been kicked in the ribs."

-E-

Ella cowered at the words she had written.

June said, "I probably don't need to tell you the rest of the story, do I? After all, you wrote it. And so you know, a copy of this diary entry has been mailed to both Davis and the police" She knew this was a lie, but Ella didn't.

"Oh," she continued, this time telling the truth. "I also sent the original to Cristiano for good measure. Sorry, I ruined your pretty journal by tearing a page out of it, but I thought Cristiano would want to know his damsel is in distress. Maybe he will be able to save you. After all, Davis needs to be held accountable for the way he has treated us."

The words resonated with Ella.

This IS about another woman-- this woman, June, Ella realized. *Davis had some sort of relationship with her, and he treated her poorly. Had he physically, sexually, and/or emotionally abused her also?*

The words forced Ella to accept that Davis had done all those things to her, and she knew that the strange woman on the other side of the wall literally held the truth in her hands. June had repeated so many times, *And the truth shall set you free.*

Who has to be truthful? she wondered. *If my release is based on Davis' truthfulness, I am in grave danger,* she admitted quietly and sadly to herself.

The whispered words, "I'm sorry this happened to you!" escaped June's mouth before she could grab them back. Dead silence followed by rushed footsteps up the stairs told Ella that June was upset, and that meant there was a chance the woman had some compassion.

Maybe, just maybe, I can find a way to appeal to her compassion, Ella thought as she said her nightly prayers. Her mind, and the bright light that had not been turned off, would not allow her the gift of sleep.

35

The caller chanted the riddle and then promptly disconnected:

"Olly Olly oxen free
You get two for one in me
What does that mean?
You'll have to see."

Davis scribbled the riddle on the back of an envelope, and Emilie's face flashed through his mind. He tapped the pencil on the words, "Two for One." Was his sister-in-law behind this nightmare, or was someone fucking with him? Every riddle made him suspect a new person, and it was driving him crazy. It also brought to light just how many people hated him. As he read over the riddle, he wondered if his sister-in-law was playing him like a fiddle. And what was up with her waltzing back into his family's lives looking just like her sister?

Why did you do that Emilie? he said to himself.

The fact that there was no love-loss between Emilie and Davis was evident to most. Although he had developed many enemies over the years, Davis despised Ella's identical twin more than he hated anyone. Her newfound access to his home felt like a total invasion of his private world. He was afraid to leave her alone in the house because he knew she would snoop into her twin sister's life-- and subsequently his life.

He was between a rock and a hard place, though, because he needed her help with the children. Davis' mind was still whirring from the phone call and the newest riddle when Emilie sauntered through the back door with a bag full of groceries and began putting them away as if she had lived in the house forever. He realized he needed to get her out of his house once-and-for-all, but he had to do so without making it look too obvious.

Davis made the not-so-subtle suggestion, "Maybe it would be a good idea for you to temporarily move yourself and the children to your daddy's lake house to get them out of our house since it has so many memories of their mother."

Emilie gritted through clenched teeth, "What do you mean, memories? You have already written my sister off for dead. Is that because you know what has happened to her? Well, they say, 'Keep your friends close and your enemies closer;' I need to keep you VERY close, Davis! You are not going to go on living your sordid life while the kids and I are looking for Ella. You and I both know you are somehow behind this, and you know that I will find out what you have done to my sister. You aren't shipping your kids, or me, off, so that you can keep all of your little secrets hidden and keep going on with your fucking life. You succeeded once at keeping me away from my sister, and I may regret that for the rest of my life. But not this time, asshole; you are stuck with me, and I will use every connection I have to make your life miserable!"

With equal disdain, Davis responded, "You don't even know your sister-- or the rest of your family for that matter. Springfield, Illinois was never good enough for you from the time you were old enough to flaunt your rich-bitch attitude. You had to run off to Chicago and leave your sister to take care of your parents. You walked into the police station like you owned the world. You have been a bitch from the time you were sixteen years old"... Davis stopped, quickly, but not quickly enough.

"How would you know what I was like when I was sixteen years old?" Emilie questioned, with an accusatory tone. She had picked up on Davis' hesitation and wanted to take advantage of his off-kilter behavior. She continued her verbal disparagement of him. "My sister would have never said those things about me, so just where did those words come from unless you know more about my childhood than you should?"

Davis didn't take the bait, mostly because he had never fared very well when he and Emilie butted heads. She may have been a bitch, but she was smart and resourceful-- two qualities he didn't like in a woman. He turned, began whistling, and walked out of the room.

Emilie stood in the kitchen, a glass jar of olives in her hand, and resisted the urge to pummel the jar across the room at Davis. She recalled the glass of wine flying through the air and Davis slapping her, but now wasn't the time for revenge. She couldn't risk doing something that would cause him not to allow her to see the kids.

36

Drew Scott and Brad Gibbons continued to investigate Davis' business transactions and Gianni's possible connection to the case. They had not received any new evidence into the disappearance of Ella Masters in a few days, but all that changed when the daily mail arrived.

The small package had the same return address, but this time the package was post-marked Pontiac, Illinois. The note on top read, "Thought we would make our way a bit closer to home since you idiots can't seem to figure anything out." Under the note in the box was a small silver flip phone. The sticky note on the phone read, "Sorry I am not charged."

Scott wrote down the make and model of the phone and sent his secretary to Walmart to find a matching charger.

Three hours later, he had combed the incoming and outgoing calls, texts and photos and compared them to the other numbers they had in their files. The experience was enlightening. Several people had some explaining to do.

Agent Scott called Davis and said, "We received some new evidence that might shed light on your wife's disappearance. Can we come to your house at 4:30 today?"

Davis said, "Yes, I will call Ella's friend, Kristina, and ask if the kids can play at her house for a while."

"That would be good, Davis," Scott replied. "Is Erik Dubin available?"

Davis did not like the fact that Scott suggested he have his attorney present.

"I spoke with him this morning, so I think he is probably available."

Scott couldn't help himself from smirking as he pictured Dubin standing on a platform being fit for a brand new suit. He stifled a laugh.

"Is Emilie at the house?"

"No," replied Davis, "She is at her father's house for the afternoon and evening."

"OK, thank you, we will see you in a couple of hours. I would not say anything to Emilie about the new evidence just yet if I were you. Let's see what you think of it first," Scott finished. He hoped his words would insinuate they had evidence against Emilie, so Davis' defenses were not heightened.

Davis, in his paranoid state, did not get the insinuation. Instead, his first thought was that they had new evidence that might incriminate him. When he replayed the agent's words, he breathed a little easier, thinking maybe they did have evidence that might confirm Davis' suspicions about his sister-in-law.

At 4:25, the back door shut, and Emilie walked through the kitchen.

"What are you doing here?" Davis said, startled.

Emilie saw his confusion, "Agent Gibbons called to tell me they received new evidence and asked If I could meet them here at 4:30."

"What are you talking about? Agent Scott called me with the same information, only, he told me not to mention anything to you," he said hesitantly. As he said the words, he realized the agents were setting both of them up. By the look on Emilie's face, she had arrived at the same conclusion.

Before the two could process or discuss what was happening, the front doorbell rang. Davis and Emilie saw Scott and Gibbons through the frosted glass of the front door.

Davis took a deep breath and opened the door.

"Good afternoon, Mr. Masters, thank you for your time," Scott began.

Agent Gibbons followed with, "And good afternoon, Ms. Randolph, thank you for your time."

Davis stopped dead in his tracks as he eyed the small flip phone, carefully protected in a plastic evidence bag. His already weary face showed a combination of worry and disbelief. If the police had found his phone in Florida, why would it have taken them eighteen days to bring it up.

Agent Scott caught the shock as Davis' wide eyes locked on the phone, and said, "This must look familiar by the surprised look on your face, Mr. Masters. Maybe you better have a seat! You look like you've seen a ghost."

Agent Gibbons turned to Emilie, who also glared at the small flip phone. "Maybe we can get a glass of water, or maybe some tea if you have any made. How about we sit outside on the back patio? It is such a nice day that I hate being stuck inside."

The knock on the front door caused Emilie and Davis both to jump. "That must be Dubin." Davis said. He raced to the front door, with a nervous energy that caused him to have an awkward gate. Scott wondered if he had already been into the sauce.

Emilie did not like the feel of the situation. She poured five glasses of iced tea. She took three glasses to Davis, Dubin, and Agent Scott, who had retreated to the living room. She glared at Davis when she handed him the tea. She retrieved the final two teas from the kitchen and tried not to spill them in her shaking hands as she made her way outside, where Agent Gibbons awaited her.

The two sat at the wrought iron table in the shade of the warm summer day, and Agent Gibbons said in a gentle voice, "Emilie, things aren't looking so great for your sister, mostly because there have been more lies in this investigation than truths. Whoever kidnapped Ella has made it clear that if any family member receives three strikes in whatever game we are all part of, your sister will be killed; Davis has already received two strikes."

"It is time you come clean with me. We had a nice visit with Gianni Cristiano Russo a couple of days ago, and he told us all about your relationship."

The color drained from Emilie's face.

Gibbons was surprised by her extreme physical reaction. "Did Gianni not tell us everything?" he wondered.

Aloud, he said, "Emilie, your color does not look good. Are you feeling OK?"

"I'm fine," Emilie stammered, "What did Gianni tell you?"

"Well, Miss Randolph, he told us everything, but I would like to hear your version of the story."

Was this a setup? she questioned inwardly, *But how would they know Davis had a throw-away if it wasn't legitimately his phone?* Her thoughts spiraled like a tornado as she tried to decide just how honest she needed to be with the FBI agent.

As if Gibbons could read her mind, he said, "Emilie, we know everything, and the longer it takes you to confirm Gianni's story, the longer it will take us to find your sister, and the more likely the result won't be good. That could leave you in a heap of trouble. I don't think I need to give you the laundry list of ways you will be implicated in your sister's disappearance and death, if, God forbid, something like that happens."

Emilie took in a deep breath, looked through the French doors of the kitchen as if she feared Davis could hear her. She told her story of hating Davis, reuniting with Gianni Cristiano Russo, and devising a plan to get Davis out of her family's life once and for all by landing him in jail for embezzlement or at least making her sister see the thief she had married for who he was. Emilie, however, told Agent Gibbons the whole story, including the part about her one-night stand with Gianni. She left out the part about the abortion.

Gibbons thought, "Ahhhh, I thought Mr. Russo was sincere, but he left out one major detail."

When a visibly shaken Emilie finished her story, Gibbons gently said, "Emilie, that is the exact story Gianni told us...only, he didn't mention the intimate relationship between the two of you. It is interesting that, as honest as he was, he left out that part."

A mixture of regret and sadness welled up in Emilie. Gibbons read the emotion on her face and explained, "I am sure he thought it might put the spotlight on you if he told me. It might look like a classic jealous sister situation, you know what I mean?"

He felt genuinely regretful saying the words he didn't really believe, so he quickly said, "The information you and Gianni gave us match almost exactly with the details we gathered from the cell phones. I wish you would have been more forthcoming during your early interviews; we have lost nearly three weeks in the investigation, and in crimes like these, every minute counts."

Guilt riddled Emilie, and she broke down in tears. "I love my sister, and I just want her back."

Gibbons said, "I'm not sure how Davis is going to handle the interview, so I think it is best that you leave now. You probably need to stay at your father's house until this whole thing is over. We will make arrangements to have your things taken there. I don't want you to have any more contact with Davis until the investigation is complete."

Emilie nodded in understanding, but said, genuinely, "But what about the children? They have been through so much, and Davis is not equipped to take care of them. I know Davis and I have had our disagreements, to say the least, but right now, my only concern is that my niece and nephew are ok... Well, that, and seeing my sister again."

Gibbons silently agreed with Emilie. He said, "We will come up with an arrangement with Davis for the two of you to split childcare. I don't think he will have a problem with that because he seems overwhelmed with the task. We will have an agent pick the kids up from here or your father's house to ensure you don't have to interact with Davis."

Emilie thought about Davis' suggestion of this very situation only a couple days earlier, and she wondered if he would still think it was a good idea. For the kids' sake, she hoped so.

Emilie slipped back into the kitchen, grabbed her purse and keys, and did as Agent Gibbons had suggested; she drove to her daddy's house. She wondered if she would have any more contact with Davis.

Oblivious to the fact that Emilie had left, Davis tried to control the wringing of his sweaty hands as Scott carefully placed the clear evidence bag on the table. Davis' eyes were locked on the throw-away phone that lay encased in the sealed bag in front of him.

Agent Scott had not jumped right into questioning Davis about the phone. Instead, he updated him on the generalities of the investigation of his missing wife and asked about the children's physical and emotional well-being.

After several minutes of sipping cold tea and watching Davis appear as though he was about to experience internal combustion, Scott spoke, "Mr. Masters, would you like to tell us what you know about this phone?"

Dubin interjected, "Agent Scott, let's not play games. Why don't you tell us what is on the phone, and then you can ask my client specific questions."

Scott didn't take the nibble. "No, thank you, I would prefer that Davis provide us with the information."

Dubin sat back, slightly deflated, but unsure about how to proceed.

Davis tried to discern if the agent knew what was on the phone, or if Scott was calling his bluff. If the cell phone had been destroyed and Davis spilled his guts about the numbers on the phone, he would seal his own fate for no reason, but if the cell phone had not been destroyed, Davis was in a hell of a lot of trouble. It was a kind of trouble he knew Dubin probably couldn't get him out of, because every lie he had told would now be refuted.

Agent Gibbons joined Scott and Davis in the living room. Gibbons explained that Emilie had to go to her father's house, which was evasive, but not a lie. He explained, "Your sister-in-law will be staying at her father's house for the time being. She and I discussed the possibility of the children spending part of their time here with you and part of their time with her and their grandfather. I think it will be good for them to be able to spend time with their grandfather, and it will give you a chance to have a break from childcare."

Davis didn't like the idea of Emilie having contact with the children outside of his control, but he also knew he needed help with the kids.

"That would probably be best for the children," Dubin spouted.

Agent Gibbons continued, "We will make arrangements to transport the children back and forth, so you and Emilie no longer need to be in contact with each other."

This caught Davis off-guard. "OOOO-KKKKK," he responded, with a clear questioning tone. His stomach churned at the thought of what information Gibbons and Emilie's interview produced.

Getting back on track, Agent Scott said, "Mr. Masters, Ella's captors have told us about the "three strikes" game, and they recently let us know that you have two strikes. Emilie and William have not received any strikes. If you are not forthright with us today, you might put the final nails into your wife's coffin."

He knew this was a harsh statement, but he wanted Davis to talk. "So, how about if you tell me what you know about the flip phone I have in this evidence bag."

"Where did you get that?" Davis asked, almost defiantly.

Dubin placed his hand on Davis' forearm; it was a silent reminder for him to settle down.

"Davis, I think you should be the one to answer that question," Scott said, just as defiantly. "I will, however, answer your question of whether or not it is in working condition." Without compromising the evidence by opening the bag, Scott opened up the flip phone through the plastic, and the phone lit up. "This phone is your phone; it is very much active, and your phone calls and text messages up until around 8:00 p.m. on Monday, June 2nd are still on it," Scott said matter-of-factly.

He continued, "We can do things a couple of ways here. You can tell me about the texts to Natalia, in addition to your phone calls to the sister-in-law you supposedly can't stand, all on the day of your wife's disappearance, or we can arrest you right now for obstruction of justice. It makes no difference to us.

Before Dubin could object, Scott said, "And we have plenty of evidence to put your client in handcuffs right now."

Dubin's mouth hung open.

Davis was glad he was sitting, because his legs tingled and went limp. He took a drink of tea, but it did not quench his cotton mouth. His words feel like gravel.

Davis reluctantly told the agents about his relationship with Natalia, brushing it off as a short-term affair that meant nothing.

Dubin cringed as his client spoke.

Masters gave a less-honest explanation about his calls to Emilie. He told the men that she had been harassing his family for years, insisting that he and his wife had been pilfering funds from family accounts. His phone call, he lied, was in response to her most recent tirade. He called his sister-in-law to tell her to quit harassing his wife.

After a forty-five-minute interview, the agents saw themselves out the front door. Gibbons filled Scott in on his interview with Emilie on the drive back to the agency. When they returned to their office, they added notes from the interviews to the large whiteboard, titled "Ella Masters." Once they updated the notes, they sat back and analyzed the composite of information.

Back at the Masters' residence, Dubin was trying to put a plan together to do damage control for his train-wreck-of-a-client and thinking about what color his new suit would be.

37

June decided she had not tortured Ella enough. She belted Alan Jackson's "Who's Cheatin' Who" through the speakers. A women's duet, "Does He Love You Like He Loves Me?" immediately followed. Ella recognized the latter song, because she had seen it performed by different female duets throughout the years on various music award shows. Cheating songs, most of them of the country western variety, continued for the next thirty minutes.

The last song Kenny Chesney rang out, "A Woman Knows When There's Another Woman," and Ella contemplated Davis' many late nights at the office and business trips.

June said, "I told you I wear many hats. Not only do I clean houses, but I also assist with mail delivery. Speaking of mail, Ella, I have a question for you. Do you know the Dick and Jane series? You know, the one that starts out with 'See Dick?'"

June saw that Ella immediately made the connection she hoped she would make.

Ella's memory returned to the day as if it were yesterday. With an armful of groceries, Ella had maneuvered the door to prop it open with her foot while she grabbed the mail from the box. Many of the houses in nearby neighborhoods had mailboxes on the street, but her road still had the traditional metal mailbox right next to the front door. She often found herself thankful for this little luxury on frigid days when she didn't have to put on an extra layer of clothes just to get the mail. She strategically placed the envelopes between her teeth in order not to lose grip of the two recycled bags of groceries she held in each hand. She dropped the mail on the table in the living room as she entered the house and proceeded to take the groceries to the kitchen. Ella put the groceries away, put a chicken in the crockpot, and started a load of laundry; she then put water in the tea kettle and waited for the sound of the whistle. She scooped her favorite organic peppermint tea into the tea strainer and let it steep. Finally, she sat down with her cup of tea and the mail and leafed through the four pieces of mail. Two of the pieces were lawn service advertisements, and one was propaganda for a local attorney. She saw the heart-warming card addressed in crayon to her. Although she hated a stack of paper wasted on junk mail, Ella still loved sending and receiving cards via snail mail. It felt so much more personal. This one must have been a thank-you card from Willow's friend, Ren, who had recently celebrated her eighth birthday with a princess party. Ella briefly thought it was odd that the card was addressed to her instead of Willow, but she guessed that Ren thought that the letter had to go to the moms or dads of a house. The thank-you card also didn't have a return address or a stamp. Ella chuckled to herself, thinking about Ren's mom juggling five kids' schedules. She was amazed the lady even had time to plan birthday parties, much less send thank-you notes.

As she sipped her peppermint tea, Ella opened the card with a cozy feeling in her stomach. Her first glance at the homemade drawing on the front of the card brought confusion and chaos to her brain. It took her several seconds to process the image. There, in front of her, was the image of two stick figures in what was undeniably a sexual position. The top of the card in colorful crayon read, "See Dick... See Jane..." Underneath the image read, "DO YOU SEE WHAT DICK AND JANE ARE DOING?" As she reluctantly opened the card, the message written in large crayon letters stated, "Your husband is cheating on you. I want to and will take care of you." The hot tea turned to a cold chill in her throat, and she felt as if she could barely swallow. *Who would have sent something like this?* The cold chills extended to her arms, and her legs felt hollow and wobbly. She couldn't process the ironic visual image of such an exploitive message glaring her in the face in a child's crayon handwriting. *What sick son-of-a-bitch would do something like this? But, more importantly, WHY?*

Panic raced over her as she realized that the person who sent this was on her front porch at some point between yesterday's mail and her arrival home from her errands today. Ella thought she might be sick, physically sick, at any moment. The rush of negative adrenaline gave her an immediate anxiety headache.

Ella didn't know where to turn in this situation. She obviously couldn't show Davis or her parents, and the uneasy wedge between her and her sister would make it awkward to call Emilie. It was at that moment that Ella realized how alone in the adult world she was. Sure, she had many acquaintances and mommy friends through her children, but her life revolved around her children and the adult social life of her husband's world, of which she hovered on the outskirts. Ella felt utterly alone, helpless, and sick to her stomach as she read the card over and over. Her thoughts traversed from, "Is he cheating?" to "Who would send me this letter?" She knew the possibility of her husband's infidelity always lingered in the back of her mind. "Was this a horrible trick from someone with whom he had slept? Was it someone I have pissed off?" All Ella knew was that she had to compose herself quickly because she had to go pick the kids up from school in twenty minutes.

She took the card up to Willow's bedroom and carefully added it to a small gathering of papers that were well-hidden between the mattress and box spring of her daughter's bed. She knew this was the safest place in the house to put important items until she had time to take them to her lock box at the post office in Lincoln, Illinois. It would have been much more convenient to use one of the many P.O. boxes in Springfield, or in nearby Chatham, but she knew too many people who might innocently and nonchalantly mention to Davis that they had seen

Ella at the post office. At that moment, her legs became weak again. *When did I start having to be so secretive? WHY have I had to start hiding things?*

She glanced at her watch and realized she should have left five minutes earlier to pick the kids up from school. Her favorite part of the day was now clouded over with a very dark cloud, and it unsettled her.

As she backed her SUV out of the driveway, she noticed, with a keen sense of awareness, her surroundings that she had been oblivious to less than an hour earlier. She looked around for strange vehicles but saw nothing out of the ordinary-- just a bicyclist speeding down the street sporting one of those goofy, brightly-colored, skin-tight unitards and fancy bike helmets. Their neighborhood was part of a greenway, so their street was a popular path for the bicyclists to get from one path to another.

Ella was so deep into the memory that she didn't hear June come down the stairs. June's voice, just on the other side of the door, reading another one of Ella's intimate journal entries in a sultry voice, forced her back to the present and then on to another memory.

My Dearest C,

A soft southern breeze sends fresh cottonwood tufts dancing like fireflies over the lake. They shoot in and out of the sunbursts. I am sitting on the dock of my childhood home, with my feet splashing in the water. "Sunday Fundays is part of our family traditions. Rain or shine we come to what the kids have termed, "Momma's lake house"' every Sunday after church. Davis and I started the tradition when we were first married, but since the children have come along, he has gotten too busy with work. Now, the children and I attend church alone, pick up lunch, and take it to Papa. Momma used to cook a big southern-style lunch, complete with homemade biscuits, homemade jam, and Georgia sweet tea for the family before she died. I miss Momma more than words will ever express.

-E-

Tears pooled in Ella's tired eyes as she thought of her babies, her daddy, and mostly her momma.

June said, "Ella, I have a little something to reveal to you, and before you panic, no it isn't about your mother... NOT YET! See, you spent all those Sundays without your husband because Davis said he was working. Well, this is a list of Davis' Sunday work activities. He certainly was doing a LOT of work."

June slid the piece of paper through the door and said, "Ella, I know you will want this for your scrapbook. That way you can remember what a gem your husband truly was." She quietly watched the monitor as a mix of disgust, disbelief, anger, and hurt twisted Ella's beautiful face, as she read the names of the women on the list, a couple of whom she recognized. She had suspected Davis' infidelity for years, but seeing the evidence written in her husband's handwriting was more than she could handle.

June gave Ella ample time to soak in the information and fully process the experience. Then, she said, "Poor Ella, not only are you facing the sins of your husband's ways through the fruits of his labors, but you also are finding out that this is your second strike because your hubby has not been completely honest. He forgot one person.

Ella looked at the ten lines; only nine of them had a name on it. Ella wondered if June was the tenth person. "Is this what this is about?" she spoke to June. Her eyes pierced the eye of the camera. "Did my husband have an affair with you, and this is your way of getting back at him? Is this why you hate me so much and are doing all of these cruel things to me?" Her voice rose to a scream as a barrage of questions spit out of her mouth like snake venom.

June watched the metamorphosis of the sweet soccer mom turn into a crazed monster. In a fit of rage, Ella lost it. She grabbed fistfuls of the little bit of her short hair that remained, and she screamed, "Let me out of here! I want to see my babies!"

"Your anger is not becoming of you," June mocked. "For that, I need to take your gift back. Slide the newest page back through the slot. I am going to give it to someone who will appreciate it."

With shaking hands, Ella slid the page back through the hole.

"My work here is done, sweetie!"

Ella heard June gather the paper up and head back up the stairs.

38

Sifting through the daily mail, Agent Scott called Agent Gibbons into his office and said, "It looks like we got another present." He struggled to get the latex gloves and opened the large envelope with the familiar return address, Ella Masters, Somewhere, Il. 32847, post-marked Chicago, Il. The note on top of a collage of pictures was addressed to Scott. He read the letter aloud while Gibbons struggled with his own gloves.

Dear Mr. FBI Agents,

We keep asking you what's in a name, and you keep failing to come up with the correct answer. It seems like we may have taken you on a bit of a wild goose chase with a couple of clues. Maybe we can redirect you... or, maybe not. Anyway, here are some names that might interest you, but what might interest you more is...well...I can't do your whole job for you. Let me just say, that your man has taken the best years of my life and thrown me away like the other women on this list."

-J-

The page was titled, "Cheater," and it contained several pictures of Davis, all with different women. On the back side of the page was an 8x10 piece of paper that had the names of nine women on it. The agents recognized the writing as Davis'.

Scott handed the page to Gibbons, "What is odd about these pictures?"

Gibbons replied, "Are you referring to the fact that Davis didn't appear to know the pictures were being taken or that not one of the women is his wife?"

"Bingo!" said Scott. We either have one bitter ex-lover or, more likely, an ex-lover's angry husband.

Gibbons agreed with the ex-lover theory, "But I don't see a man going through all the trouble of putting this together. I feel like it's too artsy-fartsy to be a man's work."

Scott analyzed, "Whoever abducted Ella has interchanged 'I' and 'We' in different pieces of mail. We need to figure out who the mastermind behind the game is, but maybe if we can figure out the Why, it will lead us to the Who. If you look at the list, there are ten lines, but only nine names. Our abductor indicated that this is what caused Ella to receive a second strike. I'm assuming the reference is to the missing name. But, who did Davis leave off…and WHY?"

Gibbons said, "Davis is an asshole; I think we can both agree on that! But would Davis send incriminating pictures of himself and a handwritten list of his affairs to the feds? I don't think so. This confirms the other leads we have; someone is trying to pay Davis back. Some of Davis' and Emilie's stories link Ella's abduction to money, but I'm beginning to think this is much more than money. Someone wanted us to get off track by spending our time investigating Davis' finances. I think we need to turn our attention to people, instead of money."

Scott agreed, but with a nonplussed look on his face, he added, "What about this angle. I keep going back to the whole 'shadow' riddle. What if Gianni has been in Davis' shadow with Ella all these years, and deep down he is a bitter man. Maybe he is trying to expose all of Davis' skeletons to make him look guilty or make Ella leave him. He has the resources to get information, and he DOES have a motive. Maybe his hooking up…OK, perhaps not the best choice of words…his relationship with Emilie was more about obtaining information about the woman he never got over. And maybe, just maybe, the missing name on the list is Emilie, and Gianni KNOWS it.

Gibbons replied, "I don't disagree with you, although Emilie despises Davis. Do you really think she would sleep with him?"

Scott said, "I don't see it, but people get themselves into all kinds of situations when alcohol or money are involved." The words rolled off his lips before he could stop them.

Gibbons gave his partner a sympathetic glance.

Scott pictured his baby girl, Reese, in her pink tutu, with a face full of cake and melted ice cream running down her naked, chubby belly, and he wondered how a year could go by so quickly. He wished he had full custody of the love of his life, but that would come with her mother attached. And Drew had NO interest in that package. Scott had met Brooke Lawson at the gym he no longer used. They were on the same 6:00 p.m. workout schedule three days a week. Drew ran or biked in Washington Park the other days of the week. He and Brooke made small talk at first, and Drew helped spot her on some of the equipment. Their physical attraction heated up, as they each looked forward to seeing the other at the gym. At the end of their workout one fateful Wednesday, they walked around the corner to a local watering hole, where one too many drinks led to a walk back to her apartment. It was an evening he would never forget. She became obsessed with him from that night on, calling him at all hours to ask where he was and what he was doing. The following week, he dropped his gym membership. He had to threaten her with an Order of Protection if she didn't stop harassing him. Two months later, she told him she was pregnant with his child. It was like an atom bomb had fallen out of the sky. It wasn't a pretty situation, but every time he looked at his daughter, Reese, he had no regrets. Lately, Brooke had asked him to keep Reese more and more. He wondered if she had a new boyfriend. Part of him hoped she did, so maybe he could have his daughter closer to full-time, but the other part of him couldn't imagine Reese calling another man Daddy.

Gibbons brought his partner's thoughts back to the investigation. "I think we need to keep Gianni Russo at the forefront of our radar. He may have used Emilie to get closer to Ella, and he may have strung Davis on for the same reason, but my gut tells me he wouldn't harm Ella, and I don't think he is the kind of man who would put Ella's kids through this. I don't know, maybe he is pulling the wool over all of our eyes, but I want to believe the guy is telling the truth."

"Davis, on the other hand," Scott interrupted, "has slime-ball written all over him. I will be interested in how he weaves his newest web of lies when we sucker punch him and his cocky attorney with this piece of paper."

Gibbons said, "I would like to give the guy a lot more than a sucker punch! I would love to find a reason to kick his ass."

Scott agreed.

Agents Scott and Gibbons decided not to share the newest piece of mail with Davis Masters quite yet. Now that his attorney was involved, every conversation they had with him had to be in the presence of his attorney, Erik Dubin. Agent Scott took half the list of names that had been thrown in their laps, and Agent Gibbons took the other half, minus one blank line. The agents had pondered the possibility of the tenth name being Emilie Randolph, but they decided to put that lead on hold while they sifted through the other women. After all, they speculated, that would be too obvious.

Each man made his way through his list of women and found that five of them were located in Chicago and four were in the Springfield area.

"I say it has been too long since we have had a Chicago-style hot dog," Gibbons said, his mouth already salivating, as he imagined a big bite of the loaded hot dog. They managed to schedule interviews with all five women for the following day, telling each of them that they had some questions about their relationship with Davis Masters. They assured each of the women that they were in no way in any kind of trouble but that the agents needed assistance with a missing person's case, and any information they could provide would be much appreciated. All five women agreed to be interviewed, and only one indicated that she would bring her attorney along.

Beth was first on their schedule. She was in her mid-thirties, attractive, and married. She was tall and thin, with what Gibbons described as "various physical alterations to enhance her appearance."

Agents Scott began, "Good morning, ma'am. I am Agent Drew Scott, and this is my partner, Agent Brad Gibbons. Thanks so much for your time. Can you tell me how you know Davis Masters and describe your relationship with him?"

"You know how it is." she began, "We met at a party, and one drink led to another. We were both single, so we hooked up. We talked occasionally and got together when he came to Chicago. That's really about it. I wasn't interested in dating at the time because I was doing too much traveling for my job. He had just come out of a nasty divorce, so neither of us was looking for anything permanent."

Scott and Gibbons gave each other knowing glances.

Beth described a one-year on and off affair with Davis in 2007. She said, "I'm happily married now, and we have a two-year-old little boy. I have to admit, I had forgotten about Davis until you called. Is he in some sort of trouble?"

Agent Gibbons said, "We aren't sure quite yet, but we greatly appreciate your time and the information you have provided." The sound of her little boy calling "Momma" through the baby monitor that sat on the nearby table was their signal to head out and move on to the next woman.

Scott handed Beth his business card and added, "If you think of anything else that might seem important, you can reach me at this number."

The next woman on the list was Collette. She was the youngest of the women at only twenty-eight, according to information they gathered from their Google search. The two men debriefed as they drove to the Corner Bakery near Collette's apartment in the heart of downtown Chicago where they had agreed to meet. They battled bottle-necked traffic, blaring horns, and pedestrians who ignored traffic signals. They parked in a nearby public garage and walked two blocks to the Corner Bakery.

They saw her sitting alone at a table at the perimeter of the outdoor seating area. Again, by the images they found on the internet, they assumed she was their girl. She had her face in her phone texting and did not see the agents approach her table.

Agent Gibbons cleared his throat, so as not to startle her. She jumped slightly and said, "Sorry, I didn't see you walk up."

"Are you Collette?" Scott said quietly, as he inconspicuously revealed his badge.

"I am," the young lady said with a nervous smile. "Am I in some kind of trouble?"

"No, not at all," he reassured her.

"Wheww. I have been worried sick since you called me. I Googled Davis Masters right after I hung up the phone with you, and, well, I am just sick to my stomach. I had no clue he was even married. He told me he had just gone through a bad divorce, and that his wife took him for everything he had and moved his kids all the way out to California. I felt sorry for him. I mean, he was REALLY convincing. He cried real tears and everything."

"Ma'am, we are going to have to ask you a few questions that might be difficult to answer, but we need you to be perfectly candid with us."

Collette nodded in understanding. The three conversed in whispered dialogue so the other patrons couldn't overhear the awkward admissions.

Collette admitted seeing Davis on several occasions during the past four years. "We met in a bar a few years ago. I knew he was older, but he was in great shape, and he had money. I don't mean to sound shallow, but I was only twenty-four, and I didn't have much of a bank account. He took me out to nice dinners when he came to town for business, and we usually ended up back at his hotel. Neither of us was looking for anything long term, so it was just a convenient hook-up," she blushed at the admission.

"Did he talk much about his family?"

"Not really-- just that his wife had taken his two young children to California after she took him for everything he had. He said he missed his babies but that it was lucky for him that he had money she didn't know about, so Davis was able to rebound pretty quickly financially. I wondered how a woman could do that to such a nice man."

"Well, Collette, I am sure you know by your Google research that Mr. Masters was not honest with you."

She hung her head and nodded, embarrassed at her gullibility.

"When is the last time the two of you…saw each other?"

"About eight months ago. Davis came to the city for the weekend in the middle of October. He called me up on Saturday night and asked if I wanted to grab dinner. We met at Dugan's for dinner and drinks and then went back to his hotel room."

"Where was the hotel?"

"It was the Crowne Plaza."

"And that is the last time you talked to him or saw him?"

"We have sent a few texts back and forth since then, but I haven't seen him."

"Do you still have the texts?"

Collette nodded. Her face turned red and then white. She felt like she was sitting at the kitchen table with her father. She knew these two guys were probably younger than Davis and to show them the chain of texts would be mortifying. Collette reluctantly sifted through her text messages, and, like a terrier not wanting to give its ball back to its owner, she handed Scott her phone. Gibbons looked on as Scott scrolled down the text exchange in disgust. The girl was nearly half Davis' age.

Collette looked away from the two men and the other patrons in hopes that nobody saw her tears.

Scott spoke, "Collette, I know this is uncomfortable, and I am sorry you are in this position. You have done nothing wrong legally."

His word choice stung.

"Can you forward the texts to me. I promise nobody will see them unless it becomes absolutely necessary, but we have a mother of two young children out there somewhere, and we need all the leads we can get to find her."

Collette whispered, "My dad is a cop here in this city. It wouldn't be good if he somehow got hold of these texts."

Scott said, "I have a little girl of my own; I get it."

Collette winced at the comment, feeling embarrassed over the age gap between her and Davis.

He continued, "You may not see it this way, but Davis has lied to you and taken advantage of your naivety, whether or not you see it that way. Now, I will do my best to keep the details of the texts among the three of us, but I can't make any guarantees. I would rather not have to take your cell phone as evidence."

"I would appreciate that. I am still on my dad's cell phone plan, and I don't really want to have to explain why the FBI has my phone."

She knew they were trying to work with her. She had been around the legal system all her life, and she knew how it worked. As far as they knew, she would erase the texts the minute they left. She liked these two guys, and she trusted they would keep their word. She highlighted all of the texts, selected copy, opened up a new text message, punched Scott's number in, and clicked paste. His phone buzzed in his pocket. He pulled it out to confirm they came through. He didn't want to put anyone through the discomfort of rereading them, so he quickly said, "OK, they came through, but I am going to ask that you not delete the messages until this is all over. Can we trust you to comply?"

"Yes," was all she said.

As they wrapped up the interview, Scott said, "Here are our business cards. If Davis contacts you at any time, we need you to call one of us, OK?"

In an apologetic tone and with a single tear trickling down her face, Collette said, "I had no clue he was married. That is not the kind of girl I am. I know it doesn't look like that, but I don't want you guys to think that about me."

Scott gently replied, "I believe that. Life is about choices, mistakes, and lessons. I am guessing that you have learned a valuable lesson here.

Collette nodded.

They finished up the three remaining Chicago interviews, grabbed hot dogs to go, and headed down I-55. They discussed the case on the long drive home through rush hour traffic. Scott drove, and Gibbons took notes.

They interviewed the rest of the women in the Springfield area during the next two days. All of the women had similar stories. They had met Davis at parties, bars or social events. Drinks and flirting were followed by various versions of his marital status. The flirting led to the women taking him back to their places if they didn't have a husband or roommate; otherwise, they went to his hotel. Many of the women knew he was married, but that didn't seem to bother any of them. Others received the same divorce story as Collette. He told two of the women he was a lifelong bachelor. A couple were one-night stands, but the rest reported hooking up with him occasionally. Three of them admitted to having longer relationships with

Davis. Two of them revealed they had a bitter end when Davis did not come through on his promises of leaving his wife for them. The agents couldn't find a rhyme or reason to the variations in his marital status, but they had learned that Davis was a calculating man, so they assumed he switched up his stories based on the woman's personality.

Their last interview was with Natalia Hunt. She was a tall, lean, buxom, blonde-haired beauty, and the agents could understand Davis' interest. She had an edgy look and an even edgier attitude.

Before the agents could begin with their questions, Natalia spouted, "I know why you are here, and I didn't have anything to do with Davis' wife's disappearance."

Surprised by her directness, Gibbons found himself at a temporary loss for words.

"Why would you say that before we even ask you a question."

"I am not stupid. I watch the news, and I know how you guys work. I know you aren't here to ask me about the weather."

"Well, then, Ms. Hunt, how about if you tell us why we are here."

Natalia didn't take his bait. She offered only, "Well, the fact that you showed up on my doorstep tells me you know about my relationship with Davis, so get along with the questioning. I have things to do and people to see."

The agents knew they had a wildcat on their hands, and they knew this was probably what attracted Davis to her. They continued the same line of questioning they had taken with the other women on the list, but she had a tinge of anger in her voice the others did not have.

"Ms. Hunt, do you have any knowledge of the whereabouts of Ella Masters?"

"No."

"Do you have any knowledge that Davis is involved in his wife's disappearance?

"Nope."

"Ma'am, did Davis plan on leaving his family to be with you?"

She did not answer. Instead, a mix of anger and angst washed over her face. Scott acknowledged that Natalia was not good at hiding her emotions. He imagined she was a woman who got what she wanted, whatever the cost.

I will ask you again, "Did Davis plan on leaving his family to be with you?"

She blew up. "That mother fucker has been promising me for nearly a year that he would leave his family, so we could start a life of our own. I have wasted a good year of my life sitting on the sidelines being played like a fiddle for his sexual pleasure, while he played the family man. I should have known he would never leave Ella, but he was good. He promised me the moon, and I believed him. "

Gibbons digested the information before asking, "Would you describe your relationship as more physical or emotional?

Gibbons felt the flush in his cheeks as Natalia described in more detail than necessary the physical relationship she and Davis had engaged in the past year. There was a glint of excitement in her eye knowing she was unhinging the agents. She left no details out.

"Does that answer your question?"

Trying to keep the smirk off his face, Gibbons said, "Yes, we get the gist."

"When is the last time you spoke with Mr. Masters? Have you talked to him since he returned to Springfield?" Scott asked.

Natalia knew Davis said he had gotten rid of his burner phone before the police interviewed him, but she didn't know what to believe anymore. She got the sense that the investigators were checking out Davis more than her, so she figured she didn't have any real reason to lie.

"I talked to him a couple of times soon after he got back in town, but that's about all."

Scott added, "Have you seen him?"

"No. Davis said he was afraid you guys would be tailing him, so he didn't want to take a chance."

"How did you respond when he said that?"

"I called him a no-good bastard for leading me on for the past year. I mean, that is a year I can never get back. And, just so you know, Davis and I are over."

Scott raised a quizzical brow.

"Well, I haven't had a chance to tell him yet because the fucker didn't answer when I tried to call him, but I am finished with the asshole. He has used me long enough, and I didn't bargain for all this shit."

As the agents finished up the interview, Natalia looked at Gibbons coquettishly and said, "Let me know if you have any more questions for me. Maybe I can answer them over drinks."

Gibbons felt the heat in his ears, "I think you have answered all of our questions."

"OK, but you have my number in case you forgot anything."

Oh, I have your number, he thought.

The agents rose and shook Natalia's hand. She held on to Gibbons' a little tighter and a little longer than was comfortable. Heat transferred from his ears to his hands.

Natalia gave him a knowing smile and questioned, "You do have my number, correct?"

Scott knew he should intercede to help his buddy out, but he was having too much fun watching his partner squirm.

"Yes, ma'am. We have your number. Thank you for your time."

As with the other interviews, Scott handed Natalia both of their business cards. He knew he shouldn't go there, but he couldn't stop himself.

"Now you have Agent Gibbons' number if you remember anything else. My card is there also, in case you can't get hold of my partner." His stomach ached at trying to contain his laughter.

Gibbons gave him a look that said, "I will get you back for this one."

The agents got into the car before Scott burst out laughing. Gibbons knew what was coming and tried to cut him off, but Scott was relentless.

"Let me know if you have any more questions for me. Maybe I can answer them over drinks." He mocked in a high pitch voice as he rubbed his hands up and down his body.

Gibbons volleyed back with, "Dude, you are just jealous that she didn't invite you for drinks."

Scott teased," She saw the wedding band on your finger and realized you are her type."

Gibbons laughed, "Right, keep justifying why she came after me over you. Just admit it, partner, I've got it going on and you…well, not so much."

Scott landed the final blow, "You, my friend, can have all of the Davis Masters sloppy seconds you want." He shuddered in an exaggerated manner.

Both men laughed.

"Wow, was she a piece of work, or what?" Gibbons chuckled. His hand still felt hot from her touch.

"It sounds like she's looking for a husband…but she needs a rebound guy first; that's where you come in."

Scott started laughing so hard that he brushed tears from his eyes. "Let me know if you have any more questions for me. Maybe I can answer them over drinks." He mocked again in a seductive voice.

"OK, OK, I'm finished, I promise," he laughed, but then he went right back to the seductive voice, "but you do have my number, right?"

Gibbons said coyly, "Yeah, I've got your number…I've got your mom's number, too."

"Hey, hey, hey, Dude, you just crossed the line," he teased.

"Oh, no, my friend, there are no lines." Gibbons teased back.

As they pulled into the agency parking lot, Scott broke into another fit of laughter, "I cannot WAIT to tell the guys about this."

Gibbons knew it was going to be a long day.

39

The melodic sound of music gently made its way through the speaker as the song, "Holes in the Floor of Heaven," played. The beautiful song brought tears to Ella's eyes and a sense of panic that she was about to find out something that would forever change her mental status.

June said, in a gentle tone, "Ella, I have alluded several times to the fact that you and I are much closer than you realize, but you just can't seem to figure it out. Today, you are going to tell me the tragic story of your momma's death."

Just the fact that June referred to Ella's mother as "momma" sent shivers up her spine. She didn't have the emotional strength to get through this story, especially to a total stranger who was mentally torturing her, but she knew she didn't have a choice.

Ella reluctantly and tearfully recanted the details of her mother's car accident. "Momma was coming home from church choir practice late one evening. She was driving around the winding lake roads when she lost control of her car and went off the road, flipping a couple of times before resting upside down in a ravine. By the lack of skid marks, the police determined she must have seen a deer and jerked the wheel to miss the animal, but she was going too fast to correct the movement. Because it was night, and the road wasn't highly traveled in the late fall, it was hours before anyone found her. Daddy got worried when she didn't arrive home by 10:00 p.m. It was about that time that the police showed up at his door with the horrific news."

Ella broke down sobbing as the memories of the night rushed over her.

June laughed a hearty laugh as she watched Ella's meltdown.

Chills ran up Ella's back and down each arm as she said, "How cruel can one person be? How do you live with yourself? Do you not have a mother of your own? How can you, as a woman, be so cold that you can't comprehend the love between a mother and her daughter? Was your childhood that bad?"

With this, June snapped! "You have no fucking clue what you are talking about, bitch, and if you ever say something like that again, I will blow your pretty little brains out myself!"

Ella had struck the wrong cord on a broken piano. She realized she was dealing with a woman whose moral character had been replaced by aggressive malice, and Ella knew she wasn't playing games.

June emotionally gathered herself. Ella could hear the malicious smile return to her voice, "I know I gave you William's journal, but I thought it best to give you your husband's and sister's journals a little bit at a time, so as not to overwhelm you. Davis wrote a special letter to you in his journal, dear, but instead of giving it to you, I think I should read it because I love story time!"

June paused long enough to see Ella close her eyes and take a deep breath. "Let's hear his version of your mommy's untimely death."

Ella went white as she was forced to listen.

Dear Ella,

I will make this admission short, as I realize it will likely be the end of our marriage. It wasn't a deer that caused your mother's accident; it was a black cat. I knew your mom would be coming home from choir practice; the man I hired hid in the high-grass ditch on the precariously winding bend near their house. Right when her car made the curve, he threw the black cat into her headlights. You know the rest.

Davis

Ella flinched and gasped. "BUT WHY? This is unfathomable! You must be making this up! What kind of cruel monster are you?"

Ella's eyes darted for an escape route like she was in a small cage with a tiger, "WHYYYYYYYYYYYY?" she screamed.

"You see, Ella, your momma was on to Davis' affairs, and she was on to the fact that he was stealing money from your parents. She came to the house the Saturday before her 'accident.' You and the kids had gone for a hike at Carpenter Park, so she knew he would be alone. The confrontation got a bit heated, and I got it all on tape. The funny thing is that I wasn't even trying to get that kind of information, so it was an extra bonus. I have to tell you, though, I thought your mom was so sweet and innocent, but the words she flung at Davis..."

June whistled. "She didn't sound very church-like; in fact, your momma could cuss like a sailor. But, that is neither here nor there now, is it? Of course, he denied it all, but your momma made a mistake because she didn't realize how truly evil her son-in-law was. She told him she planned on telling you everything. His response was simple, 'You will die trying.' Your momma scolded, in her southern Georgia accent, 'Young man, you just watch me!' Four days later, your momma was dead!"

She paused to allow Ella to once again process her words. Finally, she said, "Allow me to provide confirmation of the truth I speak." She slid the scrapbook page through the slot. Ella's tears fell onto the pictures of her mother as she re-read the accurate account of her momma's senseless death, all in Davis' handwriting. Ella melted into the fetal position with her face turned away from the eyeball of the camera and threw up.

June said resignedly, "Just so you know, he took my momma away from me too; that's what we have in common.

Ella shook her head in disbelief.

"Ella, you have no clue about the monster that you allow to be in the same home as your children. This is the man who, as we speak, is in charge of your children's welfare. It isn't good, Ella…it isn't good at all. Right now, a murderer is taking care of your children. I would tell you about my own momma, but I am too exhausted."

With that, the room went black, and June was gone. Hollow rage consumed Ella's emaciated body, and she began screaming at the top of her lungs. She kicked and flailed her arms as if she was being attacked by a swarm of bees. Her knuckles opened up as her fingers hit the walls. She shrieked so loudly that she didn't hear the sound of water. It wasn't until the powerful spray of the hose slapped her in the face that she realized what was happening. She attempted to cover her face, but the water stung her bloody fingers.

"Let me know when you are finished with your two-year-old tantrum, and I will turn off the hose," Jax said in a calm, paternal voice from outside the closet."

Ella fell silent, acknowledging that at every moment her captors had the upper hand. She knew they would stop at nothing to keep her silent.

She lay shivering in the dark, on the now-soaked towel that was the only barrier between her bony body and the cold, concrete floor.

40

William heard the mailman's truck leave their sleepy cul-de-sac. He raced down to the front porch to grab the mail before baseball practice. Each day since his mom had been gone, he secretly prayed she would send him a letter. He nervously shuffled through the envelopes, hoping his father wouldn't pull up in the drive and catch him rifling through the mail.

He saw it, right there, in the middle of bills. His name was written in bright blue crayon on the yellow envelope. The return address read, "Mommy, Somewhere, Il. 32847. He studied the address and memorized the zip code. He knew that Illinois zip codes began with a six, so whoever sent the letter was not being honest. His heart pounded. He had prayed for this moment. He needed so badly to hear from his mom, and God heard his prayers. He kissed the letter and said, "Thank you, thank you, thank you, God, for this letter. William left the other mail untouched in the mailbox, so he didn't get screamed at by his father, who had, of course, "stepped out" for a bit. He scanned the cul-de-sac one last time, hustled back into the house, ran up to his room, carefully opened the envelope, and read the note.

Dear William,

I know you have had to be strong this past couple of weeks, but I know I can count on you to continue taking care of Willow. As you know, your father is not fit to take care of the two of you, and your Aunt Emilie is, well, too self-centered to think about anyone but herself. I am sorry I have left you in such a situation that has forced you to be the responsible one in the home, but I know you will man up and accept the challenge. Do not tell your father or Aunt Emilie I said these things, and remember, TAKE CARE OF YOUR SISTER. IF ANYTHING HAPPENS TO HER, YOU WILL BE RESPONSIBLE.

Love,
Mommy

A wash of pride, followed by an extreme sense of responsibility that bordered on fear, fell over William. He realized his mom was putting so much trust in him that he had to do everything he could to take good care of his little sister.

He was relieved that she had seen through his father and Aunt Emilie. He wondered if he would ever tell her about what he saw the first night Emilie came to "help" Davis out with the kids.

He tucked his special letter into the pocket of his winter coat. The zip code bugged him. He felt as if it were some sort of trick. He picked up the house phone to call his friend, Abe, to see if he could get a ride with him to baseball practice. As he looked at the portable handset, the numbers lit up and jumped to life.

"What if my mom is sending some kind of code in the zip code?" He questioned aloud. He looked at the letters, "Friend-- no, that didn't work." As if he were working a word puzzle, William continued analyzing the combinations to see if he could establish a word. Within five minutes, he realized 32847 was the numerical value for DAVIS, his father. William knew this couldn't be by chance.

William had thirty minutes before Abe would be there. He remembered seeing a business card for Agent Drew Scott in the kitchen catch-all drawer. He rushed down to the kitchen and took the card out of the drawer. He was glad Willow had accompanied his Aunt Emilie to their papa's house. He didn't want to have to explain anything to his little sister, and he was horrible at lying to her. He knew if she were home, he would be forced to come clean with her; but she wasn't back, so he didn't need to worry about it.

With shaky fingers, he dialed the number on the business card.

A gruff voice answered the phone after just two rings, "Agent Drew Scott."

William's voice quivered, and he considered hanging up, when the voice repeated, "Hello, this is Agent Drew Scott, can I help you?"

William said, "Good afternoon, sir, my name is William Masters."

Scott assumed it was their caller again, so he was surprised when he heard William's young voice. In a gentler voice, Scott said, "Well, good afternoon, young man, how can I help you today?"

William looked at the clock, knowing Abe's mom would be there to pick him up in less than fifteen minutes. As quickly as he could get the words out, he said, "Mr. Scott, sir, I'm sorry to bother you, but I think I figured out the zip code thing with my mom's letters."

Surprised, Agent Scott said, "Really, young man?"

William continued, speaking faster than he wanted to. "I think the zip code might not be real, sir. I looked at my phone, and I think my mom, or somebody might have meant the zip code to mean something else."

Agent Scott took out his own cell phone and looked at the letters that corresponded with 3. D-E-F.

Before he could analyze the other letters, a nervous William said, "Sir, I think it is supposed to say, Davis."

Scott was speechless. He shook his head. He and his men had spent nearly three weeks, and they still hadn't figured out the damn numbers," he mused.

"William, is your dad home?" Scott asked as he waved Agent Gibbons into his office.

"No, sir, he stepped out again."

As William explained that his father had left a note saying he had business to take care of and would be back later in the afternoon, Scott noticed the irritation in the young boy's words. He wrote the zip code down on his legal pad, and underneath each letter matched the letters D-A-V-I-S. He pointed to the phone and mouthed, "William Masters. Can you believe a twelve-year-old figured it out? It has to be that, don't you think?"

Agent Scott heard the angry male voice yell, "Who are you talking to?" in the background on the other end of the line.

Click! William Masters was gone.

Without missing a beat, William quickly dialed Abe's number, and coolly said to his father, "Just trying to get hold of Abe to figure out when his mom is picking me up for baseball."

Abe heard him on the phone and said, "Be there in five, dude."

"Great," William said, as he grabbed his ball glove off the counter, the business card now tucked inside of it, and ran out the back door, all without even saying goodbye to his father.

Davis thought his son's behavior was odd, but he didn't have time for any of that right now. He had the house to himself for the time being since Willow was with Emilie for the day. He needed to find Ella's damn diary.

41

William's phone call had broken up the monotonous chore of finding Davis' father. They added the information to the whiteboard, mulled over possible connections, and got back to their search for Thomas Brown. Scott had taken the first half of the list of the Thomas Browns in Chicago, and Gibbons covered the second half. They created a script they knew would reduce the number of questions they had to ask to find their man. Thomas Brown had spent a week each year at the Master's Golf Tournament throughout his younger life, so they began each call with the same general question to see if they could get a nibble.

"Good day, Mr. Brown, my name is Drew Scott. I am an official searching for the Thomas Brown who was involved in the Master's Golf Tournament in Augusta, Georgia as a young man. The responses ranged from, "What is the Master's?" to "Dude, I wish I were able to go to the Master's."

They had whittled away seven of the names, but none of their phone calls produced their Thomas Brown. At 5:30, they called it a day, agreeing to meet early the next morning to take another drive up to Chicago. The agents knew the man had to be in Chicago, and they were confident he was one of the remaining fifteen men on their list. The agents wanted to be in the city when they found the guy, so they could interview him quickly after they contacted him. They wanted the element of surprise to work in their favor for once.

The sun peeked over the horizon, as the agency-issued Ford Taurus whirred up Interstate 55. The drive was becoming an all-too-familiar one, and the two men were over the novelty of the Chicago-style hot dog. They decided their splurge today would be a Gastone's Pizza. This sent them into their familiar discussion of food. They argued between thin and thick crust and debated which beers went best with each type of pizza. They agreed to wait until 7:30 a.m. before they started making calls. They figured their man would be up by 7:30, so they wouldn't piss him off. They didn't care if they pissed any of the other Thomas Browns off, as long as they found their guy.

Brad drove while Drew made phone calls and scratched his way through the list. The agents could see the Sears Tower building on the horizon. Finally, after nine misses, Agent Scott found the man he thought might be Mr. Thomas Brown. He didn't actually locate the man himself. Instead, he found Mrs. Brown, who indicated that Mr. Brown was at work. Scott presented the spiel he now had memorized to the sweet, female voice on the other end of the line. When the woman asked the nature of the call, Scott assumed this meant there was a chance that they had found their man.

He quickly gathered his thoughts and the notes he and Gibbons had written about Davis Brown.

"Good morning, Mrs. Brown, I am wondering if you can have your husband give me a call when he gets home from work. We have some information about the Master's Tournament he might be interested in exploring."

"Oh, Tommy has loved the Master's since he was a kid. His parents took him every year throughout his childhood, and now he takes our boys. It has become quite a Brown family tradition. We have many fond memories of Augusta, Georgia."

Scott thought, *And you are about to get a few unwanted memories.* He felt bad for the woman who had no clue her world was about to crash in on her, and once it did, it would never be the same. *Augusta, Georgia*, he thought, *is about to put a bad taste in your mouth, lady.*

Although Mrs. Brown indicated that her husband wouldn't be home for lunch for a couple of hours, Thomas

Brown returned Scott's phone call within ten minutes. "When my wife said officials from Augusta wanted to meet with me, I knew this must be big. See, my family, well, we live and breathe Augusta, Georgia and the Master's Tournament."

Agent Scott felt a little sorry for Thomas Brown that the man thought he and Gibbons were officials from Augusta. He hadn't lied when he told Mr. Brown's wife he was an official, but when she heard Master's Tournament, she made the assumption he was that kind of official, not an official FBI investigator. Scott thought, "Whatever it takes to get you to meet us."

He casually asked, "Is there any way we can meet with you for thirty minutes regarding Augusta, Georgia and your experiences at the Master's Tournament."

Thomas was intrigued and asked, "Have I won some special contest or received special tickets for next year's tournament?"

Scott coolly responded, "We can discuss all of that when we meet, Mr. Brown, but we have several people to contact, so time is of the essence."

Without hesitation, Brown said, "I can leave work now and meet you at Starbucks on North Lasalle. Is that convenient for you? If not, I can meet you somewhere else."

Scott wrote down the address, and Gibbons put it in his phone map. Gibbons nodded, and Scott said, "My colleague and I can be there in twenty minutes. We are both wearing navy suits and green ties."

Gibbons said, "No wonder there are so many Starbucks in this city; it is where everyone wants to meet."

Scott replied, "Lucky for us, we like our Joe."

Brown was giddy with anticipation as he hailed the first available cab. He called his wife and told her about the meeting. His excitement radiated through the telephone, and she said, "I can't wait to hear all about your meeting."

Thomas identified the two men immediately as he entered Starbucks, He addressed the barista by name as he briskly walked to the corner table. Both men stood and extended their hands. They introduced themselves, using only their first and last names. Thomas was clammy with the excitement of a school girl on a first date. He rushed into a monologue about all he knew about the Master's tournament and how many years he had attended the event. Scott and Gibbons listened patiently, as they took mental notes that might bridge the connection between Thomas Brown and Davis Masters. When Thomas realized he had been rambling, he apologized and asked, "So, gentlemen, what do you want to meet with me about?"

Based on the information Thomas voluntarily shared, the two agents realized they had their man. Agent Gibbons pulled out his FBI credentials and apologetically said, "Mr. Brown, we have some questions about your early years at the Master's Tournament in Augusta, Georgia."

Thomas looked around to see who else heard the words that exploded in his ears. Only a few other patrons sipped coffee or slurped smoothies as they worked feverishly on their computers with their earbuds drowning out the noises of other patrons. He was momentarily relieved, but sickness filled his gut at the wonder of what was about to come.

"Hhhoowww can I help you, gentlemen?" He spoke in a nervous but hushed voice so as not to draw unwanted attention. Suddenly, he wished he had chosen a place he didn't frequent.

Scott felt for the man whose world was about to change forever, so he crafted his words carefully, "Sir, you are in no way in trouble, but we are going to have to share some difficult information with you and ask you some tough questions."

"Mr. Brown, do you know you have a son who is now fifty years old?"

Thomas nodded and lowered his head in acknowledgment that the past he had hidden so well was about to bite him in the ass. His thoughts went straight to his beautiful wife, who would be anxiously awaiting him at the door to hear his news. Many times in their marriage, he had wanted to tell her about the mistake he made a lifetime ago, at a time when he had the world in his hands. The mistake had gnawed at his gut when he witnessed the birth of his two sons or watched them play one of their many sports. Each Augusta visit was bittersweet; he loved the place but knew it wasn't without the heavy baggage that he alone carried all these years. He knew his wife would have ultimately been supportive, but he didn't want to cause her the initial pain, so he buried his secret deep in his heart, hoping he would carry it to his grave.

As if Agent Gibbons could read Thomas' mind, he said, "I am guessing your wife is unaware that you have a son."

Again, Brown nodded.

"Mr. Brown, have you ever contacted or been contacted by your son, sir?"

Thomas said, "I never reached out to Davis' mother or attempted to contact him, but Davis has called me several times at my office. He called me within weeks of my boys' births. Davis had obviously been drinking, and he berated me for being a dead-beat dad. He asked me how I sleep at night knowing I had thrown him away. Periodically, he would call out of the blue and ask if I ever saw his face when I looked into my sons' faces."

Gibbons felt like a therapist instead of an investigator. "What did you say to him when he contacted you? How did you respond?"

Lowering his head again, Brown said, "I just hung up the phone. I never once responded."

"When is the last time you heard from your son, Mr. Brown?"

Thomas winced at Gibbons' chosen words. Secretly, he wished he had used Davis' name instead of "your son." He took a deep breath and released it as if to prepare himself for what he had to say.

"About six months ago, I got an ugly voicemail on my answering machine at work. It was Davis, and I assumed by his slurred words that he had been drinking. He told me it was all my fault that his life had turned out so badly. He said he was in real financial trouble and that it might be time for my wife and perfect boys to find out their perfect family isn't what it seems. My sons are grown and have families of their own. I am involved extensively in my community, and I have a good reputation. If something like this became public, it would affect many more people than just me and my wife. Anyway, he told me he needed fifty-thousand dollars in silence money; otherwise, he would show up on Christmas morning to give my family the gift of truth."

"That's extortion," Scott interrupted.

"I am very aware of that, sir, but I had little time to process his request before my children arrived for the holidays, so I liquidated one of my investments, met him in an underground parking garage downtown, and gave him the money. When I told him I better never hear from him again, he responded with an evil laugh and said, 'I'm the one calling the shots now, Daddy.' I guess deep down I knew this day would come. What has he done that got the FBI involved?"

Brown's face appeared to age years as he listened to the agents sketch the details of his daughter-in-law's disappearance and his son's failed business endeavors and less-than-stellar actions as a husband and parent. The latter had not surprised him. He admitted following Davis' business ventures and knowing he was more talk than action when it came to his business success. He was, however, distraught over Ella's disappearance. He thought about his grandchildren-- the ones who called him "Grampy." He felt heartache for the grandchildren he had never met as he imagined them wondering where their mommy had gone.

Thomas Brown removed a hanky from his pocket and wiped the moisture away from his eyes.

"What do you want from me?" he asked resignedly.

"Mr. Brown, you have told us everything we need to know. We have suspected Davis had money issues from the beginning, and we believe this might be behind Ella's disappearance. We will contact you if we have further questions." Gibbons hesitated, "Sir, we will contact you at your office from here on out. We are sorry for any problems this has caused you," Gibbons' words were genuine. He pictured a scared eighteen-year-old boy as he looked into the sad eyes of the sixty-seven-year-old man.

Scott and Gibbons made their way through rush hour traffic in an attempt to get out of Chicago. Both men were silent; both envisioned the conversations that were most likely taking place in the Thomas Brown home at this very moment, and they felt genuinely sorry for the gentleman.

Scott finally broke the silence, "Damn, it would have been so much easier if the guy was a jerk. It pisses me off that Davis has held this over his father's head for so many years, and the fact that he extorted fifty-thousand dollars from Brown makes me want to kick his ass even more. Gibbons, I really want to nail this son-of-a-bitch." Their silence continued as they each reflected on the meeting.

42

Olly, Olly Oxen Free
You may not know it, but you've seen me.
Your house may be open
But here you're not free.
Olly, Olly, YOU'RE NOT FREE!

Ella listened to June's light steps as she made her way down to Ella's prison. Ella felt less afraid when she heard her footsteps than when she heard the heavy footsteps of the two men. A cold bottle of Mexican Coca-Cola rolled through the food slot. A bottle opener dropped in the closet right behind it. The Coca-Cola was so cold that it was sweating from the temperature change. This was precisely the way Ella loved the one treat she periodically allowed herself to have.

June encouraged Ella, "Go ahead, open it up while it is nice and cold. There's nothing like a crisp Coca-Cola, fresh out of the freezer on a breezy spring afternoon. Fifteen minutes is just about the perfect amount of time. I know that is how you like it best. I am enjoying one also."

She opened the bottle and took a sip of the sweet, dark, syrupy drink. The cold burn slid down her throat. It tasted so good that she wanted to savor it, but she realized it was not merely a gift with no strings attached. Everything June said or did had strings. She was correct.

June began in a sing-song tone, "The kids were at a birthday party, and Davis was in Chicago for a couple of days, probably with your sister or former lover, or maybe one of his many women. Anyway, you decided to splurge on a Coca Cola--

not the high-fructose corn syrup kind, but the real Mexican Coke, made with real sugar. It wasn't often that you indulged in such pleasures; in fact, it was like you hid your secret addiction...sort of like Davis has hidden his secret addictions. You chilled it in the freezer for fifteen minutes-- just long enough to give your mouth a cool burn as it slipped across your tongue and down your throat. You loved to sip your drinks to make them last longer, as if it was a pure summer delight."

Ella recalled the odd experience, in which her mind seemed to be playing tricks on her.

June continued, "You went down to switch laundry, and when you returned to the computer, you said aloud, "Did I really guzzle that much without totally enjoying it?"

"You just got settled back into paying your bills, when the chirp, chirp, chirp of your cell phone in the other room pulled you away from the computer yet again. I knew you wouldn't ignore it because it might be one of your kids. You rifled through your purse and answered the unrecognizable number, only to realize it was a telemarketer. You weren't very friendly when you explained that you were quite satisfied with your current cable and internet plan, but that they would be the first ones you called should you become dissatisfied. You returned to your online bill-pay to finish your financial chores, only to realize you had been logged out. Oops, that might have been my doing," June added with a giggle.

"You assumed it was due to inactivity, so you logged back in and mindlessly reached over for another drink of Coke. As you brought the drink to your lips, you realized the bottle was empty. Again, you chastised yourself out loud, 'How could I have finished that entire bottle of coke with so many distractions? I don't even remember enjoying it!' You were beyond irritated!"

June's next words froze Ella, and she carefully placed the bottle on the ground next to her. "I had become a pro at getting in and out of your house, but I had to be a bit more clever with your daddy's home. I had to come up with other ways to get into his house. It worked out in my favor when you decided to put poor forgetful Daddy's house on the market. I love open houses, don't you?"

June's mention of the open house flooded Ella's memories back to the beautiful April Sunday. A strange wash of relief made its way through her body. First the Coke and now the open house. Ella remembered thinking she was suffering from her own kind of mental breakdown. Now, she knew this lady had been toying with her, like a cat toys with his mouse.

June remained silent and watched her victim connect the dots. They had put her daddy's house on the market, for sale by owner. Several people looked at the beautiful home on Lake Springfield, but there had been no offers. Ella wasn't all that upset because she knew the sale would force her daddy into an assisted living facility, and she wasn't ready for that.

Ella sat rocking on her daddy's front porch swing, anxiously awaiting the Sunday house tour groups and prospective buyers. She had just opened up a Good Housekeeping magazine when a newer-model, navy blue Chevy Malibu pulled up the drive. She watched the young mother reach into the back seat and scoop a toddler out of his car seat. She walked up the steps to the front porch with the toddler on her hip and smiled "Hi, my name is Amber, and this is Oliver."

"Well, hello, Oliver and Amber," said Ella, as she stood to introduce herself. Her phone vibrated, and she took it out of her pocket. She gave the young mother an apologetic smile followed by the words, "Excuse me, it's my little boy."

"Hey, Mommy, can I go to Abe's to swim?" Father is busy on the phone with an important client, so he shushed me away and told me to call you. "Please, his dad is going to play water basketball with us."

As the young mom waited patiently for Ella to finish her conversation with her son, the slight-figured lady, with a baggy denim dress, ridiculously large sunglasses, and an even larger sun hat, rushed right past the trio and into the house. Ella didn't like having multiple people in the house at a time, but Davis was in the middle of another important deal, so he insisted she would have to take care of her parents' open house alone. "Sure, baby, you can go to Abe's. I will pick you up when I leave Papa's house," Ella quickly conceded. She then rustled the young mom and baby through the front door of her childhood home. Ella tried to focus on Amber's questions, but she was distracted by the woman who had just disappeared into the dining room. "Excuse me, one moment, Amber; feel free to look around the first level. I will be right with you."

Ella nearly collided with the other lady as they met at the kitchen entryway. "Hi, I'm Ella." Ella spoke with an energetic tone as she stretched out her hand. The woman did not return the courtesy. Feeling the discomfort of the moment, Ella asked, "Are you familiar with this area? I can…" She was cut off by the curt words, "I grew up around here." Ella couldn't see the woman's eyes behind the dark sunglasses, but she felt her stare into her eyes a little longer than felt comfortable. Then the lady walked past Ella and, just like a bee, made a direct line to the upstairs level, leaving Ella with the awkward desire to rush after her and ask her to leave. At the same moment, Amber returned from the kitchen. *Thank goodness she was not subject to the odd interaction,* thought Ella. Now, Ella felt torn; she wanted to give Amber her undivided attention, but she didn't want a complete stranger having free-rein of the rest of her family home, especially a person who felt comfortable enough to ignore all social rules of an open house. Within minutes, the lady hustled down the stairs and out the front door. Amber and Ella gave each other quizzical looks as the woman walked down the lane and disappeared around the corner of Lakeshore Drive. Later in the day, the interaction gnawed at Ella. *Was the lady a drug addict looking for prescription drug medications in the medicine cabinets?* Ella wondered. It was incredibly odd that she wasn't driving. Lakeshore Drive was a busy and dangerous place to be walking, with all of the twists and turns and low visibility. Ella knew the dangers of the winding road. Immediately, Ella's thought returned to the present moment, and to the bitter truth behind her momma's car accident.

Ella shook her head in confusion. "You came to my open house, didn't you? You looked straight into my eyes. THAT was you! You weren't there looking for prescription medications like I thought. You were there to see ME." Ella began to freak out as the walls of her prison closed in on her even more.

The sweet laugh resonated over the speaker. "Ella, dear, I keep telling you I have been part of your life for more years than you can imagine. We have spent family time at the park and your daddy's house, and…but those stories are all for another story time. Sweet dreams, Ella, sweet dreams."

Ella was now able to put a face to her monster, but it didn't do her any good.

It had been several days since she received William's journal, and she was slowly getting pieces of her husband's and her sister's journals. She still had not yet received a journal from Willow. The painful truths that were being revealed each time a scrapbook or journal page was slipped through the door were, at times, more than Ella thought she would be able to endure, but William's journal was raw and precious. As June dealt out her daily torments, Ella asked, "Why haven't I received anything from Willow? I have received items from Davis, Emilie, and William-- but not Willow." Ella feared the answer, but she had to know the truth; she had to know her baby girl was OK.

June chuckled, "Ella, dear, don't you worry your pretty little head…well…minus the hair. After all, you wouldn't want to be a part of one of those…what do you call them…self-fulfilling prophecies where a mom feels guilty for leaving her beautiful little girl and something nasty happens to her, would you?"

"PLEASE TELL ME MY BABY GIRL IS OK," Ella screamed, as she uncontrollably grabbed at her short clumps of hair.

June shook her head for effect, knowing Ella could not see her, "Poor William, he is trying so hard to be the man of the house-- with your absence and all, and with Davis spending so much time away from home or locked up in his bedroom with your sister. He REALLY is trying to protect beautiful little Willow, but he just can't be everywhere at all times."

The speaker clicked off momentarily, but then Willow's giggles filled the small space.

Ella crumbled into the fetal position and bawled.

When she awoke, Ella knew it was the middle of the night, and she had surmised that June and Jax were the only two who watched her on the video monitor. She wasn't sure why she was doing it, but she ripped out a piece of paper from her journal. She folded the paper, so it became a box shape, and carefully slipped it over the eye of the camera. Immediately, a piercing alarm screamed through her ears and rattled her brain. Within minutes, Ella heard the rushing of footsteps down the stairs, followed by a slur of cuss words. Without warning, the lights were cut off, and she couldn't see two inches in front of her startled face. She heard the clip of something plastic hit the floor outside the closet, followed by the release of an aerosol can that had been put through the door slot. Before she could process what was happening, Ella smelled the chemicals that were now filling up the small space around her. Trying to adjust to the blackout, she had not closed her eyes soon enough. The burning sensation made her scream, and as she did so, she tasted the bug spray that now covered every inch of her hell-hole. She banged into walls as she tried to take refuge under her damp towel. After what seemed like forever, the aerosol can fizzled out. Ella did not raise her head from under the towel. Chemical tears uncontrollably ran down her face, as she spat and threw up the poison in her mouth.

June's voice raged through the speaker, "Don't ever try a little stunt like that again, or I will continue to exterminate you like the roach that you are."

"What kind of ruthless animals are you?" Ella shrieked, as she choked on the bug spray. It was with this incident that she realized the destitution of her reality. She was in serious trouble.

June's only response was a boisterous laugh through the speaker in unison with Jax's heckling on the other side of the door.

Several hours later the lights flicked on, and June returned to the basement. Ella could sense the anger in her voice.

"Ella, you have been a naughty little girl. Just for that, I sent the police your journals…that's right…BOTH OF THEM. They are going to know everything soon, and they are going to go looking for your lover boy. You see, they have been focusing on Davis, but now your sweet Italian man is going to start feeling the heat, and it is ALL your fault. The next time you do something stupid, you won't get off this easy. I see your fingers are just now healing. Instead of sending hair and journals to the police, we will start sending body parts. If you think I am in the least bit kidding, you have another think coming. Go ahead and try me. Or better yet, Donny has been begging me to let him spend some time with you. Come to think of it, that is probably better than sending the police a finger or an earlobe."

Ella instinctively squeezed her thighs together. She looked around her prison. A powder coating covered her belongings. Dead bugs gathered in the corners and along the wet edges of the closet; even the ones she had put in the plastic dish were dead. The taste of chemicals lingered on her tongue and burned her throat for hours.

43

With coffee in hand, Drew made his way to the front porch to retrieve the morning paper. The paper was sitting precariously in the bush next to his front door, but the two journals that had been neatly placed on the wrought iron bench on the front porch grabbed his attention. One journal was labeled "real," and the other was labeled "fake." The note stuck to the real journal read, "This package is symbolic of Ella's life...and very telling. The two objects you are looking at look the same on the outside, but they are oh so very different on the inside...just like Ella and Emilie. But my question, Mr. Policeman, is why did Ella go through the hard work of keeping two diaries? I'm not telling you how to do your job, but if you check them for prints, you will see that Davis is a nosey man. Ella, however, realized this, so she was very careful with her true thoughts. It's kind of a sad story, Ella's perfect life. So, how about you grab yourself a fresh cup of coffee and spend a little time relaxing with a good book."

Scott went inside and grabbed a gallon-sized Zip Lock bag and a sandwich bag. He unzipped the gallon bag, put the sandwich bag over his right hand and carefully placed each of the journals into the larger bag. He went into the house and checked his perimeter security camera. At 3:23 a.m., a puffy figure in all black with a black hoodie and large sunglasses, the kind people wear after eye surgery, slipped into view of the camera, placed the journals on the bench and rushed down the street. The person was bulky but had a swift gate.

Scott was pissed. His baby lay five feet away from the person who had violated his personal home. He fed and dressed his little girl, loaded her in the car, and dropped her off at his mom's. He was grateful his mom had offered to take care of her during the day, and he was more grateful Brooke had agreed.

He called Gibbons while he pulled out of his parents' driveway.

Gibbons barely got a "Hey, Partner" in, when curse words he had never heard Scott use, tumbled out of his mouth like a drunken sailor. Gibbons gathered what he could from his partner's incoherent words and said, "Settle down while you are driving. We can talk about this when you get here."

As he pressed the car speaker off, Scott mumbled, "Fucking settle down? That fucker was right outside my baby's window. I'm not going to fucking settle down. This JUST got personal."

Gibbons was waiting for him outside the building. "Listen, brother, I know you are pissed."

Scott interrupted, "Oh, I am more than pissed. I am going to find the son-of-a-bitch who was at my house, and I am going to make him wish he had made a better choice."

"How about we go inside and see what is in the journals and then take a closer look at your video surveillance, OK?" Gibbons was trying hard to cool his partner down, but he understood. Agents were all big and bad until they felt a threat to their family. Then, it got real ugly REAL fast.

With shaking hands, Scott unlocked the journal labeled "fake" first. The entries, each labeled, "Dear Diary" were vanilla. Ella shared her love for her children, her sadness over the loss of her mother, the strained relationship with her sister, her fear of losing her father, and her frustration with her husband, who, as she put it, was growing more distant by the month. He learned very little new information from the journal.

Scott feathered the pages of the second journal, he noticed a few pages had been torn out, and knew the tears in the journal would most likely match the entries they had previously received.

Ella began each entry, "Dear C," He knew who the C was by now. He recalled the two interviews he and his partner had with Gianni. The man was smooth, disarming, and humble. Scott could not fathom his being behind the abduction. But had the man charmed them as he had charmed Ella so many years earlier? Had his and Gibbons' objectivity been clouded by this suave man? Had Gianni lied to him? Had he and Ella been in contact with each other? He believed Gianni when he said he had no clue what had happened to Ella, but the guy's name kept coming back to him like a bad penny.

He said, "What is in the corridors of these pages that is so private that Ella had to create a fake decoy journal? Talk to me, Ella. Give me some clues. I presume that whoever sent me these diaries also read them, so who else knows your deepest darkest secrets, and how did he or she get hold of them?"

He looked at a picture of the pretty mom flashing a beautiful, toothy smile and said, "Talk to me, Ella. Give me some sort of clue that will help us find you."

He felt like a peeping Tom peeking into the bedroom window of a woman he had never met but felt like he knew so intimately. He began reading her private thoughts. The entry was dated July 25, 2012.

My Dearest C,

You would think that after twenty years, I would get over you, but I still see your face everywhere I go. I took a rare trip to Chicago, Illinois with Davis. Of course, he worked the whole time, so I entertained myself with outdoor activities. After a morning run along the lakeshore, I rented a kayak to enjoy the city from the Chicago River. I was soaking up the warm summer sun when I looked up at the Bridge House Bar and Grill to see a grown-up version of the man I fell in love with so many years ago. I was glad I had sunglasses on, so the man didn't catch me staring, but I swear he stared back through his own sunglasses. I'm sure, Mr. Montague, that you are still sipping wine at outdoor cafes, most likely with a beautiful Italian wife, but you can't blame a girl for dreaming.

-E-

Scott said, "Ella, maybe you weren't going as crazy as you thought. I assume you hid this journal very well; so how the hell did somebody find it?"

He took his notepad out and began scrawling notes haphazardly on the paper. "Davis would not hand us this. Maybe Ella had the journal with her." He scratched the second note out, knowing that the journal would not have fit in her small purse. He scrawled, "Could Emilie have found it and sent it to us? Handwriting is same as other mail, so don't think Emilie would have sent the diaries. Someone else knew where she hid it, but who is that someone else? Don't think Gianni would have had access to her home."

He called Davis. "Davis, I have a question for you." Without giving him a chance to respond, he continued, "Do you know anything about Ella having a diary or a journal, sir?"

Davis' heart dropped into his stomach. He had been looking high and low for Ella's journal since he returned home. *Did Agent Scott somehow have the journal?* he wondered. *If he didn't have it, how would he know to ask about it?* Davis wasn't sure how to answer the question. If the agent did have the journal, his fingerprints would be all over it; if he said "no," he would be caught in yet another lie. If he admitted he knew about a journal, the agent might wonder why he hadn't mentioned it before.

Davis decided to remain ambiguous. "I know over the years Ella wrote in a journal. Sometimes she wrote in bed at night while I read, and on a few occasions, she had me read her entries."

There, he thought, that covered any of his fingerprints that might be on it.

Agent Scott said, "Can you describe the journal to me?"

Davis hesitated as if it had been a very long time since he had seen the journal. "I think it had a brown leather cover, with a single word in yellow on the front. I can't recall the word, but I actually think there might have been a flower on it also."

Agent Scott looked down at the twin diaries; both of them were brown leather-bound diaries with a simple yellow flower and the word "Wanderlust" imprinted on the covers.

"Davis, I am holding a journal in my hand that fits that exact description".

Davis was silent. He knew Ella did not have the journal with her at the restaurant, so someone had to have stolen it from their hotel room. He wondered if she had even taken it to Florida. If not, that meant someone had been in their home while they were on vacation. A feeling of violation engulfed him either way.

"Are you still there, Mr. Davis?"

"Yes, yes, sorry. I was just thinking. I don't have an answer for you, sir."

"Ummm, Mr. Davis," Scott hemmed and hawed, it wasn't the only item we received. Davis' heart dropped.

Scott said, "It seemed Ella had two identical journals. Both were dated around the same time, but the contents were very different, Mr. Davis...I mean VERY different. Whoever sent the journals labeled one 'fake' and the other 'real.'"

Davis was momentarily unable to breathe.

"Do you know why your wife might have kept two identical journals, sir?"

Davis couldn't find the words to respond.

"Mr. Masters, the journal labeled 'real' provided a much deeper understanding of your wife. I have to tell you, as a husband, it was difficult to read. As an investigator, it has provided us with additional evidence as far as motives for your wife's disappearance, but at this time we are unable to provide you with those details.

Davis' voice returned in a fury, "You mean to tell me I am not privy to information my wife wrote in a journal? How do you even know she wrote it? Maybe someone is trying to set me up."

"First of all, Mr. Masters, you are assuming that the journal includes negative entries about you. Why would you jump to that conclusion?"

Davis did not answer the question, so Scott continued.

"Second, trust me when I say that the details of the real journal are specific. Someone couldn't have made up the stuff on those pages." He let his comments linger in the air for a moment.

"Mr. Masters, we would like you to come down to the station for some more questioning, and I suggest you bring Dubin with you. Are you available later today or tomorrow morning?"

Davis weakly replied, "My attorney is not available today, but I will see about tomorrow morning." He didn't want to wait, but he didn't want to subject himself to their questioning without Erik Dubin present. He knew it was going to be a long day and night.

It was his day to take care of the kids, but he reluctantly called Emilie and asked if she could keep them again. He was in no shape to deal with them.

Emilie acted irritated that Davis was once again shirking his parental duties, but deep down she was glad to keep the kids with her. They kept her mind preoccupied, and she knew it is where her sister would want them to be. She knew she wasn't good at the kid thing, but Emilie was learning...and she was starting to like it.

44

A ripped piece of paper floated to the floor at Ella's feet, and the clunky boots ascended the stairs.

June's words burned through Ella, "It is time for another story to help remind you of the gem of a man you call your husband. Now, I didn't lie to you when I said I gave the pigs your journals. I really did give them both of them, and let me tell you, they are having a hay day with them. I did, however, keep a few select entries back for us.

Ella knew she was watching her every move. Ella looked at the ripped journal entry; it was dated, April 13, 2014.

"Go ahead, sweetie, read me a story."

Ella's weak voice began,

My Dearest C-

I hate when Davis suggests the kids go to their papa's for the night or weekend. Don't get me wrong, I love for them to spend time with him, but I have come to learn that it means Davis has plans for me... and they are not nice plans. Last night was no different. Earlier in the day, he suggested to Willow that she call her papa to see if she could spend the night. He knew I wouldn't go against this because I would never want William or Willow to think I didn't want them to spend time with their papa. Daddy's memory is beginning to fail, so I want the children to be around him as much as possible. With Emilie so far away, Daddy's care is all on my shoulders. I'm not complaining, but I wish Emilie and I had a better adult relationship and that she was more involved with Daddy. I miss my sister. We haven't talked much since our big blow up. I pray nothing happens to me because I don't know what would happen to the children. Emilie wants nothing to do with kids, and Davis seems to have developed the same mindset. He has little to no interaction with the kids. The man does not possess one paternal instinct, nor does he make an attempt. He diminished his need for responsibility when William was a baby by explaining that the boy needed his mom during the first couple of years. Then, when I told him we were expecting baby number two, Davis spewed a string of slanderous accusations about how the baby was a trick and probably wasn't even his, and then he disappeared for a whole weekend. To this day, I have no clue what would possess him to think that the baby wasn't his. I have no desire, or time for that matter, to have an affair. Not to mention the fact that I have never gotten over you. From the time Willow was born, every time we got into an argument, he insisted that he knew I was cheating on him.

Ella stopped reading. The entry had new meaning, and her confusion now made sense. All these years, her husband really did believe Willow was another man's child. She felt sadness for her daughter.

June impatiently cleared her voice to encouraged Ella to continue. Ella did so.

"Within minutes of the children leaving yesterday, Davis got out the Crown Royal and downed a shot on the rocks. He usually added a bit of Coke to dilute the drink, but he wasn't in the mood to sweeten up anything. He told me his week had been exceptionally rough with several business deals going south, and he needed to tie one on and let off steam. I knew the Crown Royal would provide the means to tie one on, and I would be the means to let off steam. As he smacked my bottom way too hard, I recognized the kind of mood he was in. I had a long night ahead of me.

I wasn't wrong. Davis actually had the nerve to say, 'I have to tell you, things are much better when the kids aren't around-- not great, but better.'

What kind of man says that to his wife?

He was in rare form because of those damn Chicago investors. He said they were putting more pressure on him to come up with more money than they had initially agreed on."

June laughed mockingly, causing Ella to stop reading. "Those damn Chicago investors. Your lover boy was the reason for a lot of the things you had to endure with your hubby." As if she realized she had not minded her manners, she said, "Oh, sorry about that, PLEASE continue."

Ella felt shame and embarrassment, and she wanted this woman to leave her alone. Her words were barely audible.

"I lay there, unable to move. My head was splitting, and my stomach churned from what he had just done to me. I need to get out. I need to get away from this monster. He is not a nice man. These occurrences are increasing in number and in degree, and it is just of matter of time before Davis drinks more than he should and doesn't realize his own strength. He pushes the threshold of pain a bit further each time. I am afraid that one of these times Davis will grasp my throat a little too long or a little too hard- and I will die. If something happens to me, who will take care of the children?

You will always be my only true love!"

-E-

June watched the broken woman crumpled in a bony mound on the concrete floor for several minutes. She was amazed at what three weeks could do to a person.

"Ella?"

No response.

"Oh ELLLAA?"

Still, no response.

"Bitch, when I talk to you, you better answer."

Ella lifted her haggard face, looked straight into the eye of the camera, and gritted, "What do you want?"

"Goodness, I just wanted to say nighty-night. Sometimes you are so cranky."

Ella did not take her hollow eyes off the camera. The room went black.

45

Ella had just drifted off into another restless sleep when she heard the familiar clunky boots on the creaky stairs. She feared it was Donny. She lay quietly on her filthy towel, her heart pounding out of her chest, and waited for a voice. The heavy breathing on the other side of the thick wooden padlocked door was unnerving. Ella lay in frozen silence for what seemed like an eternity. In reality, it was only a few minutes. The male voice finally spoke. "Olly Olly Oxen Free, how would you like a piece of me?"

Ella did not respond, but her heart beat loudly, and her breathing became shallow.

He chanted, "Olly Olly Oxen Free, you know I know you recognized me."

Still, Ella said nothing. She knew this was the man who first took her from the bathroom, and she knew it was the man from the pickup truck, but she was not going to take his bait.

Her captor grew impatient. "Bitch, you think you are all high and mighty in your fancy little Mercedes Benz. You got lucky once before when the fucking police saved your pretty little ass from what I was going to do to your hot little body. Now, there is nobody to protect you. June and Jax are fast asleep, and it seems like it's just the two of us here to play games in the night."

Donny continued in a hushed whisper, "I will fucking wipe that look you gave me off of your fucking face after I have my way with you."

Ella's head was throbbing from fear, and it was debilitating her ability to think.

As if her captor could read her mind, he said, "Think, Ella, Think!" He knew Jax would kick the shit out of him for giving up so much information, but he also knew Jax would never know about this little side game because he wouldn't be awake for several hours.

The more silent Ella was, the more pissed he became. "We are going to play a little game," he continued. "We have been playing by Jax and June's rules, but now, we are going to play by my rules."

She heard his taunting anger as he continued, "I'm sure it was love at first sight for you when our eyes locked on each other-- you in your fancy little car, and me in my buddy's less-than-fancy pick-up truck."

His laugh curdled the contents of her dinner in her stomach, as the memory flooded back to the month before she disappeared.

This was the revelation that confirmed her thoughts that she was back in Springfield, presumably somewhere on the east side. Her heart pounded. How could she be this close to home, and nobody know it. Was everyone still looking in Florida, or had these people provided unintended clues to her husband or the police. She guessed this was not the case. They may have figured it didn't matter what they told her because she was stuck in this prison.

She totally visualized the man in the rusty Chevy truck. She remembered his disgusting sexual innuendoes, and again she felt like she had an elephant on her chest.

He jiggled the lock again and taunted her, saying, "I am going to do to you tonight what my buddy and I were going to do to you before, but this time I have you all to myself!"

Connecting the two situations put the fear of the devil in her. The jostling of the lock shook her back to her frightening reality. Her eyes frantically darted around the room looking for anything to use as a weapon to fend off the man who was about to open the wooden door.

She gripped a pen in her right hand, but she knew it was no defense for this man. The wooden door creaked open, and Donny smiled his wicked smile.

"Here I am to keep my promise, my love."

He moved quickly and was on top of her in seconds. His dirty hands covered her mouth. His fingers tasted of cigarette smoke and onions, and as his sloppy lips touched hers, the addition of his raunchy stale beer breath, cigarettes, and unbrushed teeth nauseated her.

The moment she had feared for weeks had come to fruition. Ella tried to wriggle herself free from his grip, but it was everything she could do not to pass out. Her once healthy body had become withered and weak.

His wet, slimy kisses moved from her mouth down to her neck as he ripped her t-shirt open, exposing her braless breasts. As his mouth moved down to her right breast, she used her left hand to reach over and knock the camera to the floor in hopes that it would alert June to come downstairs.

Ella continued to writhe under Donny's weight in an attempt to buck him off of her, but her lack of nutrition left her weak and helpless. She had flashbacks to the many times Davis had forced himself on her when he was under the influence of too much alcohol. She tried hard to muster up a fight, but the more she struggled, the more aggressive Donny became. She collapsed weakly underneath him; she had no more fight in her.

The man pulled Ella's yoga pants and underwear to her knees, and as he held her down by the neck with his right hand, he undid his belt buckle and wriggled his own pants down to his thighs.

Ella squeezed her thighs together tightly, closed her eyes and prayed it wouldn't take long. As he forced her legs open, the wooden door flew open and the female voice that had spent so much time on the other side of the door, grabbed the man by the hair and screamed, "What the fuck are you doing?"

He backhanded June, and she hit the wall. Like a chain reaction, Jax grabbed him by his hair, pulled him off of Ella, and threw him up against the opposite wall, causing the few items in her prison to break and scatter. As both men threw punches and bellowed cuss words at each other, Ella gathered her underwear and yoga pants and huddled in the corner, her hands shielding as much of her frail body and face as possible. The two men spent the next several minutes intertwined, knocking over the makeshift toilet and sending urine and wet cat litter all over the floor. They were an even match, Ella determined, by the length of time it took for Jax to take Donny down. June wiped the blood from her already-swollen busted lip as she kneeled in the doorway and coached her boyfriend to kick the shit out of the son-of-a-bitch.

She spewed profanities at Donny. "You mother fucking pussy ass son-of-a-bitch-- what the fuck did you think you were doing? I swear, if you fuck this up, you will spend the rest of your life trying to remember what it was like to have a dick."

Ella took several elbows and kicks to her fragile body as she tried to recoil into the wall.

One final fist to the jaw left Donny still. Jax had knocked him out cold.

June's profanities turned from Donny to Jax. "I told you he was a loose cannon. I fucking told you we shouldn't involve him because he would somehow fuck things up. You knew Donny was a risk factor because of his sexual past."

Jax dragged his buddy out of the closet and up the stairs. June locked the closet door and followed them, slinging profanities with every step she took.

Ella shook uncontrollably as she put her underwear and pants back on. Every muscle in her body ached, she was bleeding in several places, and she thought her ribs were broken. But she was alive and safe for the moment, and that was all that mattered. She thanked God for his hand of protection and pleaded for the nightmare to end.

46

William and Willow spent their weeks being transported back and forth by strangers as various FBI agents picked them up and delivered them between their home with their father and their papa's house with their Aunt Emilie, so Davis and Emilie didn't have to have contact with each other. Whichever adult had the kids during their activities would transport them to and from the events. Neither Davis nor Emilie were very good at shuffling the kids from activity to activity, and as a result, William and Willow missed several practices, birthday parties, and other events, or they waited anxiously to be picked up long after the other children were gone.

The morning sun glistened off the lake, and the sound of motorboats and jet skis filled the air. The weather forecast indicated clear skies and temperatures in the 80's. William had stayed the night at Abe's because they had 9:00 baseball practice. Emilie had assured him that she would pick him up at 11:00.

As usual, Emilie rushed around the house in a flurry to get out the door to run her errands before she had to pick William up from practice. "Willow, I need to run to the grocery for a few things, and then I am picking William up from baseball practice," Emilie yelled across the lawn, as her keys jingled in her hand. Your papa is watching a movie, so he is fine for a while. "I won't be gone more than an hour, OK, sweetie?"

Willow nodded as she sat on her plaid blanket under the weeping willow tree that had been planted as a gift to her from her Nana and Papa when she was born. Next to her was her favorite doll, Morgan, which her Aunt Emilie had given her three years earlier. Morgan was an American Girl doll, but instead of being Willow's twin, Emilie had created the doll in her own likeness and given it to her niece for her fifth birthday. The doll had long blonde hair and big blue eyes. Emilie sent her stylish outfits for the doll every holiday. Emilie had told Willow, "This way, even though I live far away in Chicago, you will be able to see me every day."

Willow waved as her aunt's car zoomed down the lane. As the nearby cottonwood trees scattered billowy cotton flowers all around her, Willow reassured Morgan that their mommy would be home soon. She consoled her baby, telling her everything was going to be OK.

Her father despised Willow's dolls and was blatantly obvious about it. Willow never understood why, but her father seemed to hate Morgan more than any of the others. When Willow was seven, Davis told her she was too old to play with dolls, so her mom had secretly taken them to Papa's house, where she could play with them all she wanted when her father wasn't around.

Willow gently sang,

> Oh, precious little baby, I love you so much
> Your smile, and your giggle, and your warm, soft touch,
> And I love the way your precious eyes, they smile up at me
> As I hold you…and rock you… and sing you to sleep.

Tears streamed down her rosy cheeks, wetting Morgan's dress.

She heard the tires on the black pavement before she saw the vehicle. Willow's heart raced from worry to relief to panic as the unfamiliar black car with black tinted windows pulled up the lane, around the circle drive, and half-way back down the driveway.

Just as she let out her breath, thinking the car must have turned into the wrong driveway, the car stopped, and a lady in a black skirt and matching jacket got out of the driver's seat.

Willow's eyes darted from the woman to the side door of her papa's house, which now seemed miles away. She knew she couldn't beat the woman in a foot race. As Willow racked her little brain to figure out what to do, the woman said, "Good afternoon, Willow, is your Aunt Emilie here?"

Relieved that the lady knew her aunt's name, Willow said, "No, she ran to the grocery store."

"What about your papa? Is he resting?"

"Yes," Willow responded.

The stranger needed to hear one more bit of information, so she gently said, "Willow, you and William need to come with me to the police station; we have found your mommy. Your daddy is already there waiting for you."

Willow's blue eyes became the size of silver dollars with the news that her mommy had been found. "William isn't here; he is at baseball practice,"

The woman responded, "Very good, we will go pick him up right now and give him the good news."

Willow hopped off the blanket, grabbed Morgan, and bound for the black car. At the last minute, she decided she better not take Morgan. She didn't want to ruin the happy family reunion by making her daddy mad. She ran back to the blanket and carefully kissed and hugged Morgan. "I told you they would find our mommy!" She carefully placed the doll on the red and gray checked blanket and ran back to the open back door of the black car. The lady closed the door behind the little girl. As Willow buckled her seatbelt, she heard the "click" of the locks. A sick feeling made its way through her body as she looked into the eyes of a strange man in the front passenger seat, who was staring at her with a creepy grin. The woman made her way around the front of the car, the locks clicked unlock, and she hopped into the car. With a final "click" of the locks, the car sped down the driveway and turned right on to Lake Shore Drive.

Fear pounded through every inch of Willow's little body. "You didn't find my mommy, did you?" her shaking words squeaked out of her tiny mouth. The man in the passenger seat laughed a menacing laugh. "We found your mommy all right! We just aren't the police!" June joined her boyfriend in laughter as the car headed down 1-55 south.

Willow crossed her little legs and squeezed her thighs together as she wiggled her bottom into the back seat, but she couldn't stop the stream from flowing. She wet herself, and the pee soaked into the dark cloth seats. She sat paralyzed with fear that the strangers in the front seat would hear her or smell the pee and punish her for wetting her pants. Neither noticed or said anything as they continued down the highway, leading her further and further away from her papa's house.

47

Emilie's errands took longer than she planned, so she called Kristina before she stopped at the grocery store.

"Hey Kristina, my errands took a bit longer than I had anticipated. Would you mind dropping William off at his papa's house?"

Kristina replied, "That is no problem. Would it be OK if we stop for a treat first?"

"Sure, thanks for all of your help."

Emilie wasn't used to having to juggle her daddy and the kids' schedules, so her time management was off. She didn't feel too guilty, though, about being gone longer than she had planned. Her daddy slept most of each afternoon, and Willow would be lost in her own world, playing with her doll, Morgan.

Emilie pulled up the long drive of her childhood home at 11:30. A sense of nostalgia washed over her when she saw the special American Girl doll she had given her niece, sitting upright on the plaid blanket underneath the willow tree as if she were patiently waiting for her mommy to return with her tea set.

A pang of sadness rippled up and down Emilie's arms at the thought of the child she never had. The emotion caught her off guard; she thought she hated kids, but her niece and nephew were growing on her. William had softened a little toward her, and Willow had taken to her like she was her mother. Emilie felt a mixture of pleasure and guilt over the comfort she received from the kids.

Her twin sister, Ella, had struggled for years to get pregnant, and Emilie got knocked up after a one-night stand she had unrealistically hoped would turn into more. She wondered if she would have kept the baby if the child would have had a different father. "Maybe," Emilie thought. She cringed at the thought of her sister knowing about her relationship with Cristiano, and the resulting pregnancy of the one-night stand. The twins' relationship was already hanging on a thread; this information might break it beyond repair.

She balanced the recycled grocery bags to free up her hands to open the back door, but the door was already cracked open. She pushed the door in and yelled, "Willow, silly girl, you forgot to close the door." There was no response.

Emilie checked in on her daddy, who was sleeping in his bedroom with the door closed. As Emilie turned the corner to the living room, she realized something didn't feel right. Beau had not bound out to her car to welcome her home. She had assumed he was inside, but she searched the entire house, and there was no Beau…or Willow. She tried to remain calm, telling herself that Willow must have taken her dog for a walk. She went to the back patio where they kept Beau's lead; the bright red leash was sitting right on the table.

Emilie couldn't swallow. She could not breathe. As she walked around the perimeter of the lakefront property, she began talking to herself, "There has to be a reasonable explanation here. Willow knows how to swim, and there is no way she would ever get into the lake without an adult around. Maybe Davis picked her up." She knew this last explanation was unlikely.

She stopped in her tracks and listened. She heard something…whining. "Willow, where are you? Have you gotten hurt sweetie? I am right here. Keep making noise." The whimpering increased as Emilie got closer to the shed, where they stored lake toys. Sickness filled her. The padlock that secured the double doors was on the ground, and a green zip tie replaced the broken lock.

Emilie cried, "Willow, talk to me. Are you OK? Sweetie, I will be right back, I promise. I am going to go get something to get the door open."

The whining sounds continued.

Emilie raced to the house, through the back door, and into the kitchen. She grabbed a steak knife out of the butcher block holder and ran back out to the shed. She stood in front of the shed, momentarily frozen in fear of what was behind the closed door. The whimpering was now barely audible.

"Stick with me, Willow," she reassured the girl as she took a deep breath, cut the zip tie, and threw open the doors.

Emilie would never be able to erase the sight in front of her. Her sister's beautiful golden retriever lay soaked in blood from multiple stab wounds. His mouth had been duct- taped. The tinny smell of blood warmed by the summer heat overwhelmed her. Her eyes frantically looked around the shed for Willow; she was not there. A mixture of relief and fear coursed through her body.

Blood-curdling screams built in her gut and moved their way to her lungs and flew out of her mouth. Beau tried to lift his head to console her, but it fell to the concrete floor, as he struggled for his last breath. She reached over and gently cut the duct tape from his mouth, hoping it would somehow bring her sister's beloved dog back to life. Instead, Beau took his final breath and died. The pool of blood flowed toward the slanted entry of the door, and Emilie's white flip flops turned crimson.

She stood at the door of the shed with the bloody knife in her hand. She heard tires on the warm summer blacktop. Petrified, she backed out of the shed and turned to see Kristina's car. She slowly walked toward the car, still holding the bloody knife, with a hollow look on her face. William saw her first and jumped out of the car, followed by Kristina and Abe.

"Emilie, what are you doing?" William screamed.

Emilie could not respond. She had no words. She had gone into shock. Kristina saw her drop the knife and begin falling forward. She raced to her, but not before Emilie's face planted itself into the concrete sidewalk. She was passed out cold. Kristina saw the blood that covered Emilie's flip-flops and hands and put her owns hands to her mouth to stifle her screams.

As calmly as possible, Kristina said, "William, I need you to call 9-1-1. Do you know the address here?

William closed in on his aunt to see the knife and her bloody feet.

He began yelling at his unconscious aunt, "What have you done to my sister? Willow, where are you Willow? W-I-L-L-O-W," he screamed desperately.

Kristina had already dialed the emergency number. She grabbed him by the shoulders, "William, I NEED the address here! What is the house number?" William stood helplessly, unable to come up with the address. Abe ran to the front of the house and yelled back to his mom, "114."

Kristina repeated the house number to the call center operator, "114 Willow Lane."

The operator said, "Ma'am besides the woman that has passed out, has anybody else been hurt?"

"I don't know, but her hands, feet, and shoes are covered in blood...and she had a knife in her hand."

Kristina continued rambling, "I pulled up the lane to bring William home from baseball, and I saw his aunt walking toward us with a bloody knife."

"Is there anyone else at the property or in the house?"

Kristina asked William if Willow and his papa were supposed to be there.

William nodded.

"Yes, there are two other residents on the property. An older gentleman and a little girl, but I don't see either of them because we are still outside."

"Kristina, do not go into the house! Stay put. We have already dispatched a squad car and an ambulance your way. You should hear sirens momentarily. I am going to keep you on the line until they arrive, but I need you to make sure nobody goes inside."

Focused only on her conversation with the 9-1-1 dispatch operator, Kristina had not noticed William was no longer at her side. She heard William's blood-curdling screams as a band of sirens made their way up the drive.

William exited the shed, covered in blood and still screaming. He ran at Emilie, who lay knocked out with a pool of blood next to her head. He began kicking her and yelling, "What have you done to my sister?" What have you done to my sister?"

Scores of police, firefighters, and ambulance personnel stormed the yard, and a sea of confusion ensued for the next several minutes. A husky officer grabbed William from behind and restrained his flailing body.

"Easy does it, little buddy, let's figure out what is going on here."

"She killed my dog! She's done something with my sister. She probably murdered my mom!" he spouted as he continued his rant.

Two officers cautiously approached the shed, with weapons raised. They saw bloody tracks on the round, decorative stones in front of the shed and in the grass. The first officer glanced inside and quickly withdrew.

"Damn." Officer Cookson blurted as he quickly retreated from the shed. "Whoever did that needs to be shot."

Officer Pohlman looked in and said, "Awww, Man. You have got to be kidding me. Who would do something like this?"

The firefighters had already begun treating Emilie's wounds, while two police officers, with weapons out, entered the house through the open back door. Nothing in the house was disturbed or amiss.

The sirens awakened William's papa out of a sound sleep, and by the time he woke up enough to know something was wrong, the police were making their way down the hallway toward his room.

"Mr. Randolph, this is the Springfield Police Department. Sir, are you OK?"

A confused elderly man made his way around the corner to see weapons raised and pointed in his direction.

"What is going on?" he asked, with a shocked look on his face.

"Sir, are you alone in the house?"

"I don't think so. My granddaughter is here, and my daughter should be here. My grandson went to ball practice, so he probably isn't back yet. What seems to be going on, officers?"

"Have you heard any unusual noises in the past couple of hours, sir?"

"I took a short nap, but I did not hear anything until about ten minutes ago when sirens woke me."

"Sir, we have a situation here. We think you need to sit down."

Randolph said, "What has happened? Has something happened to one of my grandchildren?"

The officer led Mr. Randolph to the couch and slowly explained the limited information they had about the series of events that occurred right outside his house.

In the meantime, smelling salts revived Emilie and paramedics carefully loaded her onto a stretcher and into the ambulance. They tended to her face wounds, which would require several stitches.

The police officer who had restrained William took him around to the front of the house away from the crime scene.

They sat on the front porch as William continued, in a more subdued tone, telling the officer what was going on with his mom's disappearance. The officer knew the case, and he called Agent Drew Scott at the Springfield FBI office.

A hunt of the entire property did not produce Willow Masters, either dead or alive, and Emilie Randolph seemed to have lost her ability to form a coherent sentence. She kept mumbling, "Willow, I am so sorry, Willow. I didn't mean to..." She closed her eyes, and her world went dark.

The police determined by the wound marks on the golden retriever that they were made by the same serrated steak knife as the one in Emilie's bloody hand.

Officer Cookson climbed into the ambulance. Emilie wildly opened her eyes and looked around the ambulance as if she had forgotten where she was. She stared at Cookson blankly.

"Would you like to tell me what happened," Cookson asked, with a hint of accusation.

Emilie squinted her eyes and furrowed her brow in confusion, and then her eyes slowly widened. She realized that he thought she had killed Beau. She rapidly shook her head from side to side and said, "I did not do what you think I did." She could tell the officer didn't believe her.

The ambulance whirred down the driveway and to the hospital. Emilie attempted to tell the officer what happened, but her thoughts jumbled, and her memory faded in and out, along with her consciousness. She continued her apologies, "I am sorry, Willow. I am sorry, Ella. I am sorry, William."

In the emergency room, doctors tended to Emilie's injuries and gave her a sedative to calm her down. Officer Cookson continued questioning her about how long she was gone, where she went, what exactly happened when she returned to her father's house, and most importantly, questions about Willow. She provided as many details as she could about the day's events, but everything was still foggy. Her head pounded from the fight she had lost with the concrete. The emergency room nurse told her she had suffered a concussion from the fall and that she had received several stitches. A uniformed officer remained seated outside the hospital room while she dozed in and out of fitful sleep.

Agents Scott and Gibbons arrived at Mr. Randolph's house. The animal rescue vehicle pulled away with Beau's dead body wrapped carefully in a sheet.

Agent Scott interviewed Kristina, Abe, and William to establish a timeline of the crime. William was inconsolable.

He said, "This is all my fault! I should have never trusted that woman with my sister and my dog. I knew something like this would happen if I left Willow. I should have never gone to baseball practice. That was so selfish of me!"

Agent Scott responded, "Maybe there is some explanation to this whole mess." He knew his words of comfort were hollow, and he knew William was smart enough to know that. Nothing he could say would take away William's guilt over his sister's disappearance.

Scott finished up his interviews with William, Kristina, and Abe.

"Kristina, I hate to ask this of you, but would you be willing to take William back to your house?"

"Sure," she said, "I can do that," but she gave him a concerned look.

Scott knew she wondered if she was putting her own children in jeopardy by keeping William.

"We will post a patrol car at your house to ensure your family's safety."

Relief washed over her. She walked over to William, who was now sitting alone on his papa's porch.

"William, I am going to take you home with me. You can borrow Abe's clothes until we can go to your house. I have extra toothbrushes and anything else you need. You will be safe with us, I promise."

Kristina questioned whether or not she would be able to keep her promise, but she knew she had to give William some sort of hope in this horrible moment. She reached down for his hand, and he took it. She pulled him into her and promised him again through a tear-filled voice, "I will keep you safe! I promise!

And we are going to find your mom and sister, OK? Do you hear me?"

The two broke down as Abe watched awkwardly from a distance, his own eyes filling with tears. She loaded the boys into her Volvo and drove down the lane. The Springfield Police cruiser followed behind her.

Meanwhile, Agent Gibbons called Davis.

"Good afternoon, Mr. Masters, are you at home?"

"Yes."

Agent Scott nodded to the SPD officer, indicating that Davis was at his residence. He continued, "We need you to get over to your father-in-law's house. We have a problem. A squad car will be pulling up momentarily to drive you here sir."

"What is going on?"

"We will explain everything when you arrive."

Davis' mind raced to every imaginable scenario, and dread engulfed him. "OK, sir, I will be waiting out front."

The squad car arrived before Davis had time to finish putting on his shoes. He rushed to the car and headed for the back seat. When the officer said, "You can sit up front, sir," Davis thought of his Orlando experience.

"Good afternoon, Mr. Masters, I am Officer Leach."

"What in the hell is going on?" Davis demanded.

"Sir, I was instructed to pick you up and drive you to your father-in-law's house."

"I know that, but what is going on that I need to go to my father-in-law's house?"

Officer Leach hopped on I-72 and merged onto I-55. "I was not given any other information, sir. Just that I am supposed to take you…"

Davis cut him off. "I know…to my father-in-law's house…but WHY? What has happened? What are you NOT telling me?" Davis continued his barrage of questions, but the officer explained that he was not at liberty to provide specifics about the situation. Davis wondered if he were being set up.

What if they had set a trap and he was about to walk right into it?

When he arrived at the Randolph home and saw the plethora of squad cars, he gasped, "Oh, my God, what is going on?"

Agent Scott greeted him with an apologetic handshake.

"Mr. Masters, let's find you a seat."

"I don't need a fucking seat. Just tell me what the fuck is going on here!"

"Well, sir, your sister-in-law ran a few errands, and when she returned, she found the door open. Your father-in-law was sleeping, but, well, sir…"

Scott hemmed and hawed before spitting out the last part of the story.

"Your dog was stabbed to death and your daughter… well…she seems to be missing. It looks as if Emilie might have been somehow involved, but we have not confirmed that at this time."

"That bitch! I knew she was behind this, but none of you bastards would listen to me, and now my daughter is missing, too! This is your fault! All your fault! If you assholes knew how to do your job, it would have never come to this."

Scott did not have a response. Instead, he said, "Sir, we have asked Kristina if William can stay with her family for a while. We will have a car stationed outside their house, and at any events he attends. We think it is important to have him stay with a stable family for the time being."

Davis stared at the agent, but he heard nothing the man said. Moments later, Agent Scott said, "Mr. Masters, is that OK with you, sir?"

"Is WHAT OK with me?" he barked.

"That William stays with his friend, Abe's family?"

"Yes, sure, that's fine."

Agent Scott knew the man was not thinking about his son; his mind was elsewhere, but on what, the agent wondered.

What could be more important to the man in front of him than the whereabouts of his wife and daughter, and the safety of his only son.

News crews showed up within two hours. The local internet headlines included, "Mother taken, and now eight-year-old daughter disappears," "Search begins for local eight-year-old," and "Did local child drown in Lake Springfield?"

Information about Beau, the family dog, had not made its way to the news, and if local authorities had any influence on the media, it wouldn't. They didn't want to feed the ego of or provide critical information to whoever abducted Willow.

A Springfield Police Department patrol officer was posted at the end of the long driveway to keep the press from intruding on the Randolph family's privacy. A couple of ballsy reporters tried to slip through the wooded area surrounding the Randolph property, but they were caught and arrested for trespassing, since the properties belonged to Randolph or his neighbors.

Although nobody in Kristina's family posted anything about Willow's abduction, nor did they post that they were keeping William safe at their house, news of Willow's kidnapping began popping up on social media platforms, including Facebook and Snapchat. The various posts included sordid accusations of Davis and Emilie, as well as fake news about scheduled manhunt searches and fundraisers.

Against their wishes, Scott and Gibbons provided a short statement to the public. Scott offered limited details about the investigation, and Gibbons urged citizens not to participate in any of the activities promoted online, reminding viewers that they were scams by individuals who were using a tragedy to benefit their own agenda.

Scott couldn't wait to get the cameras out of his face. He just wanted to get home to his baby girl. He still burned at the thought of these people being on his front porch, and he knew he wouldn't get over it for a while. He felt guilty that he had not spent his Saturday with his daughter. She was only with him two nights each week and every other weekend, so he was careful never to make plans on those days. Today's absence from his baby couldn't be helped, but it didn't alleviate the guilt he felt on his drive to his parents.

He decided to stay at his parents' house for a few days. He had to do everything he could to keep his own daughter safe. Drew's mom had set up Reese's pack and play, but Drew tucked her into bed next to him and held her tightly. He tried to forget the day's events, but he wondered where Ella and Willow Masters were. His sweet baby patted his face with her chubby fingers and closed her eyes in a gentle slumber.

48

Hours seemed to pass. Willow knew her Aunt Emilie would have returned to find her missing. What would she wonder? Would she think she had drowned? Willow pictured Morgan, sitting pretty on the red checked blanket as if waiting for a tea party to begin.

She knew William would be back by now also. He would know that she wouldn't just leave her Morgan sitting alone out in the summer heat.

If only she had dropped Morgan in the grass or along the side of the driveway; then Emilie would have known something terrible had happened! Why did she go willingly with this strange lady? Her mommy had always told her not to talk to, or go with, strangers, but the minute she had heard that her mommy had been found, all she wanted to do was go see her. Now she was stuck in a new nightmare. It was the same nightmare her mommy must have faced when they took her.

As the female figure eyed Willow in the rearview mirror, it was as if she were reading the little girl's mind. "You look just like your mommy, sweetheart, sitting helpless in the back seat of a strange car. She was brave, though, and she would want you to be brave too, Willow. Remember what your daddy says about crying; crying is for babies, and we need for you to be a big strong girl for your mommy, do you hear?"

Each time Willow heard her name, her tiny body shuddered, but she did not allow one tear to fall as she meekly looked down at the wet seat, nodding in understanding.

As day became evening, Willow's tummy rumbled with hunger pangs. The car pulled into a truck stop and parked out away from all of the other cars and trucks. As the driver went into the Arby's that was attached to the truck stop, the man turned to Willow. Panic engulfed her, as she recoiled in her seat.

"Damn," he said, as he got a whiff of the urine smell that became strong as the car heated up from the summer heat. "Fuck," he muttered. "These are fucking cloth seats, and you have drenched them with piss. This is going to add a fee to the rental cost if I don't get the stench out of here." His words sent a chain reaction, and like a puppy who was in the middle of being scolded, Willow began peeing again as she cupped both of her hands in between her legs in an attempt to both stop and catch the pee.

The man continued quietly cursing at the little girl, who, for the first time, had crocodile tears gripping tightly on her lower lashes.

The woman hushed the man as she struggled to open the driver's seat door with her hands full of food and drinks.

"She just pissed all over the cloth seats," he hissed.

The lady threw napkins at Willow and told her to soak up her pee, as she quickly closed the door, so nobody could hear the fiasco.

While the eight-year-old was doing her best to clean up the mess she had made, the woman walked to the back of the car and opened the trunk. Fear, once again, gripped her tiny body; she didn't know if she could survive this. Uncontrollably, she urinated again at the thought of ending up in the trunk. Luckily, the guy was busy organizing the food in the front seat, so he missed the additional accident.

The woman brought a towel and a blanket from the back of the car and threw them in the back seat. "Sit on the towel to soak up the mess you made," she barked at Willow.

Willow silently wondered what the blanket was for; the temperature on the rearview mirror read "86." She didn't want to think about what they might do to her. She imagined them forcing the blanket over her head and suffocating her to death.

The man handed Willow a kid's meal and a Sprite and told her not to make any more of a mess than she already had. Willow quietly picked at the food as the trio made their way back onto the highway. Her stomach was telling her she was hungry; her mind was convincing her otherwise. The frightened little girl had looked at the letter on the rearview mirror several times throughout the afternoon and early evening. It said "S" most of the day; she knew that meant south. The direction letter on the rearview mirror now read N. It was like they were backtracking. "Maybe," she hoped, "they are taking me back to my papa, and my brother, and to Aunt Emilie." But she knew that wasn't going to happen.

She watched the cars full of families heading to and returning from vacations, and she realized she looked just like them. Through their car windows, she was just another little girl heading home from vacation, with her parents in the front seat; only, this was no vacation, and these weren't her parents. The thoughts screamed through her head, *This isn't my mommy! This isn't my daddy! These aren't my parents! I'm NOT on vacation! Somebody, please help me!* She knew there was no use in picking the thoughts out of her head and placing them on her tongue and out of her lips. Nobody would hear her; she had no voice.

Out of sheer exhaustion, Willow finally fell asleep. When she awoke, she had something covering her eyes and duct tape over her mouth. As she instinctively moved her hands to remove the duct tape, male hands stopped her tiny fingers from reaching her mouth, scooped under her arms, and lifted her out of the car.

He whispered into her ears, "You need to remain quietly still or else something terrible will happen to you while your mommy watches, and then something even worse will happen to your mommy; you don't want to be the reason your mommy dies, do you?"

Willow's heart stopped, and she slowly shook her head from side to side.

The car turned abruptly and came to a stop. The man gave Willow further instructions, "I am going to pick you up and carry you into our warehouse. If you so much as make a whimper, remember what I told you just a little while ago. Now, you haven't forgotten, have you?"

Willow shook her head quickly this time. Donny liked the way her ringlets danced from side to side. She was cute, he thought. She looked like her mom.

He opened the door, reached in and scooped the little girl up in his arms, her legs and arms dangling. He carried her through the open door and down the steps.

Ella heard the heavy boots and the creak of the steps; her breath caught. She hoped it was just Jax coming down to do laundry. She prayed Donny was gone for good. She sat perfectly quiet in hopes that whoever it was would think she was sleeping. She heard items being shuffled in a nearby room for several minutes, and then the heavy boots ascended the stairs and left her in cold silence.

The gentle words of the Steve Martin and Edi Brickell song, "My Baby," rang through the speaker. Ella writhed in emotional turmoil as she listened to the words.

Oooh, my, my, my baby, I can't wait to see you.

Oooh, my, my, my baby, I can't wait to see you.

49

Emilie looked into the dark sky through her hospital room window. The sedative was beginning to wear off, and the haze of the day's events hung over her head. She could still see Willow's doll on the blanket and Beau's bloody body. She could feel the effects of William's kicks to her thighs and hips, and she couldn't blame him. She was now able to realize what he, Kristina, and Abe saw-- a crazy woman with a bloody knife coming from a shed where her sister's beloved dog lay dead from stab wounds, presumably from the blade she was frantically wielding in her clutched hand.

Officer Cookson sat outside her hospital room, partially to ensure she didn't flee, but partly to protect her from becoming a victim if she really was innocent. She had told the officers the series of events, and Officer Cookson appeared to believe her. The fact that the groceries were still in the bag and Gelato was still frozen gave the investigators a timeline for her return home, and further inspection of the knife showed it had not entered Beau's flesh. Her story seemed to pan out, but that did not explain Willow's disappearance.

Traffic around the lake was busier on summer weekends, but there had been no reports of suspicious activity. The driveways on the lake road were not close enough to each other for any of the neighbors to have seen anything. Mr. Randolph slept through everything, so his granddaughter must not have screamed. This could have meant that Willow knew the abductors or was caught off guard and didn't have a chance to scream. The careful placement of her doll, Morgan, also indicated that either she went willingly or was not on the blanket with her doll when she was taken, unless the abductor took the time to carefully set the doll upright on the blanket.

Emilie coughed, partially because her throat was dry and partly because she wanted to get Cookson's attention. He heard the clearing of her voice and slowly entered the room.

"How are you feeling?"

"I have had better days," she replied. Tears hung on her lower eyelashes. "I have let my sister down so many times throughout our lives, but nothing comes close to the pain I have caused our family. It is my fault that Willow has disappeared without a trace. If I had only insisted she come with me on my errands, none of this would have happened. But she was playing so contently with her Morgan. Besides, Daddy was at the house. I assumed the two could take care of each other for a while. I just didn't think about it. She is a smart kid, so she wouldn't have gone somewhere on her own. She is an excellent swimmer, but the kids have been told from the time they were old enough to walk that they must not go near the water unless an adult is with them. I just don't understand."

Cookson could tell she was trying to make sense of it as she spoke. He continued listening in hopes that something she said would spark a memory or a connection.

"Do you think the same people who took Ella also kidnapped Willow? If so, wouldn't it be very likely that they are somewhere close? Do you think Davis is doing this? Is he picking off each of us, one person at a time?" A tinge of fear rose in her voice. "I need to get out of this place. My daddy needs me, and I need to protect William. That is if I don't screw that up, too."

William is going to stay with Abe Patton's family for a while, and we have police cruisers keeping an eye on their house. We also have arranged in-home care for your father until you are released from the hospital. You took a pretty good blow to the head, so they are going to monitor you overnight. If your vitals look good in the morning, you will be released and able to go back to your father's house. We will have cruisers drive by his place several times each shift as well."

"Can you please have Agent Scott come to visit me? I need to talk to him."

A concerned look crossed Cookson's face. "Sure. I will give him a call now."

An hour later, Agent Drew Scott peeked around the corner of Emilie's hospital room to see the battered woman staring blankly at the white wall. Emilie saw the look on his face at her appearance and weakly joked, "You should see the other guy."

"How are you holding up?" he asked, more tenderly than he had meant to.

"Well, let's see. My sister has disappeared, my niece has disappeared, my daddy is being cared for by total strangers, my nephew thinks I am a murderer, my face looks like this, and my asshole brother-in-law, who I know is somehow behind all of this, is running around Scott free…No pun intended. So, Agent Scott, maybe you should tell me how I should be holding up."

Scott regretted the question and quickly said, "Officer Cookson said you asked him to contact me. What's on your mind?"

Emilie took a deep breath. "I know everyone has an opinion about me, and many of those opinions aren't flattering. People really think I did those heinous crimes. That is the kind of person many people think I am. I used to be so good at brushing people's judgments off as jealousy or insecurity, but for some reason, your opinion of me matters. I am not a kidnapper or a killer. I may not seem like I care much for kids or animals, but I would never harm my family…or their dog, for that matter."

"You know, it has been like this since Ella and I were young. She was the sweet one, who would help little old ladies across the street or return a person's grocery cart. For the longest time, I convinced myself that my life was so much better than her life because I took the bull by the horns and made things happen. I brushed my bitchy attitude off as a necessity to keep from getting taken advantage of or walked over in a male-dominated business world. I have always been successful because of my feisty personality, and I criticized my sister often for letting people take advantage of her. I was especially hard on her regarding Davis. I knew from the time they got married that he did not deserve her, and I let both of them know exactly how I felt. I probably should have kept a few of my opinions to myself, but then I started noticing strange activity on the trust account our parents had set up for us. Anyway, I questioned Ella, and things went downhill from there."

"A couple of years ago, I came to Springfield to celebrate our birthdays. Ella went all out to prepare a fancy dinner for us, and that asshole didn't even show up until a good hour after dinner was over. I had imbibed in one-too-many glasses of wine, and I told him exactly what I thought of him, including the fact that I knew he was pilfering our family's finances. It ended with him throwing a glass of wine across the room at me and me telling my sister that as long as that bastard was part of her life, I wouldn't be."

"I haven't seen her since that night. We communicate via email and text unless I call her to accuse Davis of something. I can't figure out how he is doing it, but I know money is being shuffled around somehow, and the son-of-a-bitch keeps getting away with it."

"I don't know why Ella is protecting him. It makes me wonder if he is physically abusive also. I mean, I know he is emotionally abusive to her and the kids, but now I am afraid he has turned to physically harming her. I'm wondering if he went too far, and that is what happened to Ella."

Emilie recalled the conversation she and Kristina had engaged in at Wm. Van's and Kristina's confirming words of her suspicions. Kristina had told her she shared the information with the police, so she didn't elaborate further. She liked Kristina, and she didn't want to drag her name into the conversation. The woman had already done so much for her family.

Scott listened quietly without interrupting.

"Since Ella's disappearance, Davis has hardly acknowledged he has children. He disappears for hours on end, and leaves me with the kids, wondering where he is."

In a softer voice, she said, "I just want it to be like the old days when I had a relationship with my sister. I just want my sister back."

Tears danced down her cheeks. She brushed them away. "I used to be such a badass, but this thing has gotten the best of me. I have never in my life felt so helpless."

"Emilie, why are you telling me this? I mean, as opposed to your friends or other law enforcement officials?"

"I don't know. I guess I like you, and I don't want you to think I am a bad person. As you can guess, I'm not a religious woman; Ella got that gene, too. I guess this is my version of a Catholic confession," she mustered a weak laugh.

"Well, I am glad you had Officer Cookson call me. Trust me, I'm no priest, but I hope it helped to get some things off your chest. We are not giving up on finding your sister. The fact that the abductors are still communicating with us is a good sign. I know we haven't been able to share a great deal about the investigation with you, but I will tell you in confidence that Davis has definitely made somebody mad."

"He has that effect on people, Agent Scott," she said with an exasperated sigh.

"Listen, Lady Jane, you need to get some rest. That pretty face of yours needs to heal…and it WILL heal, you know."

"It might leave a nasty scar though." She unconsciously touched the bruised side of her face and winced.

"At least you didn't knock any teeth out of that smile of yours," he teased.

"My smile isn't half as beautiful as my sister's! I want, more than anything, for you to meet her. You know, they say you don't realize what you had until you lose it. That's how I feel. If I am ever given a chance to make all of this up to Ella, I..." Her voice trailed off to silence.

Agent Scott patted her hand and said, "Get some sleep. Maybe the next time I come to see you, I will bring you a milkshake."

"Hopefully, I will be back at Daddy's house by tomorrow. I worry about him."

As Scott rose to leave the room, Emilie said, "Agent Scott, there's something about my daddy."

"What is that?"

"It's just that...oh, never mind. It is probably silly."

"Emilie, nothing is silly. Talk to me."

"It's just that I have been giving Daddy the prescription drugs for his early onset dementia, but the pills in one of the bottles were all crumpled at the center like they had been bent. I mean, every single one of them; so I quit giving that prescription to him. I didn't tell anyone because I thought if something happened to him because he wasn't getting the medicines he needs, it would be my fault. I already take the prize in that category. I don't want to add one more person to that list."

"What is the prescription?" Scott asked.

"It is called Aricept. I Googled the name, and the search indicated that it helps improve the memory of individuals with signs of early onset dementia, so I know the prescription is legitimate. But when I Googled the images of the pills, it showed small white or yellow chalky pills, but the pills in the bottle were powder-filled capsules, and, like I said, they were crumpled in the middle. I hid the bottle in a basket of rolled towels until I could take the pills to the pharmacy, but, well, as you know, things have been rough. I will try to clear it up with the pharmacy when I get out of here."

The confused look on Emilie's face did not sit well with Agent Scott.

"Let me know what the pharmacist says," he said as he left the room.

"Sure, I will do that," she assured him, but her mind was somewhere else.

Agent Scott knew he wasn't going to wait until Emilie contacted the pharmacy. He called Agent Gibbons and asked him to meet him at Charles Randolph's house.

Agent Gibbons was waiting in his car when Scott pulled up the lane. The skittish, temporary in-home healthcare employee cautiously opened the front door with her cell phone in hand as if she was ready to dial 9-1-1. She yelled, "Who are you and what do you want?"

Scott flashed his badge, and it seemed to appease her.

Gibbons said, "What is this all about, Drew?"

Scott explained Emilie's quandary with her father's dementia medicine. He said, "Emilie is a smart woman, but Ella has been the one who has had to bear her father's illness. In light of everything that is happening, she is ultra-sensitive about questioning Ella's administration of her father's medications.

"Emilie also indicated that her father's symptoms seemed to appear within a short time span. The man is a heart surgeon, so of course, he has received top-of-the-line health care. Initially, his colleagues assumed he had suffered a stroke, but tests indicated that was not the case."

"Drew, what are you getting at? None of this has anything to do with Ella's disappearance. You aren't going soft for that sister of hers, are you?"

"That has nothing to do with this. I am telling you; something is amiss with Dr. Randolph. Just humor me with this one, and if I am wrong, then I owe you a beer."

"Well, you better buy a six-pack of Stella Artois and get them chilling now."

Agent Gibbons sat down with Dr. Randolph and fumbled his way through an awkward conversation about his family. They had been told about his early onset dementia that forced him to prematurely give up his career as a heart surgeon, so Gibbons was surprised that he saw few symptoms of the disease that robs so many families of their loved ones.

Dr. Randolph said, "Sir, I know you think I'm just an old goat that can't remember where my underwear drawer is, but I know something is going on here that everyone is trying to keep me from finding out. I lost my wife a couple of years ago, and it broke my heart. But I kept going because I have two beautiful daughters and two perfect grandchildren. If something is wrong with any of them, I need to know. I will use any resources I have to keep my family safe and healthy."

Gibbons admired the man. They had initially not told Ella's father about her abduction because they didn't want to upset him, but he was more on top of things than people gave him credit for.

He told Gibbons, "I knew something wasn't making sense because Ella never took a vacation without the kids, and she has been here for me through thick and thin; I love her sister, but Emilie is just not the caretaker in the family. She is trying hard, but it just isn't her thing."

Gibbons decided to come clean with Dr. Randolph, providing just enough details to appease him without sending him into a coronary attack. Randolph shook his head in disbelief. He grasped Gibbons' hands, "I am begging you, one father to another, please find my daughter and my granddaughter."

Gibbons gripped his hand in return and thought of his own father. "I will find Ella and Willow, and I will bring them safely back to you." He prayed he could make good on his words.

Scott found the bottle of Aricept tucked into the back of a towel basket, just like Emilie had indicated. He opened the prescription bottle to find vegetable capsules which all had slight bends in the middle; again, just as Emilie had reported.

He dropped the bottle into an evidence bag and placed the bag into the breast of his suit coat. He opened the medicine cabinet in Dr. Randolph's bathroom, took out his cell phone, and took pictures of all of the contents in the cabinet. He rejoined Agent Gibbons and Dr. Randolph in the living room, nodded to let his partner know he found what he was looking for, and reminded Gibbons that they needed to get back to the office.

On the way back to the agency, he called the lab to explain what they were bringing in. The following day, the lab result revealed just what Emilie had suspected. The medicine in the capsules was not Aricept. Instead, someone had mixed a combination of Doxepin, Xanax, Valium, Chlorpheniramine, and Detrol. Each of these medicines had the individual potential to cause dementia-like symptoms in older adults, but the combination of them was sure to do so. The combination could have proved deadly, and Dr. Randolph was lucky his daughter had quit giving them to him.

Emilie was released from Memorial Hospital the next morning, with instructions not to drive for a week. She called a cab, but when she walked out the main entrance, the cab was gone, and Agent Drew Scott was standing there with a Krekel's milkshake. Emilie smiled a crooked smile as a result of her still-swollen face. The bruising had turned a deep shade of purple, and it drew unwanted stares from other hospital visitors. She was used to gathering stares by others, but this was a new experience, and she became keenly aware of the awkward stares.

Without missing a beat, Agent Scott told one gawker, "You should see the other guy! This little lady looks good compared to what she did to him." The man laughed awkwardly, knowing he had been caught staring at her malady.

"A little birdie told me you might need a ride."

Emilie put her hand on her hips. "I called a cab, but somehow it seems the cabbies around here aren't reliable."

"Well, I don't want to give them a bad name, so I will be honest. A guy in a yellow car with a little light on top of it might have shown up, and I might have given him a twenty-dollar bill, and he might have left right before you exited the hospital."

"Uh huh." She said. She broke into a smile, but then grabbed her face, remembering how much it hurt to smile.

"Let's get you out of here," he said in a suddenly serious voice, "I need to talk to you."

Emilie gave him a quizzical look and got into the passenger seat of his car.

"Let's get you to your father's house, and then I will fill you in on the updates of the case."

As they drove up the lane, Emilie's anticipation grew.

"What is going on? Did you find something out about my sister or niece?"

"Sorry, no, but you might want to consider a career in law enforcement."

Upset at herself for jumping to some conclusion that her sister or niece had been found, she snapped, "Let's not play guessing games, Agent Scott; If you have something to share about my family, please tell me."

Scott was visibly hurt by her outburst. "I am sorry; I went into FBI agent mode without taking your feelings into account."

Emilie slumped in her seat. "No, I'm sorry for snapping. You brought me a milkshake and everything, and I jump all over you."

Scott became serious, "Emilie, you were completely accurate about your father's medications. I went straight to his house from the hospital yesterday evening, and Agent Gibbons met me there. He spent time with your dad to try to assess his cognitive functioning, while I found the prescription. It was right where you said you put it. I took it straight to the lab, and they had the results by this morning. It was a homemade concoction of five different prescription and over-the-counter medications. It was causing his dementia, and it would have eventually killed him.

"Oh my God!" Emilie gasped. My father is the sweetest, most caring man in the world. Who would do that to him? Agent Scott, there is no way my sister would have ever willingly given my father those pills. I am telling you, Davis has to be behind it!"

"Emilie, I don't disagree with you, but we can't confront him until we have more evidence. Your whole story about him taking your family's money is making more sense by the day, but unless we have substantial proof, our hands are tied."

"That is bullshit!" she spouted. "You know damn well he did something with Ella…and now innocent Willow!"

Emilie burst into tears. Surprising himself, Agent Scott reached over and took her into his arms. "I want the son-of-a-bitch who has done this to your family as badly as you do, but we have rules and regulations. If we don't follow those rules, the bad guy walks. I know you don't want that."

He added with emphasis, "But, you need to listen to me; if Davis is capable of everything you say he is, he won't let you get in his way. My guess is that he would find pleasure in getting you out of his way. William is safe with the Pattons, so I do not want you to leave these premises without a police escort. Do you understand me?"

"Look at this face, Agent Scott, do I look like I'm going to be going anywhere anytime soon?"

Scott waved his hand. "First, a few scrapes and bruises don't define you. Second, you may not agree, but your beauty is deeper than you think. You are a good sister, daughter, and aunt, and when this whole thing is over, you will be able to mend those relationships. Now get inside and take care of your father before he comes out with a shotgun thinking I am a suitor."

She smiled a hopeful smile. "I know you won't let us down. I know you are working hard to bring Ella and Willow home. I have faith in you, Agent Drew Scott."

As he drove away, Scott prayed he wouldn't let her down. He was beginning to like Emilie.

50

June zoomed in on the monitor of her homemade command station and watched Willow in the small reinforced portable plastic dog crate that had become the little girl's new home, and a sickening wash of emotion rushed through her. Years of watching the interactions between Ella and her children had caused June to develop a bitter resentment toward the trio. She recalled the times she wanted to bash Willow's head in because she was just so perfectly cute. Her brown ringlet curls framed her big blue eyes and long lashes. She was not too fat or too skinny but had cute little cheeks that made old people want to squish them. Over the years, as June watched her on the playground at school and at the park in the summertime, she vacillated between adoration of the little girl and bitter resentment. All of the other children flocked toward Willow, who willingly invited them into her world. June knew the little girls who were the mean girls on the playground who snickered behind covered mouths as they whispered hateful things into the ears of those elite enough to be part of their cliques about those not quite fortunate enough to join the ranks. Willow was not one of those girls. June admired that in Willow, but at the same time, it made her hate her more.

Willow began to stir out of her Benadryl-induced sleep, a trick June had learned by listening to the mommy conversations at the local park during her many observations of Ella and the children playing from afar. She recalled thinking, *That's genius and fucked up all at the same time! Mom needs some time to herself, but little Johnny doesn't want to sleep, so she says, 'Johnny, it sounds like you have a little sniffle,' and she gives Johnny some Benadryl-- and*

Johnny falls fast asleep. Now Mommy can paint her toenails or read her Cosmopolitan magazine. Brilliant! She knew, however, that perfect Ella would never give her kids unnecessary medicine. She would only use all-natural products like a lavender bath if they were cranky, or eucalyptus steam if they had a stuffy nose. Plus, she seemed to enjoy spending time with her children.

June unconsciously rubbed her stomach, feeling her loss more than ever. Hurt, emptiness, and anger cut through her veins. She needed to project that hurt onto someone else; that someone was Ella. Ella heard June descend the stairs, but she did not come to Ella's door. Ella assumed she was going to do laundry. That was the only other activity any of her captors seemed to do in the basement.

Instead, Ella heard a loud muffled grunt followed by June singing, "Hush, little baby, don't say a word." Ella had no way of knowing the painful grunt she heard was the result of June ripping duct tape from her daughter's tender mouth.

The sound that followed induced a fear Ella didn't know she was capable of feeling. The room around her began to spin as the sounds of a whimpering puppy grew into the muffled sounds of a child. By the time Ella wrapped her head around the sounds that were coming from somewhere else in the basement and not through the speaker, they formed into words, "Mommy. Mommy, Mommy!" The squeaking, panicked, tiny voice was calling for her mommy. Ella's worst fear had come true.

"Give me my baby!" Ella screamed uncontrollably.

June smiled at Ella's revelation that Willow was in the basement.

She said to Willow, loudly enough for Ella to hear, "Now hold still for a minute, and this won't hurt too bad. The scissors are very sharp, and if you move, they will cut you."

Willow froze, and several brown curly locks of hair fell to the ground outside the dog kennel.

"Good girl, Willow, that's a good girl." She spoke as if Willow were a dog. "Now, you must be punished for making a mess in the rental car. If you want to act like an animal by pissing all over, then that is how you will be treated, little bitch!"

"Stop it!" demanded Ella. "Take anything you want out on me, but I am begging you, please leave my baby alone."

Ella heard June approach her closet. She pushed open the small slot, and a clump of Willow's hair fell to the ground by her feet.

"Ella, your baby girl is so close to you...yet so far away. As you know, when people do things wrong, there are repercussions. Your daughter pissed in my rental car, and I had to pay extra to have it cleaned. Now she has to have consequences. Maybe if her father would have had more punishment for his actions growing up none of you would be in this situation."

"PLEASE give me my daughter, PLEASE! I will do anything you ask," Ella pleaded in a more humble voice.

June replied, "I can't hand your beautiful Willow over to you just yet, but now maybe you know what it is like to have your child taken away from you. Each day, I feel like we begin to connect more and more to each other and feel each other's pain. Let's be honest, though; we both know Davis isn't missing the little bitch. Now, if somehow he could get rid of William, he would be quite content. But you don't need to worry about any of that. I am not going to give him that much freedom. If I did that, he might quit looking for you altogether, and I need him to keep looking for you."

Ella lost control. "Give me my child! If you hurt her, I swear I will kill you!"

"You are in quite a predicament to be throwing around idle threats, and this behavior is not becoming of you. If you continue your temper tantrums, you will be forced to listen to us do gruesome things to your daughter, and when this ordeal is all over, poor William will know it was all his fault. Do you really want your son to carry that burden around the rest of his life? I mean, really, his only job was to keep Willow safe in your absence, and he couldn't even manage to do that. He put a silly baseball practice in front of his sister's safety. He left your sister, Emilie, in charge of her for two hours, and poor Willow disappeared. Isn't that a bit ironic, Ella? Your sister had only two jobs: to tend to your father and to watch your brat daughter. It might make one question her family loyalty. We know how watching Willow worked out for her, but what about Daddy? I wonder if he is OK? His mind might be slipping, but he has his faculties enough to know pain. I bet William is at home right now crying his eyes out over letting everyone down, and poor Willow is just as frightened as she can be," she mocked.

June knew she could say anything because Ella knew nothing. She could make any cockamamy story up about how she got Willow, and if Ella thought William felt like he was to blame for his sister's kidnapping, it would turn the knife even more.

Ella fell silent, and June smiled. She had won this match.

Willow also fell silent. She had heard the conversation, and the words, "You will be forced to listen to us do gruesome things to your daughter," raised every hair on her body. She began shaking uncontrollably. She wrapped herself as tightly as she could in her own arms and started rocking. It was a futile attempt at self-soothing.

Willow felt the lady's presence outside her crate, and she heard the metal rattle. She felt fingers at her face and then on her mouth. The still blind-folded child felt the tip of a straw hit her dry, chapped lips. She parted her lips and desperately began sucking at the straw. She was weak, and the liquid tasted good. Willow thought it might be apple juice. The drink was followed by small pieces of cheese. She didn't like the feel of the woman's fingers on her lips, but she was hungry, so she relented. June squished Willows cheeks a bit too hard and placed a blanket over the small kennel. Willow and Ella heard her footsteps fade up the steps.

A rage Ella did not know she was capable of was building inside of her, but she had to contain it. She had no other options. The helpless mother had no reason not to believe June would harm Willow. She could hear the faint whimpering of her little girl. Ella had never felt so powerless.

"Willow, I love you. Mommy loves you!" She spoke in a voice loud enough that she hoped her daughter could hear.

"Shut the fuck up, Ella," June calmly requested through the now-familiar speaker. "The longer you disobey me, the longer Willow will have to stay in her dog crate. I was going to buy a fancy new one, but when I was alley picking, I saw a small kennel that was free for the taking. It smelled like the dog who had used it might have died in it, so it was thrown out. I thought that was a good deal. Of course, I reinforced the opening clasp, just in case Willow has her mommy's resourcefulness."

Ella squeezed her eyes tightly and tried to erase the image of Willow locked in a small, smelly, dirty dog cage. She knew she had to remain silent if she had any hope of seeing her daughter. This was June's game, and the monster had complete control.

June continued, "Willow is a little dirtier than I am used to seeing her, but at least her hair is no longer a matted mess! She stinks to high hell, though. You would think you would have taught her not to piss herself by the time she was eight years old. I tell you…parents these days. They just aren't what they used to be, are they?"

Ella closed her eyes and breathed. She knew June was not looking for an answer; she was merely adding to the emotional torture.

51

June watched Ella's emaciated body writhe in physical and emotional anguish. She couldn't see Willow because of the dirty blanket that covered the dog crate, but she heard occasional faint whimpers.

June sang through the speaker, "We are going to play the game, 'Let's Make a Deal' today; here is how it works. You have won several prizes, including scrapbook pages, journal entries, drawings and such from your family members. These prizes tell a very impactful story. If you are willing to give up all of that evidence in exchange for your choice of door number two or three, you can do so. Now, behind one of the doors is your sweet Willow, but behind the other door is…absolutely nothing. If you want to play the game, you must push all of your artifacts through the slot. Once you have returned all of your gifts, you will tell me door number two or door number three. This is going to be such a fun game."

Ella sickened with grief over the realization that she might be trading evidence that could put these people away and connections to her children for nothing, but the moment she heard Willow say, "Mommy, please try to choose another door," the decision was made. She began pushing all of the memorabilia through the door as quickly as she could. When the last scrapbook page was through the slot, she said with a desperate plea, "Can I please choose another door now?"

"Of course, Ella. I always keep my promises, but if you choose the wrong door, your poor little girl will remain locked in her cramped cage. She has to be feeling all cooped up in that thing. I have written the correct answer on this piece of paper I have in my hand, but oh, I keep forgetting, I can see you, but you can't see me. Hold on a minute; we will make this game fair."

Ella heard June descend the stairs. She also heard, "Momma, please pick the right door."

Her heart shattered.

"Ok, Ella, I am putting a sealed envelope through the slot. If you open it before you guess, I will stick a knife into Willow right here and now, and you will hear the whole bloody fiasco."

As the white envelope made its way through the slot, Ella wrung her hands and blurted, "I choose door number three."

"Why door number three, Ella?"

"Because we came through door number one into this building. I am in door number two, so Willow must be behind door number three."

"You think you are such a smart cookie. I thought you would say door number two since you might have considered yourself being behind door number one. Well, go ahead, silly, see if you are correct."

Ella's trembling, sweaty hands tore open the end of the envelope and the small, folded slip of paper fell into her lap. It had the number "three" on it. Ella broke down in tears.

June said, "I wish you would have chosen door number two. It has been fun watching the two of you in such turmoil. All these years of watching your cheesy relationship got old. This has been a fun twist to the game. I am, however, a fair game player, unlike your husband. Cheating is not cool with me, so I will honor the fact that you chose the correct door."

June went to the dog crate that had become Willow's new home. She removed the blanket that kept the frightened child hidden. She reached in and covered Willow's mouth with a fresh piece of duct tape so the little girl couldn't scream or bite her. She rebound her wrists. She decided not to take Willow's bandana off because she thought the girl might recognize her.

Ella heard whimpering from the other side of her wooden door. Minutes later, Ella listened to the clink of the metal lock and then the clatter of metal on the concrete. Her little girl was shoved into the closet. Ella caught her daughter just before her face planted into the concrete floor. Willow's hands were tied with twine, her eyes were covered with a red bandana, and gray duct tape covered her tiny mouth. She was filthy and covered in dog hair, and she smelled like a combination of urine, fecal matter, and old dog. Ella scooped her baby girl up and held her so tightly that she was afraid she might break her fragile body. She noticed the large clump of hair missing from the side of Willow's head.

Ella untied the tight bandana to reveal Willow's bloodshot eyes, but when Willow saw her mommy nearly-bald head and skinny body, her eyes became the size of silver dollars. Tears streamed down her dirty face, streaking her chubby cheeks.

Ella carefully removed the duct tape as Willow winced from the pain. When her mouth was free, she mouthed the word, "Mommy," and cupped her mommy's face in her tiny hands. Ella and Willow broke into soft cries at the same time. For the first time in nearly thirty days, Ella had a purpose; she had to keep her little girl physically and emotionally safe.

The reunion was broken up with the sound of a barking dog. Both looked around frantically as if they expected to see their Beauregard bound through the door. Soon, however, they realized that the sound was coming through the speaker. The incessant barking went on for five minutes, and it became louder as each minute ticked by. Willow covered her ears and buried her head in her mother's emaciated chest.

When the barking stopped, June's voice came through the speaker. "Poor Beauregard seemed to have fallen onto a knife...several times... when you left your papa's house, Willow. You can't just leave kitchen knives lying around, silly. The whole scene was a bloody mess, and poor Emilie got blamed for it. Really, though, it is all William's fault. He couldn't keep a good eye on you, Willow, much less, Beau. Poor, poor Beau. He bled out all over the shed; you know, the one you keep the pool toys in? Golden Retrievers have a lot of blood in them, I must say."

Willow wailed! Ella squeezed her little girl's face into her chest in a futile attempt to cover her ears and console her. Her daughter cried herself to sleep in her mommy's arms.

A few hours later, the recognizable pair of plastic scissors made their way through the slit in the door. June said, "Ella, you and Willow have always been like-mother-like-child, so I think we need to keep the two of you looking alike. You did such a great job on your new haircut that you should cut little Willow's locks off just the same way. Your sister seemed to treasure your locks of love, so I know she will treasure little Willow's tiny curls."

Ella responded, "Please, don't make me do this, June!"

June laughed in response, "Ella, must I remind you that I am running the show here. You really need to be a bit more appreciative of the fact that I have allowed you to have your daughter with you…ALIVE. It would be very easy for me to make her dead!"

A panicked look came over Willow's face as she looked up through alligator tears into her mommy's eyes and said, "It's just hair, Mommy. It will grow back."

Ella squeezed her daughter tightly and said, "You are the bravest little girl I know."

For the next twenty minutes, Ella carefully cut her daughter's curly locks under the instruction of June's words through the speaker, which repeated, "Shorter, shorter, shorter," until Willow had nothing but peach fuzz covering her entire head.

Willow said, "I look just like you now, Mommy! Lucky me!" Mother and child looked at mirror images of the other, and tears turned to laughter. It started with Willow's small giggle, which made Ella giggle. It became a chain reaction as the laughter grew louder and heartier. It was the first time Ella had shown any positive emotion in weeks.

The cacophony of laughs pissed June off, and she screamed through the speaker, "Both of you stop your fucking laughing NOW, or I will rip Willow right out of your arms, and you will never see her again."

Laughter turned to fear, and the duo became mute. Ella lay her little girl on the towel and snuggled next to her. She wrapped her cricket-like legs around her daughter and quietly sang her bedtime song into Willow's ears quietly enough that June could not hear, and she gently soothed her nearly bald head.

June continued to watch them as the two slept, wrapped safely, for the moment, in each other's arms. Tears streamed down her face as she realized she would never experience this kind of love; Davis had robbed her of that chance.

When they awoke, they faced each other, their faces planted into each other and whispered about what had happened in Ella's absence. Her eight-year-old looked older and harder than she did less than a month ago when she waited impatiently for her mom to put sunscreen on her face. Ella knew she had been forever robbed of her innocence.

June said, "Willow, I got a journal from your brother, and I have been getting bits and pieces from your father and Aunt Emilie, but I did not get anything from you. Did you write a journal to me?"

Willow responded, "Yes, Mommy, I did exactly what father told me to do."

The way her little girl said the words made Ella cringe. To hear Willow refer to Davis as "Father" made her sad, and her heart broke as she imagined William being stuck, frightened and alone in the house with Davis. Davis had been especially unkind to William over the years.

As if on cue, the wrapped package made its way through the mail slot. Willow recognized the crayon writing on the tissue paper.

"That's it, Mommy! That's my present to you."

The two quietly looked through the journal without speaking. Ella squished her daughter closer to her with the flip of each new page.

In a quiet, worried voice, Willow said, "Mommy, do you think Father is angry at me because I was playing with my doll, Morgan, at Papa's house? I left her on the blanket out under my tree, so now he is going to know I was playing with her."

Ella's heart broke as she observed the worry that washed over her little girl's face. *What have I put my children through*, she thought.

"Oh, no, baby, your father won't be the least bit angry," she lied. She could hear his scornful words at the sight of Willow sitting on the picnic blanket, talking to Morgan as if she were her best friend. The thought pained her.

She pulled her daughter closer to her. They lay back down on the towel and wrapped themselves into each other's arms, fearing they might be ripped apart at any moment.

52

Scott returned to his house early Monday morning to retrieve his newspaper. It had been a daily ritual since he started staying at his parents' house. He felt like such a pansy-ass staying at Mommy and Daddy's house, but the agent really didn't care, as long as his baby was safe. He thought about Ella and Willow Masters on the drive. Ella had been missing for twenty-eight days, and Willow had disappeared without a trace, four days ago. He couldn't begin to fathom what the two might be experiencing.

He saw the brown cardboard box peeking out from under the front bush when he pulled into the driveway. "Mother fucking, son-of-a-bitch," involuntarily flew out of his mouth. Relief that Reese was not in the car washed over him. He hopped out of the car and rushed to the bush. He kicked the box out and slung another line of curse words.

In black marker were the words, LAST PRESENT. Scott cautiously picked up the box and carried it to the trunk of his car. A momentary fear that it might contain an explosive device, sent a panic through him. He tossed it into the trunk like a hot potato, slammed the lid shut, and locked the car. He grabbed the newspaper, looked around the house, and went inside to check the security camera images.

Scott had put his own security system in, with the help of his buddy, T.J., and he had not had time to connect the system to his cell phone. He wished he had made time for that, but balancing his time between this most recent investigation and his daughter didn't leave much time for extra chores.

He pressed rewind on the video until he saw the familiar image in the exact same clothes. The person, a man, Drew thought, jogged down the street at 3:52 a.m., ran up through his yard, dropped the box, kicked it under the bush, and continued down the street.

Scott called Gibbons, who had to hold the phone away from his ear because Drew was yelling and cursing so loud.

"OK, buddy. I understand you are pissed, but get in here so we can see what is in the box. Remember, we have a missing mom and little girl to think about here."

Drew knew he was right.

Scott walked into Gibbons' office and dropped the box on his desk.

"Excuse me, but I need a few minutes to gather myself; otherwise, I might start punching holes in walls."

Gibbons replied, "Go do what you gotta do, but when you get done, can you bring me a cup of coffee?"

Scott shook his head in frustration at his partner. He didn't understand how this father of three, could be such a hardass.

Gibbons put on a clean pair of latex gloves and opened up the package; it was larger than the previous ones they had received. He stared at a pile of hand-written letters, children's drawings, pictures, and pages ripped out of journals. The mound of evidence they had received over the past several weeks pointed to Davis Masters, but none of it was specific enough to put the bastard away. On the very top of the newest pieces of evidence was a typed letter.

Dear Mr. FBI Agents,

Children are but innocent victims of a cruel, cruel world. They don't ask to come into this world, and they certainly don't get to pick their parents. Then, once they are here, they get caught up in all of their parents' shit. Trust me, this is exactly what happened to Davis' children. Speaking of shit, there is a LOT of that in this box. It looks as though Ella's family members were feeling a little guilty-- maybe even responsible-for her mishap. But I will let you be the judge and jury once you check the evidence out for yourself; after all, isn't that your job? By the way, this is the last help you will receive from me. I am sick and tired of having to throw you people bones to help you figure out one simple crime. By the way, you may not agree, but I am not the real criminal here. True, I may be guilty of a little abduction, but it isn't like I have killed someone!!??"

-J-

Gibbons found an odd comfort in the words. They may have revealed that Ella and Willow were still alive. He completed another Chain of Custody form; he had become a pro at filling out the forms. He poured over the stack of photographs. They included family snapshots that did not include Davis, pictures with Davis' face cut out of them, and additional images of Davis with women that the agents now recognized. There were pictures taken, presumably of Ella, years earlier on a college campus, and snapshots of other children who looked like Davis. There were additional pictures of Davis and Gianni, Emilie and Gianni, and Davis with Emilie. Gibbons determined the female was Emilie and not Ella because she sported blonde hair in all of the images. Most of the shots were not posed, but rather taken from a distance with a zoom camera. It was clear that the majority of the subjects did not realize they were being photographed.

He stared at newspaper clippings covering Ella's mother's car accident and the obituary that had been placed in the *State Journal-Register*. Each of the clippings had a small red question mark in the very center of the page. Gibbons re-read the articles, which all provided the details of the accident. Was someone trying to tell him it wasn't an accident? He made additional notes on his yellow tablet.

Agent Scott returned with two fresh cups of coffee. "OK, I've cooled down, but I am STILL pissed." Looking at the pile, he said, "Damn, did someone clear out a storage unit?"

Gibbons took a cup out of his partner's hand and said, "It looks like it." He picked up a white business card and read, "Dr. Joseph Smith." He thought about the interview with Dr. Smith, regarding Davis' vasectomies. He shook his head, "What a weasel. He was full of excuses, and he was smart enough to know we couldn't prove anything." He instinctively wriggled his hips. "I sure as hell wouldn't want that worm-of-a-man cutting on my nuts… No pun intended."

Scott commented, "It is like they are giving us enough to look at Davis, but not enough to put him behind bars. Why don't they want him in custody?"

Gibbons waved his hands around the room at the piles of evidence they had amassed. "It isn't for lack of evidence, but nothing is specific enough to warrant an arrest; everything is circumstantial. We both know you can't arrest a guy for being an asshole or a cheater; otherwise, we would have to open up a lot more penitentiaries."

Gibbons sipped his coffee and continued, "The more evidence we receive, the more this looks like it is a crime of passion! We have looked closely at Gianni Russo, but he is squeaky clean, and none of the leads we had on Emilie went anywhere. The biggest pile of shit is all around Davis, and he smells as guilty as anyone, but we don't have enough to arrest the guy."

Scott set his coffee down and put on latex gloves. He sifted through the mail Gibbons had already gone through. "I think maybe we need to ask a few more questions about Patty Randolph's car accident. Whoever is sending us all of these artifacts is either trying to lead us on a major wild goose chase, or they might know more about the Randolph and Masters families than we realize.

Gibbons made his way to the bottom of the box. He picked up three envelopes, which were carefully labeled DNA evidence #1, DNA Evidence #2, and DNA Evidence #3. He cautiously opened the first envelope. It had short brunette curls, with a note labeled, "Ella Masters." The second envelope had longer gentle locks. Scott didn't need to read the name; he knew the hair belonged to Willow. His stomach ached! The third envelope also had brown hair. The note in this envelope read, "Riddle me this, Riddle me that, Whose hair did they not see-- because of the hat?"

Scott and Gibbons thought back to all of the women they had interviewed from Davis' past. None of them had hats on during the interviews. They both scoured their legal pads full of the chicken scratch notes they had gathered over the past month. Nobody stuck out. They couldn't figure it out.

Gibbons hesitated a moment before saying, "Do you think the hair in the third envelope could be Emilie's? I know you are sweet on the woman, but do you think that is clouding your objectivity? I mean, think about it. She hates her brother-in-law, she would have access to all of this information, and she does have a motive. What if her innocent, broken-hearted sister act is just that. I don't think we can completely rule out her involvement in the case. I mean, think about it, she admitted that leaving Willow alone at her father's house was not a smart move. Maybe it was just the alibi she needed. She goes shopping, and Willow disappears. How did whoever killed Beau and took Willow know Emilie and William were not at home and that Daddy sleeps a lot? Even Davis couldn't have been certain about that."

Scott kept looking down at the pictures to avoid eye contact with his partner.

"Come on, Drew, you have to agree that it is a little fishy. She could have people working with her. We know Gianni knows we are monitoring him, so he might be lying low, but Chicago is a big place, and I would guess that Emilie Randolph has lots of connections."

Scott locked his jaw, "First of all, I resent the accusation that my objectivity is being clouded. You know as well as I do that we have looked high and low to connect Emilie to her sister's disappearance, and there just isn't anything there. Before you jump in and remind me about the lies she told us about her relationships with Davis and Gianni, let me remind you that she did come clean, and all of her stories were corroborated with everyone except Davis. We both know he can't stand her, so of course, he is going to try to deflect the blame from himself onto her."

Gibbons interrupted, "So, are you telling me that none of this…" he splayed his arms out in a grand gesture, "points to Emilie Randolph?"

Scott continued to avoid eye contact.

Gibbons added, "I am just saying that we need to keep the investigation…well…formal, Drew. Plus, I don't want to have to listen to your sob stories if we find out she is involved, or if she breaks your heart. You don't fall often, but we both know that when you do, it is hard. Let's be honest, Emilie is a Chicago chick all the way, and you live in Springfield. You may be eye-candy and a shoulder for her to lean on throughout this crisis, but we both know that this is probably just an emotional bond brought on by the stress of the crisis.

Scott brushed Gibbons' comments off like an annoying fly at a picnic. "Emilie is a captivating woman, but I know we are not in the same league, and I am NOT falling for her. The only female I have room for in my life right now happens to still wear a diaper. My only goal is to bring her sister and niece safely home and to keep her from being abducted. If these people would kidnap two people, what will keep them from kidnapping her or William? This is especially true if Davis is behind the abductions. As we have pointed out multiple times, there is no love loss there.

This evidence, however, does make me hopeful that Ella and Willow are still alive. Do you agree?"

Gibbons nodded in agreement. "I think it is time we interview Davis and Emilie again."

"I agree, boss!" Drew said sarcastically. He added, "Thanks for looking out for me, but I am a big boy. I know when I am playing with fire; this is just a little match. You can call Davis, and I will call Emilie." He paused momentarily, "Unless you prefer calling Emilie, so I don't get…burned." The corners of his mouth turned up into a wry smile.

Gibbons replied, "You can call Ms. Randolph, but just remember, it is all fun and games until somebody gets hurt. I just don't want to listen to your whining ass when it is you."

Both agents used their cell phones to call Davis Masters and Emilie Randolph.

Davis answered after three rings, "Hello, this is Davis Masters."

Gibbons jumped right in, "Mr. Masters, we have received a large package with quite a bit of evidence. We need to talk to both you and Emilie, separately, of course, about the contents of the package. We would like to talk to you first, and then we will meet with Emilie."

Gibbons paused long enough for Davis to process what he was hearing, and then added, "It might take a while, and, Mr. Masters, you will want to have your attorney present. Can we come to your place, say at 3:00?"

Gibbons waited for a beat for Davis to digest his words. He knew he and Scott wanted to interview Emilie before they talked to Davis, to ensure he didn't have an opportunity to compare notes with his sister-in-law. Plus, he wanted Davis to have some time to stew about what the agents wanted to discuss. He was tired of this man always thinking he was the one in charge.

Davis sunk into his chair. He could only imagine what new information the investigators had, and he panicked that his past had finally caught up with him.

"Let me call my attorney and make sure he can make that time, and I will call you right back," he said weakly.

Within five minutes, Davis hit redial on his phone, and Agent Gibbons picked up. "Does 3:00 work?"

"Yes, Dubin will be here at that time as well." he added, hesitantly, "Is there anything you can tell me over the phone?"

"No, sorry, Mr. Masters, we need to speak to you in person."

Momentarily, Davis Masters thought about taking a bullet to the head or getting in his car and heading straight to the airport, but he didn't have the guts to pull the trigger, and he knew he wouldn't make it out of Chicago or St. Louis by the time authorities realized he was gone. He was screwed, and he knew it.

He grabbed his car keys, got in his car, opened the garage door, and raced backward out of the driveway. He needed to get to Emilie. He dialed the familiar number, but it rang several times before her chipper voicemail sounded, "You have reached the voicemail of Emilie Randolph. If you would like to set up a rental consultation, press the pound sign; otherwise, leave a message, and I will return your call as soon as I can pull myself away from the party." The message ended with a flirtatious giggle.

"Bitch!" He pressed the end button. He waited a few minutes before hitting redial.

Agent Scott reached Emilie on her cell phone after only one ring. He explained that there was new evidence in the case that they needed to share with her in person. Moments after she answered Scott's call, another called beeped through.

Scott grabbed his keys and motioned to his partner to hustle, when he heard Emilie say, "Shit, it is him again. He is calling again. I ignored a call from him a couple of minutes ago, now he is calling again!" her voice was quivering.

"Davis?" Scott questioned.

"Yes!" Emilie replied with an apprehensive tone.

"Whatever you do, do NOT answer any calls from him. I want you to make sure all of your doors are locked. We are heading your way now."

"But he has a garage door opener and a key to the house. What if he tries to get in? What if he is already on his way? There is no way you will beat him!" Her voice raised a panicked octave with each scenario.

"Emilie, I need you to settle down, OK? I will keep you on the phone until we arrive. Davis knows we have something serious enough to say to him that warrants his attorney be present so he might feel that he is entering a trap. I wouldn't think he would be so bold as to come to your father's house, but he did try to call you immediately, so we can't put anything past him."

Emilie screamed, "Shit, he is here. He is banging on the door."

"I want you to get your father and hide in his bathroom. I will have Gibbons call him and divert him."

Agent Gibbons was already dialing Davis' cell phone.

A breathless Davis answered, "Masters here, what do you want?"

"Mr. Masters, you sound out of breath. Are you OK?"

"Yes, I am fine." He responded, as he placed the key into the doorknob and began to turn it.

Emilie had barely gotten to her father's room when she heard the front door creak open.

"He is in the house!" she whispered, "He is in the fucking house!"

Agent Scott mouthed Emilie's repeated words.

Gibbons quickly said, "Mr. Davis, I'm calling you back to let you know we might be a few minutes late. We are almost to Dr. Randolph's house now to speak with Emilie about the mail we received...Hello, Mr. Masters, are you there?"

The phone went dead.

Scott spoke into the phone, "Emilie, I need you to whisper, but tell me what is going on. We are six minutes away."

"I heard the front door slam. I don't know if Davis is inside or if he left."

Emilie looked at her frightened father as he sat on his bed. She quickly locked the bedroom door, put his desk chair underneath the doorknob, and closed the bedroom curtains. She hustled her father into the bathroom and listened intently. She thought she heard a car engine start and tires in the driveway. Moments later, she listened to the peeling of tires down the lane.

"I think he is gone. How close are you? Please get here fast. We are scared."

"We are three minutes away. My guess is that Davis will turn left onto Lake Shore Drive to avoid seeing us."

"Should you chase him and see what he was going to do to me...to us?"

"Right now, it is about keeping you safe. We will have our time with him this afternoon. We can question him then. We are pulling up now. I will see if the front door is open. You will know it is me because I will keep you on the phone until I reach your father's bedroom. Only then do I want you to unlock the door."

The front door was still unlocked. The two agents made their way down the hallway to Dr. Randolph's bedroom.

"Emilie, we are right outside the bedroom door."

Emilie exited the bathroom. She heard the familiar voice through the phone and also on the other side of the door. She removed the chair from the door, threw open the door, and flung herself into Agent Scott's arms and sobbed.

Dr. Randolph, clearly confused by the commotion, exited the bathroom and said, "Sirs, I am not sure what just happened, but I think I owe you two a big Thank You."

The agents smiled at the gentleman's words.

Agent Gibbons replied, "No problem, sir, we are glad everyone is OK."

Emilie peeled herself out of Scott's arms and with a bright red face, admitted, "I may have over-reacted a little."

Gibbons replied, "No, I don't think you did."

Scott raised his brow to his partner, "I told you she is a smart woman."

Agent Gibbons directed his attention to Charles, "Dr. Randolph, what would you think about the two of us dropping a line. I haven't fished in a long time."

Charles' eyes brightened, and he said, "Why, son, I would be delighted to teach you a few of my fishing tricks."

Gibbons winked at Emilie, who had finally stopped shaking, "I guess I am going to fishing school."

Emilie winked back. Gibbons flushed. He could now see what his partner saw in the woman.

Emilie poured two glasses of iced tea, and she and Agent Scott made their way to the back-patio table to watch the two men fish. He showed her copies of some of the items they had received earlier that morning.

Uncomfortably, he said, "Some of the evidence we received today does not bode well for you, but the fact that you were forthright with what you have told us thus far helps your case. Right now what we need from you is to help us put the pieces of this most recent delivery together."

Emilie nodded in understanding. She wondered if somehow the confessions she had written to her sister had made their way to the FBI.

Scott jumped right in, knowing they didn't have a lot of time. "Emilie, I know you admitted that you and Gianni are friends, but is there anything else you did not share with us about your relationship?"

The color drained from Emilie's cheeks, and she looked down at the ice cubes in her glass. She was afraid to answer because she didn't know how much Scott knew.

Scott sensed her hesitation, and he understood why. He said, "Emilie, we received a letter that you wrote to your sister. The letter was dated June 8, 2014; that was only twenty-one days ago." He cocked his head in confusion. "Why would you write a confessional letter to your sister after she disappeared, and how would it end up in our hands?"

Emilie recalled the specific journal instructions: under no circumstances were any of the family members to share the journal assignment with the police or Ella would be chopped into little pieces and fed to their dogs. She closed her eyes and prayed, something she had done more of in the last few weeks than she had done all of her life.

"Agent Scott, I want to help you. I really want to tell you everything, but we were given specific instructions that if we shared information with you that they would kill Ella. They were very graphic in their details."

"What are you talking about? Who gave you specific instructions? How did they communicate with you, and how did they get this pile of letters, pictures, and drawings?" Scott pointed to the plastic bags full of incriminating pictures of Emilie and Davis, as well as her and Gianni.

Emilie looked spooked, "I have no clue how they got all of the pictures. I know I didn't put any pictures in my journal." As she looked more closely, she said, "Who could have taken all these? They are all taken in Chicago. Do you think these people are in Chicago?"

"We don't know, but the more you can tell me why you think we would have received incriminating mail involving you, the sooner we can figure this case out. It seems as though you and Davis have really pissed somebody off. We need to figure out who that somebody is."

"I have no clue. These people want it to look like Davis and I have plotted to get rid of my sister, but I swear that is not true, Agent Scott."

"Do you think Gianni could somehow be behind it all?" Scott inquired.

"I don't think so; these people know things about our family that can't be explained. It is like they have been watching us all our lives."

"Have any of your family members had home invasions where somebody might have taken personal memorabilia?"

"No, none of us have ever been robbed."

"Would Gianni have had access to any of these items when he...visited you? Maybe he is getting revenge on you and Davis at the same time?"

Emilie's cheeks now reddened. She knew Agent Scott must have seen her letter to her sister. She did not know the contents of Davis' journals, but she was sure they were just as confessional as her admissions.

She blurted out, "It was a one-night stand that went as badly as it possibly could have. I knew Gianni was thinking about my sister when he was having sex with me, and then I ended up pregnant. The last thing I wanted was a kid, and to know my sister would never forgive me for my mistake was more than I could bear! I had to get an abortion. I didn't have a choice."

Emilie looked at Agent Scott for agreement, approval, or anything that would make her feel better. She got nothing but a dead-pan look. He thought about Reese and was overwhelmed with relief that Brooke had not made the same choice.

Quietly, she said, "Do you think my sister received the letter? Do you think she knows?"

"There are also pages torn out of a journal your sister has been writing in, so, yes, she knows."

"Can I see the journals?" Emilie asked.

"Emilie, right now, that doesn't serve a purpose. We just need to focus on bringing your sister home. Then the two of you will have an opportunity to mend your relationship, but that can only happen if we figure out who has your sister and why."

They spent the next hour looking through the additional evidence in an attempt at figuring out the missing puzzle pieces. Emilie provided insight into the pictures, including valuable timelines. She had been correct when she said these people had known her family for a long time or had stolen the items from her family.

She said, "Momma always kept our keepsakes downstairs in the wooden cabinet Daddy made from scratch. We used to sneak down there when we were kids and go through them. The last time we looked at any of that stuff was when Momma passed away." Her voice faded, and she left him for a minute. He knew she was thinking about the day she buried her mother.

Agent Scott chose not to mention the newspaper articles with the red question marks that had been included in the package. He didn't want to go there with her right now; that would be for another day.

"Can we go down and take a look at the boxes?"

"Sure, they may be a bit dusty, but they are neatly organized by years and events."

Emilie led Agent Scott to the basement; it was nicer than his whole house. Beautiful walnut wood trimmed the white walls, which were tastefully covered with family portraits and collages of family memories. He felt the bounce of the lush carpet under his feet, as he glanced at the pictures.

Emilie opened a beautiful, large cabinet, also made of walnut. The boxes were all lined up by date and event, just as Emilie had said they would be. She pulled out the first box, which was labeled 1963-1966. She carefully opened the lid of the box…and gasped. Sitting right on top of the box was a small white Post-it that read, "Olly, Olly, Oxen Free."

Emilie and Agent Scott opened the remaining boxes. Each of them had a white Post-it placed gently on top that created the message:

Olly, Olly, Oxen Free.
You're getting closer to finding me.
Sorry I borrowed a few of your things.
Just needed you to know you have some loose strings
I should have been part of the pictures, too.
But none of you knew-- nope, nobody knew.

Emilie questioned, "Could this be Gianni? Could he be angry that he has not been part of our family? But how could he have gotten into Daddy's house and taken items and left these notes? It doesn't make sense."

"Would you have had copies at your place?" Scott asked.

"No, I have always lived in smaller spaces, so I kept all of my stuff here. I have a handful of pictures, but that is about it. They are all still intact in my Chicago condo."

She mused, "This can't be Davis. He has been part of our family…unfortunately."

Scott asked, "Was there anybody else in either Ella's or your lives who wanted more from a relationship than they got? Maybe a bitter ex-boyfriend?"

"No, I have never gotten myself tied down in a relationship, and Ella was always too busy with her head in a hiking book to even date. Besides Gianni…or, Cristiano as Ella knew him, the only other person Ella ever dated was Davis… and we know how that one turned out."

Emily shuddered, and goosebumps made their way up and down her arms. "I can't believe someone had enough time to come into Daddy's house, take sentimental items but not steal money or any other valuables, AND leave us notes. Agent Scott, with all due respect, that is FUCKED up! It makes me want to pack Daddy up right this minute and get the hell out of here."

"Emilie, we will have a cruiser stationed here until this is over. I just hope it is soon. The longer this goes, the more I think we are dealing with one sick person. It is almost time for our visit with Davis to see how he can enlighten us on the newest information. Let me run out to the car to get an evidence bag. I will be right back."

Emilie looked around the room. She felt like she was being watched. The house that had provided years of love and physical and emotional comfort now felt creepy and invaded.

Scott returned moments later, placed the items into a clear bag, labeled the bag, took some pictures of the cabinet and its contents, and filled out another Chain of Custody form. The two returned upstairs and stepped out the back door.

Agent Scott and Dr. Randolph were coming up the hill with no fish, but the smile on her daddy's face slightly warmed the cold chill that filled Emilie's body.

Randolph said, with a wry smile, "Don't judge us; we practice the catch and release motto." After a pause, he added, "If we would have caught them, then we definitely would have released them."

Agent Gibbons thanked the older gentleman for taking time out of his day to show a young buck how to effectively bait a hook.

Randolph said, "You come back anytime you like, but if you want dinner after a day of fishing with me, you might want to bring a pizza along."

They all chuckled again, but then the mood turned somber. "Dr. Randolph and Emilie, we know Ella and Willow are still alive, and we are going to do everything we can to bring them back safely to you. When we do that, we will ALL spend the whole day fishing, and if need be, I will pay for the pizza. How is that for a plan?"

Tears filled Dr. Randolph's crystal-blue eyes, and he choked out, "I will hold you boys to that."

Emilie turned her gaze toward the water, so her father didn't see the tears streaming down her own face. She brushed them away quickly and said, "Daddy, let's get you inside for a rest. I think Agent Gibbons might have worn you out."

Gibbons promised the Randolphs they would be in touch with any updates. As the duo drove to Davis Masters' house, Scott filled him in on the notes left in the boxes of memorabilia. Gibbons looked at the evidence bags and the images Scott had taken with his phone.

"I think the biggest question we need to answer is this: Who wanted to be part of the family but did not get to be? To me, that sounds like a bitter ex-boyfriend. According to Emilie, the only boy in Ella's life besides Davis was Gianni. If he knew the whole truth about Emilie, it might have sent him over the edge. We know he already has a motive for bringing Davis down; he wants his wife. I can't figure out how he would have gotten into their parent's home, though, and stolen all these pictures and sentimental items."

Scott interjected, "Emilie would have a key to her parent's home. He could have easily taken it, made a copy of it, and returned it without her having a clue. The only time she would need it is when she was in Springfield. We know she didn't come here often."

The agents pulled into Davis Masters' driveway, promptly at 3:30. Gibbons said, "Maybe Davis can shed a little more light on the case with the new evidence."

They decided not to mention the incident at his father-in-law's house because it would take too long for them to prove his presence at the house, and they knew their time was running out.

The FBI agents were greeted by Davis and his attorney, Erik Dubin. After a few formal niceties, they made their way to the dining room. Agent Scott placed the large stack of evidence, all carefully sealed in bags, on the dining room table. With an exaggerated splay of his hand, Drew Scott said, "This, Mr. Masters, is what a lifetime of lies looks like!" He paused for effect and then continued in an accusatory tone, "Because you have lied multiple times during the past month, you have put your wife and daughter in grave danger. Whoever has taken the two of them means business, and without a clear motive, we have nowhere to turn and no bargaining chips. All of the evidence, however, keeps circling back to you, Mr. Masters."

He glared at Davis with a disgusted look.

Dubin spouted, "If you have questions for my client, sir, then get to asking them; otherwise, he and I are both busy men!"

Gibbons took over, "We need you to tell us everything you know that you have been withholding, Davis, and let us show you a few things that might help jog your memory."

Rattled, Davis' jaw dropped as his eyes gazed at the letter he had written to his wife earlier in the month, as demanded by Ella's abductors. He saw the word vasectomy. It wasn't the contents of this letter that bothered him; it was the fact that the piece was sitting back in front of him. That most likely meant his confession of his mother-in-law's murder had also been sent to the agents. This, he presumed, is why they told Davis he better have his attorney present.

He sat, speechless, waiting to be read his rights and handcuffed; neither happened. Instead, Agent Gibbons said, "Mr. Masters, you already told us this story, so our question is this: Why would we receive this same information, along with a GREEAATTT deal more leads? He stretched the word, great, to make Davis squirm."

Dubin spoke up, in his arrogant tone, "Sir, let's stop playing games. If you have additional evidence that proves my client has committed a crime then please, by all means, be forthcoming."

As Scott breathed in a deep breath as if he was about to provide a five-minute speech, Davis closed his eyes and held his breath.

Scott began, "Mr. Dubin, we have received an abundance of evidence that, at the least, questions the moral integrity of your client. At the most, it might give probable cause for us to arrest your client for the abduction of his wife and daughter."

Davis still did not breathe.

Scott continued, "We also have these, sir."

Agent Gibbons lay additional bags, which contained hand-written letters, directly in front of Davis, as if he were dealing cards at a poker table.

"Mr. Masters, does this handwriting look familiar?"

Davis knew the handwriting was his wife's. He quietly read the salutation, "My Dearest C."

A mixed bag of anger, fear, and deception stirred in Davis' gut. He wished he had eaten lunch. It might have soaked up the bile that made him want to run to the restroom and throw up.

"Mr. Masters, are you OK, sir?" Gibbons asked, half-serious and half-cocky, "You look a bit green."

"I'm fine," barked Davis.

"Mr. Davis, is this your wife's handwriting?"

Davis nodded.

"Then, sir, you can guess who Ella's Dearest C. might be, correct?"

Davis scowled, "I told you I thought she was sleeping around on me. I told you those kids can't be mine. See, all of this proves it...all these letters. She is probably sitting by some pool in a hotel with her lover boy, right now!"

Davis spread both hands in a grand display as if to say, "See, I just solved your case for you, you incompetent bastards!"

"How then, Mr. Masters, do you explain the disappearance of your daughter?" Gibbons snapped back.

"She probably arranged for her to be "taken" also. Davis put both hands in the air in a quotation gesture to indicate that the abductions were planned by his wife.

He continued, "She is probably biding her time for the right moment to do the same with William. Only, now you guys have pigs all over the place, so it doesn't fit into her little game so well."

Even Davis' attorney, cringed at his client's use of the word, "pigs". He stepped in, "Clearly, agents, my client is under a great deal of stress. You have just presented him with information that his wife is in love with another man. He did not mean to offend you, gentlemen."

Agent Scott couldn't help himself, "RIGHHHTTT, that is so much more difficult than knowing your spouse has had multiple affairs."

Neither Davis Masters or Erik Dubin had a response.

Scott saw Davis trying to nonchalantly read bits and pieces of the journal entries, without looking obvious, so the agent said, "Don't strain your eyes trying to read the entries. I will summarize them for you in a minute."

Gibbons took over, "We thought it was strange that several of the pages were ripped out of the journals we received the other day. Well, those missing pages were shared with us this morning, and they provide graphic details about your relationship with your wife, at least from her standpoint. They do not paint an upstanding picture of you, sir."

Davis still waited for the hammer to drop about Ella's mother, but the agents were toying with him. If they had all of this evidence, why would they not have been given that letter? He wondered.

Agent Scott said, "Mr. Masters, we have all of these journal entries and pictures. With all due respect, sir, we disagree with your theory that your wife left voluntarily, and we have evidence, which we are not at liberty to share because it might jeopardize the investigation, that tells us otherwise. Your wife did not go willingly, and let us not forget the unborn fetus that was left at the crime scene."

Scott paused for effect, "OR the brutal killing of your family dog, Beau, whom Ella loved dearly. Now, are you certain there is nothing more you can provide that you have left out in previous interviews? Are you sure you have told us everything you need to tell us about your wife and her family?"

Fuck, here it comes, thought Davis. His heart thumped loudly, and his head pounded. His mouth was like cotton, and he couldn't muster up enough saliva to answer.

He merely shook his head no.

Dubin said, "Gentlemen unless you have any further business with my client, I am going to have to wrap this little visit up. As you can see, he is under a great deal of stress, and I have other clients who need my services. I am a busy man, you know, keeping innocent men from being falsely accused of crimes they did not commit."

Agent Gibbons said, "I have one more question."

He paused long enough that urine dripped down Davis' inner thigh.

"Awww, Never mind. We will have that discussion another day." Gibbons decided not to mention Davis' recent visit to his father-in-law's house, nor did he want to show him the newspaper clippings that covered Adeline Randolph's car accident. He wanted to keep a few details in his back pocket for another day. Besides, they needed to gather more information about the accident before they could accuse the son-of-a-bitch for being responsible for that, too.

Davis did not move, and he hoped the three other men would not notice the puddle at his feet.

Dubin walked Agents Scott and Gibbons around the corner to the front door.

Scott spoke loudly enough for Davis, who was quickly wiping the mess up off the floor, to hear, "I am sure we will be talking again real soon."

By the time Dubin returned to the dining room, Davis had retreated into the bathroom.

"Davis?"

"Hey, Erik, I'm not feeling well. Can you see yourself out?"

"Sure," he called through the door, "but call me if those assholes try to harass you anymore, OK? A few whiny letters from an unhappy wife aren't enough to convict a man of anything."

Davis thought to himself, "No, but a letter admitting I was responsible for my mother-in-law's murder is." He pulled off his wet, navy shorts and Calvin Klein underwear, sat on the toilet, and defecated, while simultaneously bringing the garbage in front of him and vomiting up the bourbon he had downed, right before the agents arrived.

Dubin pretended not to hear Davis in his misery. He hustled around the corner and yelled, "We will talk soon." He let himself out the front door, locking it behind him.

Scott cranked up the air conditioner in the hot car. He pushed the button on the door handle and the windows closed. "Damn, this is going to be a hot summer! It is 92 today, and the temperatures are supposed to reach 97 by the weekend."

Gibbons took a big swig of his lukewarm water. "So, what do you make of Davis' reactions to the newest evidence?"

Scott responded, "I think Davis is all about Davis. As long as it doesn't affect him, he doesn't care. Can you believe the asshole is still trying to play the "Woe is me. My wife left me" card. And, he didn't even ask about or mention his son! What father does that?"

"A father who doesn't think he is the father," Gibbons said, raising a brow.

"Come on, Gibbons, you can't look at the pictures of Davis as a kid and deny William is his son."

"I agree, Drew, but Davis has a narcissistic personality. I think he finds a way to convince himself of a lot of things, including the fact that he is a victim of his wife's infidelity, but his multiple affairs are somehow justifiable. I mean, I think that in his mind, he really believes his wife's disappearance is her own doing.

Gibbons switched gears, "You know, I don't think Davis is right, but allusions to Gianni Russo do keep coming up. It has been a little while since we have called her high school sweetheart; maybe we need to check in on him again."

Drew agreed, "I really want to like that guy. He seems like the perfect guy to catch a baseball game and a few beers with, but maybe he is too perfect."

Both agents had grown to like Gianni Russo, but they knew they had to remain objective, and the newest evidence gave them a reason to once again question a possible motive with the suave Italian businessman. It was late in the day, so they decided to wait until the next morning to contact Gianni Russo.

53

As they sipped their morning coffee, Scott pondered, "Do you think there is a remote possibility that he and Ella planned her abduction, and he has her and Willow safely tucked away somewhere?"

Gibbons shook his head, "I don't see it; there is too much evidence that shows foul play, and even more evidence that a woman is behind it."

The two agents kept going back to the bitter message about not being able to be part of the family.

Scott analyzed, "Ella has led a vanilla life, with little drama, besides the stress of being married to Davis Masters. In her life, it seems as though Gianni Russo is the only person who hasn't been part of the family, but we have not witnessed a bitter attitude in any of our conversations with the man. He is a humble and soft-spoken man, who brushes his successes off by saying he has surrounded himself with good people with good intentions."

"What doesn't make sense," Gibbons added, "is that Emilie reported that it was a female who called her the first night she arrived at Davis' house, and we both know that Davis had plenty of women. Let us not forget that we still don't know the name of the empty number ten spot on the list of women with whom he had affairs. I know we initially questioned Emilie, but with as much bad blood as the two of them have, I just don't think it is her."

The two men discussed Emilie and Gianni's relationship. They considered telling Gianni about his unborn child but decided against it.

Gibbons said, "Either he already knows about the abortion and is keeping it from us, or he doesn't know at all. Either way, I don't believe this case is about an abortion Emilie Randolph had a few years ago."

"I agree, but we can't forget the miscarried fetus left in the toilet at Gastone's the night Ella disappeared. I am telling you, this case has to be about mystery woman number ten. I think she is giving us just enough information about herself to keep us questioning, but she is peppering it with information about Davis, Gianni, and Emilie to stump us up. How is it that she knows so many intimate details about all of them, but none of them have provided information that would lead to her. Whoever she is, she is beyond bitter, and I think her goal is to knock as many people off their pedestals as possible."

Gibbons asked, "But what is her connection with Gianni, and why would she want to bring him down? He is a great guy who doesn't seem to have a bad bone in his body."

"Dude, I swear you have a bromance going on with this guy." Scott teased.

"Come on, you know you get the same vibe from the guy as I do. Either he is a freaking saint, or he is a world class liar who has us all bamboozled. If he truly is a shyster, somebody would have uncovered his character flaws long before we came along. You don't make that much money and get involved in that many community outreach programs without someone uncovering who the real person behind the action is. I mean, come on, he earned the 2008 Chicagoland's Most Eligible Bachelor, and six years later no woman has been able to snag him. I am telling you, the guy is squeaky clean. I think we are barking up the wrong tree putting our focus on him."

Scott nodded, "You are probably right, but let's just give the guy a call and check in with him."

They closed the door to Scott's office and made the call. Russo's secretary, Kathy, answered in her chipper voice,

"Revitalize Chicago, Inc., where we are revitalizing Chicago, one block at a time, this is Kathy, how may I direct your call?"

"Hey, Kathy, this is Agent Scott, is Mr. Russo available for a telephone call?"

"Good morning, Mr. Scott," she said hesitantly, "How are things going?"

She wished she wouldn't have asked the uncomfortable question for which she knew there probably wasn't a good answer.

"We are still plugging away," was his only response.

"Let me buzz Mr. Russo's office," she said quickly as if to let the agent off the hook, to have to further explain what was clearly not her business.

Moments later, Russo picked up. His voice seemed weary. "Good morning, Agent Scott, please tell me you have good news," he said in a pleading tone. Although he had not had any verbal interaction with Emilie, he had seen the information about Willow's abduction on the news and in social media feeds.

"Mr. Russo, I also have Agent Gibbons on speaker phone here."

Silence filled the phone lines. Russo was afraid to hear what he was sure would follow, but before he could question the news, Agent Gibbons said, "Good morning, Mr. Russo, we don't have bad news or good news, but we did receive another package that had a great deal of potential evidence."

"OOO-KKK," Russo responded, in a concerned voice.

"Whoever sent the package has a plethora of information about Davis, Emilie, and you, sir. There were multiple pictures of interactions between you and each of them in various settings. This all corroborates your story about your relationship with each of them, but Mr. Russo, we have to ask, have you received correspondence from, or had any interactions with Ella Randolph over the years that you have not shared with us?"

A rock formed in Russo's stomach. He visualized the crumpled letter he had read and reread nearly a hundred times.

His silence spoke volumes.

"Mr. Russo, we need to know if you have had contact with Ella Randolph; do you have knowledge of her whereabouts?"

"Oh, my God, NO! I would never put Ella or her family in jeopardy like this."

"We didn't say you would, but would you and Ella have planned this elaborate abduction to finally be together?"

"Agent Scott, I feel like I have aged ten years in a month. I would not willingly put my body through this stress. If I had any kind of clue where Ella was, I would do everything I could, to share that information with you."

Scott replied, "Then why the hesitation when I asked if you have had contact with Ella?"

"OK, OK, I received a letter in the mail. It was a ripped-out page from a journal or something. It was written as a letter, and the salutation was 'My Dearest C.' I didn't tell you about it because I thought you guys would think…well, exactly what you are thinking, that somehow, I am involved in Ella's disappearance. I love that woman like nobody knows. I wouldn't harm her, and I would never do the worst thing a person could do to her: keep her from her children or put them in harm's way."

"Mr. Russo, we are going to need that letter, but can you give us a brief summary of what it said?"

Russo unashamedly explained, "I was afraid if I told you about the piece of mail, you would insist on taking it. It is at my condo underneath my pillow."

"Is this guy serious?" Gibbons mouthed, "Under his pillow?"

He wrinkled his eyebrows and then raised them. He shrugged his shoulders and again mouthed, "He really is in love."

The agents and Russo exchanged a few more questions about his activities and connections since Ella's disappearance. Russo agreed to take a picture of the letter and email it to Scott, and he assured them that he would send the actual copy via FedEx before the day was over. He didn't want to part with the only connection he had with Ella, but he knew it wasn't an option.

Russo said, "I would give every dime I have ever made to get Ella and Willow home alive. I am begging you guys not to give up. Please don't let this case get pushed into the back of some filing cabinet."

Gibbons assured him, "We are doing everything we can, Mr. Russo, but you need to be forthright if you have any more information already or if you receive information in the future. We can only figure out the puzzle if we have all of the pieces."

Russo felt chided. "I am sorry. I will run home now to get the letter."

Russo grabbed his umbrella from the coat stand at the entrance of his glass office doors and told Kathy he would return within the hour. Typically, she asked where he was going; this time, she didn't.

The humid air felt stifling, as he maneuvered his own umbrella through the parade of multi-colored umbrellas protecting people hustling from one building to another. He was in great shape, but he was having a difficult time catching his breath. The oppression of Ella's disappearance was getting the best of him.

He gave his umbrella a final shake as the doorman opened the door for him, took the umbrella, and placed it in the umbrella holder.

"Are you feeling well, Mr. Russo?" Oscar asked, in his British accent. "You look a little under the weather."

"I am fine," Gianni lied, "I am just in a rush, and I forgot something for an important meeting."

"Very well, good day, sir."

"Good Day, Oscar."

Gianni pressed the up button and waited for the elevator to make its way to the lobby. He pushed "30," and the elevator doors closed.

He followed the agents' instructions and returned to work within an hour. Kathy gave him a concerned look when he walked into the office. "Do you need me to make you some tea?"

A weary Gianni mumbled, "No, thank you, Kathy. Thanks, though." And he disappeared behind the large mahogany doors that separated him from the rest of the world.

54

The caller I.D. read, "blocked," and the message was short. In a soft female voice, Agent Scott heard,

Riddle Me This, Riddle me that,
Nobody looked beyond the hat.
Let me whisper a new clue in your ear.
They talked to me the night Ella disappeared.

Scott recalled the three envelopes of hair and said, "Wait, the earlier clue about the hair didn't say, 'Whose hair did YOU not see,' but rather 'Whose hair did THEY not see.'"

Gibbons nodded, "Good catch on the wording. I am telling you, this perp is quite the wordsmith. I'm not dogging the male population, but the psychology behind all of this feels like a woman's touch."

"I agree," Scott nodded, "We have checked Davis' phone records, and we have interviewed every woman we have leads on, so, who the hell is woman number ten?"

The lightbulb went on, and Drew snapped his fingers. The woman had to have been part of the restaurant interviews in Florida the night of Ella's disappearance. He pulled up the Florida police reports. After ten minutes of searching, he yelled, "Gibbons, get Agent Austin from the Tampa department on the phone right now, and transfer the call to my office. I think I have something," Within minutes, Scott's phone rang, and Gibbons joined him in his office.

"Agent Larry Austin here from Tampa, what have you come up with?"

Scott said, "I need you to talk to Officer Rick Thompson of the Orlando Police Department about the young lady he interviewed at Gastone's Pizzeria. Then, can you question the girl? Her name is Brandi Conrad at 610 N. Miller Ave. in Orlando, Florida. I think she might somehow be involved in the missing person's case of Ella Masters.

"Will do. Do you have any other leads in the case that we need to be aware of?"

Scott snorted, "We got the mother-load of evidence dropped in our laps; it all points to her husband and sister, but it's just too good to be true. I will say that her husband is a real piece of work. You know the saying 'Keep your friends close and your enemies closer'? Well, I think they are one-in-the-same with Davis. Whoever is feeding us all the evidence wants us to question Davis and Emilie, but the leads around Emilie haven't really gone anywhere." He did not make eye contact with Gibbons.

Two hours later, Austin called Agent Drew Scott back. "Well, that lead went nowhere."

"What happened?" Scott replied.

"It seems as though Brandi Conrad had her purse stolen the very day Ella disappeared. So, your Goth girl was a fake. My question is, why would a young girl go to such great lengths to hide her identity if she didn't have something to hide?"

Drew slammed his fist down on the table, causing Gibbons to jump. He asked, "Are you sure this girl wasn't lying to you?"

Austin replied, "I'm sure. She even showed me a series of text messages to both her mom and her dad that showed how distraught she was over the theft of her purse the day of Ella's disappearance. She explained that she had just cashed her McDonald's paycheck, and the only thing in the purse was her driver's license, library card, and the money. I checked her parents' phones to confirm the texts were actually sent to them.

They checked out. Our mystery girl stole Brandi Conrad's identification to back up her 'I'm a local kid' story."

Scott questioned, "Did Brandi have brown hair?"

"Yes," Austin replied. "I'm assuming our girl chose Miss Conrad because they looked enough alike to actually pass for each other on a driver's license. I took a picture of Brandi. Maybe that will give us a little something to go on."

"Send me her picture, will you?"

"Sure will, Drew. Do you think Ella Masters is still alive?"

Scott sighed in frustration, "I have to think she still is; otherwise, why would these people still be toying with us? All I know is that whoever is behind this keeps saying it is one big game. It has turned into quite an ugly game."

55

Davis awoke at 5:14 a.m., unable to sleep. He knew his wife had been gone thirty days, and he knew whoever had her, told him their game would last thirty-two days. He felt like he had only two more days to figure this asshole's game out if he ever wanted to see his wife alive again. He grabbed a cup of black coffee, while he waited for his toast to pop up. He carried his breakfast up to his bedroom and flipped on the television to see if there was any coverage of his wife and daughter's disappearance. There wasn't. He briefly thought about Natalia and wondered if she had thought about him.

Davis reluctantly took out the manila folder from under his mattress. It contained all of the notes he had written and gathered, and he recalled the phone calls he had received. Each time, the numbers were different. He did not recognize the male voice, and the female voice was distorted. The callers were obviously using throw-away phones. A sting of guilt coursed through him. He was familiar with throw-away phones.

After two hours of studying the information, his head felt like it was going to explode, and he began to feel claustrophobic in his house. He had stayed close to home because he assumed every law enforcement entity was watching his every move, but now he needed to get away from the oppression of this place.

Davis showered and dressed. The digital clock on his nightstand read 10:45 a.m. He figured by the time he got to Longview Country Club, it would be 11:00, which meant he could order a stiff drink. He had heard the bartender at the country club makes comments to the waitresses about members who drink their breakfast, and he didn't feel like enduring the judgmental glances of a lowly bartender or waitress.

He grabbed the previous day's mail before he left. He remembered the chore only every second or third day. He flipped through the pieces. Stuck onto a 5x7 advertisement for a local attorney was a yellow sticky note. The words on it nagged at him the whole way to the country club.

He found a quiet corner in the bar area, ordered a Jack and Coke, and studied the note that read, "What did you do under the Friday Night Lights in September of 1981?" He immediately knew the reference was to football, and he knew he didn't play football. Sickness filled his stomach as he racked his brain to remember the girl's name. Finally, Lisa Brown's chubby cheeks and beady eyes came to him.

"No fucking way," he said aloud and louder than he had intended, as he slammed his hand on the table. The waitress rushed to his table, tucked into the corner of the bar, to ask if everything was ok. She saw that he had a couple of pages of scribbled notes and the familiar yellow 3 x 3 Post-it pad. He had written one word in big letters on a fresh Post-it, and he was circling it repeatedly, unaware that Allie, the waitress, was even there.

"Mr. Masters," he finally heard through his fog. "Are you OK, Mr. Masters? Is there something wrong with your drink?"

"Oh, no, Allie, everything is fine. Sorry about that."

Allie had been watching Davis come in and sit quietly in a back-corner table once or twice a week for the past couple of weeks. Each time, he took out the same small yellow post-it note pad and scribbled as he drank his bourbon and Coke. He placed and replaced the Post-it notes on an opened manila folder. Each time Allie came to check on him, he closed the manila folder.

As he left the restaurant, one of the Post-its fell to the floor. Allie picked it up and started to call after Davis to retrieve the note, but he had already raced out the door. She looked at the single word that had been circled several times on the Post-it. "Lisa," was all it said.

Davis drove to the nearby Walgreen's pharmacy and asked to borrow a telephone book. The cashier looked at the man oddly and said, "Who uses a phone book these days? Don't you own a smartphone dude?"

Davis looked at the acne-covered freckle-faced redhead teenager, who was annoyingly chewing gum through metal braces, and said with a disdainful tone, "As if it is any business of a punk teen, I have lost my phone, but maybe I need to speak to your manager to explain that you are harassing me."

The scrawny boy quickly reached under the counter and produced a yellow phone book and apologetically handed it to Davis. Davis yanked it from his hands and walked over to the empty counter across from him.

Davis quickly found the B's and then moved to Brown. There were two pages of Browns, and just seeing the last name conjured up hate, anger, and a tinge of sadness. He quickly looked at the T's for Tommy Brown, but that wasn't who he was trying to find. He moved back a page to the L's, specifically to Lisa Brown. There were three Lisa Browns, and there were five L. Browns. "Damn, this is like finding fur on a rattlesnake," he thought to himself. Taking a Post-it note out of his pocket, he wrote down all eight of the numbers.

Geek-face, he was aware, was watching his every move. As Davis handed the phone book back to the kid, he made a note of the boy's name tag. "Anthony," he said to the boy, looking intently at his pocked face. "Well, Anthony, I can't say this is the best fit for a job for you. You might say you are better suited for radio." Davis picked up a pack of gum and tossed it on the counter. Anthony's freckles and acne seemed to blend together as his faced brightened with embarrassment; he took Davis' $3.00 and the change clinked into the return tray. Davis said, "Keep the change; put it towards a bottle of Proactive."

Davis laughed to himself as the electric door slid open, and he walked out of the pharmacy.

He sat in his car for a long while and devised a plan. He had to come up with a reason to call the eight numbers that were staring at him. He decided the most logical and believable reason would be a class reunion. He picked his throw-away phone out of his left pocket and realized the chance of Lisa's last name still being Brown was pretty unlikely, but he had nothing else to go on; he had to at least give it a shot. The first phone call was uncomfortable, as Davis awkwardly muddled through his schpeel. "Good afternoon, this is Larry James. We are working on our class reunion for the Class of 1982, and we are wondering if this is the correct number for Lisa Brown. He crossed the first Lisa Brown off the list when the man explained he hadn't graduated from high school. He moved on to the next one. No luck, and he crossed off the second name. The third Lisa Brown was a young girl, who politely said, "I just graduated last year."

He made his way down the list, and he was more convincing with each call. He called two of the L. Brown numbers and got no hits. With only three names left, he got a possible hit. The lady had a deep, throaty cigarette-damaged voice. Davis got all the way to "class" before he heard the phone go "click." He called the last two numbers, circled the two names on the Post-it that were hang-ups, and drove to the nearest McDonald's.

The teenage girl said, "Welcome to McDonald's, may I take your order."

Davis shook his head at how ridiculous the girl looked with her red weave and fake eyelashes, that made it nearly impossible for her to keep her eyes open. Davis ordered a large unsweetened iced tea and asked the girl if he could please bother her for a phone book. The girl handed him an empty cup and the thick phone book. Like the kid at the pharmacy, she looked at Davis quizzically as if to ask, "What does a person even do with one of these things?"

Davis was sick of stupid teenagers. He filled his cup and made his way to a corner table as far away as possible from the other patrons and repulsive homeless people, who were finding a cool reprieve from the summer heat. He opened the phone book up, matched the two numbers and wrote the addresses next to each of them. One of the addresses was on Lowell, and the other was northeast of Springfield. He was still taking a long shot in the dark that the "L" might actually stand for Lisa, or that she would even have her maiden name, but time was running out, and he had no other leads.

Davis knew he couldn't share this information with the police. He didn't think Lisa Brown would have had the guts, brains, strength, financial means, or know-how to be a mastermind behind something this big, but at this point, he couldn't eliminate any enemy he might have made over the years.

Davis stared at the address and devised his next plan. He knew there was a good chance this was the Lisa Brown he thought she was. He spent the evening, alone in his house, and devised his next plan. He finished off his bottle of bourbon and made a mental note to make a trip to the liquor store the following day. He knew he didn't need to write it down. That was an errand he wouldn't forget.

Lisa Brown was glad she had been sitting down when she heard his voice on the other end of the phone because her legs turned to rubber. She would never forget that voice as long as she was alive, and now he was calling her. The shaking woman wished she would have hung the phone up sooner. She replayed the words in her head, "Hello, my name is Larry James, and I am calling in an attempt to contact Ms. Lisa Brown, regarding our upcoming class…".

"Larry James, my ass," she had said out loud to herself when she clicked off the phone, as she sat alone and lonely in the front yard of her run-down trailer. But now, as the dark blanket of night enveloped her and she lay huddled in her bed, she felt fear. Memories of Davis rushed over her, causing a nauseous wave to rise from her stomach. Lisa Brown was afraid to close her eyes.

The moon went down, and the morning sun awoke. Lisa's night-time fear turned back to anger, as the safety of daylight surrounded her. She continued to mumble obscenities at the man she loathed. She sat in the same rickety lawn chair with her Pit Bull, Brutus, by her side.

The Mercedes Benz slowly crept up the barely graveled dirt road. She sat frozen. The last time a car pulled up the lane was to arrest and take away her deadbeat boyfriend for the manufacturing and sales of Methamphetamines, that unbeknownst to her, he was cooking in her boarded-up childhood home at the back edge of the property. The faded yellow police tape still lay blowing in the wind around the perimeter of the house.

Lisa sat paralyzed in her lawn chair as the familiar face stepped out of the car. Brutus stood on his rear haunches and snarled as the frail woman struggled to hold onto his collar. Lisa spoke first in a quivering voice, "I don't know who the fuck you are," she lied, "but you better just back that fancy-ass car right out of here and get on your way before my husband comes out with his shotgun."

Davis smiled a wicked smile-one that Lisa had seen on multiple occasions. "Lisa, darling, we both know you don't have a husband. I told you I would be the only man you ever had, and I was right. No other man would ever want you, and you know it. You are just rotting away in this pigsty of a place."

Davis' words once again cut her to the core, but she tried to keep her composure.

Davis said, "You know why I am here, and I am not leaving until we resolve our little issue."

Out of desperation, Lisa said, "Brutus, here, doesn't much like strangers, especially assholes like you, so, unless you want to be his lunch, I recommend you get back in your fucking car and pull away."

Davis wasn't sure whether or not Lisa lived alone, but the longer he kept her talking, the more convinced he became that she was alone at the moment. He knew there was a male involved in this fiasco, so at this point, if his guesses were correct, he was on the right trail. Davis chortled a hearty arrogant laugh. "You better be careful with your idle threats, Lisa. I made a promise to you a long time ago that I haven't forgotten. Now, maybe time and distance have made you forget how powerful I am, but let's be honest. Look at me and look at yourself. You may think you are running the show here, but I am very much in control, just like I was that hot Friday night."

They played chicken for the next several minutes in a verbal standoff. Each had enough information about the other to do damage, but neither knew the extent of the other's resources.

Lisa broke the silence that hung over them. She said, "If I call the cops, the whole truth about Davis Masters, or should I say, Davis Love-Brown, will be revealed." With this admission, two things caught his attention. First, she called him Davis Love-Brown, so he had the right woman. Second, he knew if the police came, he would have a great deal of explaining to do, at the very least.

Davis took in the surroundings of the property. He saw only the run-down trailer and a dilapidated, boarded up, old house way in the back of the property. He noticed an old faded yellow police line around the perimeter of the ramshackle house; it gave him a momentary sick feeling.

He mentally recovered and quickly said, "By the looks of that rat trap out back, it seems like the police have already been here, Lisa. Maybe they will be interested in coming back and taking another look at that old house out back."

A startled look took over Lisa's face as she recalled the parade of police cars that followed the unmarked car the night they took Leo away and cleared out the meth lab in her childhood home.

Davis said, "It looks like you have made quite the life for yourself here. I see your mommy and step-daddy set you up quite nicely in this fancy little place."

Lisa could not hold her anger back any longer. She let go of the Pit Bull's collar, and it bounded toward Davis.

Davis barely escaped the snarled teeth as he jumped into the car through the car door he had purposely left open. The dog jumped and scratched at the shiny paint of the E- Class Mercedes, and Lisa laughed her own laugh. She could not hear Davis, but she could see him screaming profanities at the dog as he sped back out the driveway in reverse. The last image she saw of Davis was his imitation of shooting Brutus and then her; it was only when the car sped down Sangamon Avenue that the dog retreated and returned to a visibly shaken Lisa.

As night fell, Lisa started to walk out to her broken-down childhood home, but she turned around after only a dozen steps. She couldn't will herself to go out there. She had been watching the news about the disappearance of Ella Masters, but she couldn't figure out why Davis would come looking for her after all these years.

Lisa double checked the locks on the trailer doors. Instinctively, she pulled the cigarette-stained curtains the slightest bit to make sure Davis had not returned. Her psyche had not yet recovered from his surprise visit. She grabbed a metal cup and the bottle of cheap whiskey. She had not yet come down from the events of the day, and she justified the drink by telling herself she just needed to take the edge off. She called for Brutus to join her as she shuffled to her bedroom in the rear of the trailer, ice cubes tumbling in her cup, as she made her way down the narrow hallway. When her dog refused her verbal command, she closed and locked her bedroom door. The frightened woman pulled her Glock 43 out of the drawer and placed it on the nightstand beside her bed. She turned on the old television and adjusted the antenna wires to clear up the picture. She idly watched local programming and continued to fill her cup, as her mind went to another place and time she so longed to forget. She finally cried herself to sleep.

Davis parked his car and waited for the trailer to go dark. He didn't have to wait long.

The burning splash of whiskey in her eyes followed by the pressure of a gun in her temple shook Lisa out of her drunken sleep. When she awoke enough to fathom what was happening, she realized it was her own gun that was being driven into the side of her head.

"Get the fuck up now, or I swear I will splatter your brains all over this bed! You don't have to worry about me fucking you first! You are too fucking ugly to fuck! You are going to take a little walk with me down memory lane, do you understand me?"

Breathless, Lisa nodded.

Not giving her a chance to even put her slippers on, Davis dragged her out of her bedroom. It was only when they passed through her bedroom door that she wondered why Brutus didn't stop Davis. Davis shoved the shaking woman to the couch and explained that he knew everything. Lisa saw her beloved, Brutus, lying in a pool of his own blood. It was at this moment that Lisa sobered up and began facing her worst nightmare.

Davis began by telling a stunned Lisa that he had not gone to the police with his newest revelation. "You see, this way, I can get rid of Ella, Willow, you and anyone else involved, and make it all look like a homicide-turned-suicide. This is, assuming you have not already killed my beautiful wife and daughter."

Lisa tried to shake the bourbon fog from her brain as she took in his words.

"What kind of monster are you?" she slurred.

His voice was cold, and his words were calculated. "In a couple of days, I will go to the feds and inform them I think I might know who has Ella."

He fantasized briefly about letting them know he was superior to them in that they couldn't figure the crime out, so he had to figure it out himself.

He continued, "Of course, I will play the mournful husband and father. I know I won't get as much of Ella's daddy's money as I had hoped for, but lucky for me, I took out two-million-dollar policies on myself and Ella. Young William will continue to receive financial benefits from his grandpa, so I will be able to skim off the top of those funds also, while I ship him off to a boarding school. You see, the events of the past month were a bit untimely, but at least now I will be able to produce my wife's dead body, and maybe even sweet little Willow's, which will definitely legitimize my insurance claim."

He picked Lisa up from the couch by her hair and said, "We are going to go see just what is in that old shack out back."

The walk to her childhood home seemed to take forever. Davis had to support her frail body much of the way as her legs continued to give away. Lisa knew what would happen when they arrived inside the house. Her worst fears would come true.

The entire time Davis was dragging her to the dilapidated house, he was calling her everything from a cunt bitch to a no-good whore. He took her to the back of the house and kicked in the locked back door with the heavy boots he had purchased just for the occasion. The sound of the door crashing down made Lisa cringe and buckle to the ground.

Davis yelled to anyone in the house that he and little Miss Lisa were now entering the building. Lisa scrambled for words as she yelled, "Jax, Leroy, Jimmy, Mike - he has a gun to my head. He must know what you have hidden here."

Davis hesitated as Lisa rattled off the four names. In an instant, he wondered what trap he had just fallen into. He remembered the note that said, "Davis, you don't even realize that you are a mouse (or should we say RAT) in your own 'Mouse Trap.'"

Quickly, he recovered from the uncertain fear her words evoked. "That is fucking right! I know where you all are, and I am coming to take what is rightfully mine."

Stillness filled the stuffy house. Davis dragged Lisa by her thinning greasy hair, with the gun shoved to the side of her head, through each of the first-floor rooms, he kicked open each door. He looked in closets and underneath beds that were so old that the exposed rusty coils hung down. The rooms were all empty. He forced her down the creaky basement stairs. Besides the remnants of a busted-up meth lab, the basement also had no signs of Ella or Willow.

"Well, old hag, I know you are somehow behind the kidnappings of my wife and daughter."

"I have no clue what you are talking about," she said, now visibly shaking. "Look at me. Do you think I have the resources to pull something like this off? Plus, as you already said, I am a washed-up woman, old before my time thanks to you."

Lisa gathered as much smoker's phlegm as she could muster in her dry mouth and spit directly into Davis' face. He smacked her so hard her neck jerked back, and she went sailing to the floor. He kicked her hard in the side and said, "Bitch, that's for old times' sake. I keep telling you, I have all the power and you have none. When will you learn that?"

Lisa did not respond. The fall to the cold concrete floor left her unconscious. Blood pooled at the side of her head. Davis wiped his face on his sleeve, kicked her one final time to release his rage, and walked back up the creaky stairs. He left her to die in the damp basement; he didn't care. He muttered to himself as he made his way back to his car, "That's one less person sponging off our welfare system."

56

The cacophony of heavy metal music broke through the speakers like fingernails on a chalkboard. Ella listened to the words of the unfamiliar song through the screeching of guitars. The female singer sounded like she was eating the microphone. She covered Willow's ears to protect her from the sound. Ella could not discern many of the words, but the chorus that repeated through her head was "Unforgiven, you are unforgiven." She was too tired to make even the most feeble attempt at figuring out the meaning behind this most recent song.

The music cut off, and it was replaced by June's voice. "Good morning, girls. I thought I would wake you early. We have a big day ahead of us, so I have a special breakfast for you."

Ella knew it was day thirty-two. She knew this because she had carved a notch into the wall of her prison every day since she had been held hostage in the dark hell of her 4'x8' cubicle. She scratched hearts around the notches of the days Willow was with her; there were six hearts.

She was languid with the fear of what today would hold for her and Willow. Her captors had repeatedly told her that she had thirty-two days before she was released…OR KILLED! Ella was well aware of the three strikes game these monsters were playing. She feared William would never see his mommy or sister again. She knew he would never survive a tragedy like that.

They smelled fresh-baked cinnamon rolls and listened to the key turn in the metal lock on the other side of their prison. Willow pressed herself into her mommy's ribs. Fear wrapped its arms around Ella. Besides when June shoved Willow into the closet, Ella knew the only other time the door had been unlocked was when Donny had tried to rape her. She clung to her daughter.

June set down the plate of cinnamon rolls, followed by three boxes of milk. "This is just like the old days, isn't it? I know these are a rare treat saved for special occasions. I thought we might have some time to recap the fun we have been having."

June made her way into the cramped space and handed Ella the final scrapbook page. Ella's eyes locked on June. She clung tightly to Willow, who was also staring wide-eyed at their captor.

Each previous scrapbook entry had induced anguish, heartache, and fear. Ella's heart pounded at twice the speed of a normal heartbeat. The newest page had several pictures of her cheering at the football field where she had spent many Friday nights cheering for her St. Frances football team. She couldn't figure the connection between her abduction and this final scrapbook page. She wondered if June had wanted to be a cheerleader but didn't make the squad.

June picked up a cinnamon roll, took a bite, and said, "Here's to Friday Night Lights." She motioned her hand toward Willow, "Maybe this little lady will get to be a popular cheerleader like her mommy was, instead of some nerdy band geek."

Tears streamed down June's face. Instinctively, Ella reached over and touched the woman's arm, "June…"

"What in the fuck are you doing?" June screamed as she drew her fist back and clocked Ella in the jaw. "You better NEVER fucking touch me again, do you understand me?" A startled Ella retreated, apologizing for her actions. June continued attacking Ella, grabbing her by the throat and squeezing the breath out of her.

Willow screamed, "Please stop hurting my mommy!"

Jax reached through the small door, grabbed June by the shoulders, and shook her back to her senses. "Don't fucking screw this up now, baby! You are going to get yours in a few hours. Don't ruin the show by starting it early!"

June looked at Ella with something just short of rage, as Ella rubbed her neck and regained her breath. "Bitch, birth and death will smack each other in the face tonight, and you have a front row seat at the show to see your fucking family destroyed! Your precious baby girl will remain here while you go watch the final game. If things don't go as we plan, nobody will see sweet Willow until they decide to take out the concrete wall we will build all around her."

Willow recoiled into the corner, put her thumb in her mouth, and watched the puddle pool around her.

June grabbed the plate of cinnamon rolls and pummeled them at Ella. She climbed out of the closet and left Jax to lock the door.

Jax had a remorseful look on his face as he watched Ella wipe the blood from her mouth. He said, "You know, she isn't a bad person. Your husband made her this way, and she needs to make it right. She needs to face the man who ruined her life. You and your children just happen to be innocent victims of Davis' evil games."

The door closed, and they heard the click of the lock.

"Sorry, I piddled, Momma!" Crocodile tears pooled in Willow's eyes.

"Oh, baby, it's OK."

Willow cuddled into her mommy and whispered, "Do you think they can hear me if I tell you a secret?"

"Maybe not if you are very quiet," Ella whispered back.

"Momma, that lady that came in here...well... I have seen her lots of times, but she looks a little different."

"What are you talking about, baby?" Ella whispered with a concerned look. Her mind went to her husband. She wondered if Willow had seen the woman with Davis.

"Are you sure?" she questioned her daughter.

"Yes, Momma, that lady is at the park all of the time, but at the park, she looks different; she looks like a big kid."

Ella knew her daughter was referring to teenagers.

"She sits on the big rocks that we climb on. She wears hats and pants with lots of holes in them like big kids wear. She sits and draws, and..."

"What, Willow? What is it?"

"Well, Momma, sometimes she gives me mean looks."

"Are you sure?"

"Yes, and a couple of times, when I got too close, she whispered, 'Get away, ugly little girl.' Why did she take us, Mommy? What did we do to her?"

Ella recalled the regularly scheduled playdates twice a week at Washington Park, and she could suddenly picture the misplaced girl, sitting on the top of the rocks or loafing on one of the swings, her skateboard always nearby. She looked like a grungy street kid or an eccentric artist. Ella recalled her being there often. Sometimes the girl would find shade on a park bench near Ella and the other moms who showed up a couple times a week. She remembered thinking the girl looked a little old to be hanging out at the park by herself, but she had never given it much thought. Now, she wondered if her family was the reason June had spent so much time at the park.

Willow tugged her mommy out of her thoughts. She reached up and whispered into her ear, "I don't think we should tell her we have seen her before."

June bellowed over the speaker, "Secrets don't make friends!"

Willow froze and clung to her mommy.

June continued, "You have a smart little girl there, Ella. The only problem is that she might be a little too smart for her britches. She recognized me, and now she can identify me. That's a real problem, now, isn't it?"

Willow's eyes widened, and Ella sputtered, "She doesn't know who you are."

"Now, you are lying to me. I thought Davis was the only liar in the house. I am most disappointed in you. What kind of role model is that for your daughter? Her asshole father has never been a role model for his daughter, but I thought you were different. I might have to punish you for lying."

Ella said, "OK, OK, she thinks she has seen you before, but she isn't sure. That's all she was saying."

Willow had a white-knuckled grip on her mommy's arm.

"We both know you have seen me before, don't we, you ugly little girl."

Willow's eyes widened more.

"Yes, Ella, I told you a long time ago that we have been hanging out together for a long time."

Every hair on Ella's body stood at attention at the realization that this woman had been so close to her children in a public place with people all around, and now she was physically and emotionally torturing them.

"The problem we have with this little situation is that now you know where we are, and precious Willow can identify me, so it seems as though I am going to have to punish her now."

"No, Mommy, please don't let her hurt me." Willow cried.

"Shhhh, it's OK. I've got you, baby girl."

June sang her way down the wooden stairs,

"Olly Olly Oxen Free, I'm taking Willow away with me."

Willow grabbed Ella around her skeletal waist and screamed, "Don't let her take me away, Mommy. Please Mommy, PLEASE!!"

The lock jiggled, and the door creaked open. June snatched Willow's leg and pulled her body toward the door. Willow's fingers gripped her mother's arms. June peeled each of Willow's white-knuckled fingers off her mother and dragged her kicking and screaming body out of the closet, scraping her belly as she pulled her across the concrete floor, and back into the dog crate.

She whispered to Willow as she locked the dog crate, "Stop crying, ugly girl! If you make one peep, I will go shoot your mommy right this minute." Her words silenced Willow into verbal paralysis.

Ella listened, but she heard nothing…no cries or screams or pleadings. She only heard June's whistles as she ascended the stairs and closed the door at the top of them.

"Willow, please talk to Mommy. Are you OK?"

She got no response.

"Willow, tell me you are OK."

Still nothing.

She melted to the floor like a rag doll and sobbed. She had let her daughter down, and it might have been the last time she ever saw her.

57

Davis woke to the ringing of the telephone. He blinked several times to read the time on his iPhone before he answered the call.

The voice on the other end sang,

"Olly Olly oxen free, do you remember what you did to me? Today is Independence Day, Let Freedom Ring, I will be free!"

Before Davis could shake the fog from the previous night's booze, the song, "Janie's Got a Gun" belted out in his ears.

In a raspy, morning voice, Davis barked, "Who the fuck is this and what in the FUCK do you want?"

The male voice on the other end of the line whispered, "You've got mail. I just dropped it off on my morning jog. If you hustle outside, I can give you a good morning wave."

Davis threw off his covers and rushed to the front door in his underwear. As promised, a small white envelope with a red and blue-ribbon bow, neatly tied around it, stuck out of the mailbox. He got chills, as he saw the figure in gray sweatpants with a matching gray hoodie pulled over his head, jogging out of his cul de sac. Davis took the envelope in the house and returned to his bedroom.

The note was clear. "If you ever want to see your wife alive (which I don't think matters to you) and you want any chance of getting her daddy's money (which does, however, matter to you), you will follow every instruction you are given today. Lucky for us, today is a holiday, so your buddies, Agent Scott and Agent Gibbons, are spending quality time with their families. If you notify the police or the agents, you will get your third strike. We have already given you one too many breaks, but our patience and time have both run out. Ella's time will also run out if you don't follow our instructions, which will be forthcoming. Do not leave the house until we tell you to do so, and do not contact anyone. If you cooperate with us, this whole misunderstanding will be over tonight."

Five hours later, Davis was instructed by the muffled male voice on the telephone to come alone to the football stadium by Central High School at 8:45 p.m. sharp, if he ever wanted to see his wife alive again. He was going to find out once and for all what the hell was going on. At 8:15, Davis packed his Derringer in the waist of his pants and slipped out of the house. He thought about calling his buddy, Frank, to drive his car, but decided he still wasn't sure if Frank was in on the plot. He parked on Klein Street by the practice field and waited nervously for further instructions.

The minutes seemed like hours, while he waited for another call. Davis hadn't realized how many enemies he had made until his wife's abduction. The asshole police seemed only to be focused on him, but he realized there were a lot of people who wanted paybacks over bad business deals, unpaid gambling debts, and broken promises. That's why Davis HAD to find his wife. He was drowning in financial misery, and without her inheritance to get him out of the mess of a life he had created, he might be the one who disappeared. He imagined being tied to a concrete block and tossed into Lake Springfield, only to be found by a fisherman months later, who would cuss when he snagged his line on Davis' body parts. This thought shook him back to the reality that there were people out there who wanted their money badly enough to kill him. As darkness settled in the air, he suddenly questioned not calling Frank.

The door of Ella's prison opened, and a bright light

shone in, blinding her. She threw her scrawny wrists up to block the light, but Jax grabbed them. He tied her wrists together in front of her with a blue bandana. June held the flashlight, while Jax held a roll of duct tape and the remaining red and white bandanas. He blindfolded her with the red one. He cut a piece of duct tape and covered Ella's mouth. Then, he tied the white bandana over her mouth for extra assurance. The song, "Independence Day," screamed through the basement.

"Today is Independence Day, sweetheart," June whispered in Ella's ear. "And freedom will definitely ring tonight. My question is this: Will it be your freedom, Willow's freedom, or your bastard husband's freedom? With freedom comes responsibility, and if Davis wants freedom, he will have to admit and take responsibility for his actions."

Ella tried to ask what was going to happen to her daughter, but she could only make animal-like sounds through the bandana. Her stomach churned.

As if June could read her mind, she said, "Willow will be staying here tonight while we go to the show. She will be fine with Donny. I know we had a bit of a misunderstanding with Donny, but he has seen the error of his ways and promises he is a changed man. I guess tonight will be a real test to see if he has changed."

Ella heard her daughter's cries in the nearby room.

June said, "Hey, Ella, your daughter is a feisty little wildcat, like her mommy. You know what Donny will do to her if she keeps this behavior up."

June laughed the meanest laugh Ella had ever heard in her life and spouted, "Then you will know what it is like to have a man come between a mother and her child; there is no worse crime."

June fitted flip-flops onto Ella's feet. They had replaced her broken flip flops with a new pair of cheap rubber ones. As she did so, she reminded Ella, "If you make a silly mistake of trying to use your feet to kick or run, we will hog tie you up so tightly, you will wish you had made a better choice."

That wasn't a problem because when Jax pulled Ella out of the closet, her legs did not cooperate. She had not stood in so long that her muscles had withered. He grasped her under her arms and dragged her limp body out of the closet, up the stairs and outside. A car door opened, and he flung her into the back seat. He squished her legs in and slammed the car door. The two front doors opened, and she heard Jax and June get into the car. Sickness washed over her at the realization that Willow was alone in the house with Donny. Guttural cries were cut short by the bandana that filled her mouth.

Ella guessed it was night-time because she knew she had been held captive in a populated area by the sounds of traffic at all times. The reality of June and Jax taking a gagged and blindfolded woman out of the house during the daytime was too risky.

The smell of hot summer filled her nasal passages. She already seemed like she was miles away from her daughter. She had never felt helplessness as she did at this very moment. As she lay in the backseat, powerless and fearing for her little girl, tears soaked the bandana.

As they drove, Ella made mental notes of which way and how many times the car turned. She repeated in her mind, *Right out of a driveway, straight less than a minute, smell of greasy food, straight for a minute. Stop. Wait. Turn left, count of ten. Turn right. Count of five, turn right, count of three. Stop. Count of five-still stopped.*

Jax's taunting words, "We're HERE," confirmed that they were at her final stop. The drive was short, maybe three to four minutes. She carefully repeated her notes in her head.

"This is the end of your road, Ella," Jax said as he dragged her limp body out of the back seat. Her legs still did not cooperate, but Jax cursed in a low whisper, "You better get those legs stepping, or I will shoot you right here and now."

Fear enveloped her. At this moment, the words of her self-defense instructor rang through her head, "No matter how bad the situation seems at the moment, it is better than where you abductor wants to take you. The only reason he wants to take you someplace else is that it is a better place for him and a worse place for you. You need to kick and scream and make as much noise as you can. He will tell you that if you do so, you will die, but that is probably what he has planned for you anyway." She never thought she would be living out her instructor's words. However, she knew she didn't have the strength in her wilted legs to do enough damage, even if she wanted to.

Ella willed her legs to put one in front of the other, and through wincing pain, she walked arm in arm with Jax as he half dragged her through what she guessed to be some sort of parking lot. Her feet stepped off of the concrete and into lush grass. Her only surroundings for the past month had been concrete and wood, so the grass seemed to spring a bit of life into her feet.

As they walked a short distance across the grass, she heard, "pop, pop, pop." She recoiled as if to shield herself from gunshots.

Jax cursed at her to pick up the pace. "Damn, are you afraid of a few fireworks?"

The terrain under her feet changed once again. She now felt rocky gravel make its way between her flip flops and her toes as she shuffled her feet. Her attempts to shake the gravel free as she walked were futile, and she felt the tiny stones bruising her malnourished feet with each step. Jax guided her up what felt like a set of rickety metal bleachers. Her sore legs knocked against aluminum, as she navigated her way in the dark. Jax finally jerked her arm to make her sit down. He drove the pistol with which she had become very familiar into her ribcage and whispered in her ear, "You better not make one peep or the pop, pop, pop will be real." He continued, "Your only role tonight is to see how this game ends. As you know with every game, someone wins, and someone loses. June lost her first game with your hubby; I can guarantee you, she will not lose this one. Now, I am going to take the bandana off your eyes, so you can watch the show, but remember… shhhhh!"

It took Ella's eyes a few moments to focus once the tight bandana was removed. It was the first time in weeks that her eyes had taken in the outdoors. She recognized the location and felt slightly relieved at it being such a public spot. She sat on the same bleachers of Central Stadium that she had cheered in front of nearly thirty years earlier.

Ella's vision had been restored, but she was still bound and gagged so she couldn't ask Jax what came next; she wasn't sure she wanted to know. All Ella could envision was Willow back alone in their prison. She prayed like she had never before prayed, "Father, God, you are bigger than Satan, and you are bigger than these evil people. Place your hand of protection over my baby girl." Tears streamed down her face, and her bound hands were drenched with sweat; not from the summer heat, but from nerves.

From around the corner of the bleachers, Ella saw the dark figure she knew to be her husband come into view. He glared up at his wife. His eyes burned with an anger Ella couldn't quite read, and he looked like hell. Was his anger directed toward her or toward her captors, she couldn't tell. Jax pressed the Smith and Wesson into Ella's temple and yelled down to Davis, "Take a seat on the third row of the bleachers." Davis followed his instructions.

Suddenly, a face with whom Davis was familiar appeared three feet in front of the bleachers. The woman held a Springfield Armory pistol in her shaking hand. Confused, Davis questioned, "Allie, what are you doing here? What in the hell is going on?" He added, with a cocky, throaty laugh, "You certainly can't be behind all this."

Ella was confused. The only name she had heard during her thirty-two days in captivity was June; now, she was hearing

Allie. Everyone seemed to know the girl except Ella, who was forced to sit and watch and listen to this nightmare of a movie, wondering if she would ever see her children again.

"June," Jax said in a much steadier voice, "Remember what we talked about. This is your game, sweetheart. Remember, the best offense is a good defense. You have the upper hand with this mother fucker for the first time in your life. I have your back, baby, but this moment is all about you. You don't have to be afraid or sad or guilty. I love you, and I am right here for you!"

Ella was caught off guard by the gentle interaction. Tears once again burned her eyes, as she tried to repress her emotions. Ella couldn't fathom what her husband had done to June to cause such vehement actions, but at that moment she realized Davis had never spoken to her with such gentle and tender words. Jax loved June so much that he was willing to risk everything for her happiness.

"Who the fuck is June?" a nervous Davis said as he looked around for another woman.

"I'm June, you fuck head... Allie June! You would think you would know my name as much as we have experienced together," June said with a condescending laugh.

Ella cringed at the fact that Davis did not deny knowing the woman.

Davis said, "OK, Allie, you have had your fun and games, but now you will play my game."

Her only response to him was, "Oh, I don't think so; I am still running the show, and let's start with you calling me by the correct name. My name is June."

Davis sneered, "June, Allie, whatever... whoever you are, you are nothing more than a no-good waitress with no place to go but down. You are all big and bad with your boyfriend and your guns, but I have the police on their way right now." He knew he was bluffing and the bluff might cost him his life, but, besides the small gun he had in his waistband, it was all he had.

Without missing a beat, June responded, "Do you mean a no-good waitress like your mom? The one you left to rot of a broken heart because you, her only child, spent your adult life telling everyone she was dead."

Before Davis could process what he heard, a biting sensation on the back of his ankle took his breath away and caused him to grab his leg. "What the fuck?" he yelped. He felt the wet liquid drip through his fingers as he tried to figure out what caused the pain.

From under the bleachers, Davis heard the familiar, raspy female voice, "Davis, I have a gun pointed right at your testicles. We had so much fun last night, I thought we would do it all over tonight... only... I have the gun now. I am in control now, and you are at my beck and call to sit quietly and listen."

Lisa dropped the knife, replaced it with the item from her jacket, and stepped out from behind the bleachers, with the Glock 43 in her hand.

"WHAT are you doing here?" June screamed through gritted teeth. "You are going to fuck everything up."

Lisa's slurred words interrupted June, "Alice, I have been watching the hubbub of Davis Masters' wife's disappearance since she went missing. I guess you could say it brought back memories. So I went to get my diary, but it was gone. I put two and two together and realized that since you are the only person who had been in my house, there was a good chance that you took my journal and were somehow behind her disappearance.

She tried to contain her anger. "Then, Davis paid me a visit; It wasn't a good visit. I knew I needed Jax's help to keep him away, so I took a cab to your house tonight. That is when I saw you putting the woman into the car. I had already figured out that you held her prisoner for thirty-two days to symbolize how many years you have lived without a father-figure in your life. I took a guess at where you were taking her, and I guessed right."

Davis chortled, "Alice? I thought your name was Allie, and it ISN'T a house, it is a fucking trailer for trailer trash!"

Ella was so physically, emotionally, and psychologically weak that she couldn't make any sense of the horror show that was playing out in front of her. How did he know these two women, and more importantly, what had her husband done to them so heinous that they had so much hatred for him?

Lisa pointed the gun straight at Davis, and mocked, "It takes one to know one!" She loved the control she felt she had for the first time in her life, and she was going to relish in it. She had been waiting a long time to get even with Davis Brown for throwing her away, and she was in no rush to finish him off.

She started, "I was a nobody from a nobody family, just like you, Davis. My mom had four kids from four different men who threw her away when they were finished with her, just like your dad threw you away after he fucked your mom at some golf tournament."

Davis' shaky voice revealed that he was off-kilter. Ella had never seen him in this state. He tried to talk calmly. "Lisa, last night was a misunderstanding, and I apologize for that, but you don't have a dog in this hunt, so you need to get yourself out of here before you get hurt in this mess."

Davis looked at her quizzically.

"Oh, yes, Davis, I know ALL about your life. I spent a lot of time researching you, and I found all kinds of tidbits about your life that I'm certain your wife does not know."

Ella's confusion was confounded by this short interaction. "How does he know this woman, and what did they do last night?"

Lisa did not take her eyes off Davis, but she turned her conversation to June.

"Alice, listen to me. This piece of dog-shit isn't worth spending the rest of your life locked up. If he was, I would have killed the son-of-a-bitch a long time ago".

Davis attempted to regain his composure and control of the situation. He quietly asked what the two women wanted from him. Lisa took over the conversation, and June focused on keeping the red laser pointed at Davis' heart. June had not planned the attack this way, but she now realized the woman next to her needed the chance to avenge thirty years of anger.

Lisa yelled up the bleachers, "Ella, let me tell you a story about the monster you married. See, I have known Davis longer than you have, and I don't have fond memories. We sat in alphabetical order in various classes throughout our four years at Central High School. Unfortunately for me, I was stuck right in front of Davis Brown in at least one class all four years, and his obnoxious behaviors got worse as the years progressed. He was a small, quiet boy his freshman year, but when he returned his sophomore year to the seat right behind me in health class, he was quite a bit bigger and a lot meaner-- not mean, meaner, but sexually meaner. I was a little bit overweight, and I had budget eyeglasses with thick black frames. I liked learning, but I didn't always like school. I was the band girl who had saved every penny I earned babysitting for three years to buy my own flute, after borrowing one from my band teacher at East Middle School, until my sophomore year."

"During our sophomore year, Davis took his seat every third hour in Mr. Johnson's health class, and within minutes, he used the capped end of his ink pen to trace down my back. When I jerked around the first time he did it, Mr. Johnson yelled, 'Lisa, what seems to be the problem?' I knew Mr. Johnson was not able to see Davis' pen painfully digging into the soft flesh just below the clasps of my bra. I responded, 'Nothing, Mr. Johnson, it was just a bee buzzing by my head.' Mr. Johnson responded, 'Very well, let's return to the female reproductive system then, can we?' Davis whispered quietly into my ear that if I ever pulled a stunt like that again, he would catch me walking home to my rat-infested house and slit my throat! I had no reason not to believe him, so for the next two years, I lived in fear of this mother fucker right here. That was only the beginning of the many comments he whispered into my ears-- things like, 'Have you ever felt the sweat of a real man between your legs or just the deadbeats your mom sends your way as leftovers?' He told me he could show me what it felt like to have a REAL man, as he caressed his fingers up and down my back and then around the side of my body until he felt the meaty flesh of my breasts. When he was feeling especially mean, he used his pen to push my glasses off the back of my ears and tie knots into my wavy hair. He always positioned himself so no one could see him unclasp my bra through my t-shirts. Then, he watched me leave the classroom with my books covering my large, unrestrained breasts, as I raced to the nearest restroom. He chuckled all the way to his next class. While most guys bragged about their antics to their buddies, Davis never did. The biggest reason was that this loser didn't have any friends, and even if he did, he didn't want to have his fun ended by someone ratting him out. He knew he had scared me enough that I would never reveal his secrets…and I never did."

Davis still sat arrogantly and said, "Who gives a fuck if I bullied you a little when you were fifteen years old. Get over it. Everyone gets bullied!"

But Lisa wasn't finished talking, "Shut the fuck up!" she barked, "Let me get to the part that you might give a fuck about!"

She directed her words toward Ella, "You see, Ella, Davis was pissed at watching you interact with all of the Catholic School boys you cheered for at Bishop High School as the players crushed the Central High School Cougars football team yet another year."

Davis felt the sweat drip down his face. He remembered the night well. By the time the game was over, he was pissed at the way the Catholic school kids thought they were so much better than the public-school kids. He needed to release his pent-up anger. He waited in his beat-up green Plymouth Ventura until everyone left the stadium and the lights were turned off. He reached into the small cooler in his back floorboard and stuffed two Budweiser beer cans into the pockets of his jacket. He snuck back into the stadium through an open gate in between the school and the football field, sat in the lower section of the bleachers, and sucked down the first cold beer with a few quick chugs. He opened the second one and planned on drinking it a little more slowly when his eyes fell on Lisa Brown. She was frantically looking for something under the bleachers. He saw her reach down in relief and pick up a black case. He eased down the side steps of the bleachers and waited in the darkness. His heart rate began racing at the thought of what he was going to do to this ugly bitch.

Davis thoughts were interrupted by the pressure of the gun that was now in his side, June said, "Pay attention. She deserves a little respect."

Lisa continued, "I know you think you know where this story is going, Davis, but you have no clue how it ends. See, Ella, I was oblivious to the fact that he was watching me, as I snaked my way through the back side of the bleachers with my flute in hand. Davis grabbed me, cupped my mouth, and told me he knew I wanted all those things he had promised me the past couple of years. I froze in my tracks. Davis whispered into my ear as he held my hair tightly in his grip, 'If you make one sound, ugly girl, I will find both of your little sisters and rape them until they can't walk. I promise you, they will never recover from what I will do to them if you make one fucking move!'

Ella winced at the familiar words.

Lisa continued, "The next thing I knew, I was on the stinky, popcorn and soda-covered ground, underneath the bleachers, with Davis Brown unbuckling his pants. He forced himself into my mouth and then ordered me to take off all of my clothes. This mother fucker taunted me with jeering remarks with each article of clothing I removed. He kept calling me a fat, ugly girl, and he told me the only way I would ever have sex with any man was if I paid for it. He continued. 'It just happens to be your lucky night because I am going to show you what it is like to be with a real man. This will be a night you will never forget!'"

Tears streamed down Lisa's, June's, and Ella's faces. Jax' jaw was clenched like he was going to sock Davis before he put a bullet in his head. Davis' look was hard to read.

Lisa hung her head, and her next words were barely audible, "I endured the rape for no more than thirty minutes, but it felt like I remained under those bleachers for ten hours. When Davis finished, he stood up, took a few more swigs of his beer, and poured the rest of the warm beer on my exposed breasts. He calmly pulled up his pants, grabbed his jacket, and spit on me as he walked out from under the bleachers. As he walked away, I could hear his faint voice reminding me of what he would do to my adorable little sisters if I ever told anyone."

The angry tone left her voice, "See, Ella, I had been an honor student, and even though I was from an impoverished family, I was going to be the first one to graduate from high school. I was the oldest child of a single mom, and I spent most of my time outside of school, tending to my younger siblings, cooking, and cleaning. But no matter what, I never missed school. It was too vital for me to get a high school diploma and go to college, so I could make a better life for myself and my three younger siblings, one brother, and two sisters."

"Davis ruined that dream. That night, he left a broken shell of the young girl I was, and I would never be the same. My three-year perfect attendance record was shattered by the events of Friday, September 25, 1981. I missed my first day of school during my entire academic career on Monday, September 28, 1981, and I never returned to school. My mom wanted to care about my quitting school, but she was so busy trying to make her own ends meet, that deep down she was relieved by the extra help I provided around the house."

"By late November, I knew I was in trouble. I had missed my period in the middle of October, but I thought it was because I was sitting around the house more. When November's period didn't arrive as scheduled and I could barely stand facing the shower head when I showered because my breasts felt like balloons that were ready to pop, I knew I was pregnant. I was able to hide the reality of my growing belly until February because I had always been a little on the chunky side, but by Valentine's Day, my mom was questioning me. I lied to her about the identity of the father, and she was too busy tending to her three other children by three different fathers to really care."

Ella became more heartbroken with each new revelation. Davis had a disdainful look on his face. Ella could see he wasn't getting it. He wasn't getting the gist of what he had done. She was frightened because June had told her the only way Ella would be set free was if Davis acknowledged his wrongdoings. Ella looked at her husband and realized he didn't have the capability of doing that. Sickness filled her.

"I had been so determined to rise up and get out of the hell hole of my life, but when I got pregnant, as a result of the rape, I knew I was forever stuck. On June 5, 1982, while my fellow classmates were walking out onto the very football field where my child was conceived, I was delivering a 5 lb. 2 oz. baby girl, and while my friends were spending their summers getting ready to go away to college, I was hiding in my trailer from the boy I knew was still in Springfield, because he didn't have the money to go away to college either."

Lisa continued, resignedly, "So, there I was, living in an endless cycle of poverty. I fell into the smoking and drinking lifestyle of my family, who only occasionally inquired about the baby's father. This trap I call life had only begun."

Lisa tried to keep her volume from rising to a yell as she recalled how she watched Davis attend junior college and pretend to go away to Eastern Illinois University, while she bartended and waited tables to keep her young child, THEIR YOUNG CHILD, clothed and fed.

With a biting tone, she said, "I watched you return to Springfield, marry perfect little Ella, become a successful businessman, thanks to your father-in-law's money and connections, and father two adorable children, all while I continued to fail at making my financial and emotional ends meet. I wanted revenge, but I was depressed and weak, and I knew I would never have the courage I needed to bring such a pillar of the community down. I had already written the horrific details of the fateful night's events in my secret diary, which I thought was well hidden, and I continued to write down the events of your life, as I read about them in the *State Journal-Register* or on the internet when I used June's cell phone."

Davis continued to give the woman a disdainful glare.

Lisa's voice faded, "And now we are here."

Through Lisa's entire story, June's unwavering hands remained on the pistol, ready for Davis to make one wrong move. She had been looking for a reason to kill this man for as long as she knew him.

Fireworks popped and boomed around them. Ella jerked each time a new set of explosions rang in the night sky.

June took over the conversation. "See, DADDY..."

She paused long enough for Davis to furrow his brow in confusion and then look back and forth from Lisa to June with a stupid look on his face.

"That's right," June said, "I didn't stutter."

She paused again, so Ella could also comprehend her words.

Ella closed her eyes and lowered her head. It all came together. Everything June had said, and the physical and emotional torture she and Willow had endured, all finally made sense.

June admitted, "I was snooping in my mom's closet when I was fourteen years old, and I found her diary. I shouldn't have read it, but I did... and it sickened me. I couldn't understand how one human being could do those things to another human being. I never told my mom I had it, but for the first time, I understood her ongoing depression and hatred for men. For the first time, my mom made sense to me."

She shook her head as she continued, "The kids at school were always mean to me because I was dirty and poor. They called me names like 'Little Orphan Alice' because they knew I didn't have a daddy. I used to get mad at mom, but once I read her diary and knew all of her secrets, I felt awful for her, and I wanted revenge...for her and for myself."

June explained, "So, just like my daddy, I got a job at the elite Long View Country Club as a hostess at the age of 16 in order to....let's say...get to know you. You got a job as a dishwasher at that very country club, so you could stalk Ella's family, right?" June nodded up at Ella.

"Well, I wanted to be just like my daddy. I quickly moved up to waitress status, and before I knew it, I was waiting on you and your cronies several times each month in the grill room. It was rare for you to bring Ella and the kids in, but when you did, you always chose the dining room, so I could remain behind the scenes and watch your perfect family. I had a tough time hiding my anger, knowing I was part of that family. I'm sure you can understand that. Not only was I excluded from your family, but I also had to witness my mother suffer a lifetime of depression over what you did to her. She wanted to be a good mom to me, but you robbed her of that."

A lifetime of hatred spewed out of June's mouth like verbal vomit. "Then, I got pregnant a few months ago. I had found myself a good guy, and I was determined to make things right in my world by giving my child two parents who would love him or her. Jax up there would have been a perfect father." She waved the gun in Jax's direction. "Everything was going great; I was healthy, taking prenatal vitamins and everything, but then, you see, I had a miscarriage, and once again, I had you to thank for my fucked-up life!"

Ella looked over to see tears streaming down Jax's face. June's mother stared at her daughter in shock.

Davis said, "What the fuck does that have to do with me? How can you put that one on me?"

"Everything, you bastard! You patronized me to my face, but you made sexual jokes about me with the guys when you thought I was out of earshot. When you egged your buddy on to grab my ass under the table, that was the beginning of the end. See, your buddy must have liked what he felt because he was waiting by my car one night when I got off work. He told me he knew I wanted him, and he grabbed me and forced his tongue into my mouth. I responded by biting his tongue as hard as I could, and he returned my gesture by punching me as hard as he could in my stomach. I dropped to the ground, and he kicked me with his steel-toed boots several more times. I miscarried that same night."

She paused for a beat. The gun was visibly shaking in her hands. "I just snapped. I had fantasized about getting revenge on you for years, and the miscarriage ignited hate I didn't know was possible. I replaced the passion I had for being a perfect new mother into revengeful passion toward the man who had caused me so much pain. That man, Davis, is you."

Lisa cried out, "Oh June, I had no idea, baby. I am sorry. I had no idea."

Splashes of color painted the sky. With the gun pointed at Davis' head, Lisa looked into the eyes of the man who had raped her and screamed uncontrollably, "You aren't a son-of-a-bitch, but you ARE a fucking BASTARD child! Your father dumped you! He didn't want you!" she lunged at Davis.

Davis saw her come at him, and with a swift swipe of a backhand, he knocked Lisa to the ground. He began kicking her in the stomach as she lay there in the fetal position.

With every kick, she screamed louder, "You raped me, got me pregnant, and then you dumped us both. You ended up with two more brats you didn't want; you are a bastard husband and a bastard father."

She grabbed Davis' leg, and he stumbled to the ground. Lisa had regained her footing and started beating his head with the butt of the pistol.

June attempted to jump on Davis, but he knocked her off of him. Jax ran down from the upper bleachers. He grabbed his girlfriend and pulled her to safety. He said, "Baby, this is her game. She has been waiting a long time for this night, and she didn't even know it." Fighting his hold, June continued to struggle as she watched the violent battle between her mom and Davis unfold.

Davis had endured some heavy blows from Lisa, but he now had the upper hand. He pulled himself up and stood over Lisa. Just as Jax was about to grab him, Davis dug the heal of his Cole Haan shoe into the battered woman's forehead and spit on her. " You are nothing but a piece of dog shit under my shoe. You are nothing and you will…"

Bang! The first shot landed right between Davis' legs. As 195 pounds of dead weight fell on her, she got off two more shots.

Lisa's frail body lay trapped under Davis. Blood dripped from her mouth. Her past came back to her in a flash, and the panic of being stuck underneath this man again filled her with terror. She began wriggling and struggling to free herself from the man she despised more than anything.

June raced toward her mom to get Davis' heavy body off of her. She saw the terror on her mother's face. Lisa's mouth contorted to scream, but no sound escaped her lips. She had to get away from this terror, once and for all. She inched her arm free from the weight of Davis, placed the revolver in her mouth and pulled the trigger.

"NOOOOOOOO," June screamed.

She shoved Davis' body to the side and fell onto her mother's chest. The sound of sirens didn't faze her. She had spent so much of her life trying to protect her mother from any more hurt, and now she felt like she had let her down. Remorse spilled out of her mouth, "Mommy, all I wanted to do was avenge your hurt. I wanted him to pay for what he did to you when you were so young and innocent. He robbed you of a real future and left you stuck raising me, a baby you didn't ask for or want. I'm so sorry, Mommy! I'm sooooooo sorry!!! Please come back to me, Mommy!! PLEASE don't leave me, Mommy!"

The sound of sirens roared in sync with the explosion of fireworks as the grand finale lit up the sky. Ella sat frozen on the bleachers. Tears poured down her face at the realization that the man she had shared a bed with for more than twenty years had taken her own mother away from her, and now he had taken his daughter's mother away from her.

Jax picked June's limp body off of her mother's bloody body. June's gaze caught on Davis. Rage once again overtook her. Her tears turned to sobs and then to screams, "You mother fucker!!" she cursed, "You killed my mom thirty-two years ago when you raped her, and then she continued a slow death of alcoholism and drug abuse, staying alive only because she didn't want to throw me away; now, she is dead…in the same place where you first took her life away."

Jax held her bloody body in his arms, stroked her hair and kissed her forehead. "It's all over, sweetheart. It's all over. Shhhhhh. Listen to me," he whispered, "We will have that baby someday, and when we do, you will be the best mom ever." He knew deep down they would probably both end up in prison, but he would tell his girl any lie to make her feel OK.

Tears streamed down Ella's face as she watched the girl who had emotionally tortured her for the past month revert to a helpless child. She was void of any emotion toward the bloody body of the bully she called her husband.

For Ella, time stood still as police cars, firetrucks, and ambulances screamed into the parking lot, and men and women flooded into the football stadium. She knew her baby girl was locked up with a monster, and she needed to get to her. She needed to find her baby.

Several Springfield police officers stormed the stadium. Ella's eyes caught on June as officers placed handcuffs on the couple. Officer Cookson looked at the carnage around him as he made his way up the bleachers to Ella.

"I am Officer Cookson. Everything is going to be OK, now. We have contacted the agents who have been working on your case; they will be here soon." Cookson carefully removed the bandana and duct tape from Ella's mouth, apologizing when she winced in pain. He carefully untied the bandana that bound her wrists.

Ella rubbed her skeletal wrists. With a barely audible voice, Ella pleaded with Officer Cookson, "I need to find Willow. She is in a dog crate in the basement of a house nearby. She is with a nasty man who might hurt her; she is scared. Please help me find my Willow. I know how to get to where she is. I made a mental map of how I got here; all we need to do is turn it around," her voice rose to a panic.

"Agents Scott and Gibbons will be here any minute. We will find your daughter, Ma'am."

As if on cue, Agent Drew Scott hustled up the bleachers just as Ella was about to describe what she had rehearsed in her mind several times. He took out his pen and notepad and began writing furiously; Ella closed her eyes and recounted her car ride.

"I know we pulled forward out of a driveway. I felt the slight bump at the end of the driveway. We turned right and drove only a very short way, stopped briefly, and turned right again. We drove another very short distance and then stopped for a brief time; I assume we were at a stop sign. We made a sharp left and went what seemed like a block. We stopped, and Jax cussed about red lights. We made a right and then another pretty fast right…maybe a half block. We stopped, and that is where Jax dragged me out of the car. We must have crossed the practice field because I felt the grass between my feet."

As Agent Scott listened to Ella's recollection of the car ride, Emilie appeared at the bottom of the bleachers. Emilie gasped audibly as she took in the bloodshed. She ran up the bleachers and wrapped her arms around the woman she barely recognized.

Agent Scott awkwardly interrupted the reunion. He knew every minute counted. He said, "Ella, I promise you, I am going to go find your little girl." He turned to Emilie, "You can accompany your sister in the ambulance. I will meet you at the hospital with Willow in tow. We will get an agent to pick William up from Abe's house if Kristina can't bring him to the hospital. I know he is ready to see his mom. As for me, I have a little girl to bring to her mommy."

Scott rushed down the bleachers, and then quickly turned back to Ella and Emilie. "By the way, Ella, your sister did her very best with the kids, but I think she has a newfound appreciation for what you do as a mother."

Emilie responded, "Thanks, Agent Scott, and thank you for calling me."

Ella put her bruised and dirty face in her hands and sobbed. Emilie cradled her twin, and the two rocked in each other's arms and wept. Officer Leach made his way up the bleachers and, with Emilie's help, guided Ella down the stairs. Ella gave Davis' dead body a wide berth when she walked around it, and she deliberately looked away.

June sat on the bleachers, hands still cuffed behind her back with her mother's blood covering her hands, face, and shirt; she looked up at Ella and mouthed a genuine, " I'm sorry."

Ella pulled away from her sister and Officer Leach and weakly made her way over to June. She cautiously placed her hand on June's arm and whispered, "You lost your mother before you even had a chance in life. You didn't allow that to happen to my babies. For that, I am grateful. I know I am not your mother; I will never be your mother, but I promise I will take care of you!"

"Why?" June asked, quietly.

"Because you have had a lifetime of pain!"

E.M.T's gently placed Ella on a stretcher and put her in the ambulance. Emilie climbed in next to her twin sister and held her hand so tightly that Ella had to wiggle life back into her fingers.

Jax was placed in the back of one squad car, and June was put in another one. June looked over at her dead mother, covered by the white sheet. She lifted her bound hands and placed her thumb on the window, "Thumb kiss," June quietly said to herself. She mouthed, "I love you, Mommy," as the squad car drove past the ambulance and out of the stadium parking lot.

58

Donny chugged two quick long neck Budweiser beers. He splurged on the bottles instead of cans. It was going to be a special night, after all. He showered, dried off, and put on his robe. He smiled into the mirror. His crooked yellow teeth returned the wicked smile. His left eye was still swollen, and the broken blood vessels had turned the whites of the eye red. It sent a rage through his body. He had not gotten a piece of that bitch the whole time she was downstairs, and Jax had kicked the shit out of him. It was now Donny's turn to get the last laugh.

He squeezed a fresh pimple that had emerged on the side of his nose, patted cheap aftershave on his cheeks and neck, and gave himself one last approving glance. He had spent the day fantasizing about this night.

Willow's soft cries were barely audible. The diarrhea she couldn't hold back caused a gag response that sent her into dry heaves. She had no room in the dog crate to escape the mess. She tucked her body into itself and prayed.

She heard the crack of the door and Donny's voice, "Hey, ugly girl, June and Jax had to take your mommy to see your daddy, and they told me to take real good care of you."

She winced as each step creaked. She didn't hear the man's clunky boots, but rather the soles of slippers. The footsteps came closer, and her breath stopped.

"Fuck, what is that smell. You smell like dog shit."

"Willow pee'd herself."

"Well, ugly girl, it looks like we need to get you cleaned up."

The lock rattled, and the metal door opened.

Willow stiffened her entire body and tried to make it impossible for the man to drag her out. It was a futile effort.

"Damn! I just got cleaned up, so I can't pick you up and get your shit all over me."

He dragged her by her delicate wrists across the concrete floor. She finally gathered her footing and tried to keep up with his steps as they headed upstairs. Her legs failed her about every third step, and he screamed, "Get the fuck up!"

Willow's stranger-danger alert was at high level. She realized Donny was going to do bad things to her. He dragged her through the kitchen and down the hall. He shoved her into the bathroom. He looked down at his robe to make sure he didn't get any of her shit on him. He hadn't.

He wanted to go into the bathroom with her, but his own gag reflections needed to settle down. He was moments away from throwing up.

He yelled, "You have fifteen minutes to get nice and clean for me, little girl. Then, you and I are going to have the fun I didn't get to have with your mommy."

Willow froze, and the room began to spin.

"Do you hear me, ugly girl? Fifteen minutes!!"

Willow had to get away from this man. She had to find her mommy.

She caught a glimpse of the strange girl in the mirror; it was her reflection. She was an ugly girl. She was gaunt and bald and dirty. Her clothes were filthy, but at least she still had clothes on. She was glad for that.

"I better hear bath water running soon, or I will come in and stab you a hundred times."

Willow quickly reached into the tub and turned on the water.

"That's my ugly girl," Donny chanted.

Willow saw the window atop the bathtub. She looked back at the door; it had a lock on it. She splashed at the water to make it sound like she had gotten into the tub. She quietly crawled to the door and slowly turned the lock. She let out her breath when she didn't hear him touch the door handle. He hadn't heard her. She crawled back to the tub and splashed at the water.

"Atta girl, ugly girl, get real clean now, you hear," he cackled.

Willow stepped onto the ledge of the tub, unlocked the window, and attempted to raise it. It wouldn't budge. Panic coursed through her body. She knew she needed to punch at the edges to loosen it up. She had seen her papa do that in his house when he opened the windows for the first time in the spring. She needed to distract the guy.

She yelled out to him as loud as she could make her little voice go, "Please don't hurt me, mister."

He yelled back, "Shut up and get clean. You only have seven minutes left before I come get you."

She hit the right side of the window while he yelled. It seemed to work.

She again pleaded, "Please, mister don't hurt me."

He was losing his patience, "Shut the fuck up, or I will kill you right now."

She banged the back side of her hand against the window again.

"What was that, ugly girl."

The rest was a blur.

Willow heard the handle jiggle and a long stream of curse words. She mustered her strength and slid the window up. She pulled herself up through the window and dangled halfway out when the door kicked open, and she felt his ominous presence.

"Fuck! You ugly girl little bitch!" Willow looked down at the five-foot drop and felt his hands grab her feet. She closed her eyes, imagined diving into the pool, and flung her body out the window and flew to the ground.

It all happened so fast that Donny's grip was not tight enough. Her feet slipped out of his hands. He spewed another string of profanities and raced out the bathroom, down the hall, through the kitchen, and out the side door.

The agents had known they had to be close to the house by the information Ella provided, so when they saw the man in a robe race out the side door of a house and around the corner, they stopped the car, hopped out, and each ran in the opposite direction around the perimeter of the house.

Willow lay, stunned and aching, in the overgrown grass. She knew he would be there soon to get her again. She looked around at the empty lot next to the house and realized he would easily outrun her. She saw the busy street. She would run there. A car would see her. She gathered her wits and willed her wobbly legs to get up and run. She picked herself up and ran toward the street as fast as her weak body could go. She didn't make it past the house. She ran smack into the muscular arms.

Agent Scott barely saw the frame of the small child before she fell into his arms. He scooped her up and held her tight. He whispered soothing words, but she was limp and unresponsive.

Again Gibbons' steps closed in quickly on Donny as the man raced toward Willow. When he was just about to rip his victim out of Agent Scott's grip, Gibbons tackled him. The perp did not stop cursing at his victim, even when his face was planted into the ground and he was in handcuffs. Gibbons dragged him to his feet by his hair. Donny had run out of his slippers in his attempt to grab Willow; Gibbons didn't bother getting them.

Donny was, not so gently, placed into the squad car. He was wearing his robe...and nothing else. Gibbons smiled at the officer who would be driving this asshole to the station and said, "The guys are going to like this fresh meat, and he's only wearing a robe. That's nice...that's REAL nice!"

Donny's face turned pasty white, and he pissed himself.

59

Ella lay in the hospital bed writhing in her nightmares, under the power of heavy sedatives. She and William and Willow were running, running, running as Davis closed in on them. Willow tripped, and William stopped to help, but Ella said, "Run William, and I will save Willow. Don't look back, just run," William ran. Ella got Willow to her feet, and the little girl took off, but Ella lost her footing and tumbled to the ground. Ella tried to scramble to her feet, but Davis closed the distance on her as the distance between her and the children grew. Her husband tackled her and pinned her to the ground. She felt his hand cover her mouth and nose, stopping her air flow. She woke up, drenched in sweat.

Cristiano placed a wet washcloth on her forehead and hushed her, "It's going to take a while, but you will be OK. You've been through a lot."

Ella squeezed his hand and closed her eyes. She couldn't believe he was still sitting there by her side. The nurses had told her they couldn't get rid of him.

"How's my baby girl?"

Cristiano moved to the side, so Ella could see her daughter asleep in the next bed over. It wasn't hospital policy to place children in adult units, but hospital personnel decided to ignore the policy just this once. They couldn't fathom separating the little girl from her mother.

"And what about my brave William and Daddy?"

"They are doing fine, but they are ready for you two to come home. Your daddy is missing your cooking."

Ella's mood turned somber, "Can you believe my poor father's dementia was caused by…" Her voice trailed off.

"It's OK, you can talk about it," Cristiano encouraged.

Ella whispered, "I can never get my mother back. Davis took her away from me. He almost took my daddy away from me. And I was the one giving Daddy the pills.

Cristiano interrupted her, "You had no clue Davis tampered with the pills. You thought you were giving him Aricept."

"Yes, but I should have gotten a clue when Davis offered to pick up Daddy's medications every month. Who would even think about making deadly pills? What kind of person does that? I'm just so relieved and thankful that Emilie figured it out and told Agent Scott about the medications."

Cristiano brushed the tears from Ella's cheeks, "But he didn't take your daddy away from you. The doctors said he will make a full recovery. He is even talking about coming out of retirement. With you and the kids living with him, and Emilie sticking around for a while, he has all kinds of reasons to keep getting better every day. "

Ella's heart ached just a touch at the sound of Emilie's name coming out of Cristiano's mouth. She knew she and her handsome Italian man would have to talk about it someday, but today wasn't that day.

Cristiano interrupted her thoughts, "How about we get you ready to go. That way, when Willow wakes up, we can get you two out of this place."

"I think that is an excellent idea."

They turned to hear Willow's quiet voice, "I'm ready to get out of here too. I miss William and Papa and Aunt Emilie.

Ella showered and got herself ready while Cristiano read to Willow. Then, Ella got her little girl ready.

When they were about to walk out, Willow rubbed her head, and said, "Mommy, do you think people will laugh at me and call me Ugly Girl?"

Ella's heart broke, "No, baby. Nobody will say that. You are a beautiful little girl."

Cristiano stepped into the hallway and returned with three boxes, each one bigger than the next. "I want to give each of you a special gift that is very popular in Italy.

He handed Ella and Willow each a box.

They opened the boxes simultaneously to find beautiful matching straw sun hats.

"Oh, I love it," squeaked Willow, placing it on her nearly bald head

"As do I," said Ella, doing the same.

Willow eyed the smallest box that sat on her hospital bed.

"Go ahead, Willow, you can open that one also."

Willow removed the lid to see an identical, but smaller version of their hats.

Cristiano explained, "Morgan can't be out in the sun all day without a hat."

Willow looked at her doll's bald head. Earlier in the day she had told her mommy she no longer liked Morgan's long blonde hair and asked if it would be OK if she made her doll look more like her and her mommy. Ella smiled a tearful smile at her daughter and said, "I think that would be just fine."

Willow immediately placed the hat on Morgan's bald head, "Oh, thank you, Cristiano. It is perfect."

Ella smiled at Cristiano and mouthed, "Thank you!"

Cristiano made several trips to the car to carry boxes of flowers and gifts, while Ella and Willow said their goodbyes. The hugs and well-wishes from hospital staff took thirty minutes, but the trio finally got out the door.

The homecoming was simple and small and happy. Cristiano's Saab made its way up Dr. Charles Randolph's driveway. Cristiano ran around the side of the car and opened the passenger door. Ella emerged to the whoops and hollers of her family, Agents Drew Scott and Brad Gibbons, Kristina Patton's family, and some special visitors from Florida. Cristiano opened the back door, and Willow shyly got out of the car. She held her doll, Morgan, tightly to her chest as she faced the mass of smiling faces. She recognized Detectives Luke Rogers and Nathan Austin. Sgt. Pickett waved to her from the crowd, and the corners of her mouth turned slightly upward, but she hung close to the car. Ella was still too weak to pick her daughter up, but Cristiano scooped the little girl up and held her tight.

He whispered in her ear, "All these people are here because they love you and they care about you. Do you need me to keep holding you, or do you think you want to get down? It's totally up to you."

"I guess I can try to get down."

Cristiano leaned over to Ella, "It's all going to take time, but we have time."

She squeezed his arm.

William ran to his mom and sister and hugged them tightly, being careful not to knock their hats off.

Sgt. Pickett walked over and leaned down to Willow, "I am so glad I get to meet Morgan, and I love your matching hats!"

Everyone grabbed plates of food; the kids swam and played, and the adults argued over the Cubs vs. the Cardinals. Nobody mentioned Davis Masters, or June, or Jax, or Donny, or Lisa. There was no room at this party for them.

Drew Scott found refuge under a large oak tree and spread out a blanket to have a picnic with baby Reese. Emilie carried her plate over and said, "Do you have room for a guest on your blanket?"

Drew looked at Reese, "Do we have room for a fancy Chicago girl on our blanket?"

Reese giggled, having no clue what her daddy was saying.

"I guess that means we do."

"Well, I'm sure glad," Emilie said, dotting Reese's nose.

Gibbons glanced over at his partner, held up a hot dog, and smiled. He wished his own family had been able to make the party, but his son, Van, had a baseball tournament in St. Louis. He hated missing his kids' activities, but when he explained the reason he would miss the first game of the tournament, Van had said, "You can't miss that, Dad. I will have lots of games, but there is only one homecoming." Gibbons had promised his son he would arrive by the second game. Gibbons said a silent prayer of thanks. He looked around the yard, and he thought about his own family, and he realized, he had a lot to be thankful for.

William yelled, "Last call for anyone who wants to go out on the pontoon boat."

Willow carried Morgan down to the dock. She cringed as she stepped around the new piece of sod that replaced the area where the shed once sat.

Cristiano said, "I think we might have just enough room for two more guests."

"Morgan, would you like to join us on a boat ride also?"

Willow put the doll's face up to her ear, "Mr. Cristiano, she says thanks for asking her. She would like that very much."

Ella squeezed Cristiano's hand, "Yes, Mr. Cristiano, thanks for making room for one more person."

Dr. Charles Randolph walked down the hill toward the boat dock, "Cristiano, with all due respect, sir, I am not quite sure why you are in the driver's seat. The doctors have assured me that I have regained all of my faculties, and I am still very much the captain of my vessel."

Cristiano stood and bowed in a grand gesture to Mr. Randolph, "Sir, I do apologize. I was merely keeping your girl safe until you arrived. I was wondering what was taking you so long."

Charles Randolph didn't miss a beat. He joked, "I forgot where I put the keys."

Cristiano teased back, "At least you didn't forget where you put your swim trunks."

Randolph turned the key, and the engine purred. He backed out and got the pontoon turned around.

Willow wobbled her way over to her papa and asked if she could help drive.

"Why, of course, you can, Little Buddy, but I'm still the Skipper."

Willow sat on her papa's lap and guided the pontoon out of the cove and onto the main lake.

"MY SWEET ADELINE" gleamed in the moonlight as the pontoon boat danced in and out of the gentle waves.